Praise for the novels of Mary Alice Monroe

"With its evocative, often beautiful prose and keen insights into family relationships, Monroe's latest is an exceptional and heartwarming work of fiction."

—Publishers Weekly, starred review, on *The Beach House*

"With each new book, Mary Alice Monroe continues to cement her growing reputation as an author of power and depth. *The Beach House* is filled with the agony of past mistakes, present pain and hope for a brighter future."

—RT Book Reviews on *The Beach House*

"Mary Alice Monroe is helping to redefine the beauty and magic of the Carolina Lowcountry. Every book she has written has felt like a homecoming to me."

—Pat Conroy on *The Beach House*

"*The Book Club* skillfully weaves the individual story threads into a warm, unified whole that will appeal to readers who enjoy multifaceted relationship novels with strong women protagonists."

—Library Journal on *The Book Club*

"*Skyward* is a soaring, passionate story of loneliness and pain and the simple ability of love to heal and transcend both. Mary Alice Monroe's voice is as strong and true as the great birds of prey of whom she writes."

—Anne Rivers Siddons, New York Times bestselling author, on *Skyward*

"Readers who enjoy such fine southern voices as Pat Conroy will add the talented Monroe to their list of favorites."

—Booklist on *Sweetgrass*

"Monroe writes with a crisp precision and narrative energy that will keep [readers] turning the pages."

he Four Seasons

"Mary Alice Monroe is he_____ magic of the Carolina Lowcountry. _____ lt like a homecoming to me."

_____ bestselling author, on the Lowcountry Summer Series

Also by *New York Times* bestselling author Mary Alice Monroe

The Beach House Series

The Beach House
Swimming Lessons
Beach House Memories
Beach House for Rent
Beach House Reunion
On Ocean Boulevard

Lowcountry Summer Series

The Summer Girls
The Summer Wind
The Summer's End
A Lowcountry Wedding
A Lowcountry Christmas

Stand-Alone Novels

The Book Club
The Summer Guests
The Butterfly's Daughter
Last Light over Carolina
Time Is a River
Sweetgrass
Skyward
The Four Seasons
The Long Road Home
Girl in the Mirror

For additional books by Mary Alice Monroe
visit her website at www.maryalicemonroe.com.

Mary Alice Monroe

The Beach House

mira

ISBN-13: 978-0-7783-1142-3

Recycling programs for this product may not exist in your area.

The Beach House

First published in 2002. This edition published in 2021.

Copyright © 2002 by Mary Alice Kruesi

This edition published by arrangement with Harlequin Books S.A.

For questions and comments about the quality of this book, please contact us at CustomerService@Harlequin.com.

Mira
22 Adelaide St. West, 40th Floor
Toronto, Ontario M5H 4E3, Canada
BookClubbish.com

Printed in U.S.A.

This book is dedicated to my fellow members of the

Isle of Palms/Sullivan's Island Turtle Team:

Mary Pringle, Mary Ellen Rogers,

Beverly Ballow, Barb Bergwerf,

Nancy Hauser, Tee Johannes,

Marge Millman, Susan North,

Kathey O'Connor, Wanda Parker,

Grace and Glenn Rhodes, Sara Saylor,

and to all Turtle Volunteers here and elsewhere

who walk the beaches every morning

to help our beloved loggerheads.

The
Beach House

prologue

---

loggerhead.

1. Latin: Caretta caretta.

A tropical sea turtle with a hard shell and a large head.

2. a stupid fellow; blockhead.

3. at loggerheads; in disagreement; in a quarrel.

It was twilight and a brilliant red sun lazily made its hazy descent off the South Carolina coast. Lovie Rutledge stood alone on a small, rolling sand dune and watched as two young children with hair the same sandy color as the beach squealed and cavorted, playing the age-old game of tag with the sea. A shaky half smile lifted the corners of her mouth. The boy couldn't have been more than four years of age yet he was aggressively charging the water, the stick in his hand pointing outward like a sword. Then, turning on his heel, he ran back up the beach, chased by a wave. Poor fellow was tagged more often than not. But the girl... Was she seven or eight? Now *there* was a skilled player. She danced on tiptoe, getting daringly close to the foamy wave, instinctively knowing the second to back away, taunting the water with her high laugh.

How like her own Cara, Lovie thought, recalling her youngest. Then, seeing a rogue wave wash over the boy, toppling him and leaving him sputtering with rage, she chuckled.

And how like her son, Palmer. Not far away, the children's young mother was bent at the waist busily gathering up the carelessly thrown buckets and spades into a canvas bag and shaking sand from towels, eager to pack up and go.

Stop what you're doing and observe your children! Lovie wanted to say to the young mother. Quick, set aside your chores and turn your head. See how they laugh with such abandon? Only the very young can laugh like that. Look how they are giving you clues to who they are. Treasure these moments! Savor them. For they will disappear as quickly as the setting sun. And then, before you know it, you will be like me—an old woman, alone and willing to trade anything and everything for one soft evening such as this with her babies once again.

She wrapped her arms around herself and sighed. "Lovie, you do go on," she told herself with a shake of her head. Of course she wouldn't tell the young mother this. It would be rude, and of no use. The mother was harried, her mind filled with all she had yet to do. She wouldn't understand Lovie's warning until her own children were grown and gone. One day she would recall this very twilit evening and the sight of her children dancing on the shore and then… Yes, *then* she would wish she had stopped to hold their chubby hands and play tag along with them.

Lovie continued to watch the scene unfold in its predictable manner. The towels were shaken and folded, then stuffed into the bag, the children were called in from the water's edge and, as the sky darkened, the mother led her tired soldiers in a ragtag formation over the dune and out of sight.

Silence reigned once again on the familiar stretch of beach. Another day was done. Along the water's edge a sandpiper peeped as it skitted across the sand and foam line in its straight-legged manner. Behind Lovie, the tall grasses swayed in the evening breeze. She closed her eyes, acutely attuned to the night music. There would only be a few more quiet nights like this. It was mid-May and the tourist season would soon go into full swing on the South Carolina coast.

Soon, too, her beloved sea turtles would be arriving.

She peered out for a long while at the sea as the sky darkened around her. Somewhere out in the distant swells that rolled and dipped with the winds she sensed a loggerhead was biding her time. Waiting until some powerful instinct told her that the moment was right to venture ashore. Every summer for more years than she could recall Lovie had done whatever she could to help the loggerheads through the nesting season. This summer's group of mothers might even include hatchlings she'd helped scramble to the sea twenty years earlier. She smiled at the thought.

Lovie walked to the water's edge, right to where the sea stretched to her toes. When she was young—oh, so many years ago—she, too, used to giggle and run away in that timeless game of sea tag. As did her children and grandchildren. But she and the sea were old friends now and tonight she hadn't come to play. Rather, she'd come to her old friend for solace. She stood motionless, feeling each swirl about her ankles as a caress, hearing the gentle roar of the surf as loving whispers. *There, there…*

Tears filled her eyes. Seeing the mother and her young children brought back images that were both joyous and heartbreaking. The years had flown by too swiftly, slipping away like sand through her fingers. She lifted her chin and wiped away the tear from her cheek. The vast blue ahead stretched out seemingly to infinity. This was no time for tears, she chided herself. She was old enough to know that life, like the sea, didn't always play fair. Yet she'd always believed that if she played by the rules, if she persevered, one day she'd have time enough to…

To do what? she asked herself, shaken. She was still unclear as to what exactly was missing in her relationship with her children. Her daughter, especially. When they were young, Cara and Palmer had played together under her watchful eye on this very same stretch of beach. They'd been close then, had such good times together. But now her children were grown-up and she felt every inch of the distance between them, stretching further over the years.

She turned to walk up the beach toward three lots that remained vacant on this stretch of valuable real estate and climbed the small dune. Beyond the lots she could see her beach house perched on a distant dune like a tiny island, nearly obscured from view by a row of gangly oleanders. Its once vibrant yellow color was stripped by sunshine and leached into the gala of yellow primroses that grew wild over the dunes. All the angles, corners and quaint panes of glass of the cottage were dear to her. Primrose Cottage was more than a beach house. It was a touchstone. A place of sunshine and happiness, for her and for her children.

Lovie stood alone gazing toward the west. The day's light extinguished and the night grew dark and silent save for the clicking of the swaying sea oats and the gentle lapping of waves along the shore. As ghosts of the past rose up to swirl in the hallucinatory colors of twilight, she sighed deeply, clasping her hands tight in front of her as one in prayer. She was nearly seventy years old. There was no time left for regret or misgivings, no time for dreams of what might have been. There were plans to be made. The beach house—and all the secrets it held—had to be placed in secure hands. Too much had been sacrificed for too many years to let the secrets slip out now. Too many reputations were at stake.

She had but one hope.

"Lord," she prayed, her voice raspy in her tight throat. "I'm not here to complain. You know me better than that after all this time. But the Bible says You never close a door without opening a window. So I'm praying for You to open the window. You know how things are between Cara and me. It will probably take a miracle to make peace. But You're famous for those, so I'm hopeful. Please, Lord, that's all I'm asking for. Not more time. I'd go willingly if I knew things were settled here before I left." She smiled ruefully. "I'm going whether it's willingly or not—I know that, too." Her smile fell as she grimaced in pain. "Please, Lord, answer this one small prayer. Not just for me, but for Cara. Help me play with my child once more before I die. Bring my Cara home."

one

After living at sea for twenty years or more, the female loggerhead returns to the beach of her birth to nest. She travels hundreds of miles through the Atlantic, her three-hundred-pound, eddish-brown carapace filled with hundreds of fertile eggs.

Cara had begun this long journey home many times in her mind over the years, but always there was some project, some appointment, some emotional obstacle of her own construction that stopped her.

Road weary and life tired, Cara was traveling the path of least resistance as she headed south across the flat expanse of the old cotton country known as the coastal plains. It had been over twenty years since she'd driven this long stretch of South Carolina highway toward the sea. Growing up, she'd always considered it someplace to drive through on her way to somewhere else. Anywhere else.

She passed vanishing woodlands and acres of farmland for sale, huge, flat-roofed warehouses and sun-faded billboards heralding exits for boiled peanuts, tree-ripened peaches, stock-car racing and fireworks. It was late May. Spring was already giving way to sizzling summer in the South. Elderberry bushes rambled along the roadsides, and beyond in the pinewoods,

Cara knew the coral beans were aflame and swamp roses decorated the banks like some wild hothouse garden.

The thought that the sea turtles were returning home to nest sprang to mind. She laughed out loud at the irony.

If someone had told her a year ago that the following May she would be driving to Charleston for an extended visit with her mother, Cara would have tossed back her head and laughed in that throaty manner of hers. "Impossible," she would have told them, the smile slipping from her face and a flash sparking in her eyes. First of all, her schedule would never have allowed it. Every minute of her day was double booked. At best, in an emergency, she might fly in for an overnight stop, as she had for her father's funeral. Secondly, there was nowhere on earth she'd least want to visit than Charleston. And no person less than her mother. The current status of a polite truce had worked well for them both over the past years of her self-imposed exile.

But, as always, Mama's timing was impeccable. Where else would one go but home when there was nowhere else to go?

Cara tightened her grip on the steering wheel. How could her orderly life have careened so far out of control? How did it happen that, after twenty-two years of living independently, after a successful career, after complete and utter self-sufficiency, she found herself back on this damnable stretch of road limping back home?

It was her mother's letter that had lured her. The day before, Lovie had sent the customary flowers for Cara's birthday. As Cara gingerly unwrapped the purple florist tissue, the heady scent of the gardenias permeated her apartment. Instantly, Cara was back in her mother's walled garden in Charleston where an ancient magnolia spread its broad glossy leaves and the white, heavily scented flowers of the gardenias competed with the climbing jasmine. She'd opened the letter from her mother and read her familiar, feathery script.

Happy Birthday Dear Caretta!
I never smell gardenias without thinking of you.
Things have been in a state of flux since your father's death. Now it is time for me to, shall we say, put my house in order. Come home, Cara, just for a while. Not to the house on Tradd Street. Come to the beach house. We've always had the best times there, haven't we?
Please don't say that you are too busy or that you can't get away. Remember how we used to say "Take charge of your birthday"? Can't you grant yourself this one gift of time and spend a few days with your ancient mother? Please come home, Cara dear. Soon. Your father is gone and we need to sort through years of accumulation.
Love,
Mama

Perhaps it was the scent of the gardenias that prompted the sudden loneliness, or simply that someone had remembered her birthday. Or perhaps it was her desolation at having just lost her job. But for the first time since leaving her embrace at eighteen, Cara felt a sudden, desperate longing for her mother.

She wanted to go home. Home to the Lowcountry, where once she had been happy.

Cara crossed the Ashley and the Wando rivers, took a final turn off the highway, then sped over a new, graceful arch of roadway that connected the mainland to the small barrier island called Isle of Palms. The vista yawned open before her, revealing a breathtaking view of endless blue sky and watery, greening marsh stretched out as far as she could see. She felt her mind ease as she took in the wide-open space. The hustle and honking of the crowded roads felt a world behind her. Ahead, cutting a wide, blue path through the waving grasses, was the sparkling Intracoastal Waterway and parallel to it, the smaller Hamlin Creek lined with docks, one after another, most with a boat at moor. She reached the peak of the arch.

Suddenly, looming straight ahead, like a magnificent yet serene beast, lay the vast, glistening expanse of blue that was the Atlantic Ocean. It was a living thing, pulsating power beneath the quiescent surface. Her breath caught, her body shivered and in that soul-striking instant, Cara knew that saltwater still ran thick in her veins.

She was back on the Isle of Palms. Even the name was soft on the tongue and evoked images of waving palm trees and tranquil, sunny afternoons by the rolling surf. For a hundred years, the Isle of Palms was a place the folks of Charleston and Columbia escaped to when the summers got too beastly hot. They took the ferryboat over to camp in the pine and oak forests or dance at the pavilion to big-name bands. Years later, bridges and roads were built and each summer the island's population swelled along with the heat. Growing up, Cara had spent summer after summer here with her mother and her older brother, Palmer. Her happiest memories were of the three of them living without paying mind to a clock, letting the sultry light of the Carolina sun dictate their days.

She'd heard that back in 1989 Hurricane Hugo had turned the island upside down. But she hadn't imagined the extent that time could alter a landscape. This used to be a sleepy island town with a grocer, liquor and hardware store clustered together beside a small stretch of postcard-ish, islandy restaurants. Ocean Boulevard was but a line of modest beach cottages across from a wide stretch of sand dunes that rolled lazily along the ocean.

So it was all the more shocking to see that the dunes she'd played on were gone, paved flat for a row of mansions that formed a wall of pastel-colored wood blocking the view of the sea and dwarfing the once oceanfront cottages across the street. These beautiful new post-Hugo houses stood even closer to the water's edge, as though arrogantly daring the heavens to strike again. Cara could turn her head left, then right as she drove and see, in turn, an eerie picture of pre-and post-Hugo worlds.

Still, some things never changed, she thought as she spied a line of pelicans flying overhead looking like a squadron of bombardiers on patrol. She opened her window to the balmy island air and breathed deeply. Dusk was setting in, and with each moist breeze she felt a page of her history flutter back, recalling the days when she was young and pedaled this road on her bicycle, feeling the wind toss her hair like streamers behind her. She drove another two blocks south, scanning. Her breath caught in her throat when she saw it.

Primrose Cottage. As pale a yellow as the delicate evening primroses that surrounded it, the 1930s beach cottage sat back from the road perched on a small dune. In contrast to all the meticulously landscaped properties of the newer mansions, her mother's house appeared as a wispy memory of the past glowing in the twilight among waves of tall grasses, brilliant pink phlox and yellow primroses for which it had been named. Although a bit wind worn, the old frame house with the low spreading roof and the wide, welcoming verandas seemed as indigenous here as the palmetto trees. It had been twenty years since she'd laid eyes on this house. So many years since embarking on the journey from little girl to middle-aged woman. Pulling up to the curb to stare, it occurred to her that while she'd been busy with her life in Chicago, oblivious to the goings-on of the island, this charming little house was here, patiently waiting for her.

She shifted into gear and slowly drove around the block to the back of the house, pulling into the winding gravel driveway, careful when the wheels dug past the thin layer of gravel to hit sand. She released a short laugh to see the old, shiny gold VW convertible parked beneath the porch. Mama was still driving The Gold Bug? That old ragtop was like a flag. Everyone knew if The Gold Bug was in the driveway, Olivia Rutledge was in residence and ready for visitors.

Coming to a stop, Cara could feel the miles still moving in her veins. She stared out the windshield at what had always been home and wondered if *she* was now a visitor at Primrose Cottage, too. Did blood alone earn her the right to call it home? Did hours of pulling weeds from the flower beds and boarding up windows against storms, or years of swinging on the front porch count for anything? She sighed and pulled up the parking brake. Probably not. Besides, she remembered how, in a fit of youthful passion, she'd made a point of shouting to her mother that she wanted nothing at all to do with her, her damn father or anything connected to them.

Yet the connection tugged, pulling her out from the stale confines of the car into the cool offshore breezes spiked with the heady scent of honeysuckle. She stood, one foot on the sand, the other perched on the car, feeling the undertow sweep her back, back from the shoreline of the world she'd left behind.

Her memories were crowding her now and she anxiously eyed the remaining feet to her mother's door. She wanted to go in but years of anger rooted her to the spot. So she leaned against the car, formulating what she would say that could break the ice yet still allow her to keep a modicum of self-respect. She'd stay one week, she told herself, gathering courage. Maybe ten days. Any more than that and her mother would drive her crazy and they'd fall back into that pattern of bickering and harsh words followed by long, sulking silences. Oh, God, she thought, rubbing her forehead. Was it a mistake to come back at all?

All around her the sky darkened to dusky purples and blues and the birds called out their final warnings to go home. A dog howled somewhere in the distance. Then, from around the house, she heard the high melodic hum of a woman's voice.

Cara moved to peek around the corner. Ambling up the sandy ocean path she saw a diminutive woman in a big, floppy straw hat, a long, faded denim skirt and bright red Keds. Bits of the tune she was humming carried in the breeze, nothing recognizable. In one arm she lugged a red plastic bucket, a telltale sign of one of the island's Turtle Ladies. Cara's heart beat wildly but she remained silent, watching. From this distance she might have mistaken the woman for a young girl. She seemed utterly carefree and oblivious to anything save for the field of wildflowers she passed. She paused en route to stoop and snip a flower, then, resuming her hum, she continued up the path toward Primrose Cottage.

A million things that Cara had meant to say, a thousand postures she'd meant to strike, evaporated as quickly as sea foam once it hits the shore.

"Mama!" she called out.

Her mother stopped short and swung her head in her direction. Bright blue eyes sparkled from under the broad rim of the hat and her mouth opened in a gasp of genuine pleasure. Dropping her bucket, she held out her arms in a joyous welcome.

"Caretta!"

Cara cringed at hearing the name she despised, but closed the distance quickly, following the age-old path of a child to her mother's embrace. Taller by a head, she bent her knees and felt like she always did beside Olivia Rutledge—like a clambering bull next to a porcelain doll. Yet when her mother's arms flung around her and squeezed tightly, Cara felt a sweeping flush of childlike pleasure.

"I've missed you," her mother said softly against her cheek. "You're home again. At last."

Cara squeezed back but too many years of silence choked all words. She released her hold and, stepping back, it struck her like a fist's blow how much her mother had changed. Olivia Rutledge had become an old woman. Beneath the cheery straw hat her skin was pale and seemed to hang from her prominent cheekbones. The brightness of her blue eyes had dimmed, and though always small and trim, she was now painfully thin.

How could it have happened so quickly, Cara wondered? Only eighteen months ago at her father's funeral Olivia still retained that timeless quality to her beauty and grace. At sixty-nine she wasn't young, of course, but Cara couldn't think of her mother as *old*. She was one of those lucky women born with a girlish, slender body and a face that was as scrubbed fresh and naturally pretty as the wildflowers she adored. Her father used to say that he married Olivia because she was as sweet as she looked—and it was true. Everyone loved Olivia Rutledge, "Lovie" to those who knew her well. But her daughter knew the price that ready smile had cost her mother over the years.

"How are you?" Cara asked, searching her face. "Are you well?"

"Oh, I'm fine, fine," she said, dismissing Cara's tone of concern with a flip of her hand. "Nothing much one can do to stop the ruins of Rome. I've given up trying." Her eyes brightened as she looked up at her daughter. "But look at *you*. Don't you look wonderful!"

Cara looked down at her rumpled white shirt and dark jeans

that pinched her waist. She'd woken before dawn that morning, splashed cold water on her face and dressed in a hurry, not taking the time for makeup and allowing her dark hair to hang in disarray to her shoulders.

"I do not. My clothes are a wreck and I smell of fast food."

"You look wonderful to me. I can't get over it. You're here! I about fainted when you called to say you were coming. Thank the Lord."

"Mama, the Lord had nothing to do with it. You wrote me a letter asking me to come and I came."

"That's what *you* think. I'm old enough to know better. Now let's not argue," she chided, linking arms, squeezing gently. "I've prayed that you'd come back home and now my prayers have been answered." They began to walk slowly toward the house. Lovie turned her head to peer into Cara's face. "Why do you look at me like that?"

"Like what?"

"Like you're in shock."

"I don't know. You seem different. So…happy."

"Why, of course I'm happy! Why shouldn't I be?"

Cara shrugged. "I dunno… I guess from your letter I expected you to be rather lonely. Maybe a little depressed. It hasn't been that long since Daddy died."

Lovie's expression shifted and, as usual, Cara couldn't read the emotion behind her smile.

"I didn't mean for my letter to sound sad. Wistful, perhaps."

"Do you miss him?"

She brought her hand to Cara's cheek. "I miss *you*. Especially here. We had good times on the island, didn't we?"

Cara nodded, touched by the emotion in her mother's voice. "We did. You and me. And Palmer." She refrained from adding her father's name. He'd rarely come to the beach house, preferring to stay in the city or to travel. And though it was never discussed among them, it was quietly understood that the summers were all the better for the arrangement.

"Oh, yes," Lovie said with a light chuckle. "And Palmer, too."

"How is my wild and crazy brother?"

"Neither wild nor crazy. More's the pity."

Cara's brows rose. "Well, that's a bit out of character for you. I seem to remember you and Daddy holding tight the reins whenever Palmer rode the wild roads and waves of his youth. I'll have to mull that one over—once I get over the shock of you criticizing the royal heir."

Her mother only laughed. "How long can you stay?"

"A week."

"Is that all? Cara, dear, you're always so busy. Please stay a bit longer."

Cara slowed down to consider. She really had no deadline and her mother seemed so anxious. It might be nice to relax a while. "Maybe I can take a bit more time. That's what's nice about driving. No ticket to ride." She paused. "Is it all right to be open-ended?"

"It's more than all right. It's perfect." She patted Cara's arm, leading the way across the sand-strewn path into the house. "Come inside. You must be exhausted after your long trip. Are you hungry? I don't have a meal ready but I'll scrounge around and find something."

"Don't go to any trouble. I've done nothing but nibble in the car for fourteen hours."

"What time did you leave Chicago?"

"Before five," Cara replied, stifling a yawn.

"Why push yourself so hard, dear? You should have taken two days, maybe three, and stopped at a few places along the way. The mountains are so beautiful this time of year."

"Yeah, well, you know me. Once I'm on the road I like to get where I'm going."

"Yes, you do," her mother replied with a teasing glint in her eye. "You always do."

Looking at the house as she climbed the porch steps, Cara saw further signs of the house's age. It was worse than she'd first suspected. The back porch was sagging, the border shrubs were a jungle of overgrowth, a shutter was missing and in spots the paint had peeled clear to the wood. "The old place looks like it could use some work."

"This poor old house… It takes a lot of abuse from the weather. Always it's nip and tuck, nip and tuck."

"It's a lot for you to do alone. Doesn't Palmer help you keep things up?"

"Palmer? Well, he tries, but the main house keeps him pretty busy with its own list of chores. And then there's the business. And his family." Her brows knit and her lips tightened, a sign she was holding words back. "He has his own troubles. I get along well enough on my own. Oh, look at my primroses," she exclaimed, pointing at a nearby clump. "Aren't they beautiful this year?" She closed her eyes and sniffed. "Can you catch their lemony scent?"

Cara couldn't decide if her mother had adroitly changed the subject or was just easily distracted. But she could feel the miles she'd driven that day weigh as heavily as the suitcase hanging from her arm and the last thing she wanted to do was stand in the enveloping darkness and smell the flowers.

"I'm bushed. I'd really love to drop this load and have something cold and wet and alcoholic, if you've got it."

"How's a gin and tonic sound?"

Cara almost purred.

They passed through the screened porch, cluttered with old rattan furniture, a mildewed canvas beach bag loaded with miscellaneous beach supplies and assorted rusted garden tools. Lovie paused, resting her hand against the wall as she slipped her feet from her sand-crusted running shoes. Cara noticed with a start that there was a small, pale space on her mother's ring finger where a band of gold and a large, Tiffany-cut diamond had rested for forty-two years.

"Mama, where's your wedding ring?"

Flustered, her mother looked down at her hand, then began swatting the sand from her skirt. "Oh, that big ol' thing? I took it off after your father died. I only wore it to please him. I never much liked wearing it. It got in the way and was such a bother here at the beach. I expect I'll leave it to Cooper to give to his bride someday."

Cooper was Palmer's young son, and true to form, her mother was doting on the only male to carry on the proud Rutledge name.

"Scrape your feet, hear? I'll never get used to the amount of sand that gets tracked into the house."

Cara obliged. "What were you doing on the beach so late?"

"Why, we've already had two turtle nests!"

Cara's eyes glittered with both amusement and resignation. "I thought you looked for tracks in the morning."

"We do. I just wanted to check that everything was in order. You know me. I'm always a little excited when the season starts." Her face scrunched in distress. "I didn't move this nest and I'm not sure if I shouldn't have. Ordinarily I would have. It's a bit low on the tideline." She tsked and shook her head. "The Department of Natural Resources is quite strict these days and doesn't want the nests moved unless it's urgent. Oh, I don't know…" she fretted. "If the tide comes in high, the nest could be ruined. Maybe I should have moved it."

"Mama, you made your decision. It's done. Let it lie." In Cara's job she made a thousand decisions a day and never understood how some people could waffle back and forth. But she knew it wasn't just the indecision that annoyed her. It was the turtles. It was always the turtles. From May till October, every year for as far back as she could remember, her mother's life had revolved around the loggerheads. And so, by default, had hers and Palmer's.

"I know, you're right. I can't move them now anyway and I'm just fussing." Her face clouded before she turned toward the door. "Come in. Let me make you that drink."

One step and Cara was inside the house, floating back in time. Her mother's was one of the few remaining original beach cottages on the island. It was all cramped and worn, but comfortable. Tongue-and-groove walls and heart pine floors warmed the small rooms that her mother kept immaculate. Lovie's eye for comfort and charm was evident in the muted, worn, Oriental rugs, the ivory-colored walls adorned with family photographs and paintings of the island done by local artists, many of them old friends. Mismatched, plump sofas and chairs clustered in spare but cozy arrangements before a large front window that provided a breathtaking view of the ocean beyond.

The family heirloom antiques were kept at the main house in Charleston, out of harm's way from hurricanes, children and visitors in swimsuits. Only the "not-so-good" pieces were brought to the beach house. Cara's friends had always wanted to come to her house to play because her mother never said, "Feet off!" "Careful!" or "Don't touch!" Icy sweet tea was always in the fridge and sugar cookies in the pantry. Life here at the beach was so different than in the city. In so many ways.

She followed her mother single file through the front room down a narrow hall to the two bedrooms at the end—hers and Palmer's. As she walked she felt the pressure of memories lurking in the musty walls and darkened corners.

"Your room is made up for you," Lovie said, opening the bedroom door. A gust of ocean breeze whisked past them into the hall. "Do you want me to close the windows?"

"No, it's fine. I like them open." How like her mother not to use the air-conditioning, she thought, inhaling the moist, sweet-scented air that seemed to soften the bones. They stood facing each other.

"There are fresh towels in the bathroom," Lovie said with a quick gesture.

"Okay."

"Feel free to use the toiletries. There's soap and shampoo. A spare toothbrush."

"I've brought my own, but thanks."

"The hot water's slow in coming."

"I remember."

"Well then," Lovie said, clasping her hands anxiously. There was a moment's awkwardness, as though they were strangers. "I'll just leave you to freshen up."

"That'd be great."

Her mother's hand lingered on the bedroom door and there was such yearning in her face that Cara had to turn away from the bruising intensity.

"Take your time," Lovie said, closing the door behind her.

The door clicked, and in the resulting privacy, Cara took a deep sigh of relief and dropped her suitcase. It landed with a thud. Round one went pretty well, she thought, considering the ruts they'd avoided. She was exhausted from the long drive and the tension of the duet with her mother brought a worrisome throbbing to her forehead. Rubbing the crick in her neck, she slowly surveyed her old room. Amazingly, it was exactly as she'd left it twenty years earlier. The old black iron double bed covered with a pink crazy quilt filled most of the floor space. Pink-and-white gingham curtains fluttered at the single window over her sturdy pine dresser with the rosy marble top. A narrow door beside the window opened to the screened front porch.

It was a girl's room, comfy yet spare. Her posters of rock stars had been replaced by paintings of palm trees, but all her old books were still here. She ran her fingers over familiar titles that had carried her through the summers for years: *Nancy Drew, A Swiftly Tilting Planet, The Hobbit, Wuthering Heights, Zen and the Art of Motorcycle Maintenance.* Words that had helped form a young girl's mind. What books did she need to add to her shelf to help her through this next phase of her life?

She caught a glimpse of herself in the mirror and stopped short, surprised at the reflection. It was a surreal moment, one fragmented by time. Back here in her old room, she half expected to see the skinny, stringy-haired child that had once stared at this mirror with tear-filled eyes. That poor, pitiful girl.

By Southern belle standards, Cara wasn't considered the beauty her mother was. All Cara's parts were too big. At five feet ten inches, she was too tall, her body too thin and her chest too flat. Her feet were enormous and her lips too full for her narrow face. And her coloring was all wrong. She used to curse God for His mistake of giving her her father's tall, dark-haired, dark-eyed genes and Palmer their mother's small-boned, blond-and-blue-eyed genes.

Lovie, however, adored her daughter's dark looks and used to call Cara her Little Tern because of her dark, shining eyes and her glistening, black-crested cap. And sometimes, teasingly, she called her a Laughing Gull, another black-headed bird but with a loud, cackling call.

Cara leaned closer to the mirror and brought her hand up to smooth the flesh of her cheeks. All nicknames aside, the South of the sixties and seventies was not an easy place for a

skinny, unattractive girl to grow up in. But this ugly duck-
ling grew up to be a dark swan. Cara's once-mocked gangling
looks had matured into what colleagues now referred to as
"strikingly attractive" and her previously scorned aggressive
intelligence was described as "the appealing confidence of a
successful career woman."

Tonight, however, even those descriptions felt woefully out-
of-date. She was neither a child nor a young woman. In her
reflection she saw the new fragility of her skin, the fine lines
at the eyes and corners of her mouth and the first strands of
gray at the temple. She thought with chagrin that she was no
longer striking nor successful. Rather, she appeared as tired
and sagging as the old beach house.

I'll just lie down for a minute, she told herself, turning away
from the mirror and slipping from her clothes. She left them
in a pile on the floor. Wearing only her undies and a T-shirt,
she pulled back the covers and stretched out upon the soft
mattress, yawning. *Just long enough to rest my eyes.*

The old linen was crisp, and ocean breezes, balmy and
moist, whisked over her bare skin. Her mind slowly drifted
and her eyelids grew heavy as she felt herself letting go, bit by
bit. The life she'd led mere hours ago seemed as distant from
her now as the city of Chicago. As her mind stilled, the quiet
deepened further. Outside her window, she listened to the
ocean's steady, rhythmic motion, lulling her to sleep, like the
gentle rocking of a mother's arms.

Her mind floated as helplessly as a piece of driftwood
through the turbulence of the past few days' events that had
sent her on this journey. It began on Tuesday morning when
her office phone rang and she was invited, without warning,
to Mr. David Alexander's office. Dave was executive vice
president of the chopping block. Everyone knew that an in-

vitation to his office was the equivalent of an invitation for a long car ride in the Mafia.

Why didn't they just shoot her, she'd wondered wildly as she rode the elevator to the thirtieth floor. She was a workaholic mainlining hours of work and she was about to be cut off from her supply. She'd lost a major account, but that happened in the advertising business. She had a great track record. Wasn't she already hot on the trail of another account? As she walked through the halls she was aware of an unusual, tense silence in the spread of gray cubicles and cramped offices broken only by an occasional ring of the phone followed by a muffled sob. Empty file boxes lined the halls, and most frightening of all, armed guards stood by the elevators. She swallowed hard and walked stiff-leggedly through the maze of halls and rooms. The rumors were true after all. Heads were rolling on a mass scale.

By the time she'd arrived in Mr. Alexander's office, her body was moist with a fine sweat. She woodenly took a seat. Refused the offer of coffee or water. In the end, there were no surprises. He informed her in his thin, nasal voice that he was terribly sorry but as executive officer, she would bear the brunt of the loss of a major account. While listening to him drone on about the firm's generous severance package, Cara crossed her legs, folded her hands neatly in her lap and looked out the plate-glass window, numb with shock. When the humiliating session was over, she rose, politely thanked Mr. Alexander for his time, told him she would collect her personal things later, then left the building—accompanied by an armed guard.

She'd gone straight home to her cramped, one-bedroom condominium on the lake. The somewhat shabby space represented every penny she'd saved in the past twenty years. She'd bought it because it was near the water, the last vestige of homesickness after a long exile. Yet it wasn't the safe haven one returned to when hurt by slings and arrows. It wasn't a home that marked milestones or greeted family members. These walls held no memories of laughter or treasured moments. With its minimalist style, the cool colors of ice blue and gray on the walls and upholstery, and the scarcity of personal items, there wasn't a clue to her personality or interests. Her condo was merely where she went to sleep at night. It was a place to store her meaningless possessions, every bit as stark as a bank vault.

And it was all she had in the world.

It was chilling to wake up at forty years of age to find she had no friends, no interests and no investments in anything unconnected to her work. She had delayed too long, put such things on hold until she had time. She had defined herself by her job and now, suddenly, everything was gone and she was back once again in her mother's house, in the bed she'd slept in as a child, every bit as uncertain at forty as she had been at eighteen.

Cara wrapped her arms around herself and shivered, feeling the kind of bitter cold that went straight to one's marrow. The kind that felt very much like fear.

Sometime later, she wasn't sure if she was dreaming or if she really felt her mother's touch at her temple, smoothing back the soft hairs from her face, and a tender kiss placed on her forehead.

two

Female loggerheads return home to nest. Is it imprinting
or genes that prompts this behavior? Smells or sounds?
Perhaps magnetic fields? No one knows for sure.

The South Carolina moon can lull one to sleep with its silvery glow, but the coastal sun is as sharp and piercing as a bugle call. Cara pried open an eye to the glaring shine flowing in from the open window. It took a moment to place where she was and to register the contrast of blaring car horns to the relentless, cheery chirping of birds. The long drive, the lost job—it all came back in a blinding flash. Groaning, she plopped a pillow over her head just as the telephone began ringing down the hall.

When it became obvious no one was going to answer it, she threw the pillow off, tugged her T-shirt down over her panties, then scuttled like a sand crab down the narrow hall to where the cottage's single phone rested on a wooden trestle table.

"Hello?" she answered with a froggy voice.

There was a pause. "Olivia?" The woman's voice on the line was high with uncertainty.

"No, this isn't Lovie," she replied, stifling a yawn. "It's her daughter."

"Oh." Another pause. "I didn't know Lovie had a daughter."

Cara rubbed her eyes and waited.

"May I speak to your mother?"

No one had asked her that question in over twenty years. Cara blinked sleepily while she gazed around the living room. The house was as quiet as a mouse.

"She's not here."

"But… I've found turtle tracks!"

Gauging by the panic in the voice, Cara figured the woman was one of her mother's novice volunteers for the island's Turtle Team. "Uh, great," she replied. "Thanks, I'll tell her when she comes back."

"Wait! Don't you want to know where they are? I'm at the 6th Avenue beach access. What should I do? Should I wait here?"

Cara sighed and woke up a little more. "Really, I don't have the foggiest idea what to tell you to do and without coffee I couldn't even venture a guess."

From out on the porch she heard the footfall of someone trudging up the steps. Thanks heavens, the cavalry, she thought.

"Hold on," she told the woman on the phone. "I think that must be her now." Cara stretched the cord of the ancient black phone to peek around the corner. The front door swung open. Instead of her mother, however, she saw a young woman enter the house free-as-you-please. Her shaggy, blond hair cascaded over her eyes as she bent down, struggling with several plastic grocery bags. With a muffled grunt, she kicked the door shut with her heel.

The young woman was hardly threatening in appearance. Pregnant women usually weren't. She wore a pastel, A-line floral dress that was very short and cheaply made of thin rayon that lifted higher in the front where the fabric strained against her belly. When the woman raised her head she shook her hair back and their eyes met.

Cara ducked her head back behind the corner, tugging down her T-shirt. In contrast, the woman didn't seem the least astonished to find Cara in the house. Cara leaned against the hall wall listening as the mystery woman moved on into the kitchen without so much as a hello, opening and closing cabinets as though she owned the place.

"Excuse me," Cara called out with authority. "But who are you?"

"Didn't your mama tell you about me?" she called back. Her voice carried the drawl of a rural Southern accent.

It flashed through Cara's mind that she'd fallen asleep without a meal or so much as a good-night to her mother. They hadn't had a chance to talk about schedules or visitors or a girl who might stop by in the morning. Cara assumed she was either a neighbor or someone hired to help with the shopping.

From the phone, a strident voice rose up. "Hello? Hello? Is anyone there?"

Cara called out to the woman in the kitchen. "I've got a frantic phone call here about a turtle. Do you know where my mother is?"

"I'll take it."

The voice drew nearer and in a moment the face was looming before her. Cara saw that it wasn't a woman's face at all, but a teenager's. The girl had a sexy, baby-doll kind of face, all rounding cheeks and full, pouty lips. Her youth surprised Cara and her gaze dropped to the belly. Instantly the girl's hand moved to rest on the rounding curve. Looking up again, Cara saw the girl's pale gray eyes turn icy. Lined as they were by dark kohl, the challenge she read in them gave her a hardened, tough-girl appearance that set Cara immediately on edge. With a slightly raised brow that was dangerously close to a smirk, the girl returned a cool glance at Cara's outfit. For a second, no one spoke as they sized up one another.

The voice of the caller rose up between them. "Hello? Hello?"

The girl reached out her hand, palm up, and wiggled her fingers.

Cara narrowed her eyes and handed over the phone. The girl deliberately turned her back to Cara in a snub and began speaking to the woman on the phone, confirming the address and giving instructions with the confidence of someone who had done this many times before.

Why, the little punk, Cara thought to herself, affronted. Then fatigue got the best of her. "Whatever," she muttered, turning and heading back down the hall. At least the girl, whoever she was, knew what to do with the pesty phone call. En route she noticed that the door to her brother's old room was open. Peeking in, she caught a glimpse of the rumpled unmade bed and on top of it, a pink, frilly nightgown.

Cara's heart fell as the mystery was solved. The girl was a houseguest, she realized. So much for plans of a private mother-child reunion. The cottage was barely large enough for the two of them, but with three, it would be crowded. There would be no escaping the recalcitrant teen mother who appeared equally thrilled to see her. If she'd known there'd be guests…

Grabbing her pillow from the floor where it had landed, she tossed it back onto the bed, then slumped against the pillows. What was she expecting anyway? Her mother had always put others in front of her—her brother, her father and the guests who always seemed to fill the Charleston house.

But the beach house had always been different. She'd hoped that here…

Cara's mouth pinched and she thought herself a fool. She'd

learned long before her teens to take care of herself and not to expect anything. In the piercing morning light her room no longer appeared as charming. The colors in her old quilt were sun-bleached and the paint had yellowed on the walls. Although a gentle breeze still fluttered the threadbare curtains, without air-conditioning, the humidity would be brutal by midday. Cara began to regret her hasty decision to return home.

The beginning of a headache from too many days of stress and too little sleep nagged. Lying back, she punched her pillow a few times, then relinquished her troubled thoughts to a deep, brooding sleep.

Toy Sooner stood at the kitchen sink rinsing out the coffeepot, tapping her foot in agitation. She carefully spooned out six tablespoons of coffee grinds into the filter, then pushed the start button. She knew Lovie enjoyed a fresh cup of coffee when she returned from her turtle watch. Toy had gone to the Red and White to purchase a box of Krispy Kreme doughnuts. There wasn't much she could afford to do to show Miss Lovie how grateful she was, and Lovie had said a hundred times or more that she didn't expect any thanks. Things like that just made Toy want to thank her all the more.

Toy wasn't used to people giving her something without expecting something in return. To live here with Miss Lovie was like a dream come true. This was the nicest place she'd ever lived and she had a room all her own, too. Best of all, there wasn't any fighting or hollering at her all the time. She didn't know before living with Miss Lovie that mealtime could be so nice, with a clean tablecloth and napkins and a knife, fork and a spoon—for every meal!

And they had meals regularly. Not an open can of soup in front of the TV or McDonald's out of the bag, but real dinners with vegetables. Lovie talked to her, too, like she was someone worth talking to and listening to. Not just some worthless, ungrateful kid who was dumb enough to get herself pregnant, like her parents said. They'd stood at the door of the trailer and wouldn't even let her in when she tried to come back home. "If you was grown-up enough to up and move in with Darryl then you're grown-up enough to take care of his kid," is what they told her. Now what kind of parents is that? They wouldn't even help when she told them about Darryl hitting her. "You made your bed, now go lie in it." That's all they had to say. That and how she ought to go to church, too, and pray hard for the Lord's forgiveness for being such a sinner.

But Lovie told her again and again that love was never a sin. *Not* loving, now that was the very worst kind of sin, she said. Miss Lovie was the saintliest person Toy had ever met, and if she said so, then Toy believed it. She always had a way of making Toy feel better about herself instead of making her feel like nothing…worse than nothing. Something to be discarded, which is what her own mother made her feel like.

That's why it made her so mad to think that Miss Lovie's own daughter didn't appreciate how lucky she was to have someone like her for a mother. Just let Cara spend a day with my mother and see how she feels, Toy thought with resentment.

From the moment she heard that Caretta Rutledge was coming home, Toy knew it would be bad news for her. First of all, she heard from Miss Lovie that Cara was some big-shot ad executive in Chicago. That figured. Toy knew the type. It wasn't just that they grew up on the right side of Broad and went to the best schools. Or that they had nice clothes and fancy houses. It was like, deep inside, girls like Cara knew they were better. They didn't have nothing to prove.

That's how the rich stayed rich, she figured. It was like some club and they had some secret code that only they knew and that girls like her couldn't ever clue into. As if she wanted to... She could tell just by the way Cara looked at her pregnant belly that it was a royal put-down. Toy had lots of experience with being looked down on, but it hurt feeling cheap in this house where she'd finally been so happy.

She wiped up the coffee grinds with a sponge. She loved that everything was just so in this house and she actually enjoyed keeping things clean. Growing up, everything was always a mess, with clothes and papers lying all over the place, the laundry never done. She couldn't ever remember having folded towels in the linen closet or flowers on the table. Living here was like another world. Opening the cabinet, she still got a shiver of pleasure just seeing the neatly stacked sets of matching china.

She'd hate to leave. Lovie wanted Cara to stay the whole summer, but Toy didn't think Cara could last that long. For Lovie's sake, she didn't want to screw things up between them. She didn't know why, but this time with her daughter was real important to Miss Lovie and Toy would do just about anything for Lovie Rutledge.

The scent of fresh brewed coffee filled the kitchen. She'd just laid out the doughnuts on a pretty plate when she heard steps on the front porch. She quickly wiped the sugar from her hands and hurried to greet Lovie at the door.

"Hey, Miss Lovie!" she called out, grabbing the red bucket from her arm. "I was beginning to wonder if you were going to stay out there all morning."

"It's not that late, is it?" Lovie replied, pausing to catch her breath.

Toy's brows gathered as she monitored Lovie's level of exhaustion. "Why don't you sit down for a spell? I'll get you some water and a nice fresh cup of coffee."

"My, that sounds nice," Lovie replied breathlessly as she lowered herself into a chair at the small wood table just outside the kitchen.

With her eye trained on Lovie's pale face, Toy brought a tray from the kitchen and set it before Lovie. "Did you find anything today?"

Lovie's face immediately brightened. "Our third nest! Emmi and I probed and on only the third try the probe sunk right in. You should've seen Emmi's face! One hundred and fifty-four eggs. Isn't that wonderful? Unfortunately, the mother laid them directly in the middle of the beach access path. That big wide one on 17th Avenue."

"That wasn't too smart of her."

"I'm sure the poor old girl had no idea it was a beach path. So we had to move the nest. The dunes are quite high between 16th and 17th Avenue so after Emmi and I checked around a bit, we found a nice place for the nest. All in all, a good day."

"But a long one for you," she amended with a serious look.

"Oh, I'm fine, really. A little out of breath, but not the least bit fagged out."

"No pain?"

"None at all."

"And you got that message from the volunteer about 6th Avenue?" she asked, bringing a small bowl filled with pills to Lovie.

"I did, thank you. Flo passed it on to me." She looked down at the pills and wrinkled her nose.

"Come on, Miss Lovie, you know you got to. See? I bought you a doughnut to help with the swallowing. 'A spoonful of sugar helps the medicine go down,' just like the song says. Now, come on, don't put it off."

Lovie grimaced as she faced the mound of pills but Toy remained at her side, arms resolutely crossed over her chest as she waited. She hated to play the heavy but the doctor hadn't been fooling around when he'd taken Toy aside and told her it was her job to make sure that Lovie swallowed each and every one of the pills. She tried to keep the conversation about turtles going to take Lovie's mind off the swallowing.

"So, did that call about 6th Avenue turn out to be a nest?"

After a noisy swallow Lovie set the glass down and shook her head. "A false crawl. She came up the beach quite far, then wandered around a bit before turning back. We searched carefully but didn't find a nest. I suspect she's the same mother who laid the eggs a little farther down on 17th. The tracks were similar." She stared at the remaining pills with dejection.

"Come on, now, just a few more," Toy prodded. She watched as Lovie took a deep breath, grabbed the two final pink pills, then swallowed them with a shiver of disgust.

"There, that's done."

"Horrid things. I don't know why I still bother."

"Don't say that. You know why. We want you around for a long time."

Lovie's face softened and she looked at Toy with a sad expression. "At least for the summer."

"Oh, much longer than that. I'm already shopping for your Christmas present. But, yeah, summer is best. You've been so happy since the turtles came."

"And now, my own Caretta is back."

Toy's smile fell.

Lovie tilted her head and gazed at Toy speculatively. "You've met?"

The legs of the chair scraped the pine wood floors as Toy joined Lovie at the table. She sat in a clumsy flop, leaving room for her growing belly.

"Sort of. She answered that phone call about the tracks and

I walked in from the store while she was talking. I think we kinda surprised each other."

"She fell asleep early last night. I thought we'd all have a chance to meet after you came home from the movies. As it turned out, I didn't have a chance to tell her about you."

"I figured that. She looked at me like… Well, let's just say she wasn't glad to see me."

"Cara can be quite formidable."

Toy snorted. "I swear, Lovie, I can't believe that she's your daughter. I never seen two women cut from such different pieces of cloth."

Lovie chuckled, then said ruefully, "I'm sure she'd agree with you."

Toy twisted her mouth and began picking at her nail. "I was thinking. Maybe I should go someplace else, just for this week or so while she's here. Give you two a little time alone."

"Where would you go?"

"I guess I could go back to Darryl's for a week."

"That's out of the question."

Lovie's sharp tone brought Toy's gaze to her face. Lovie had straightened in the chair and her eyes were shining.

"It'd just be for a week. I know he wants me back."

"We won't even discuss the possibility of you returning to that man."

"He loves me."

They sat across from each other in a long silence. Lovie reached out and put her hand over Toy's. "When I invited you to live here, I wanted you to feel that this was your home. I think we've managed quite nicely for ourselves here, don't you?" When Toy nodded she continued. "So what made you think you'd be suddenly booted out when a guest arrived?"

"We're not talking about some guest. Cara's your daughter."

"And you have become as a daughter to me, too."

Toy lowered her head and fixed her gaze on the small hand over hers. It was a mother's hand. Though the skin was pale, almost translucent, with blue veins protruding over bones as fragile as a sparrow's, Toy saw in it so much love and strength she felt her eyes water with emotion.

Lovie said softly, "Tell me you'll stay? That you'll try to make this work?"

Toy nodded sharply, embarrassed for her tears.

Glancing at the clock Cara saw through bleary eyes that it was nearly noon. Her head felt groggy, as though she could sleep another twelve hours. But she couldn't spend the entire day in bed, could she? The thought that yes, she could, was disquieting. Her mouth felt as if it were filled with cotton and a faint thrumming still pulsed in her skull. Swinging her legs off from the bed, she slipped into a pair of boxer shorts and padded down the hall toward the kitchen.

She felt out of place in her childhood summer home, as if she didn't belong. The beach house even looked different. Her mother had gutted and redesigned the small rooms of the old cottage to create one main, airy room in the center of the house that opened up at the front and back to large, covered verandas. To the left of the house was a small hall that led to the two small children's bedrooms and a shared bath. To the right was the master bedroom, bathroom and a tiny kitchen. The clunky old kitchen she remembered was a far cry from the sleek galley kitchen with modern appliances she stepped into now.

The only thing she recognized was the dish cabinet. Through the glass-fronted doors she saw the remainders of china sets that had been handed down through generations. Choosing a blue-and-white Meissen cup, she was comforted by something at once familiar on an out-of-sorts morning.

The coffee was still blessedly hot in a thermos and someone had thoughtfully laid out a small plate of doughnuts.

Moving at a slow pace, she carried her cup and pastry to the screened porch and slumped into a large wooden rocking chair facing the ocean. Straight ahead, across the empty lot of low-humped dunes and wild, gnarled greenery, the ocean placidly rolled, distant and unwelcoming.

"Well, there you are!"

Jerking her head around, she spied her mother rounding the corner of the house. She looked sporty in khaki shorts, a sage T-shirt with a turtle emblazoned across the chest and a red baseball cap with the state's palm tree and crescent moon logo on the front. Cara lazily returned a wave.

Lovie gripped the railing and began climbing the short flight of stairs with a labored tread. Her breath came heavy. Alarmed, Cara hustled down the stairs to take hold of her arm.

"Are you all right?"

"Signs of my age," Lovie said ruefully. "Nothing more."

"When was the last time you saw your doctor?"

"I'll have you know Dr. Pittman and I are on the most intimate terms. When I sneeze, he calls to say 'God bless you.'"

"Seriously, Mother. I don't recall your ever being so out of breath."

Lovie stopped on a step and turned her head to look at Cara askance. "Cara dear," she said, a tone of reprimand in her voice, "you haven't visited me in quite a long time. Your memory banks are not that recent. These days, I'm frequently out of breath."

Chastened, Cara quietly followed her mother's march up the stairs. When they reached the top, Lovie stepped away from Cara's hold and took a deep breath.

"See? Nothing to worry about. I'm like a turtle, slow but sure. How are *you?*"

Cara noted the pearls of sweat along her mother's upper lip but said no more about it. "I'm sorry about last night. I didn't mean to conk out on our first night, but the bed looked so inviting and with that soft breeze coming in through the window... I lay down for a moment just to rest my eyes and the next thing I knew it was morning."

"Don't give it another thought. I figured you must've been exhausted after your long drive and there's plenty of time to catch up. You did exactly the right thing. Did you wake up feeling refreshed?"

"No, sadly not. I still feel draggy. I think I'm just slowing down from the rat race."

"Island time. Many of my guests from the north seem to need a few days to unwind. Give yourself time. I know, why don't you come on down to the beach tomorrow and join the Turtle Ladies? Walking in the fresh air and sun will do you good."

"I used to love sunbathing but not anymore. I've read all about skin cancer and wrinkles. These days, I like to admire the sunshine from indoors, thank you very much. Besides, did you forget that I don't want anything to do with the turtles?"

Lovie waved away the sentiment. "Come down for the company then. Do you remember Emmaline Baker? She's joined us now and she's just dying to see you."

"Emmi's here?" Cara conjured up an image of her dearest friend growing up.

"She still comes for the summers with her boys. She's been asking about you."

"I'd love to see her, too. But not today. Maybe later," she hedged. The thought of chitchat was beyond her.

Lovie cast her a sidelong glance, then walked inside the screened porch. She slid into a rocker with characteristic grace. "Sit down, Cara. We can talk a bit."

Cara followed her into the porch. Lovie removed her cap and fanned her face as she rocked. Watching her, Cara suppressed a shudder. Her mother's hair, once thick and the color of spun gold, was now so thin and white that in the harsh light her scalp could be seen. Cara licked her lips, shaken. "Can I get you some water?"

"No, I'm just about to go in and fix lunch. You must be famished."

"Don't go to any trouble for me while I'm here," she said, grabbing her mug and sitting beside her mother. "I never eat regular meals anyway. My body is used to the abuse."

"You're far too thin. And pale."

She laughed. "I was just thinking the same about you!"

"Oh?" Lovie's blue eyes widened. "Well, who cares about me? I'm an old woman. But you're in your prime!" Her gaze eagerly traveled across Cara's face to her disheveled, shoulder-length brown hair cut in a blunt style. She wore the same wrinkled T-shirt that she'd arrived in over baggy, blue men's boxers that exposed long, thin legs crossed at the ankles. "You always do find the best hairdressers," she said. "But you look tired. And stressed. Especially your eyes. They're all puffy and a bit bloodshot."

"Charming," Cara muttered as she sipped her coffee. She moved her hand to apply pressure to her forehead where she could feel tension building up.

"Are you ill? There's been so much early summer flu going around."

"No. It's just an annoying headache."

"Ahhh... So you still get them?"

"Unfortunately."

"Mmm-hmm. See? It is the stress. When you were little you used to get them whenever you had a test, do you remember? Or when..." She stopped midsentence.

"When Daddy blew his top," Cara finished for her.

Her mother smiled weakly and an awkward silence reigned.

"Oh, I forgot to tell you that you got a call while you were out." Cara reached for her doughnut. "Some lady found tracks."

"What time was that?"

"Hours ago. That girl inside took the call."

"Oh, yes. That was the false crawl." Then she asked pointedly, "*That girl?* I assume you mean Toy Sooner?"

Cara couldn't keep her opinion from her face. "Toy? Is that her name?" She bit into the doughnut, sprinkling bits of glazed sugar down her chest. "We didn't get that far," she mumbled, chewing and brushing away the crumbs. "We snarled at each other like cats for a few minutes, then I left before any damage was done." She reached for her coffee cup and took a quick sip. "Who is she anyway? And isn't she a bit young to be pregnant?"

Lovie studied her daughter's face with the same expression she had worn when Cara was young and spoke with her mouth full. "Yes, she is young. Very young, poor dear. But these things happen, you know. Even in Charleston."

Cara rolled her eyes and dabbed a napkin at her mouth. "Mother, I'm hardly shocked. I'm just curious what she's doing here. Now, of all times."

"During your visit, you mean?"

"Frankly, yes. It's not like I come that often. What? Once every twenty years?" She bit into her doughnut and chewed. Swallowing hard she added with pique in her voice, "You led me to believe you wanted to spend some time with me. Fool that I was, I assumed you meant just us."

"Cara, dear, let's not start getting snippy. I *did* invite you to be here with me."

"I see. So you invited this Toy person because…?"

"I didn't invite her. She's not a guest, Cara. She lives here. I couldn't boot her out just because you were coming for a visit."

"Lives here? Since when? The season's only just begun."

"Since I moved in last January. Toy came in March."

"January? But you never come that early. Why would you leave your house to come stay out here in winter? Did you and Palmer have a fight?"

"No, Palmer and I did not have a fight. Why would you think that? But I couldn't, or rather, I didn't want to live alone at my age. So when I mentioned my situation to Flo she introduced me to Toy." When Cara looked puzzled, Lovie asked, "You remember Florence Prescott from next door, don't you?"

"Of course I do. The upbeat woman with a great shock of bright red hair."

"Yes, but the hair is white now. What you might not recall is that she worked for years as a social worker in Summerville. Flo spent the weekdays in an apartment there and fixed up the family's old house on the island on weekends, vacations—whenever she could. Anyway, her mother grew quite frail and Flo finally decided it was time to retire and bring her mother home to live with her. Goodness, that must be ten years ago already. My, my, my, time flies so quickly. They've been such good friends. Lucky for me to have them next door."

"Mother, what has this got to do with Toy?"

"I was getting to that. Flo still volunteers her time at the Women's Shelter and one day while we were talking I told her about my wanting to live here on the island and how I should have a companion. She grew quite excited—you know how Flo gets—and told me about a young girl who would be perfect for the job."

"You found her at the shelter?"

"You make it sound like she's some dog I found at the pound," Lovie scolded. "Yes, she was at the shelter, poor girl.

That's what it's there for, thank the Lord. Women need a place to go to when they're frightened for their well-being."

"I know, I know. You're preaching to the choir. I donate regularly to a shelter in Chicago."

Her mother nodded in acknowledgment. "I'm not talking out of turn when I tell you Toy's history. She and I discussed this and she agreed that it would be best for me to tell you. Toy found herself pregnant by her live-in boyfriend and she left him when he hit her."

"Hit her?"

"Beat her, actually. The baby wasn't hurt but Toy was frightened for it and left."

"As well she should have. I give her high marks for that. But she's so young to be living with a boyfriend and pregnant. What about her family?"

"Horrible people who wouldn't take her back. They kicked her out, called her a tramp and other such cruel things you can only imagine then left her to fend for herself. Imagine, doing that to your own daughter."

Cara could indeed imagine and felt a sudden sympathy for the girl. She knew how terrifying that scenario was. The city streets could be cold and mean to a young girl.

"How old can she be? Sixteen? Seventeen?"

"She's almost eighteen, and precious. She looks quite young."

A knot formed in Cara's throat. "I left home at eighteen."

Her mother startled. "Why, that was different, Cara. You chose to leave. Your father and I were against it, but you were always headstrong and so sure of yourself. Toy isn't like that. She's insecure, a mere child."

Cara squeezed her eyes shut, feeling a sharp stab of hurt. She couldn't look at the wide-eyed expression on her mother's face nor believe she could say those words to her after what they'd put Cara through at the same age. How could Mama have forgotten that she, too, was kicked out of the house? Or had she merely preferred to forget?

"Toy had nowhere else to go," Lovie tried to explain.

Nor did I when I left. Did you worry about me? "So you just took her in?" Cara asked, opening her eyes.

"It seemed the perfect solution. I wanted a companion and Toy needed a place to stay."

"It's your life," she said, lifting her hands.

"You're shutting me out again."

"No," she replied evenly, controlling her bubbling anger. "I'm not interfering. There's a difference."

A familiar, painful silence dragged between them during which Cara's headache pounded and her mother gazed out at the sea.

"I'm certain if you give Toy a chance, you'll like her. She might seem a little hard at first, but she's rather like a turtle. Underneath her hard shell is a very sweet creature who needs to be protected and loved." Lovie reached out to place her hand over Cara's. "Won't you at least try to be friendly with Toy? For my sake?"

Cara leaned wearily back in her chair and looked long at her mother. Her rage fizzled but the hurt lingered as her heart cried in a child's voice, *Why are you defending Toy and not me? Your own daughter?* Cara couldn't help the burn of jealousy that her mother was so fond of this strange girl. Over the years, she and her mother had remained polite yet nonintrusive. It was a long-distance relationship that had suited them both. And yet, seeing her mother sitting a foot away, that space between them suddenly felt so large and empty.

Cara slipped her hand away. "Okay, Mama, I'll try."

three

---

*At last the loggerhead arrives in familiar waters. She waits in
the swells near shore as a moon rises above the Atlantic.
Her home is the sea, but instinct demands that she leave all she
knows and face the unknown dangers of the beach to nest.
Is it safe here, or should she swim farther on?*

Cara's headache blossomed into a full-blown migraine that
sent her limping back to her bed. Lovie placed a cool cloth
over her eyes and forehead and instructed Cara not to think,
to just let her muscles relax. Cara nodded in compliance but
knew that was like telling herself not to breathe. She had no
job, no income and no plan for tomorrow. Her brain would
be churning like mad for weeks to come. She shifted rest-
lessly, then pulled the washcloth off her face. A rare hopeless-
ness overwhelmed her, and bringing her hands up to cup her
face, she let go of days of unshed tears.

Sometime later, her eyes were swollen and gritty and she
felt that queer listlessness that comes when one is drained.
Turning her head, she stared vacantly outside the window at
an oleander swaying in the wind. Time had little meaning for
her now. Clouds had moved in quickly from the mainland,
changing the blue sky to gray. Outside her window she'd heard
the low bellowing of a foghorn as a huge container ship navi-

gated its way through the harbor and out to sea. She felt like one of those ships, caught in a fog as thick as pea soup, unable to see what lay ahead.

She had been only eighteen when she'd left Charleston for points north. She didn't care where she went, as long as it wasn't in the South. She'd had her fill of the unspoken but clearly understood expectations of a young woman, especially one from an old Charleston family. She would go to the college of their choice, find a husband and get married, then live somewhere in the South. Her whole life had been neatly mapped out for her.

But all along, she'd been studying maps of her own. She left home in a huff of tears and landed in Chicago. That soaring city on Lake Michigan suited her outspoken, rebellious ways more than the delicately mannered, cultured city of Charleston ever had. So she'd stayed, trading saltwater for fresh, her Southern lilt for a Midwestern twang, vowing to make a place in the world with her brains and wit, not her feminine charms.

She'd given it her all. During the day she worked as a secretary in an ad firm. At night, while roommates were having fun at bars finding mates, she went to school. To this day she was most proud of having earned a college degree by going to night school for seven long years. She went on to get a master's in business, all without a penny of support from her parents. That was her way. She believed if she worked harder than most were willing to, she'd win the race.

And she did, but the race was a marathon. It took her fifteen years to doggedly work her way up the ladder from receptionist to account director. She'd earned a full and busy life, filled with the small luxuries that she was proud to be able to afford for herself. She wasn't wealthy, but she could splurge and go to the theater, drink good bottles of wine, dabble in investments and buy the appropriate suits and accessories required of a woman in her position.

And from time to time there were men... Never anything lasting, but then again, she never expected it to be. She'd been with Richard Selby for four years, longer than anyone before. He was a lawyer for the same ad firm, surefooted, witty and handsome in a corporate way. It was as close as she'd come to a serious relationship. She wondered if this was love. They didn't speak the words—it was not their style—but she felt the understanding was there.

All in all, her life had been content.

And then, unthinkably, that life was over. She was fired and found she had no friends outside of work. She'd left town without so much as a goodbye to Richard and it didn't seem to have made any difference. She still couldn't get over that fact.

What frightened her most was that she'd had no control over what happened. She was a woman who liked control, who planned for all contingencies. But she hadn't seen it coming. She'd worked and worked, moving along on her planned trajectory and bam! Now she felt numb. Drained of everything but fear. Wouldn't they have a good laugh at work if they could see her now? The strong, tough Miss Rutledge curled up like a fetus in her mother's house.

She brought the blanket high up under her chin, burying her face in the pillow. The down smelled of the sea. Holding it tighter, she looked again outside her window. A gust of air carrying the sweet scent of rain sent the roller shade rapping.

A rain shower would be nice, she thought drowsily, closing her eyes again.

She awoke later to the sound of knocking wood. Opening her eyes, she was surprised to find the room shadowy dark. In the hall, a light glowed. Her mother stood at the window, a small, trim figure in a thin summer sweater, an apron tied around her waist. Lovie was patting the window frame with the butt of her hand, trying to close the stubborn, swollen wood against the incoming storm. An angry wind billowed the screens and the first fat drops of rain streaked the glass. At last the window rumbled closed, leaving the room tight and secure.

"What time is it?" Cara asked in a croaky voice, rising up on her elbows. Pain pulsed in her head, sending her back to the pillows with a soft groan.

"I'm sorry I woke you," her mother said, fastening the window lock and rolling the shade down. "My but that rain's coming down like the Lord's flood." Turning to face Cara again, she studied her with a mother's eyes. She stepped closer, hesitant. "How's the headache?"

"Not as bad as this morning."

"But still there?"

"Uh-huh," she murmured. "How long have I slept? What time is it?" she repeated, licking dry lips.

"It's almost four o'clock. It's been drizzling on and off all day, just teasing us. But a good storm is rolling in now from the mainland. Thank heavens. We need the rain." She reached out to stroke a lock of hair from Cara's forehead, then rested her palm to test for fever. Her fingertips felt soothing and Cara's lids drooped. "And you can use the sleep," she added, removing her palm. "But first, do you think you can eat a little something? I've made you some soup."

Cara smiled weakly but gratefully. "I thought I smelled something wonderful. And could I have a glass of water?"

"Of course. I'm on my way."

Cara dragged herself up again, wincing at the relentless pulsing in her temples. But she could hold her eyes open in the dim light and the nausea had subsided. Outside her window the wind whistled. Thunder rolled so loud and close she could feel the vibrations, but it was fast moving. She knew this storm would soon move out to sea. She walked on wobbly legs to the bathroom to splash cool water on her face. When she returned, she found her mother already back in her bedroom with a tray filled with food and fresh flowers in a vase.

"Here we are! Some nice chicken gumbo, chunks of bread, ice water and, best of all, aspirin."

Cara moved slowly, any sudden movement causing ricochets of pain in her head. She settled under the blankets and leaned back against the pile of pillows that her mother had plumped for her. "I feel like a patient in the hospital."

"You're just home, darling. Do you often have these headaches?"

"From time to time. They come if I work too late or sleep too long, that kind of thing. Chocolate does it, sometimes. Caffeine, on occasion. I've had more than the usual of all of the above recently."

"Genetics, most likely," her mother said with conclusion. She rested the tray on Cara's lap. As she spread out the napkin, she continued. "Your grandmother Beulah had headaches so bad she used to retire to her room for days with the shutters drawn. We children were instructed to play out of doors and were under strict orders to tiptoe around the house in stocking feet so as not to clomp loudly on the hardwood floors. The order went for house staff, too. I remember how we used to giggle at seeing a hole in one of their stockings."

Cara savored the soup as the tastes exploded in her mouth. "Oh, God, I'd forgotten how good this was."

Lovie's chest expanded as she watched.

"If genetics win out," Cara said as she dipped her spoon again, "then I reckon that hidden somewhere inside of me lies the knack for making gumbo like this. And greens…and barbeque sauce…and grits with tasso gravy." She blew on another spoonful. "Though very deeply hidden," she added with a twinkle in her eye before sliding the spoon in.

"Pshaw. That has nothing to do with genetics. That's training, pure and simple. Since the day you were old enough to help me in the kitchen. I wouldn't be worth my salt as a mother if I didn't pass on the family recipes."

Cara looked into her bowl.

"What's wrong, honey? You seem troubled. Do you want to talk about it?"

"Not really." She paused, realizing she'd sounded flippant. She hadn't meant to. It was more a knee-jerk reaction to anyone probing into her personal life. Even her mother. Perhaps especially her mother. Taking a step to closing the gulf between them she added, "Not yet."

Lovie unclasped her hands and made a move toward the door. "I'll be here if you change your mind."

"Mama," Cara called out.

Lovie turned, her hand resting on the doorknob.

"Thank you. For the soup."

"You don't have to say thank you. I'm your mother. It's my job. My pleasure."

"I know, but thanks for…everything."

Lovie wiped her hands on her apron and nodded, but her eyes sparkled with gratitude. "You eat up, hear? I'll be back in a bit for the tray."

Cara lay back on the pillows and sighed. These first steps could be exhausting.

The rainy weather persisted on and off throughout the Memorial Day weekend. Parades were canceled and picnics brought indoors. Lovie could well imagine the grumbles that rumbled in the hotels and rental houses on the island. As for herself, Lovie was glad for the rain. They needed it desperately. The tips of the palmettos were crisp brown. Besides, the cloudy, introspective skies were a nice change and propelled her to do more of the indoor chores that needed doing. Like her photo albums.

For years she'd intended to organize her collection of old family photos into albums but the free time never seemed to materialize. So, most of her photos ended up stashed in boxes, out of harm's way but certainly not in any kind of order. Since moving to the beach house, however, she'd put the project high on her priority list and filled up more albums in the past four months than she had in the past forty years.

On this rainy afternoon, Lovie was so engrossed in sorting through the photographs that she didn't hear the kitchen door open.

"Are you still digging through those moldy old photographs?" Florence Prescott asked as she walked into the cottage.

Lovie turned her head to smile at her dear friend and neighbor. "Still? Honey, I've more photos to sort through than I can get done in a lifetime. Or, at least my lifetime."

Flo's smile slipped and her brilliant blue eyes grew more serious. "Why? How are you feeling? Any change?"

"No, and I don't expect any."

"Well, don't sound so glum about it. That's good, I guess. Steady as she goes."

Flo crossed the room and plopped down on the sofa beside Lovie. She was of average height and build but with a runner's body—slim, wiry, darkly tanned and just beginning to give in to softness at sixty-five. Only her thick, snowy-white hair gave a clue that she wasn't a woman half her age. When she spoke it was with the same focused, upbeat energy she used in running the local races.

"Well, then! How's everything else around here? Seems pretty quiet. Where's Toy?"

"She went to the market. Said she wanted to make something sweet for dessert. I'm not sure whether it's to fatten me up or because her hormones are running wild."

Flo laughed. "Probably a bit of both. You know, I still haven't laid eyes on that renegade daughter of yours. Is she really here or are you just making that up?"

"Go on and take a peek in her room if you don't believe me. But I wish you wouldn't. She's sleeping."

"Again? All she does is sleep. Is she sick?"

"She has migraines. She spent the first several days just lying in the dark, poor thing. But I gave her plenty of my chicken gumbo and they're pretty much gone now."

"Chalk up another cure to home cooking. Then why is she still sleeping?"

"I've been wrestling with that question myself. It could be she's just exhausted. She works so hard and she claims she's burned out by the job. Do you know she travels to New York or Los Angeles several times a month? I had no idea. I couldn't imagine living like that. Back and forth, back and forth, sometimes just for the day. It suits her, I suppose, but I'm much too much a homebody for that." She pursed her lips and looked toward the closed bedroom door. She thought of the sadness she saw in her daughter's eyes...or was it defeat?

"I get the feeling that something else is wrong. It's like she's sick inside but she won't tell me what the problem is."

"She's our Caretta. I'd be more surprised if she did tell you."

"Why do you say that?"

"How many years has she been gone? Twenty? In all those years how many times has she come to you for advice? Or just to visit and hang out and, I don't know, go through those old pictures together?" Her eyes flashed. "I can't think of a single time."

Lovie turned back to the photographs, feeling the pain of the comment deeply. "She's busy and has her own life."

"I think it's because it's easier. You two fight a lot."

"We do *not*."

"Maybe not yelling or such. You're much too polite for that," she said with a nudge. "But there's always been this unspoken argument between the two of you. I suppose it's just your way. But if you ask me—and I know you aren't asking but here's my opinion anyway—the two of you could use one good ol' knock-down-drag-out fight. Spit it all out."

"What a suggestion!" Lovie replied, irked that her dearest friend couldn't understand the situation at all. "You've known us for long enough to know better. Cara's simply moved far away. It's only natural that there be an emotional distance as well. Besides, Cara's always been a loner and perfectly capable of taking care of herself."

"Being able to take care of herself and being by herself are two separate things entirely."

"What are you saying?" The notion struck her hard.

"Well, does she have a fella?"

"Who knows, though I've asked her enough times. She gets prickly when I so much as broach the subject. She mentioned a Richard Selby from her office who she's been seeing for some time. My ears perk up whenever a man's name is mentioned twice in her life. But it seems to me if he were the least bit special she would be on the phone with him. She hasn't called a soul." Lovie thought back to the empty-eyed expression she'd caught when Cara was staring out the window. "Do you think she's lonely?"

"How should I know? It's possible. I mean, she may be

superwoman at work but she's still a woman when she goes home at night."

Lovie set the photos down in her lap, flustered. "But, I just told you. She lives a busy, full life. She's always going some-place or doing something with someone. Cara loves the the-ater, you know. She's seen all the latest shows."

Flo's blue eyes seemed to burn right through Lovie's ar-guments. "You might know better than most how empty a busy life can be."

Lovie's breath caught and she couldn't reply. It felt as though her world, which just a few moments ago seemed peaceful and orderly, was thrown off-kilter.

"I'm sorry," Flo said. "You know me, I speak first and think later. You wouldn't be the first one to toss a ripe tomato my way. Go right ahead."

Lovie shook her head with a shaky smile. "It's what I love most about you. But, I wonder if you might be right about Cara after all." She picked up a photograph from the pile on her lap. It showed a dark-haired Cara at about thirteen, all thin arms and legs. She was curled up like a cat in the branches of an enormous, twisted live oak tree, reading a book.

"Look at her," Flo said with affection. "She was scowling even then."

Lovie chuckled and ran a finger over the girl's image. "I remember taking this one. That old tree was her favorite spot. She'd go up there to read or think, or just to be alone. Hiding out, most likely. She was a funny little thing. Always seemed to carry the weight of the world on her shoulders."

"Pubescent girls often behave like that. They're teetering at the edge of womanhood and are so damn moody."

"Perhaps. We used to be very close when she was little but she became so distant. I could almost feel her hand pushing me away."

"Again, that's normal for a girl that age."

"Be that as it may, it's still painful for the mother to go through." She sighed. "She's still pushing me away. But that's nothing compared to her father. She may have pushed me away but she raised her dukes to him. Went toe-to-toe with him at every chance. I was terrified for her. You know how his temper was. I daresay she enjoyed torturing him."

"Yeah? Well, good for her."

"Flo!"

"What? You know how I felt about Stratton. God rest his soul, though I hate to think where the old coot's roasting now."

Lovie frowned but let that pass without comment. The least response from her about Stratton would get Flo wound up like a top. She couldn't stand the man and the feeling had been mutual. But that was all water under the bridge, as far as Lovie was concerned.

"I wanted to capture Cara in her tree and I'm glad I did," she said, returning her attention to the photograph. "Hurricane Hugo took that oak away along with so many others. Such a pity," she ended with a sigh and set the photo aside. "I'll show this to her later. She's bound to notice her tree is gone."

"When you do, why don't you ask her what else she remembers about that time? It's a good way to open things up between you."

"Oh, Flo, those days are long gone. Why stir up bad memories? This is the first time she's come home just to visit me. I'd like to keep things cheery and positive. And who knows? You might be right and it was nothing more than teenage angst, anyway. Best to leave things lie."

"There you go, tucking everything neatly away again." She looked at her fingernails and said, "Speaking of which, have you talked to her about, well—" she raised her eyes "—you?"

"About me? Good heavens, no. She's only just arrived."

"She's been here for days! I know you, Olivia Rutledge. You'll keep mum and hold it all inside so as not to rock the boat."

"No, I won't. I've got a doctor's appointment in a few days. I've waited this long to tell her, I can wait a few days more."

"You *will* tell her?"

"Of course."

Flo's eyes bore into hers one more time, as though to gauge whether or not to believe her. Apparently satisfied with whatever she saw in Lovie's eyes, she sighed deeply, slapped her palms on her thighs and rose to a stand. "I have to go check on Miranda. She caught a slight cold but at her age everything's a worry. Oh! I almost forgot the reason I came over. There was a stranding this morning over on Sullivan's Island."

"Was it a loggerhead?"

Flo nodded. "A juvenile. Poor thing. Its carapace was sliced up by a propeller. Probably in the harbor. That's the sixth dead turtle that's washed up this season. I hate it when the dead ones outnumber the nests. What with the shrimping season getting underway, we can expect to see a lot more."

"I hope not. It's early. Our girls are still out in the swells and they're just getting started. Give them time. It might be a slow start, but it's going to be a great season. Our best." She looked at the photograph of Cara and smiled with the brightness of hope. "I can feel it."

four

The loggerhead is named for its unusually large head. She has a
powerful beaklike jaw and her eardrums are covered by skin. She
has a keen sense of smell and an even keener instinct
for survival—one that has kept the species alive since
prehistoric times.

After a week of moping about the house in her pajamas, Cara
decided she'd had enough wallowing. Today she would start
her visit over. She waited behind the closed door of her bedroom until she heard the front door close and the footsteps of
Lovie and Toy departing from the cottage. It had been another in a series of wild mornings of the telephone ringing
with reports from the turtle volunteers, followed by a bustle
of motion as Toy and Lovie gathered their supplies into the
red bucket and headed for The Gold Bug and whatever point
along the beach that turtle tracks were found.

The coast was clear, as she and Palmer used to say when their
father had left for work. She showered as best she could in the
pitiful stream of water that escaped through a faucet with a
chokehold of lime, but the French lavender soap her mother
laid out went a long way to making her feel enormously better. There were large, thirsty towels and a lovely gardenia-
scented lotion to complete her bath. Back in her room, she

saw that her mother had unpacked her suitcase for her. Inside the dresser drawer she found a fresh sachet.

Cara smiled, shaking her head and murmuring, "Mama…"

Her mother had always picked up her messy room during her teens. True, the room was vacuumed, the dirty dishes and laundry removed, but Cara knew it was really her mother's clever way of keeping tabs on her rebellious offspring. One day Cara planted a package of condoms in a brown paper bag far back in the drawer beneath her bras. Oh, how the fireworks exploded that afternoon when she came home from the beach! Lovie tried both to scold Cara and defend herself for rifling through her daughter's drawers. Cara's hand stilled on the dresser, remembering that her mother had never told her father about the contents of that paper bag.

Hanging in the cramped closet were her dressy slacks, silk blouses and one sexy black dress. Her closet back in Chicago was bulging with lovely tropical weight wool suits, silk blouses and scarves, and fine leather boots and shoes for a professional working in a city. But she had nothing for a casual day at the beach. Her life in Chicago had not been casual.

She settled on a chic mint-green silk outfit and a pair of very dressy, strappy leather sandals studded with rhinestones that looked great on Michigan Avenue. Looking in the long mirror tacked to the back of the door, she saw a tall, sleek, dark-haired woman dressed to the nines and terribly out of place on the laid-back island. Then, because she felt a need for bolstering, she added a touch of shadow and mascara and a spritz of scent. Her dark hair, still damp, was rolled into a twist and secured with a clip.

By the time she stepped into the living room, the fog had swept out to sea and sunshine poured in from the windows. Her spirits lifted at the prospect of a lovely day as she stood for a moment just inhaling great gulps of the fresh, salty air.

She took her growling stomach as a good sign and moved into the small kitchen, neat and sparkling in the sun. She helped herself to a quick breakfast, then began to prowl, glancing out the windows, peeking in all the rooms and running her fingers through magazines on the coffee table. Before long, she felt the old restlessness stirring. She wasn't accustomed to so much time on her hands. She had no agenda. She was anxious to *do* something.

She rationalized that she'd needed a long, overdue vacation. But now it was time to regroup. She'd make a few calls and develop a game plan. Perhaps set up a couple of meetings. After all, she had contacts in the business, and a solid reputation to fall back on.

Except, she didn't have her computer with her. Or her cell phone. How could she have been so dazed as to leave them in Chicago? She'd stormed out of the city, determined to disengage. But rather than feel freer, she felt totally cut off without access to her email. She was addicted to the connection. Without it she felt jittery and antsy. Marooned on some deserted island.

While she paced, her wandering gaze caught sight of a cluster of photographs on the mantel that hadn't been there before. Her mother must have just put them up. Her curiosity pricked, she walked closer to inspect.

She was drawn first to the photograph of herself, naturally enough. In a small silver frame she saw herself as a young teen curled up in a tree reading a book. She felt a ping somewhere deep inside and raised her eyes out the rear window to search for the old oak tree that had been a dear friend to her for many years. But it wasn't in the yard. "Poor old tree," she said softly, mourning its loss. A flood of memories coursed through her and, instinctively, she placed the photograph back on the mantel and moved on.

The largest was a silver-framed family photograph taken on the veranda of the Charleston house. A ruddy-faced Palmer in a navy blazer with shiny brass buttons sat with his arm around a slender, erect Julia in pale linen, every hair in place. Palmer had borne the butt of many jokes about how he'd married a gal just like mom, but Cara had never laughed. She'd always found that at the root of jokes there often lay a core of truth. On either side of them sat their children, Linnea and Cooper.

She picked up a flowery, porcelain-framed school photo of her niece to study. Linnea was a pretty girl, an interesting combination of her parents. Counting back, Cara figured her niece was nine years old now. She had Palmer's warm smile and flirtatious grin that would someday wrap a boy around her little finger. But in everything else, she looked like her mother and grandmother: petite, with brilliant blue eyes, fine white-gold hair and porcelain skin. Ol' Palmer would have his hands full keeping the boys from that one, she thought with a chuckle. And it would only be God's good justice after the hell he'd raised growing up.

But Cooper was all Rutledge, from his strong jaw stuck out at a rebellious angle, to his broad forehead with the Rutledge hairline and the hint of what would someday become a proud, straight nose. He didn't smile as much as grimace for the camera, as if to say, *Do I have to?* She tried to recall how old he was, ashamed that she didn't know. It was a sad statement about her relationship with her brother. From the pudgy cheeks and the uncertain, wobbly smile, he looked to be no older than five. There was something in his eyes, however, a dark brown like her own and her father's, that drew her in. It was the vulnerability behind the bravado that she understood so well.

She placed the photograph slowly back onto its place on the mantel, feeling very distant from these children and sorry for it. She had no children of her own—not so much by choice as by circumstance—and they were her only niece and nephew. She'd sent them gifts at Christmas and for their birthdays, for which she promptly received polite but impersonal thank-you notes. Such was the extent of their relationship. She wondered if they would even recognize her if she passed them in the street.

Making a quick decision, she walked directly to the phone and dialed Palmer's number at the family house. It was the same number she'd dialed since she was a child. It rang four times before a gruff voice answered.

"Palmer?" she asked, surprised to find him home in the morning. She'd expected to reach Julia.

There was a pause. "Mama?"

Cara laughed. "No, it's me. Cara. How are you?"

"Cara? Well, for... This is a surprise! Are you all right?"

"I'm fine, fine. In fact, I'm in town."

"No kidding? That's great. How long you in for?"

"Not too long."

"Business or pleasure?"

"Pleasure, actually."

"Really?" He sounded genuinely surprised. He chuckled softly, a low, masculine rumbling sound unique to Southern men. "Well now, that's a switch."

"Don't start in on me, Palmer," she replied, laughing. "Actually, I'm out at the beach house. Mama asked me to come for a visit and I had a few days, so here I am."

"Did she now?" He paused as though thinking that over. "So, did you meet her companion?"

By the way he said the word, she knew instantly that he disapproved of Toy Sooner. Cara sighed, remembering her promise to her mother. "I did. Briefly. She's been keeping herself scarce and, frankly, I've been grounded with a migraine since

I arrived. I couldn't open my mouth except to groan. But I'm feeling much better now. Listen, Palmer, I saw photographs of Cooper and Linnea and I was amazed at how they've grown. Actually, I'm calling because I'd like to see y'all while I'm in town." Palmer's drawl was so infectious she couldn't help the Lowcountry from creeping back into her own tone and words.

"Why sure, honey! We'd love that. Julia will cook up something real special. When can you come?"

She felt herself smiling. "When do you want me?"

"Well, here's the thing. I'm fixing to leave for Charlotte this afternoon. I've got some business to tend to up there that'll take up the week. I'm packing my suitcase right now. How about Saturday? You gonna be here that long? That's a whole three days away...."

She let the tease ride. Looking out the window she saw a brilliant blue sky. She'd spent her first week groaning in bed with the shades drawn or moping—hardly a vacation. But more importantly, she hadn't accomplished what she'd come here to do. And she wanted to see her niece and nephew.

"You can count on it, big brother."

"Well, good," he replied, and she could hear the pleasure in his drawl. "We're all looking forward to it. And bring that runaway back home with you, hear? Tell her that her grandbabies miss her. Mama hasn't been back here but a few times since she left. She's like a hermit crab, hiding out in that tiny place. I worry about her."

"Come out to the island, then. It's not far."

"Maybe now that summer's here and the kids are out of school, we'll do just that. We'll come out for a good visit."

"Mama'd like that." Then, thinking of Toy, "But it's a little crowded here now."

"Hell, I don't stay in the cottage anymore," he said, shooing away the suggestion in his blustery voice that sounded so much like her father's it was eerie. "I've got my own place on Sullivan's Island. Over by the lighthouse. Problem is, it's rented out so much in the summer we hardly ever get to come down to the water like we want to."

Cara heard the pride in his voice and thought that business must be pretty good for him to buy a summerhouse on Sullivan's. Last she'd heard, they were saving to buy a house downtown. Could be they liked living in Mother's house well enough. Then Cara knew an unsettling feeling as a new thought took root.

"Why don't y'all come around four o'clock," he said. "We'll take a spin on the boat, maybe go up the Intracoastal a ways and come around back to the harbor. I'll bet you haven't done that in a long time. We can have ourselves some drinks and watch the sun set like old times. We'll do it proper."

"Sounds great, Palmer," she said, meaning it. "Is there anything I can bring?"

"Well now, since you asked. Remember that shack that sells shrimp over on Shem Creek? Clud's?"

"No, but I can find it."

"Now, how can you forget an operation like that? Sure you remember. They've got the freshest shrimp, sell it right off the boat. You have to turn off Coleman by the gas station and wind your way round the old neighborhood as far back as you can go. It's way in there by the dock. If you can get me some of that shrimp, I'll take care of the bill when I see you. About four pounds ought'a do it. I'd get it myself but I won't be back from Charlotte until Friday and Julia and the kids are coming along to visit her mother. We'll all be back on Friday, though. Think I'll make us some Frogmore Stew."

She wondered if Palmer remembered that it had been her favorite Lowcountry meal growing up and wanted to prepare it just for her. "I sure can't say no to an offer like that."

"Well then, that's that. Say hello to Mama for me. I'll see you soon."

They signed off with the same familiarity as if they'd just talked yesterday. It was like that with family, she thought, staring at the old telephone with a grin on her face. They could be separated for years but in a few words an age-old connection was made that had nothing to do with telephone wires.

She placed the receiver back into its cradle but left her hand resting on it. The house was quiet. She was alone. In for a penny, in for a pound she decided and picked up the phone again. God, it was a clunky thing and it weighed a ton compared to her little cell phone. She dialed her home number and checked her messages.

There were the expected sympathy calls from colleagues, some of whom were also laid off, some of whom she wasn't sure about. She wrote these numbers down. Richard had called many times, asking why she wasn't answering her cell phone, each time sounding more worried and pleading that she call.

Richard. She missed him with a sudden urgency, conjuring up his strong features and dark brown hair just beginning to show dashing strands of gray. They'd shared disasters and triumphs alike. Everyone at the agency knew about their relationship and even tacitly approved of it. After all, when they weren't working together on a project at the office, they were talking about the project during their personal time together. In fact, they'd often laughed and declared that what they had was better than love.

She heard the panic in his messages and felt guilty for not trying to reach him sooner. She hadn't even left him a message that she was leaving town. Headache or no, she should have tried to contact him. Was Richard as devastated at being fired? It was a shame that he'd had to leave for New York during the biggest crises of their careers, when they needed each other the most.

She looked at her watch. It was 10:15, an hour earlier in Chicago. He might still be asleep. She yearned to call him but decided to contact Adele Tillwell first. If she didn't reach her early, she and the headhunter would begin a nagging session of lunchtime phone tag. She went to her room to collect her PalmPilot, paper and a pen, then returned to the small wooden hall table and made a makeshift desk, cursing herself again for leaving her cell phone. Pulling up a chair, she dialed the number of the trusted contact at an employment agency she'd dealt with many times before, but always from the hiring side of the desk.

Fortunately, Adele was at her desk. After initial pleasantries, they got swiftly down to business. She talked at length with Adele about her current situation, not the least surprised that she already knew about her layoff. They made a few jokes, laughed a bit, shared a little gossip, then when the chitchat was completed they dove right into what was out there in the market, appraised her résumé and considered what her next move should be.

"I'll do what I can but the hiring picture is grim," Adele concluded. "Especially at your level. Thanks to your old alma mater, the streets are flooded with applicants."

Cara felt panic take root. "But my reputation is solid. I've got an impressive list of credits."

"Yes, you do. You're a plum, no doubt about it. There's something out there for you."

She heard the uncertainty. "Go on…"

"It's just a matter of waiting it out."

Cara did a little mental arithmetic, trying to figure out how long she could survive without an income. The separation package was generous, but… "I can't wait too long or I'll lose my cushion. Not to mention my condo."

"I can't control these things, Cara. It could take months, at the very least."

"God, I hate not being in control."

Adele chuckled and Cara felt the tension easing. Adele was good at her job. "It's not totally out of our control. What I can do is work hard for you. And I will, Cara. You're now my favorite client. I owe you. You've done a lot for me in the past."

"No, you don't owe me anything, but thanks, Adele."

"What you can do is follow up on your own contacts. By the way, is there anyone or anyplace in particular you'd like me to inquire?"

They chatted a few minutes longer about possible firms to pursue.

"Okay then," Adele concluded. "Just fax me the list."

"I can't. I'm in the dark ages here. If you saw the phone I was talking on…"

"Email me then."

"I don't have a computer."

"You don't? Where the hell are you? Siberia?"

"No." She chuckled. "My mother's beach house. I left in such a fog I forgot everything that wasn't attached. Look, it doesn't matter. I won't be here that long. I'll get the list to you. There's always the U.S. Mail."

"This will be interesting. When are you coming back to Chicago?"

"Probably next week."

"I'll see what I can line up. Oh, I just had an idea. You can always call Richard Selby and see if he can pull a few strings for you."

Richard? "Uh, fine. Thanks again. Goodbye."

She slowly put down the receiver. For another minute she

sat with her hand resting on the phone trying to make sense
of Adele's parting comment. Clearly the message was that
Richard was in a strong position. Was it possible that he was
not laid off from the agency after all? Her mind spinning with
questions, she immediately dialed Richard's home number.
Ordinarily she wouldn't expect him to be at home in the
morning, but these were not ordinary times.

After the fifth ring, the answering machine clicked on. His
voice answered, clear and upbeat, but she hung up without
leaving a message. Her heart was pounding in her ears as she
thought the impossible. *Could he still be at the agency?*

Damn. The last thing she wanted to do was call there.
She cringed at the thought of the awkward condolences and
embarrassing explanations. But it was unlike her to put anything off. She needed to know. Now. Taking a deep breath,
she picked up the phone again and dialed Richard's private
number, even while wondering if the number was still valid.

"Good morning. Richard Selby's office."

Cara's breath caught and she took a second to collect herself. "Hello, Trish. This is Cara Rutledge."

"Well, hello! We've been wondering where you've been
hiding!"

She felt the sting of that comment prickle her cheeks. "I
wasn't aware that I was hiding," she replied with frost.

"Oh," the secretary stumbled, her tone becoming more subdued. "It's just that Mr. Selby tried calling you several times.
He's been worried about you."

"Has he? There was no need. My mother called and I had
to leave town immediately to see her. It was urgent family
business." She wanted the word out that there was an emergency she had to tend to rather than that Cara Rutledge was
hiding under some bush.

"I hope she's all right."

"Everything is fine now, thank you." She skipped a beat then said as casually as she could, "I take it that Mr. Selby is still with the agency?"

Trish laughed. It was a high trill sound ringing with astonishment. "Of course he is. In fact, he's been promoted! Didn't you know? Mr. Selby is now Vice President Senior Attorney."

Cara's heart beat faster as suspicion did its nasty job of creating doubt in her mind. It wasn't hard to create a diabolical picture. Richard worked in legal. He knew the mass layoffs were coming. And yet, he was promoted. That could only mean he was on the inside track on this one. He had to have known that her name was on the list. And knowing, he had left town while the dirty work was done. He let her go to the chopping block with a blindfold on.

Why, the sneaky little coward, she thought, wringing the telephone cord in her fingers. And on her birthday…

"Miss Rutledge?"

"What wonderful news for him," she replied in an even voice. "I imagine you must be very busy moving offices."

"Oh, no, we're done now. The announcement wasn't made until this week but we've known for a while and had time to get things packed up. It's just that, you know, Mr. Selby didn't want to make it official until after the layoffs and all. Oh—" She paused, suddenly unsure, as though just remembering that Cara had been one of the unfortunate ones. "I'm sorry, Miss Rutledge. But, of course, you knew all this." There was a nervous question in the statement.

"Of course," Cara replied. She needed to get some air.

"He's in a meeting now, but I know he wants to talk to you. Like I said, he's been calling and calling. I'll be sure to tell him you're out of town. Is there a number where he can reach you?"

Cara paused, feeling his betrayal claw at her heart. "No,"

she replied calmly. "I'll be on the road. Please tell him I'll call him later. At home," she added before hanging up, preserving the illusion that they were still on intimate terms.

At the moment, that's all it was. A hideous illusion. All the closeness, confidences, hours that they'd shared for four years were meaningless! She felt her fury rise up to howl in her chest. Her hand hovered over the phone as she fought the urge to call his home and leave a blistering message on that infernal machine.

She closed her hand in a fist and let it slide to rest at her side. It would be a cold day in hell before she called that bastard again. Even hurt and angry, she wasn't so stupid that she'd leave a message like that recorded for him to play over to whoever with a chuckle and a drink. He'd be patted on the back for the narrow escape he made. Cara's eyes squeezed at the pain. How could he have done this to her? She'd never known he could be so ruthless—at least not with her. No, they weren't married, but she'd thought of them as a team. She recalled the many happy occasions they'd spent together. There had been so many good memories, so many intimacies shared.

She sat on the hard-backed chair and stared out at the sea, overcome.

Then she laughed.

It started out as a short bark of laughter, a guffaw of disbelief blended with self-mockery then rolled into a choppy cadence of laughs. Oh, it was all too pathetic! This was the real top-aroo. What hellish astrological event brought all these catas-trophes her way? She'd turned forty, lost her job and now her boyfriend had dumped her. If she had a dog, it would have been run over by a car. What was next?

Lord, she thought as her laughing ended, she had to get out of this house or she'd go mad. She rose quickly from the chair, eager to put distance between herself and the phone, the beach house, everything. Outside, the late morning sun was high and cast a glistening sheen across the ocean.

She grabbed one of her mother's broad-rimmed straw hats from a basket by the door and lunged into the sunshine. Though she felt the power of a spring sun on her shoulders, she kept walking, making her way through a narrow path in the empty lots across the street. Such a broad expanse of unoccupied land was unusual on this valuable stretch of beach. Only a few beachfront lots were left on the entire island and here were three lopped together. Her mother was lucky to live across from them and keep her ocean view.

The path cut up a sandy incline and curved around a tall dune. Once again she was exhilarated at the sudden, surprising sight of the wide expanse of sparkling blue water. She heard the echoing roar punctuated by the cries of a gull. Far off in the mist, she caught the shadowy form of a cargo ship and, closer in, a line of pelicans coasted low over the waves. It was a marvel how she couldn't think about her problems or solutions while staring out at the sea. It was as if she'd pushed a delete button in her brain and the monitor had cleared. The breeze greeted her with a caress, drawing her down from her perch on the dune to the wide arc of beach.

On this side of the island, far from the hotels and restaurants, there were fewer tourists. But farther ahead, groups of sunbathers stretched out on colorful beach towels or sat in the shade under cheery umbrellas anchored in the sand. She began walking toward them, fixing as her goal the long stretch of pier two miles up where she knew she could get a cool drink and rest. As she walked along in her dressy silk outfit, she caught the idle stares of young girls in bikinis and mothers who stood by as toddlers splashed in the warm tidal pools. When she passed a small triangle of space on a dune outlined by wooden stakes, orange tape and a bright plastic warning sign, she smiled. This was a loggerhead turtle nest and it was likely her mother had marked it.

Her shoulders were beginning to burn by the time she reached the pier and the small business section of the island called Front Beach. Young, hard-muscled teens played ferocious games of volleyball before a cheering crowd. Desperately thirsty, she walked up the wooden pathway that led to the Banana Cabana. Tables under red umbrellas were available but she was hot and sweaty and longed for the cool of an air-conditioned room. Stepping inside, she faced a blessed wall of cool and blinked in the dim light of the darkly paneled restaurant.

Cara took a small table beside the wall under a neon beer sign. She didn't mind sitting alone. Her job had required lots of travel and she was accustomed to eating alone in a restaurant or biding her time at an airport bar. But on a business trip, her mind was focused on the job and her suit and briefcase made her invisible. Here, she idly stared at the walls and her dressy silk outfit screamed "Outsider!" in this easygoing crowd dressed in shorts, T-shirts and beach cover-ups.

A young waitress appeared and pulled out a pad and pencil. She already had a fabulous tan that she was eager to show off. Cara ordered a Diet Coke and a Cajun shrimp salad. It arrived quickly and she began mining through a salad the size of a small planet. As she jabbed her fork into the greens, she got the tingly sensation that someone was watching her. Quickly turning her head, she locked with a pair of eyes exactly the color of the cerulean sky she had left outside the dark room.

The spark of attraction shot straight down to her toes. He was sitting with his elbows on the bar and looking at her intently, his head turned over broad shoulders that stretched the faded blue fabric of his shirt. His thick hair was tawny colored and windblown, there was a stubble on his cheek and long lines cut through his deep tan at the corners of his eyes. He exuded a restrained power too ripe for a boy.

He sat at the bar with his three buddies, each of them a sterling example of a good ol' boy pulling down a beer at a favorite pub. The bearded redhead to his right leaned over to mutter something close to his ear, followed by a short laugh and a quick glance her way. She saw the tall man's glance slide from her face down to her shoes, then a slow, easy grin lifted the left corner of his mouth like he'd just caught the punch line of a private joke. He turned his head back to the baseball game on the TV over the bar, dismissing her.

Cara's cheeks flamed. In her mind's eye she could see that her strappy sandals with their sparkling rhinestones, which might have looked fabulous in the city, were a joke here.

"Check, please!" she called out, flagging her waitress. The girl came bouncing over, scribbling in her pad en route. Cara whipped her credit card out of her purse before the girl even arrived. The bill was soon settled and Cara hurried from the restaurant, walking swiftly past the bar without so much as a glance.

Outside the sun was blinding and stung her tender shoulders but Cara was mad now and not to be daunted. The anger felt good, the first real emotion she'd had in days. Even better, she now had a mission. Looking from left to right, she searched the lazy street. Her gaze passed over crazy murals on whitewashed buildings, ice cream and pizza parlors, a surf shop and a new, miniature chain hotel to zero in on a small boutique where a loud, raucous African parrot whistled and called. Cara smiled and made her choice, crossing the street.

"Good job," she said to the parrot as she entered the shop.

The salesgirl, though young, looked Cara over with an experienced eye. From the way she scurried around from behind the counter, Cara knew she had Customer In Dire Need of Help written all over her.

"What can I do for you?" the girl asked in a cheery voice.

"I need a dressing room," Cara replied, briskly walking through the narrow aisles of neatly folded clothes. She pulled out two pairs of shorts, four T-shirts, a thin stretchy sweat suit that would be perfect for nights on the beach, two swimsuits, a thin terry cloth cover-up, a long black flowing cotton dress decorated with red Hawaiian flowers and a blue tie-dyed beach towel that she couldn't pass by. She went into the dressing room and emerged soon after in khaki shorts and a white T-shirt with the tags hanging out. The salesgirl laughed as she snipped the tags off and carefully folded the mint silk ensemble into a bag.

"Anything else?"

"Sandals," Cara said emphatically, looking down at the now despised ones on her feet. "I need comfortable sandals that I can walk along the beach in and not worry if they get wet. I plan to do a lot of walking."

"You should get these," the girl replied, lifting her own foot.

Cara looked at the clunky, wide-strapped sandals with thick rubber soles and thought they were nothing she'd have picked out on her own.

"Size nine," she replied, slipping off the rhinestone sandals and tossing them in the trash bin.

"How about this?" the salesgirl asked with a wry smile, holding up a purple Koozie with the Isle of Palms logo. Cara laughed and shook her head, but when she saw a navy baseball cap with the South Carolina palm and crescent moon logo, she bought that, too. Placing it on her head, she handed over the straw hat to add to the burgeoning bag. Leaving the shop, she caught a glimpse of herself in a long mirror. Her neck and arms were sunburned and her long thin legs looked as pale as the underbelly of a fish.

"I scream tourist," Cara said, but laughed, pleased to see the same jaunty look she'd admired in her mother.

"Now you fit right in."

five

Though the mother loggerhead is tired and hungry, her work is just beginning. She will nest an average of four times during this season, resting two weeks between each nest.

Lovie sat slump-shouldered on the hard examining table while her shaky fingers buttoned up her blouse. These radiation therapy sessions leached the energy right out of her. If only it was as efficient with the cancer, she thought. But cancer wasn't about *if onlys*. Cancer was about what was, and the plain fact was, the radiation wasn't doing much. She'd only continued this long in hopes of prolonging her life by a few months. After such a full, active life, Lovie didn't want to spend her last days as an invalid.

Her hands stilled on her blouse as she considered again whether or not now was the time to tell her children about the cancer. When the tumor was discovered last December she'd felt shocked. Numb with fear. The tumor was already large and inoperable and the prognosis was dim. She had weighed the decision carefully, then drawn on years of experience in keeping unpleasantness from her children. So she'd kept her illness private.

Besides, Palmer would have made such a fuss. He was very attached to her and there would have been lots of his useless hand-wringing and wild declarations on how he was going to call in the experts and holler that she'd get the best damn treatment possible. Then Julia would have been pressed upon to be her primary caregiver and Lovie knew that her daughter-in-law wasn't up to the task. She was a good girl, but she would fret and worry and generally fall apart at the seams, more about how the illness was affecting *her own* schedule and life rather than Lovie's. The resulting chaos would have been too disruptive to the children. Not to mention, Palmer never would have allowed her to leave the house in Charleston and come out to the beach house to live if he knew.

And Cara… Lovie finished the row of buttons, then let her hands fall to her lap. She didn't know how her daughter would have reacted to the news. She might have taken time from work, flown in and demanded to take charge of the medical treatment in her efficient manner. Or she might simply have sent flowers.

Oh, she'd heard stories from other cancer patients. Heartbreaking tales of children who didn't visit their sick parents, of old friends who didn't even pick up the phone to chat, of brothers and sisters who pretended the cancer wasn't real or that, if ignored, it would simply go away. Did they think cancer was contagious? Were they so self-absorbed that they didn't want the inconvenience of sickness to interrupt their lives? Or were they so afraid of the very idea of death that they preferred to look the other way? It was no wonder so many of the terminally ill felt so alone.

Lovie shivered on the examining table, staring blankly at the green-tiled walls. The chill of the room went straight through her thin skin to her bones. She was so very tired, she felt like weeping and the radiation always made her stomach queasy. All she wanted was to go home to her beach house, sit in her favorite rocker on the windward porch and listen to the comforting murmur of the sea.

A brisk knock on the door brought her head up in time to see the door swing open and Dr. Pittman walk in, his long white coat billowing behind him. He always seemed to be in a hurry and when he spoke he shot out the words to get to the point as quickly as humanly possible. She found it unnerving and attributed it to him being both so smart his mouth couldn't keep up with his brain and to him being from somewhere in the North, Harvard or Yale or some such place. He was said to be the best, but nonetheless Lovie thought he seemed very young to have so many degrees.

"Good morning, Mrs. Rutledge," he boomed, his eyes still on the chart.

Lovie murmured a polite response and gathered her blouse closer around her neck.

Toy followed quietly, her eyes wide with anxiety. Bless her heart, Lovie thought. That child had been through the mill these past months, driving her to the therapy and endless doctor's appointments, waiting for hours at a time, all without a whisper of complaint. Providing transportation was important, but it was the least of Toy's caregiving efforts. She did most of the shopping, did all the housekeeping chores and even went to church with Lovie on Sundays. Most of all, Toy talked to her. When they came home from the therapy and Lovie felt more dead than alive, it was a simple pleasure to just sit back and listen to her upbeat prattle, so full of life, about whatever flitted through her young mind.

Lovie didn't know what she would have done without the girl. Toy Sooner was more than a companion. She was a godsend.

Lovie reached out her hand to the girl and Toy hurried forward to grasp it, squeezing it with encouragement and relief. Her face, however, was pale with fatigue, revealing a smattering of freckles across her nose. She didn't look old enough to be having a child.

"The Lord said to care for the sick," she said, patting Toy's slightly callused hand. "But you've taken it to the nth degree today."

"Hey, no problem," she replied, brushing away the concern with a flip of her hand.

"You'll get your reward in Heaven," she said, smiling. Then, more seriously, "I had no idea it would take so long."

"I was just sitting out there watching TV and reading. By the way, Doctor, the hospital could sure use some new magazines. The latest one is four months old. It's, like, really sad."

The doctor absently nodded as he read Lovie's chart.

"Are you tired?" Toy asked, looking closer at her face. "You look real tired. We might could stop for a milkshake or something on the way home?"

"Not for me. My stomach is still doing flip-flops. We can stop for you, though. It'd be good for the baby."

"I'd like to see you eat more," the doctor added to Lovie. "You're still losing weight."

"I'll try," Lovie replied in a lackluster tone, more to make the doctor happy. Privately, she couldn't see much point in it. She was going to die anyway. But she didn't express this so as not to alarm Toy. The girl seemed intent on keeping Lovie alive forever.

"Is there anything bothering you lately?" the doctor asked, looking up from the chart to skewer her with his dark eyes. "Any pain?"

Oh, yes, there was a great deal bothering her, Lovie thought. But the doctor knew he couldn't cure her and seemed to have lost interest in her case, eager to finish the chart and file it.

"I'm handling the pain very nicely with the pills you gave me, thank you."

"You'll call me if at any time the pills don't cover it anymore, okay?" He glanced at Toy for confirmation. She nodded dutifully. He closed the chart and rested his hand on it, shaking his thinning head of hair. "Well, that's it then. I have to say I'm not happy that you've canceled the treatment, Mrs. Rutledge. I'd rather you continued on through the summer."

Lovie closed her eyes and sighed.

"You stopped the treatment?" Toy asked, her eyes round with alarm.

"Yes, dear," she replied, then faced the doctor. "If I continue throughout the summer, as you recommend, will I be cured?"

"No," he replied cautiously. "Radiation was never the cure. But we discussed that, Mrs. Rutledge. Right?" He seemed unsettled that she should think otherwise.

"We did," she replied firmly. "I understand that completely. And I also understand that I'm not expected to last much beyond the summer, if that. Right?"

He had the grace to smile.

She felt Toy squeeze her hand, nervously.

"So tell me, Doctor, if you had one summer left of your life, would you spend it in radiation therapy?"

"I might. If it took me into fall."

Lovie shrugged slightly. "Summer's enough for me. If it's a good summer."

"But, Miss Lovie, you don't know!" Toy was revving up and Lovie knew she could go on for a long time if not checked. "You can beat this!"

"Hush now, dear. I've made up my mind." Then more softly, "Time is too precious for wishful thinking. I want to enjoy every minute the Good Lord gives me. And I can't do that if I'm sick and exhausted. Why would I want to spend what little time I have left just waiting for death? Not when there's still life in me. I'm firm, Doctor. No more radiation."

Toy was silenced and her eyes filled.

The doctor nodded in understanding. "Very well," he replied, pulling a prescription pad out from the pocket of his long white jacket. "Though our time here at the hospital is finished, Mrs. Rutledge, I do want to keep up with your progress. And, of course, I'll be in touch with your regular doctor should there be any change. But there are immediate concerns you'll have to discuss with your family about your care. We don't know the time frame of the cancer spreading. Hopefully, this last series of treatments will keep it at bay for a while. The time will come when you will need more assistance than Miss Sooner is able to provide. You'll need to gather a support system. Or you may want to consider moving into nursing care."

"No! Miss Lovie won't need to go nowhere. I'll stay with her," Toy said quickly.

Dr. Pittman looked at her with sympathy. "When is your baby due, Miss Sooner?"

"September."

"You understand that is the same time Mrs. Rutledge might need the most help? Caregiving can become extremely demanding. How can you manage all of her pressing needs plus take on the additional burdens and worries of a new baby?"

Lovie answered. "I have grown children, and as you said, there are organizations I can call. I don't want to go to a home."

"I'm writing out a phone number of a social worker who is trained to help the family make this decision. There are many considerations, of course. You may want to discuss it with your clergyman as well." He handed Lovie the paper. "I wish there was more that I could do for you. Best of luck to you. Keep in touch."

After he left, Lovie slumped her shoulders with relief. She was done with doctors, at least for the summer.

"I wish you'd have told me you were planning on quitting the therapy." Toy's tone was reproachful.

"I've only just decided."

"You'll have to tell Cara now. About being sick, I mean."

"No. And I forbid you to tell her, hear?"

"But…"

"Toy, let me be clear. I don't want Cara to know. Not yet."

"I don't know why you're protecting her," she said with a flare of temper. "She's supposed to be such a high-powered lady, right? Then she can handle it."

"I'm not doing this to protect her. It's because she *is* a high-powered lady, as you put it. If I tell her now, all we'll talk about is the treatment. Besides, she doesn't seem herself. I've more important things I want to discuss with her, and not very much time. If it gets too bad, then yes, I'll tell her. But I'll know when the time is right. You'll have to trust me. And promise me that you won't tell her."

"Okay, I promise," she agreed reluctantly. "But I don't think it's right. If it was me, I'd want to know. You should tell her."

"Oh? Have you told your mother when the baby is due?"

"That's different," she replied quickly.

"Is it? Or are you afraid that she won't care one way or the other? Toy, honey, I know what that is like. Maybe I'm afraid, too." She smiled reassuringly and put her hand on Toy's. "We can only do what we can live with."

Toy nodded, chewing her lip.

"Now I'm dog tired and want to go home to my beach house. Let's not fret about this any more today. After all, we both have the summer to think about it. And what a summer. Cara is home again! Your little hatchling is coming soon, too! There's so much good happening. What do you say? Let's make it a summer to remember."

The ladies of Primrose Cottage rallied around Palmer's invitation with an excitement that surprised them all. It had roused them from the lethargy that had hovered in the house. Part of the fun of the day was changing from the usual casual beach attire to something a bit dressy. When Cara stepped into the living room, Lovie stopped tying the rosy silk scarf over her linen dress to stare at her.

"Aren't you going to dress for dinner?"

Cara looked at her new navy sweatpants with the white racing stripe down the sides. She thought it looked rather smart. "I thought I'd wear this."

Lovie didn't speak for a moment. "For dinner?"

"Mama, we're going boating."

"You look like you're going to the gym! You can look so smart and you have all those pretty clothes. Why not wear something with a little color? High heels and a smidgen of lipstick go a long way to making a woman feel good about herself. Southern women know this."

Cara took a deep breath. "In case you haven't noticed, I've spent the last twenty years in Chicago."

"Caretta Rutledge, you were born a Southern woman and don't you ever forget it. When you left Charleston, you may have put miles between yourself and your family, lost your accent and gained a couple of degrees and titles, but where does that leave you? Where are you *from?* Darlin', you can't travel enough miles or live enough years to ever lose your heritage. You carry that with you in your blood."

"I see. Now I'm in for the steel magnolia lecture?"

A sparkle of hard-won wisdom flickered in Lovie's eyes.

"I worry about you, Caretta. You are a strong woman, true enough. But strength without flexibility makes one hard. Come September, when those fierce winds blow in from the sea, those hardwoods crack, splinter and fall. But the pliant palms are resilient and they bend with the wind. This is the secret of a Southern woman. Strength, resilience and beauty. We are never hard."

Cara closed her eyes and counted to ten. "If I dress for dinner, will you leave me alone?"

Lovie smiled sweetly and adjusted her scarf. "Why, only dress if you want to, dear."

Cara changed into her new long, cotton Hawaiian print dress and allowed her dark hair to fall down to her shoulders like a glossy mane. Gold hoops at the ears and brightly colored bangles at her wrist were her only jewelry, and to please her mother, she colored her lips with a glossy red.

"You look positively exotic," Lovie said with an approving nod when she emerged a second time from her room.

Cara had to admit to herself that she felt deliciously at ease in the loose, flowing dress and more in sync with the island mood.

Toy dressed in a long black skirt and a flowing black jersey top that strained across her middle. She was morosely silent and retiring, reminding Cara of a Japanese puppet master cloaked in black, unnoticed on the stage. Toy was nervous about going to the formal house for dinner and gave a dozen excuses why she should stay behind. But Lovie had been firm that Toy was to join them or she wouldn't go herself. When Cara tried to object, she was on the receiving end of a stern glance that told her Lovie was well aware of Palmer's feelings for her companion and she didn't care a single whit. Remembering her promise, she bit her tongue, then left a friendly message on Palmer's answering machine to set the table for one more.

The weather did its best to lift spirits for the outing. Beautiful skies, low humidity and a soft, friendly breeze sent the three women on their way to Charleston. Being a balmy Saturday afternoon, no one was surprised to find the Ben Sawyer Bridge open for a long parade of weekend boat traffic. They took their place in the line of waiting cars and enjoyed the beat of oldies but goodies music pouring out of the open windows of the car ahead.

"Hey, that song is about your name," Toy pointed out from the back seat. "Hear? Caretta, Caretta," she sang along.

"That's 'Corrine, Corrina,'" Cara replied dryly. "Which would have been infinitely more cool than being named after a species of turtle."

"Yeah, well, I wouldn't know. It's an *old* song. Before my time," Toy teased, flopping back against the cushions.

"It was before my time, too," Cara muttered, trying not to laugh.

"You should be pleased and proud to be named after the noble loggerheads," her mother said.

"I'm only pleased that you didn't give me the full Latin name *Caretta Caretta*."

"I wanted to but your father wouldn't let me. Don't laugh. I'm serious!"

"Then your middle name would have been Caretta, too?" Toy's laughter pealed like bells and Cara shook her head, resigned to the fact that, from that moment on, Toy would call her Caretta Caretta just to tease.

Cara beat the tempo with her fingers on the steering wheel, thinking how easy the mood was between them now where just a few days ago it had been so tense. She and Toy had kept a polite but deliberate distance from one another, rather like two pugilists sizing each other up before the bell. As each day passed, however, Cara couldn't help but notice how much work the young girl did around the house and her respect grew.

She turned her head to listen in on the rapid-fire conversation between Toy and her mother, who had turned around to face the back seat. Something about a marinade using sesame oil and garlic. The affection between them was obvious. Whenever those two were together they chatted away like magpies. Cara watched from behind her dark sunglasses with a twinge of jealousy. She never could be like that with her mother. Though they were trying hard, there was this deep current running between them that was too strong for idle talk and laughter.

The Ben Sawyer Bridge took its sweet time to close again but eventually they were off, over the river and across the wetlands to Mount Pleasant.

"We've got to stop for shrimp on the way," she remembered, her eyes on the lookout for the turn off Coleman Boulevard. "Do you have any idea where this shrimp joint is?"

Her mother laughed lightly beside her. "It's off Shem Creek. Just turn left at the next corner. I can't believe you don't remember all the times your father brought you there."

"Selective memory," she quipped, then turned off the main road. Moments later, Cara was lost in a winding maze of narrow roads in an old neighborhood with enormous oaks dripping with moss and charming smaller houses. She stayed to the right as Palmer had instructed, passed a row of enormous new houses on the creek, then went straight to a dead end with an old wood sign that read: Clud's Shrimp Bait and Accoutrement.

It was a long name for nothing more than a small wood shack beside a few shrimp boats docked in the rear. Several burly men hauled shrimp from a large trawler, shouting to each other and laughing, seemingly oblivious to the three women in high heels and sun dresses as they stood at a plywood counter.

Cara walked around to the rear to drum up some service. It was a shining afternoon and everywhere she looked it was like a postcard depicting an old Charleston industry. She could smell the pungent blend of shrimp, salt and sea in the air, and hear the water lapping, the boat thumping against the dock and the raucous call of gulls. She walked closer for a better view of the long, centipedelike riggings. Perched on the side of the trawler, like a model for a Wyeth illustration, stood a broad-backed shrimper in stained jeans, a red T-shirt and heavy, paint-splattered, sun-bleached boots. There was stubble on his tanned, weathered face and his brown hair fell along his brow as he bent over the nets. She was about to turn away when he swung his head around toward her.

Damn, it was the man from the bar. She knew he caught sight of her, too, because after a second his eyes crinkled in recognition and he smiled.

It was a rogue's smile, full of tease, and she turned away sharply, the mocking laugh of the seagulls in her ears. "Of all the luck," she muttered as she turned on her heel and headed back to the shack. Her mother and Toy were already collecting the shrimp.

"All set here?" she said, anxious to leave, pulling out her wallet.

"Your credit card is no good here," her mother chided.

Cara pulled out some bills and laid them on the table, but her mother, with agonizing deliberation, counted out the coins from her purse to give the exact change. Cara cast a nervous glance out back. From the corner of her eye she saw the man on the boat heave himself over the side and deliberately make his way toward the ramp.

She reached into her purse to pull out another dollar. "Keep the change." Then, linking arms with her mother, she led a hasty retreat with Toy bringing up the rear.

"I don't see what the big hurry was all about," her mother exclaimed, doing up her seat belt as Cara spun gravel and veered out of the parking lot.

"We don't want to keep Palmer waiting."

"Waiting? For heaven's sake! It just isn't polite to arrive right on the dot. Now you slow down a bit, Cara, and show your manners!"

Palmer Rutledge stood at the helm of his Boston Whaler, one hand firmly on the wheel of his powerboat and another wrapped around a beer as he grandly gestured, pointing out the new, expensive houses as they made their way up and down the Intracoastal Waterway. Lovie and Toy sat together on plush cushions under a canopy. Cara chose to sit at the rear in the sun. It was a lovely, sunny, splashy trip and Palmer was pulling out all the stops. Cara leaned far back on the padded deck chair, hung on to her cap and acknowledged his comments with a smiling nod.

More houses and docks bordered the winding waterway than she remembered and many more boats were cruising. When she was young, she and her friends could jump from the dock and swim across the waterway to a small hammock of land where they could stand for a bit to catch their breath before they swam back. To try that today would be as dangerous as crawling on all fours across a two-lane highway. The wakes of boats rocked them as they sped by, but it was all in good sport with lots of waves and smiles.

As beautiful as the houses and marshes were, she far more enjoyed just sitting back and enjoying the vision of her brother in his own element. Palmer was a Lowcountry boy through and through, in love with every square inch of land and every drop of water that made up this special place on God's earth.

He'd been a restless boy. Mama had called him Palmer the Panther because of the way he prowled with a hungry look in his eyes. But he was older now and Cara thought the paunch over the rim of his Tommy Bahama trunks and the extra roundness to his cheeks attested to a certain degree of satisfaction with his life—and his penchant for biscuits and barbeque.

"Auntie Caretta, do you want some soda?"

Cara turned her head to see a prim Linnea standing wide-legged before her, trying desperately to maintain her balance while serving a cold Coke in a Koozie in a ladylike fashion.

"Why, thank you, darling," she replied, taking the soda. "You are the sweetest, most adorable hostess I've ever seen. And you're doing a wonderful job. Palmer, do you see how wonderful your daughter is? Not spilling a drop? She's like a ballerina with all this bouncing around."

"More like a drunken sailor," he called back.

"Daddy!"

"Only kidding, sweetheart. You know I think you're the best."

"My mama told me I was the hostess," she told Cara earnestly. "Since she's back at the house fixing dinner. Do you want anything else?"

"Just a kiss."

The little girl obliged, leaning far over to give a bumpy kiss on her cheek, then she was back on duty. "Grandmama Lovie, do you want something cold?"

Linnea moved across the boat, holding tight to seat backs, knees, anything she could grab to keep from tumbling over as the boat sped along. The child was trying so very hard to do her job right.

Cooper was only interested in driving the boat. His small

but stout frame stood rigidly near his father, his round dark eyes trained on the gears and every move Palmer made at the wheel. Sadly, Palmer was too busy shouting out his comments to the adults over the roar of the engine to pay the boy mind.

"Daddy, can I hold the wheel? *Please?*" he asked for the tenth time.

"Cooper, go on over to your grandmother for a spell," Palmer shouted, shooing the boy away.

Cooper's face fell to a scowl but he obliged, moving stiff-leggedly to sit in the shade of the awning beside Toy and Lovie. Cara watched the boy as he squirmed in his seat for a few minutes, then chuckled to herself when she saw him sneak his way back to the wheel again to stare at his father, his brown eyes pleading. It was both funny and sad for Cara to watch, remembering how Palmer used to be the same way with their father, and how Daddy, too, had shooed his son away.

Palmer, Palmer, she thought to herself. Careful what you're doing.

The red sun was sinking into the horizon as they headed back to Charleston and the waters took on a marvelous, glassy pink hue. The powerful engine churned as they cut through the choppy waters of the harbor.

"Look, Aunt Cara. There's Fort Sumter!" Linnea exclaimed, pointing to a small island in the middle of the entrance to Charleston Harbor from the Atlantic.

Cara smiled and nodded, having seen the historical spot a million times in the past.

Linnea moved closer in an attempt to strike up a conversation with her. "Aunt Cara, did you know the first shot of the War Between the States was fired at that fort?"

Cara opened her mouth but was too surprised to find the words to reply.

Palmer let loose a loud belly laugh and shouted, "She thinks you're a Yankee! That'll teach you to live up north so long."

Lovie only smiled and nodded her head as if to say, I told you so.

"Honey pie," Palmer said between laughs, "if your Aunt Cara's a Yankee, then so am I."

Linnea looked at her father with confusion. "But, Daddy, *she* lives in Chicago."

"All too true, darling. But she was born and raised right here in Charleston. Just like you."

Linnea turned to look at Cara again, the wonder in her limpid blue eyes mixed with speculation as to whether Cara was to be scorned or pitied for having lost her mind and left the Lowcountry.

Cara knew that she'd become something of an oddity in the family, the exile who lived somewhere cold and unfamiliar to warm-blooded Southerners. Someone who only came to visit when duty called, wearing clothes that were different, and preferred to stay in a hotel than with the family. She felt the distance most acutely with these children who studied her now with measured glances.

"Don't you worry, honey," Cara assured her niece with a wry smile. "It's not your fault for not knowing. I left long before the *Civil War*." She exaggerated the phrase that marked her as a Yankee, just to tweak her brother.

"You just keep dating yourself, sister mine," he drawled, not missing a beat. And though she couldn't see his eyes behind his black sunglasses, she knew they were sparkling. "But I'll always be your older brother, our mother's darling and superior in every way."

Cara took the ribbing in her stride, knowing full well that this was only the appetizer portion of what was yet to come. It was his way to make light of painful subjects—and it worked.

Linnea warmed up to her once the family ties were straightened out. She took a seat next to Cara as much out of curiosity as affection. Cara felt the line of her slim body bump against hers as they headed straight for the tip of the Charleston peninsula and felt a surge of affection for her young niece. It was a new experience for her and she smiled warmly, gratified when Linnea smiled back.

Everyone in the boat quieted as they drew near to the city. Cara lifted her chin and felt a stirring of pride at seeing the cluster of historical homes along the Battery that gave the city its distinction. They loomed over the high stone embankment as pretty and desirable as a line of well-bred beauties leaning over an iron balustrade. No matter how many times one saw the view, stranger and local alike never got over the thrill of viewing the city in the same manner that travelers approaching by sea had seen the city for hundreds of years. Charleston showed herself off best from the water, she thought, still smiling.

The big motor slowed and the propellers churned the waters as the boat eased into the Charleston marina. The smell of gasoline mingled with saltwater. Cara's stomach tightened as the boat rocked.

"We're almost home," Linnea said. Then, pointing toward the shore, she added with a child's boast, "Our house is right back in there."

Cara lifted her chin to look beyond the tall masts to Bay Street and the familiar row of stately homes. *Home?* She drew in a long breath while her thoughts traveled the few blocks farther back in that cluster of brick, wood and iron to the house that she had grown up in. She looked to her mother and was surprised to see Lovie's gaze upon her, a small, knowing half smile upon her lips.

six

Under the cloak of night the loggerhead comes ashore. She slowly drags her body in a tanklike crawl to a dry site high on the beach. Only the female loggerhead comes ashore to nest. Once the male hatchling swims into the sea, he almost never will set flipper on beach again.

Her mother's house was a handsome Greek Revival located on one of the narrow, palmetto-and-oak-shaded side streets "South of Broad," that golden perimeter of blocks where affluence still reigned in splendor. *Charming* was the word most people used to describe the distinctive architecture of the historical, pastel houses, churches and gardens with their elaborate grillwork. Olivia and Stratton Rutledge had purchased the house in the early 1960s soon after Cara's birth for a fraction of its current worth and it was the only house Cara had ever lived in growing up. Her mother had fallen in love at first sight with the grace and charm of the rather dilapidated house. Owning it had been an adventure. Lovie had found countless artifacts in the yard as they dug the earth for the pool, and over the years she'd painstakingly brought the mansion, with its gracious three-story piazza, back to its former glory. It was Lovie's glory that every fall for years the house was included in the Preservation Society's annual house-and-garden tour.

Sitting at the curb looking at her childhood home surrounded by majestic oaks, Cara knew that a beautiful house
was not always a happy one. She got out of the car, stepping
into the mist drifting in from the harbor. She closed the door
and quietly walked along the crooked sidewalk toward the
front gate. Even as she moved forward she felt as she always
did the urge to spin on her heel and run. Inside this grand
house there were memories she preferred not to revisit. Nothing morbid or incestuous, nothing that would make scandal-
ous headlines. Theirs was a more quiet and insidious kind of
trauma. Palmer and she had suffered a long series of insults
and sad incidents that curled thick and musty around her like
the fog on this gunmetal-gray night.

Her chest constricted and she took a deep breath as she
stood at the front door beside her mother and Toy, waiting
for someone to answer their bell. Inside the house she heard
the sound of children's high-pitched laughter and a pounding
of feet on the stairs. A moment later, Julia swung open the
wide front door to welcome them each in a warm embrace.

"You're here! We thought y'all got lost. How long does it
take to get here from the dock?"

"I just wanted to drive around the old neighborhood,"
Cara explained.

"Well, come on in and welcome. The children are like
jumping beans." Julia was tiny and slender in her lovely floral
summer dress that matched exactly her pale blue eyes. Cara
hadn't seen her in years and thought her sister-in-law had
traded her youthful perkiness for a mature elegance that flat-
tered her. Yet behind Julia's bright smile she spotted a new
hardness, especially around the eyes where fine lines accen-
tuated the strain. She'd cut her long blond hair to a sporty,
cropped look that exposed the large topaz-and-diamond ear-
rings at her ears. Her makeup was expertly applied. Cara knew

that if she ran into her sister-in-law at the grocery store she would look as well turned out.

It seemed to her that Julia was a bit presumptuous in welcoming Lovie as a guest in her own home, but she reasoned that it was only natural for a Southern woman to do anything she could to make everyone feel welcome. In contrast, Toy was being mulish, shuffling her feet and barely muttering a halfhearted hello. Cara knew her well enough now to know that this was a mask for her insecurities.

Julia did not take offense. Laughing at something Lovie said, she guided them all through the foyer to the veranda. Cara stayed indoors to wander. The house had the look and feel of one of Charleston's grand historic houses with high ceilings, heavy amounts of wood trim, elaborate fireplaces and glossy heart pine flooring. Yet she found a difference now that was not so much in a change of furnishings as in mood. The stuffy wallpaper she remembered had been replaced by bright and cheerful colors: raspberry red in the dining room, sage green in the front sitting room, cool teal in the study. The heavy brocades and velvets on the windows were now gorgeous silk that seemed to float from the ten-foot ceilings to the floor. The brilliant colors drew attention to the antiques that had been in Cara's family for generations.

"You look like you expect to see a ghost to materialize," Palmer said, bringing her a gin and tonic. He'd changed from his boating clothes to trousers and a silk polo shirt.

Cara turned her head and broke into a wide grin at seeing him. She gratefully accepted the drink. "You mean Daddy?"

Palmer's gaze went to the large painted portrait of Stratton Rutledge prominent over the staircase landing. "He's still here, floating around. I never could escape the son of a bitch."

"You could have."

Palmer shook his head and forced a laugh, but his eyes appeared haunted. "I run the company now. I live in his house. I carry the name. Hey, what can I say? I gave up running from my destiny."

She looked her brother in the eye. "We each make our destiny."

"If you believe that, darlin', I've got some swamp land I'd love to sell you." He raised his glass for a drink of his bourbon but his eyes gleamed over his drink. Again, she felt the age-old connection they'd shared as children. "It sure is good to see you again," he said. "You're as beautiful as ever." He skipped a beat. "And as tall."

At five foot ten, Cara could almost look her brother in the eye. Growing up it had been a sore point between them that, though younger, she was taller than him. Then he hit a delayed growth spurt and beat her, but only by an inch.

"I've still got you beat," he added.

"It looks like you've beat me in the girth department, too."

He patted his belly with jovial pride. "Yes, ma'am, marriage does that to a man. Not that you'd know about that."

Cara remained unfazed. "I've managed to escape so far."

"Woman, where'd you get all those crazy ideas? Not in the South, that's for sure and certain. If you'd stayed here you'd have a strapping husband and a whole slew of babies running around right this minute. Oh, no, look out. Her back is up."

"If you only knew the third degree I was getting from Mama. I'm worn out."

He chuckled in understanding and swirled his drink. "So, how long are you staying this time?"

"Don't know, exactly. Mama wants me to stay longer but, to be honest, I'm getting a little antsy already. There's nothing for me to do here."

"Cara, Cara," he said shaking his head. "You just can't wait to leave this paradise and get back to that cold city. I'll never understand you." He inclined his head in interest. "You said Mama wrote you a letter?"

She nodded and took a sip of her drink, turning more serious. "That's right. Our usual status of a polite truce has worked well enough for us both over the years, but I sense things have changed for her since Daddy died. I like to think she's missed me. More likely she just wants me to help sort through all the stuff now that he's gone."

Palmer's face sharpened, barely perceptibly, but enough that she knew she'd hit a tender spot.

"What kind of sorting?"

"Again, I don't know. I imagine all the clutter stored up in the attic, and dividing things up from this house now that she's living at the beach house. I suppose she wants to sell this house. Hasn't she talked to you about this?"

His face clouded and he studied her with a question in his eyes that she couldn't make out. "No," he replied slowly. "No, she hasn't."

"I believe she—"

"So how do you like the place?" he asked, interrupting her and extending his arm toward the living room.

Cara was taken aback by the abrupt change of subject but she went along with it, concluding that Palmer was upset that he'd not been consulted.

"The place looks quite different," she replied, following him into the sunroom. "It looks much, I don't know...younger. Cheerful, even. The decorator was brilliant."

He beamed. "Julia gets all the credit and it'd be real nice if you said something to her about it. She slaved over every detail. And I don't mind telling you I thought I'd go cross-eyed looking at all the fabric swatches she brought home for curtains or bedspreads or cushions—you name it. And the fringe! You never saw so damn much fringe in all your life."

"I'll tell her. She did a marvelous job." Then looking at her drink she asked, "And Mama didn't mind the changes?"

He looked at her queerly. "Mind? Hell no, why should she mind?"

"I don't know. She lived in the house for so long…"

"No, no, she loves it," he said with boisterous confidence. "And Julia loves fixing it up. And I don't care one way or the other, so everybody's happy. But I don't figure this traditional stuff is your style. You prefer that modern, spare look, I hear."

Cara's gaze swept the gracious rooms and she wondered if that was still true. "Perhaps," she replied, then caught his eye and smiled wickedly. "But it's a woman's prerogative to change her mind."

"Well, you haven't changed your mind about Frogmore Stew, I hope. Man, oh, man—I've a big pot out back with your name on it. Should just about be ready. Julia!" he called out.

She poked her head around the corner. "Yes, honey?"

"Get my sister something to nibble on while I tend to the stew. I'll be ready to serve in a few minutes." He turned to face Cara with a wink. "Made it special for you."

Cara felt a flush of pleasure that he'd remembered it was her favorite after all and went to join Julia in the kitchen to help serve the feast.

They sat together in the raspberry-colored dining room while tall white candles glimmered around them and the ornate crystal chandelier glowed like the moon above. They spoke of old times. Or, for the most part, Palmer talked and she sat back and listened to him at the head of the long, mahogany table as he recounted funny tales and anecdotes of the happier moments they'd shared, both in the city house and at the beach. He had acquired their father's gift of storytelling. It was a skill with words taught to young Southern boys that improved with age. But only a few inherited the real talent for drawing out choice details, for turning the colorful phrase and for nailing a characterization with such precision that the listener could see the person as readily as if he or she were standing before them in the flesh. The listeners leaned forward as Palmer brought to life old memories. He seemed to relive them as he spoke and brought Cara and Lovie to the past along with him. They each punctuated the telling with comments of their own.

Initially, Toy had tried to act bored but she, too, got sucked in. Cara caught glimpses of her sitting wide-eyed as she and the children gobbled up the stories as quickly as the steaming shrimp, sausage and corn. At times Palmer had them laughing so hard the children had to cover their mouths to keep the food in. Even Toy relaxed enough to crack a smile and let a laugh escape.

As the evening drew late, however, and more wine consumed, Palmer's cheeks became flushed and his colorful, silken stories became fringed with bitterness. He touched on the darker side of their jangled-up histories and an uncomfortable tension crept over them. When he pushed back his chair to stand, the sigh of relief from the women was almost audible.

"I think we should open up another bottle, don't you?" Palmer asked in a long drawl, lifting the empty bottles of wine from the table. "Y'all wait here and I'll be right back."

As soon as he left the room, Lovie shot a loaded glance at Julia.

She immediately rose. "Come along, children. Hurry up and kiss your grandmama and Aunt Cara good-night. Quick like bunnies!"

There was a bustle of smooches and tender declarations of love and then Julia excused herself to put her babies to bed.

Toy took the cue. "I'm really tired, Miss Lovie. Would y'all mind if I stretch out on the couch a bit and put my feet up?"

Lovie appeared relieved. "Yes, that's a good idea. Watch a little TV if you like. But don't get too comfy. We'll be leaving presently."

Soon after Toy left, Palmer returned to the room dusting off another bottle of wine.

"Son, I think it's time to call it a night," Lovie said, placing her napkin on the table. "It's been a marvelous day. I can't thank you enough."

Palmer stopped dead in his tracks. "No, no, don't go," he replied, a petulant pleading in his voice. He brought the bottle to the table and began to uncork it. "It's the shank of the evening and we never see you anymore, Mama." Then, as though he just noticed, he looked around and said, "Where did the children go?"

"Julia put them to bed," Lovie replied.

He scowled and his eyes flashed with anger. "Now why did that fool woman hurry them off?" He took a step and craned his neck toward the staircase. "Julia!" he bellowed.

Cara stared at her brother with shock.

"Yes?" They heard her voice from upstairs, sounding a tad too cheerful.

"What the hell are you doing up there?" he called back.

"I'm putting the babies to bed. It's late."

"Hush now, Palmer," Lovie said in an easy, calming voice. "You sound like a fishmonger shouting across the room like that. Let her put those darlings to bed."

"They can go to bed any ol' time. I want them to spend more time with you."

Cara stiffened at the ugly and too familiar sight of a man turned belligerent from too much wine.

"They've had a full day and the awnings were dropping over those precious eyes. They're young and need to go to bed. And I'm old and need to go to bed as well. Besides, I'm only a short drive away. You can bring my grandbabies to visit anytime you wish."

Palmer wagged his head, frowning. "It's not the same with you gone. They need their grandmother's influence. Julia's a fine girl and all, but let's face it, she doesn't have your breeding."

Cara eyed him sharply for shaming his wife in front of his mother and sister.

"Why'd you leave us anyway?" he droned on. "This will always be your home as much as mine."

"How grand of you to say so," Cara said testily.

"Well, it is!" he replied in strong defense. "I never wanted Mama to leave." He poured more wine into Cara's glass, spilling a few drops. Then almost in a pout he added, "She insisted."

"That's true," Lovie replied in a cajoling tone while placing her hand over her glass. "I know you wanted me to stay and I'm touched, but honestly, I couldn't be happier than right where I am. I've always loved my little beach house."

"You always loved *this* house," Palmer replied, filling his own glass.

Cara and Lovie exchanged a worried glance.

"But since you brought it up," he said, sitting down and getting comfortable, "let's talk about this sensibly." He repositioned himself in his chair and placed his elbows squarely on the table. Raising his eyes to Lovie's he said in a congenial tone, "Okay, here it is, plain and simple. Mama, I want you to come back here to live with us. I don't like you so far out there on the island. I want you right here where I can keep an eye on you."

"I'm quite content where I am."

"In that ol' place? First off, that place is a firetrap. It's barely standing. Hell, one good wind will take that cottage straight off from its foundation."

"That little cottage has withstood more hurricanes than I can count," Lovie replied in ringing defense.

Palmer put up his hand. "Maintenance is just one thing. Hiring this girl when you could be living here with us is another. But those are small potatoes compared to the whopping hit we took from the recent tax assessment. The value of that little piece of land has skyrocketed in the past few years." His eyes gleamed and he leaned forward on his elbows with import. "That worthless little cottage sits on prime ocean real estate. There's not much of that left on the island anymore, and you know that's true. The new tax bill made my blood pressure shoot sky-high."

Lovie seemed agitated and she leaned toward her son. "But Palmer, didn't you apply for the tax cap? I told you to do that for me last December when I moved out there."

"I did, but it was still a sizable increase. Your money is largely invested, Mama, and with the stock market the way it is your cash flow is severely limited. It just doesn't make sense to hold on to that place any longer."

"I don't need much."

"That's not the point, Mama. Now, don't you get up on your high horse. Hear me out. I did my own investigating and I know for a fact that no matter how sorry a shape that cottage is in, it's worth at least seven, maybe eight hundred thousand. Maybe even more. See, the thing is, there's those three choice lots sitting across from you. Two of them were gifted to the Coastal Conservancy as open parkland forever."

Cara's brows rose. She didn't know that. If so, that would add a great deal to the value of her mother's site.

"Now the way I see it," Palmer continued, "if I can buy that third lot that's right smack in front of your place, then between them we'd have two prime lots. I could build two houses on spec, situating one on the ocean in such a way as to guarantee ocean views from the other. The land would be priceless then. Worth millions."

"The land is already priceless to me," Lovie said in a quiet voice.

"Why, sure, Mama, I know you love it. But we should strike while the iron's hot. We need to buy that land before someone else does."

"Do you know who owns the third lot?" Cara asked.

Palmer shook his head. "No, but I've got my people on it. It's only a matter of time till I find out."

"So, I gather you want me to sell now?" Lovie asked.

There was something about her mother's tone that alerted Cara, an iron strength hidden in the question. She glanced at Lovie's face. It was solemn and pale. Palmer's face, in contrast, was beet red and his eyes were alive with the look of a bloodhound on the scent.

"I think we should talk about it. See what our options are."

Lovie turned to face Cara. "Do *you* want me to sell?"

Cara didn't expect the question. "It's not up to me."

"Why are you asking *her?*" Palmer interjected with heat.

Cara bristled. "As a member of the family, I have a right to at least an opinion."

"A right? Hell, after twenty years' absence you feel you still have a right?"

"Cara," her mother said and her tone drew Cara's attention back. "Do you want me to sell?"

Cara pursed her lips, considering. One of her strengths in business was her ability to remove herself from an equation and think objectively. When she replied, her voice was calm and decisive. "If what Palmer says is true and those two lots are deeded as a park, then your land is like gold in the bank.

It's safe. And money isn't the issue, or it shouldn't be." She looked at Palmer. "If I recollect, Mama is invested in blue-chip stocks. If they go under, the country goes under. So," she concluded, turning again to her mother, "as far as I'm concerned, you should do what makes you happy, Mama. It's your land. Your life. Enjoy it."

Lovie's face eased into a soft smile and her eyes seemed to express relief and even, perhaps, hope.

"And you don't have any interest in the beach house yourself?" Palmer asked.

It was an ugly question and Cara was sorry to hear it. She looked at her mother. Lovie was leaning forward, intently focused on her answer.

"No," Cara replied honestly. "It belongs to Mama. I hope she'll live there happily for a very long time."

Palmer leaned back in his chair and laced his fingers across his belly. "Oh, do you? Well, I think it's odd that you come home now, after all these years, with a sudden interest in sorting through this house and the beach property."

It was the drink talking and she didn't rise to the bait. "I've told you, Palmer, I'm home because Mama asked me to come. Let me put any fears you have of my being a mercenary to rest. I'm well-off, Palmer, not rich, but comfortable. I've always been able to fend for myself, as you well know." She leaned back in her own chair and with a wry smile added, "I've made my money the old-fashioned way—I earned it. I don't need anything from Mama."

"Honey," Palmer replied with a long drawl, "*I* made my money the real old-fashioned way. I inherited it." He laughed and managed to diffuse the tension between them, though it was still there, simmering under the surface. He turned again to Lovie, his face appearing sincere. "Mama, be sensible. Aside from the financial picture, we have to be realistic about your health. As pretty as you are, you're not getting any younger. It's just not safe for you to be living out there by yourself. We're downtown. Your doctors are downtown. If you should have some sort of emergency, you'd be too far from real help. What kind of a son would I be to leave you on your own at this point in your life?"

"I appreciate your concern," she replied stiffly, "but I'm not alone. The Turtle Ladies look out for me and I've Toy to see to my everyday needs." Lovie seemed to regret mention of the girl's name because she closed her mouth quickly.

Palmer seized on this. "That's another thing! What do we know about that girl? Why, she could be robbing you blind."

"Oh, for pity's sake…" Lovie said, shaking her head in her palm.

"Even if she's not rifling through the silver, what kind of help can you get from a girl who's so far pregnant she can barely walk? How can she take care of you? She's barely old enough to take care of herself. I mean, hell." Palmer slammed his hand on the table. "I'm not sure I want my children associating with her kind. I don't even want her in my house. Who knows where she's from? What kind of an example is she setting for Linnea?"

Cara looked over her shoulder, wondering if Toy had heard, doubting she could not have what with the way Palmer was shouting. She waited for her mother's stinging defense, but when she turned to see her slump-shouldered again, she knew none was forthcoming and felt an old disappointment rise up. When she could hold out no longer, she burst out in a voice that had stopped boardrooms cold in Chicago, "That's enough, Palmer! You don't even know this girl but you condemn her because she's pregnant? Isn't that the pot calling the kettle black? I seem to remember an incident years back…"

His face mottled but he had the decency to duck his head.

"So, you do remember," she said, not dragging out the old scandal. She knew he was remembering years back to the high school girl he took out to their daddy's hunting lodge every chance he could. It ended in the predictable manner, money passed hands and Palmer got off lucky. Which was more than she could say for the girl involved. Cara couldn't remember her name and she'd wager Palmer couldn't either. Some things never changed, she thought with a sigh. It was always the girl that paid.

There was an awkward silence during which Palmer downed his glass and Cara took a deep breath. As far as she was concerned, the evening was over.

"I think we've tripped down memory lane enough for one evening," she said. "Mama has decided to stay at the cottage and has chosen this young lady as her companion. And for what it's worth, from what I can tell Toy is a decent, hard-working young woman and she's doing a fine job. Her very best, which is more than I can say for myself these past few days." She turned to Lovie. "I'm sorry, Mama, that I've been such a slug lately but this fine meal and repartee seem to have revived me. I'm remembering exactly who I am and why I left here in the first place. Palmer, if you don't mind my saying so, you've become every bit as much of a heavy-handed chauvinist pig as Daddy ever was. I hardly know you."

Palmer looked temporarily broadsided, then his expression hardened. When he spoke again, his voice turned low and icy despite the charm of his smile. "I'm sorry if your opinion of me has diminished, but the fact is, dear sister, you've been out of the picture for some time now, living your own kind of lifestyle, taking care of your own business. It fell to me to take care of our mother."

"You treat her like a child!" she exploded. "You're not her husband, you're her son. Show her more respect. It's *her* money after all. Mama is perfectly capable of handling her own finances. I think you enjoy the control you exercise over her. Just like Daddy did."

Palmer's face froze for a moment, and despite the truth in her statement, she realized a momentary pang for him, remembering the boy he once was. Then she watched his face ease into a starchy smile.

"I'm just being a dutiful son. Ask her."

Cara turned to her mother.

"You know that I don't have a mind for figures," she replied in a distant voice, appearing to shrink within herself.

"You compare me to Daddy?" Palmer said, returning to the sore point. "Well, maybe I am. The apple doesn't fall far from the tree, isn't that what they say? But *say* what you will, the fact is, while you were in Chicago, I was here, dealing with his reeking alcoholism and his plain cussed meanness. After he died, Julia had to paint the house just to get the stink of bourbon and cigars out of it. I was here with Mama, watching out for her, and we both know I'm not just talking about money." His eyes glared as he worked himself up into a state of agitation. "He left the business to me, not you. He left the estate to me, not you. Why? Not because he loved me more, we all know that," he said bitterly. "But because you turned your back on him, on all of this, and shoved it down his throat. He never forgave you for that."

They stared at each other in a heated silence.

"And I never forgave him for the way he treated us, either," Cara said at length. "Or the way he treated you, Mama."

Lovie's eyes dropped.

Cara couldn't bear to see her mother shrink inward again. It physically pained her. This meek creature sitting at the head of the table was the mother she'd grown up with, but the woman at the beach house was someone else entirely. When she thought of her mother, she thought of words like *hover* and *subservient*. During family dinner conversations at this same long, polished table, Olivia Rutledge had usually sat quietly and listened, or moved silently from kitchen to dining room to serve. Only when asked a direct question did she participate in the debates that usually raged over some point no one could remember or even cared about. And never did she contradict her husband, no matter how cruel. For Cara and her father, debates were all about firing shots and winning. For her mother and, to a lesser degree, Palmer, it was about dodging the bullets. They thought she was so strong. What they never understood was that, for her, firing back was a means of survival, too.

She faced her brother, the embers of an old, cold fury sparking in her chest. "Let's not bring up the past."

"Unfortunately, the past has repercussions into the present," Palmer continued, all trace of drunkenness gone. "Allow me to bring you up to speed on what's transpired here while you've been away."

"Palmer..." Lovie broke in.

"Now Mama, it's clear to me that our Caretta here has no notion of the way things are. There should be no secrets. It's not right she doesn't know."

"Know what?" Cara asked. "We all knew long before he died that Daddy was leaving you the company. Primogeniture or not, in this case it was just. I didn't want it and you deserved it. You put up with a lot and worked hard for it. I was happy for you."

Palmer registered this with a curt nod. "But that wasn't all he left me, which you would have known if you'd stayed around for the reading of the will."

"Let's not get into that now," she said.

"You need to know he left me the lion's share of his wealth."

Cara looked at Lovie for confirmation. She felt disgust at her father's final abuse against her mother. "You didn't get at least half? But, Mama, it was your money to begin with."

Palmer answered. "By the time he died, it was all in his name. Even the house."

"No." It came out on a breath. Cara's face stilled and she looked again at her mother uncomprehendingly. Lovie sat looking at her hands. How could she have been so weak as to let him take everything away from her? The several odd comments Palmer had made about the house earlier in the evening suddenly made sense. Cara swung her head back toward Palmer and her voice rose.

"You took Mama's house?"

Fury streaked Palmer's features. "Hell, no. What do you take me for? Of course I didn't take it. The son of a bitch gave it to me in his will just to spite her. I tried to give it back." He faced Lovie for confirmation. "Didn't I?"

Lovie nodded and tears moistened her eyes.

"I don't understand," Cara said.

"He—" Palmer began.

"Let me explain," Lovie broke in. Her voice was quiet but level. "I wouldn't take the house back. I gave it to Palmer, lock, stock and barrel." She looked into Cara's eyes. "You never wanted any of it, Cara. You made that point crystal clear over the years. Palmer did want it. He wanted it for Julia and the children. They took care of the house, loved it and deserved it. And they've been very happy here. Ultimately that's what I wanted, too. For happiness to return to this house. For a family to laugh again in these rooms." Her blue eyes, paler with age and illness, gazed around the room in a bittersweet sweep. "For whatever his reason, your father set this decision into motion. But in the end it was my decision. Not Stratton's. Not Palmer's. Mine. And mine alone."

Cara looked into her mother's eyes. The hurt struck harder and deeper than she would have imagined. Not that Palmer had inherited the house. She heard her mother's reasoning and it made sense to her—and more, it felt just. But not to even have been considered? That hurt. In her heart she blamed herself. She was honest enough to know it was all her own doing. Sure she'd been young and headstrong when she left. Who wasn't at eighteen? But to have been ignored…? She knew her reasoning was emotional but she couldn't help it. When her father died, she had been secure in her career and strong enough to walk away from everything. But she was on soft ground now. In less than two weeks she'd been fired from her job and dumped by her boyfriend. Now, coming home for solace, she found her family had discarded her as well.

Her mother's eyes were filled with concern. "If there is something you want from the house, a piece of furniture, a painting, whatever…"

"Why sure, Cara," Palmer interjected. "Just tell me what you want."

She glanced at him, unable to respond to his offer of a small afterthought that represented her worth in the family. Cara felt a deadening inside that she recognized as a time-tested self-defense mechanism. It was as though a steel wall dropped down between herself and them, one that had saved her from spears many times in the past. The first time it dropped was at this very table twenty-two years earlier. She was just eighteen and had informed her father she was going to Boston University. Her father was sitting where Palmer was now, drunk again, his eyes seething. Her mother sat at the opposite end, where she sat now. As usual, her eyes were cast down at her plate. Palmer was frozen across the table from her, begging her with his eyes to be quiet and to just go along.

"Who the hell do you think you are, little girl?" her father had roared. "You'll do as I say. And if you step one foot out of this town—out of this house—that'll tear it between us, you hear? You are not going north and that's final. I'll not tolerate this arrogance. Especially not from some blunt-mouthed teenage girl who won't act like the lady she's been bred to be. You're an embarrassment to your mama. And to me. Where do you think you're going? Come back here! Caretta Rutledge! You leave and you'll not get one dollar, not one stick of furniture, not so much as a nod of the head when you pass the street from me, hear?"

Instinct reared now as it did then. She knew that no matter how much she'd admired, even treasured, the family antiques, if she took one piece it would be like a heavy stone tied around her ankle, dragging her under. As much now as then, she needed her freedom.

"Thank you, but no," she said in a steady voice. "It was given to you and Julia. I don't want anything. Thank you for explaining things to me."

All she wanted now was not to humiliate herself further. The oppression she'd always felt in this house closed around her, choking her, and she was afraid lest she lose control and release either a bitter laugh or a painful cry.

She ended the labored silence and stood up. She woodenly went through the usual polite motions and mutterings of a farewell. Toy was called, Julia came down to join them, and flanked by Lovie and Palmer, Cara walked blindly through the house. At the door, Palmer bent forward to kiss her cheek.

Before the door closed behind her, she heard the sudden gust of wind as the mocking howl of a ghost.

seven

If the site doesn't feel right or she encounters a root or rock,
or if she senses an intruder, the loggerhead will return to the sea
without laying her eggs. This is known as a "false crawl."

They rode home in silence. Perhaps because too much had
been said already, or perhaps because not enough. In any case,
no one felt compelled to talk as they drove back over the rivers and across the still marsh and Sullivan's Island to the Isle
of Palms. The clouds were low and thick and few house lights
pierced the velvety blackness.

Lovie sat in the back seat with Toy and saw the silhouette
of her daughter in the dim car. Cara's shoulders were back
and she held the steering wheel with a tight grip. Lovie knew
this pose so well. When she was upset as a child Cara would
become quiet and rigid, thoroughly unapproachable. Palmer
used to cry and make a fuss, but if anyone asked Cara how she
was, she'd simply look away and reply, "Fine."

When they arrived at the cottage, Cara politely opened
the door for her mother, then moved quickly into the house,
avoiding any discussion. By the time Lovie was inside, Cara
had a glass of water in her hand. With a quick "Good-night"

and a wave of her hand, she slipped into her room and closed
the door.

"Well, I guess I'll go to bed, too," Toy said, cool and distant.

"Are you all right?"

"I'm just tired," she replied, but kept her eyes averted.

Lovie watched her leave, saw the sway of her hips under
the increasing weight of her growing baby. "Good night then,
dear girl."

Toy only nodded and went to her room.

Lovie walked slowly to the kitchen stove to light a kettle for
tea. She laid out two mugs, spooned out the herbal tea into the
pot, then she wiped her hands on the towel. When done, she
leaned them against the counter and lowered her head with a
ragged sigh. Her heart was breaking. These silences between
herself and Cara were no good. There had been enough silence
between them over the years. Too much, if truth be told. She
couldn't be weak any longer. Flo was right that they needed
to talk. And there was no more time.

With new resolve she walked across the sisal rug directly
to Cara's door and knocked once. "Caretta?"

There was no answer.

"Cara?"

She heard the sound of footfall, then the door opened.
Cara appeared in pale blue silk pajama bottoms and a cotton
camisole top. Her face was scrubbed clean and her dark hair
gleamed from a good brushing. Behind her on the bed Lovie
saw a suitcase spread open. It was half-packed. Cara ran her
hands through her hair, then let them drop with an exasperated sigh.

"What is it, Mama?"

"I thought we might have that chat."

"Now?" She paused, looked up at the ceiling, then shook
her head. "I couldn't. I'm too tired." But, seeing the disap-

pointment on Lovie's face, she added more gently, "You must be, too. You look exhausted."

"I am, rather. But I won't sleep a wink unless we talk."

"Talking has never been our forte."

"No, it hasn't."

"Why now? Why tonight?"

Lovie's gaze moved to the suitcase. "I should think it's obvious. Besides, better to start late than not at all."

"Maybe it *is* too late."

"It's never too late as long as there is breath in us to speak. Come. I've got a kettle on."

They carried their mugs of steaming tea to the living room. Lovie turned on two small lamps that created soft, yellow pools of light and made the room feel cozy. Cara went to the sofa and eased onto the plump upholstery, curling her long, slender legs under her catlike in the corner. Her beautiful, dark eyes were watchful and wary. Lovie took the armchair across from her. Sinking into the cushions, she suddenly felt the weight of her fatigue and yawned.

"Do you want to do this tomorrow? It's almost eleven o'clock," said Cara.

"No, no, I'm just getting comfortable."

"You should have told me," Cara said when her mother settled.

How like her, Lovie thought, to jump right in and voice what was on both their minds. "I know. I meant to. But I hardly thought it would come up tonight."

"Palmer thinks the reason I came home was to collect the family goods."

"He's a dear boy, and I don't know what I would have done without him these past years, but he does keep his hand in the cookie jar. It's his insecurity, I suppose. I'm partially to blame

for that. I've given him whatever I could because Stratton…
Well, you know how your father was. As hard as it was for you
being his daughter, it was doubly hard for Palmer as his son."

"Mama, I realize all that. But he is far too heavy-handed.
Why do you put up with it? I mean—" she dropped her hand
in exasperation "—it was one thing with Daddy. But Palmer
is your son! Don't you ever want to be independent? To know
where your own money is?"

"I couldn't care less where my money is," she replied with
astonishment. "I never have. Why should I? It's nothing but
a hassle and a headache. Your father always took care of the
finances and bill paying when he was alive, and now that he's
gone, Palmer continues to do it for me."

"And look what good all that trust has done you."

"Palmer's a good boy. He's been here, Cara, all these years
while you were away. I'm not saying that to berate you for
your choice, but to defend Palmer."

"Dear, dear Palmer."

"Cara…"

"That's always been the problem, hasn't it? You taking
Palmer's side against mine."

"I'm not taking sides," she said wearily.

"Yes, you are! You just don't realize it. You've done this all
your life and it drives me crazy. You just sit there, Mama, and
let them run over you. I can't stand by anymore and watch
you just cave in to the men in your life. Why can't you be
stronger?"

"Like you? I'm not like that. You're very much like your
father in that way."

Cara stiffened as though slapped. "I am *nothing* like him."

Lovie blinked at the vehemence of Cara's response. "Does
the comparison bother you so much? I'd always thought you

preferred being compared to him rather than to me. Powerful rather than weak."

"I'd rather not be held up to anyone for comparison. Least of all him."

"Well," she said dazed, exhaling a puff of air. "Well, well, well. Good for you. I don't mean that snidely, I'm being quite honest. I wish I had been as strong when I was your age."

"You should have been."

Lovie closed her eyes.

"I'm sorry, Mama," Cara said after a beat, her voice beginning to rise with emotion. "I know the way he was. I know you loved him. I just never understood how that was enough for you to put up with his goddamn abuse for so many years."

"You couldn't understand," her mother said in a strained voice.

"Why couldn't I? I'm not a child. You loved him. I know that." She brought her hand to her forehead and closed her eyes tightly before tearfully blurting out, "But I hated the son of a bitch."

Lovie's breath stilled, then she replied evenly, "Why, so did I."

Cara dropped her hand and swung her head up. Neither spoke as they stared at each other, their thoughts journeying on separate paths. With a jerky motion, Cara turned to stare out the window.

Lovie quietly observed her daughter's profile. With her proud, straight nose, high cheekbones and full lips, she strongly resembled the father she claimed to hate.

"Cara, can't we talk through some of our misunderstandings?"

Cara wiped her eyes, then turned around again to face her mother. It pained Lovie to see the tears. She could count the times on one hand she'd ever seen her daughter cry.

"I came home hoping for just that. I actually had some silly vision of a mother-daughter bonding. Imagine that?" Her quick smile fell and she added wearily, "It's okay, it doesn't matter." She took a deep breath. "I'm going back to Chicago tomorrow."

Lovie heard the north in her voice already. "So soon?"

"It's clear you don't need my help here and frankly, I left a mess I need to clean up at home. I can't sit around here any longer."

"Oh, Cara. You're hurt."

"No. I'm fine. I just need to refocus."

Lovie took a long shuddering breath. "You think you've been abandoned. That everything has been handed to Palmer and nothing to you."

"Mother, please..."

"You asked me what I meant when I wrote to you that there were things to sort through. There are." She drank some tea, was comforted by it, then set the mug on the table. She felt secure in this little cottage, better able to speak her mind than in the Charleston house.

"After your father died," she began, "I decided to move out here to the beach house. It wasn't an impulsive decision. It was a promise I'd made to myself long before. Sort of a gift that I kept in the back of my mind to unwrap and think about in difficult times."

Cara looked into her mother's pale blue eyes and wondered about those *difficult times*. "Why did you wait so long?"

"I had my reasons. But I planned for it. Why do you think I redid the kitchen years back?"

"I'd assumed to make it a rental."

"That's what I told Stratton. I knew he'd agree if I presented it as an investment." She smiled conspiratorially. "But it was for me. I wanted to live alone and the beach house is much more manageable for someone my age. Without all those fussy antiques. Here I'm free of all the..." She sighed, grasping for the word.

"Hassles?" Cara prompted.

"Distractions. You always understood that, I think. You never put much store in a house or furniture. I admire that about you."

Cara was surprised by the unexpected compliment.

Lovie's expression shifted as she reflected on private thoughts. "I spent forty years in that big house," she said slowly. "And let me tell you, those charming old houses everyone always admires are not easy to maintain. I was a slave to it. There's always painting or wiring or plumbing or plasterwork that needs doing. I promise you, a good plasterer is worth his weight in gold in this town. Women I've known for years have gone to the grave without whispering their source. I'd had enough of worrying and dusting antiques and drawing shades against the sun. And Lord knows I'd had enough of entertaining."

"I thought you loved that house."

"I did, for a while. I'm talking about more than just the house. There, I had a role to fulfill in society as your father's wife, your and Palmer's mother, an active member of my church, schools, business. There was an endless demand on my time. Invitations and thank-yous, political drives and cultural events, endless telephone calls and meeting someone for this or that, preparing meals, cleaning up after meals, doctors, dentists, the garden, shopping. There was always a button that needed sewing or a plant that needed watering. And driving. Lord, the driving! I spent years in carpools, then more years worrying about you and Palmer driving, and then the final insult, worrying about Stratton's and my own skills behind the wheel as we aged.

"A woman's life has so many demands because she is the axis around which so many little planets spin. I did it and, yes, there were countless delightful moments. But that part of my life died when Stratton did."

Her voice was firm on this point. Lovie turned to allow her gaze to travel lazily over the yellow cottage. She breathed deeply and when she spoke, it was heartfelt. "If I made one mistake, Cara, it's that I did not allow enough time for solitude every day. A quiet time to reflect, to pray, to refill my well. I was so very busy. In that big house every minute was so consumed that I simply dried up inside. I suppose I could point to people and events and cast blame, but in my heart I know that this was my own responsibility, not anyone else's." Her face brightened. "Except, I did come here in my summers. This place saved me. I love it here. I always have. I feel freer, happier. Like it's summer inside of me every day of the year."

Cara leaned forward, peering into this window to her mother's personality that she'd never looked through before. "That's the way I've always felt here, too."

"Is it? I always believed that about you. And that you understand how important Primrose Cottage is. To us and to the family."

"Hmm," Cara replied, not willing to link herself to strong family sentiments. "It's nice, talking with you like this. We don't do it often enough."

"Then stay."

"Mother, I can't. I'm not a little girl anymore. I don't get summers off."

"You're still *my* little girl."

"This isn't a good time for a vacation. I have a lot going on. I can't explain it all right now. Maybe next year."

"No. Not next year, Cara. This year."

Cara uncurled her legs, rose and walked to her mother. Reaching out, she took Lovie's hand. "I'm sorry, Mama. I can't. I'm all packed up and will leave at dawn."

"You're going so early?"

"I really must get back."

"If you stay a few more days, we could—"

"I left my home, my bills... I have to earn a living, Mama. If I leave tomorrow real early I can get back in a day."

"I see. Will you come back soon?"

"I'll try."

Lovie dropped Cara's hand. She knew it wouldn't happen and felt inexpressibly old and woeful. "You go on to bed, dear. I'm just going to finish my tea."

The night was blowsy but it was a good thing. The wind moved the clouds that had blanketed the sky earlier like a giant eraser. The stars now sparkled in a clear sky and made one understand why generations had so often compared them to diamonds.

Stepping out from the screened porch Lovie raised her chin and saw that the Big Dipper was so clear little Cooper could play connect the dots. Still, the path through the tangled lot would be treacherous. Lovie flicked on her special flashlight that glowed a soft red that would not disturb the turtles, wrapped an old sweater around her shoulders, then headed out toward the beach. It was very late, past midnight, but she was deeply troubled and overcome with lassitude.

She needed to walk. Being old, she couldn't walk as far as she would have liked. Being tired, she would most likely just rest a bit on the sand. But this pacing in the sand was the only easing of her soul she had at her disposal now that Russell was gone.

Dear Russell... Oh, how she missed him and his gentle

counsel. He had been her dearest friend and love, and if he were alive she would tell him all about the mess she'd made of things with Cara and ask for his advice. Her thoughts were full of him as she followed the thin stream of light that snaked ahead of her. She walked one foot in front of the other along the narrow path, careful for vines that could trip her and leave her stranded all night with a broken hip. Wouldn't Palmer have a fit then!

She climbed the small dune that peaked where the beach stretched up to meet it. At the top she sank gratefully to her knees, warm with exertion. It was horrible, this getting old. She used to run along this same path to the beach then straight into the sea for a long, vigorous swim before she even felt the need to catch a breath. Putting her hand to her chest she chuckled. Goodness, it didn't seem all that long ago.

She slipped off her Keds and dug her toes deep into the cool sand, then flexed her fingers to do the same. This was her favorite roosting spot. On this bit of land she could sit for long periods of time and feel close to all that was dear to her heart: the sea, the sand, this land. And all this was dear because it brought her close to Russell.

She lay back into the sand and, closing her eyes, imagined she felt his arms around her again. The older she became the easier it was to feel his presence. It was a game she allowed herself to play more often now. She couldn't see the harm. If she was going senile, what of it? She'd likely die before she went totally gaga. Besides, it was too much of a comfort to resist.

In her imagination, she and Russell were lying together again on the old black-and-red-checked blanket she'd always dragged along from the cottage when she met him on this dune. Back then, Russell's hair was so blond it appeared white against his leathery tan from hours of field research in the sun.

She remembered how his skin was both smooth and callused in spots. Her own skin was soft and pliant in those days and she wore her long, thick blond hair twisted in a braid during the day. At night, however, Russell would slowly unwind the skein and spread her hair out upon the blanket to look at it. He said it reflected the gold of the moonlight.

She had been only thirty-nine and he forty-one. She'd clung to him with the knowledge that they had only that one golden summer to treasure. For she had a husband and he had a wife. They had families and social standing. Commitments they could not—would not—break, no matter how tempted they might be. They had both understood from the onset that their love affair could not continue into the fall.

This small bit of land on the deserted bit of island had been their oasis. Back then, no houses overlooked their haven. No lights shone except for the moon. Around the lovers the sea oats clicked. Above them, the stars watched and winked in sympathy. If she closed her eyes tight, Lovie could imagine he was here with her. If she let her mind go very still, she could hear Russell's voice, his delicate Southern accent that was sweet to her ears.

"Russell, I am all confused," she said aloud. "Did you hear Palmer tell how much this piece of land is worth now? I had no idea it would ever be so valuable. You know what a comfort it has been to me all these years of such loneliness and want of affection. I feel close to you here, and wouldn't part with this land for the world. But I am dying now. I will be leaving this world soon. What am I to do with this land? I have to decide. Did you hear Palmer go on about wanting to buy this land? Should I tell him that it's mine? He would surely sell it—after he danced a jig. It would break my heart, but it would be a lot of money. Just think what I could do with so much money!"

What would you do?

"Oh, if I were only young again, I would travel! There's so much of the world I would like to have seen. But I'm too old for that now and too ill to manage the trip. I don't care much for clothes. I'm giving away all my jewelry. At this point in my life, I see all possessions as just more stuff, as Cara called it. Meaningless! Worse than meaningless. They are distractions. Yet I feel so responsible. It *is* an awful lot of money that might mean something to my children."

You will have given them each a piece of property.

"That's more than many children ever get. Then there are my grandchildren. The money could give them a leg up when they're grown. Help them with tuition, a down payment on a house, that sort of thing. It would be nice to be remembered fondly. And, of course, there's Toy. I really must help Toy.

"Oh, but what should I do? If I leave the land to my grandchildren, people will wonder where it came from. Questions would be asked and eventually answers would be uncovered. I've sacrificed too much for too long to lose my dignity, our privacy, at the end."

Privacy or secrecy?

"Is there a difference?"

Privacy is something that we maintain for the good of ourselves and others. Secrecy we keep to separate ourselves from others, even those we love.

"But I only want to protect my family!"

But you have succeeded in dividing them.

"Tell me, my love, what do you think I should do?"

You know what I would do.

"I do. You always intended to leave the land to the Conservancy. I want to, but I'm not sure if it's the right thing. And I'd need someone who I can trust to help me."

Cara?

"Cara is leaving."

She is still here now. You should talk to her. You know you want to.

"There's no time. She's leaving tomorrow. It would take a miracle."

Miracles happen every day.

"Where are you going? Please, don't leave me."

I'll never leave you.

"Russell!" She sat up and reached for him. Lifting her hand, the sand sifted slowly through her fingers until it was gone.

She was alone again and knew that she could not wish him back. Bereft, she leaned her elbows against her knees and tightened the sweater around her shoulders. The bright moon gave the beach a silvery glow and the earlier wind had swept the sand like a broom, leaving it smooth as pavement. The tide was coming in. She could see the white ruffled edges of the waves as they cascaded upon the shoreline.

With a jolt, she peered at the edge of the water. She thought she saw something moving out there. The waves rolled in, then back again, leaving bits of luminescent plankton, shells and seaweed in its wake. Lovie remained quiet, her heart pounding, not daring to move and scare away the large, shadowy hulk emerging like a great, prehistoric creature from the sea.

Yes, it was a loggerhead!

At the water's edge the turtle lifted her head, arching her neck as if sniffing the air. Then she lowered her beak, poking it into the sand. Lovie could only guess she was tapping into some ancient, instinct-stored information that would guide her. She waited breathlessly for the turtle to make her decision. At last, with a slow, dragging shuffle, the loggerhead plowed her way onto the beach straight in Lovie's direction. Every few steps the turtle stopped, contending with the effects of gravity on her three-hundred-plus pounds of weight.

Foot by foot the turtle persevered in her sluggish gait, lurching forward, then stopping to gasp for breath.

It would take time for the loggerhead to make its way up the beach and Lovie had a moment's inspiration. Very slowly she swung her legs around and crawled down the opposite side of the dune. With a hunched back she hurried down the dune, not turning on her flashlight lest she scare the loggerhead. She scurried across the path as fast as she could back to her beach house.

This time she didn't knock on Cara's door. She went into the bedroom, past the suitcase at the foot of the bed, put her hand on her daughter's shoulder and gently rocked her.

"Cara. Cara, wake up."

Cara awoke with a jolt, her breath hitching and her eyes opening wide in a startled expression.

"It's me, honey. Wake up. There's something I want you to see. Hurry now."

"Whatisit?" she slurred, looking around the room.

"Come on. Put on your jeans. A turtle has come ashore. You don't want to miss this."

"Oh, Mama…"

She cajoled and hurried a sleepy Cara into her jeans, T-shirt and sandals, and with her heart beating joyfully in her chest, led her daughter out into the cool, moist night. In single file they hurried along the path to the sea. Lovie's eyes were accustomed to the dark and she led the way quickly. As they neared the dune, she turned to put her finger to her lips and slowed to a crawl as they rounded the hill and came out on the beach.

The tide had inched back and the smooth sand was scarred by a long, wide furrow of turtle tracks from the water's edge high up near the dunes. In the silence, Lovie could hear the scrape of the turtle's digging. Following the line of tracks, she found the loggerhead. The creature was magnificent. Sand flew into the air in great gusts, spraying sand like confetti.

Lovie heard Cara's gasp behind her and guided her to a spot hidden by a dune. The turtle worked without pause to dig the egg chamber, using one rear flipper to scoop out the sand and another flipper to brush the mound away in an ancient ritual, over and over for almost an hour. Then she stilled and a deep silence again reigned. Signaling with her hand, Lovie led Cara closer now, for it was said that, once the mother began laying her eggs, she went into a trance and was less likely to stop until her work was done.

It was a perfect night, with little wind and a bright moon to light the area like a theater. Lovie felt the excitement she always felt at the sight. No one knew at what time or where a loggerhead would come ashore. Even with vigilance, seeing this was a matter of luck.

And God's grace, she thought, whispering a prayer of thanks for this small miracle. She looked at Cara's face. It was as still and watchful as a child's and Lovie smiled to herself. She'd made the right decision to fetch her, she thought. She knew her daughter would always remember the night they shared this ancient ritual of the loggerhead for which she'd been named.

They sat shoulder to shoulder during the next hour and Lovie felt that their silence bonded them now rather than divided them. From time to time Cara would look over to her to exchange a glance, their eyes gleaming like the moon overhead. The loggerhead was steadfast as one by one more than one hundred leathery eggs slipped into the sand. While she worked, great streams of salty tears flowed down from her eyes.

A mother's tears, Lovie thought to herself. The tears of duty, love and commitment. The tears of resignation and acceptance.

And, too, the tears of abandonment. For this sea turtle would finish laying her eggs then leave the nest, never to return.

Don't cry, Mother, she silently said to the turtle. Didn't all mothers abandon their children at some time? Soon she, too, would leave her own children, never to return.

What did scientists know, explaining those tears away as a mere cleansing of the eye? A woman saw those turtle tears and instinctively knew that the turtle mother wept for her children. A mother knew of all the predators that awaited her young, of the swift currents that might lead them astray, of the dazzle of dangerous lights, of the complicated nets that could entangle them and of the many years of solitary swimming. She wept because she could not protect them from their fate.

Lovie lifted her hand to wipe away the tears from her own face, feeling a powerful kinship with the beautiful beast before her. They were like old friends, having a good cry together.

Then Cara squeezed her hand and all at once it no longer felt so sad. Such was the way of nature. Like the Bible said, there was nothing new under the sun. There was a time for being born, for giving birth, and a time for dying.

The turtle finished laying her eggs and began shoveling sand into the nest with her hind flippers. Then she turned and tossed sand violently to camouflage her treasures. They stepped back, giving her a wide berth to finish hiding her nest and crawl back to the sea.

Lovie and Cara were her honor guard, walking quietly behind her. Each movement seemed a colossal effort and her shell scraped the sand as it dragged. She paused frequently to breathe and raise her head as though sniffing out the sea. The nearer she drew to the water, however, the more vigorous she became. The new energy and excitement in the turtle was contagious.

Lovie sensed the turtle's relief when it reached saltwater. A wave washed away the coating of sand and her gorgeous red-dish-brown carapace shone like fabulous armor in the moon-light.

"You're home free!" Cara called out to the turtle.

The moon was now high over the ocean, creating a long ribbon of light that appeared as a road for the turtle to follow home. Lovie and Cara had walked all this way to the water's edge with her, agonized each step with her, but now they could go no farther.

Lovie watched the turtle lumber forward into the sea. As she became buoyant in the saltwater, her strong flippers began to stroke and in that miraculous instant the turtle shed her earthly burdens and was transformed from a plodding, hulk-ing beast to a creature of great grace and beauty. She raised her head once more, as though to say farewell, then dove be-neath the surface and was gone.

Lovie stepped forward into the water after her. She felt an inexpressible urge to go with her. Beyond, she sensed a great, deep unknown. Out there, under the surface, lay a vast other-world filled with mysteries and beauty. Transfixed, she wanted to follow the turtle down that ribbon of moonlight.

"Mama? Come back. You're going out too far."

Lovie blinked and looked down. The water was up to her knees and the hem of her skirt floated around her.

"Why, I've barely noticed. I was watching her. But she's gone now."

"Here, take my hand."

"Wasn't she beautiful?"

"Breathtakingly beautiful. I never imagined it could be so magical."

Lovie came out from the water to stand by her daughter. "It is, isn't it? I've seen it many times, but each time is like the first."

"I wonder what it's like out there," Cara said wistfully, standing at the shoreline with her arms wrapped around herself and her eyes searching the sea. "Look at it. It's so vast. To just slip under like that... I can't imagine."

"I imagine it's rather like death. You want to go with her, you're curious, but to do so you'd have to cross that slender, elusive barrier that separates the two worlds. A little death, that's all it would take. One step, one final breath, then you'd be floating."

"Well, I'm not ready for that particular journey yet, thank you very much. Just making it back to the house seems far enough for tonight." Cara turned and took a few steps back up the shore.

"Cara?"

She stopped and looked around. "Yes?"

"I'll be making that journey soon."

Cara's face froze in puzzlement. "What?"

"I have cancer. I know that sounds dramatic but I can't think of an easy way to say it. So, there it is."

In the stunned silence myriad emotions flickered across her face. "No!" she exploded. Cara took a step forward, then stopped abruptly, shaking her head in confusion. "Cancer? What kind of cancer?"

"It's lung cancer."

"But you don't smoke! Not for years."

"I know, I said the same thing when I found out. But the damage was done. I've already gone through a round of radiation therapy." She heard Cara's sharp intake of breath. "It was never the cure. We were just buying a little time."

"How long have you known?"

"For some time. Since December."

"How bad is it?"

"I'm afraid it's quite bad. Simply put, I'm dying."

Shocked, Cara said nothing.

Lovie reached out her hand. "My dear, you've gone white."

Cara brought her own hand to her head to clutch her hair in a fist. "Dying. Dying? Why didn't you call me? I would have come home immediately!"

"I didn't want you to come home only because I was sick."

"Sick? You just said you're dying."

"Yes."

"Wait. Let's back up a minute," she said in a tone that Lovie recognized as her daughter's effort to table her emotions and be practical and efficient. "How do you know you're dying? Who have you seen? There are new procedures. Other hospitals we can go to. I know of an oncologist—"

"Cara, stop. There's nothing that can be done—other than to put my house in order. That's what I've been trying to do, though I've been making quite a mess of it. I'm sorry about what happened at Palmer's tonight. I should have told you but I simply wanted for us to have a little time together first without bringing up the topic of who gets what after I die. That's such a waste of time, and I have so little time left. Oh, Cara, don't you see? It's like watching that turtle slip into the sea. She's finally free of the earthly burdens. That's what I yearn for. But I know I have to settle my affairs before I go. I want to spend what time I have left getting to know you again."

Cara went very still and tears glistened in her eyes. "That's why you wanted me to come home? That's the sorting out?"

"Yes."

"Oh, Mama..." Cara slumped down onto the sand and covered her face with her hands. "It feels as though the earth just dropped away from my feet. It's so unreal. Just the other day I was feeling so sorry for myself. I wondered what else the gods could do to me. But I never thought it could be this. Not now. Not yet."

"Don't cry," Lovie said, crouching close to her daughter. Her own tears streamed down her cheeks. "Didn't we have fun tonight? I thought we shared something very special."

Cara nodded, wiped her face with her palms. "We did. Yes, we did."

"I wish Palmer could have been here, too."

"Does Palmer know?"

"No one knows except Florence and Toy. They've been helping me through these past months of treatment. But the radiation is finished now and I hope—I pray—I have this one last summer."

"This summer? That's all?"

"It's enough. Cara, I know I'm terribly selfish to ask this, but please stay with me. Just for this summer? I know how difficult it is for you to get away from work for so much time, but if you could see your way clear to do it…"

Cara took a long ragged breath and looked out at the stars. All the crazy pieces of the past few weeks tumbled together to guide her to this answer. She took her mother's hand and squeezed it gently, causing her to smile with hope.

"Of course I'll stay, for as long as you need me. I'll take care of you. I won't leave you, I promise."

"But your job?"

"Don't worry about that. Oh, Mama, I have a lot to explain to you, too."

eight

The turtle uses her hind flippers in an elaborate digging ritual,
alternately digging out scoops of sand to create an egg chamber
eighteen to twenty-two inches deep.

Toy woke early. She couldn't sleep in even if she wanted to.
The baby was growing fast now and pressing down on her
bladder so that she had to pee all the time. There was so much
that was changing in her body. Her belly was really starting to
stick out there and her breasts were enormous. Darryl would
have liked that, she thought, then her smile fell.

Last night she'd sat alone in the Rutledge's TV room while
in the dining room the others talked and talked. She'd hated
being stuck in that house, hated having to wait, then pretend
she didn't hear nothing. Well, she'd heard plenty. Every word
that pompous, pig-faced Palmer had said about her. And she'd
heard what wasn't said, too.

It was Cara who stood up for her. Cara who let her brother
have it right between the eyes. Toy still felt the same wonder
and awe just remembering it. The ice queen—who'd have
thought?

All night long she'd wrestled with the thought that she

should go back to Darryl. She'd dreamed about him, too. His nice smile, the way he was so protective of her and was always looking out for her.

He'd never let someone talk about her the way Palmer Rutledge did. But that wasn't the only reason she was thinking of going back to Darryl. Her insides hurt so bad that Lovie hadn't said a word to hush up her son. He'd said some real hurtful things that were not true. Did he think that just because she was poor she would steal? That's what so many rich people thought, that poor folks didn't know the difference between right and wrong. She'd never steal from Miss Lovie! As if! It sounded to her like *he* was trying to steal from his own mother, taking something that didn't belong to him out of pure and simple greed. To her mind, that was as low as anyone could go, rich or poor. It wasn't as if he didn't get nothing already. Jeez, if someone gave her a house like that she'd be set for life.

Not that anyone ever would. People like her didn't live in houses like that. She didn't want it anyway. All she really wanted was a nice, clean place that was sunny and she could fix up the way Lovie taught her with pretty tablecloths and matching dishes and some lace at the window. She'd make it a happy place, too, for her baby and Darryl. She was good at making people happy and knew he'd want them both back. He just needed a little time to get over the shock of her being pregnant and all. 'Cause that's all it was, a shock. He didn't mean to hit her or say those things. He was a good man and she knew he loved her. He'd love her baby, too, once he saw it. She just knew it.

So she thought maybe she should call him today and sort of see how he felt about her coming back. Even if she'd told Miss Lovie she wouldn't.

She thought these things while she washed her face and squeezed into one of her A-line dresses. She tsked when she saw the seam tearing at the waist. Walking down the hall she tried reaching down her back to tug on the zipper that strained at the task. Then she stopped, sniffing the air. Was that coffee she smelled?

"Good morning!" Cara looked up and smiled when Toy stepped into view.

Toy was so taken by surprise she didn't know what to say. This was the first morning she'd even seen Miss Caretta Rutledge before 11:00 a.m. much less in the kitchen brewing coffee and making toast. She'd have rubbed her eyes if it wouldn't have smeared her eyeliner.

"Want some coffee?"

"Why, uh, sure. Thanks." She reached for the cup but Cara already pulled one from the mix-and-match sets in the cupboard. "Want this one? The Meissen's always been a favorite of mine."

"I'm partial to those pink flowered ones."

"Limoges. You have good taste. Those are Mama's favorites, too."

Toy basked in the compliment, but remained wary.

The toast popped up, and with the speed of a short-order cook, Cara had it buttered and placed on two plates, one for each of them. She then carried a platter of jam, sliced cheddar and Jarlsburg cheeses to the table.

"I'm not a gourmet cook, but this should settle us for a while. Do you want anything more? Cereal? Eggs? A growing baby must need a lot."

"I can fix it myself later. This will hold me just fine for now." She looked at Cara, unsure of what to expect next. Cara looked lean and fit in her khaki shorts, like one of those ladies in Miss Lovie's *Town and Country* magazines. Feeling self-conscious, Toy reached her arm behind her back for the zipper, feeling as gangly as a walrus.

"Here, let me get that for you." Cara moved behind Toy and with a few struggles, tugged the zipper up the track. "I'd tell you to tuck in your stomach but I don't think it'd do any good. I hate to tell you this, sweetie, but this dress isn't going to hold you much longer. What do you say we go to the Towne Center and pick you up a few maternity things?"

"I'm okay," Toy replied quickly. "I'm fixing to sew up a few dresses. By the way, where is Miss Lovie? She's usually the first one up."

"She's pretty tired this morning. I'm glad she's sleeping in." Cara moved toward the table and gestured for Toy to follow her. They sat across from each other, Toy a bit uneasy but Cara more relaxed than she'd ever seen her as she applied a thick layer of strawberry jam to her wheat toast and bit into it with relish.

Toy watched every move Cara made, painfully aware of her natural elegance. Toy sat straighter in her chair and imitated her movements as she spread jam on her own toast.

"You'll never guess what we saw last night," Cara said, her eyes sparkling. When Toy shook her head, Cara exclaimed, "A turtle! We saw the whole thing—the digging, the laying of the eggs. Then we followed her back to the ocean. What a gorgeous creature she was."

Toy bit into her toast, then said while chewing, "I thought you didn't like turtles."

Cara wiped her mouth with a napkin, emerging from the white linen with a smile. "I do now. How could I not after that spectacle?"

"This happened last night? Where was I?"

"Fast asleep. I hope you aren't upset we didn't call you. Actually, Mama woke me up and we hurried out there. I think she wanted to spend some time alone with me." She set down her toast, wiped her hands and gave Toy her full attention. Her face was serious. "Last night Mama told me about the cancer."

Toy put down her own toast and just stared back at Cara.

"We talked about a lot of things last night, things we should have talked about long before. She told me about how you've taken care of her all these months. Taking her to the hospital for all those treatments. Waiting for hours at a time. That couldn't have been easy."

"It was nothing compared to what she's done for me."

Cara seemed to take this statement to heart. "You did a lot, and I thank you for it. I can't tell you how much. But that's going to change now. I've decided to stay for the summer and I'm here to help. Don't worry that I'm taking your job away from you. I'm just making it a little easier. I figure I'll do some of the outside chores that need doing, the driving and maybe the shopping when you're tired. I can't cook worth a darn, so you'd best keep that up if you don't want to starve. And Mama can tell you I'm not exactly a neat housekeeper. Frankly, I've no skills whatsoever in the house and hearth department. So, believe me, we need you. We can work out all the details later. I just wanted you to know."

Toy sat silent for a moment, ruminating all she'd been told. Cara seemed so confident. So efficient. So different this morning than she had been since she'd arrived. She figured Cara must really love her mother after all.

"I'm glad Miss Lovie told you. I've been wishing she would. It didn't seem right me knowing and not you. Made me feel like we had some secret and it wasn't like that at all. I think she was protecting you."

"Mama has a habit of doing that. She likes to keep things inside and pretend everything is just peachy keen. I guess now it's my turn to protect her. No, not from you!" she said with a smile.

"From Palmer?"

Cara's brows rose at this. "Maybe. He doesn't know about the cancer yet. I'm worried how he'll take it."

"Do you think he'll make her go back into the city?"

"Not if I can help it. But he'll try and I admit I'm worried. She defers to him now like she deferred to my father. I still get mad just thinking about it." She sighed and stared into her coffee. "I'm sure growing up seeing my mother kowtow to my father is one reason why being independent has always been so important to me. A woman shouldn't expect a man to take care of her."

"Why not? I do."

"Don't. If you're waiting for a man to sweep you away and make your troubles disappear, then you'll be disappointed. I found it was much more likely to happen if I depended on myself instead."

"That's fine for you and all, but I guess I'm more like Miss Lovie. You know, kinda old-fashioned. I don't want a big career. I just want to be married and have a nice family. That's all I ever wanted. And I know my Darryl will take good care of me and my baby someday."

Cara didn't reply. She sat listening in that way of hers that made Toy feel like every single word she said was being chewed, swallowed and digested. Unaccustomed to such focused attention she found it unnerving. She got up from the table and took her plate to the sink. Carrying the coffeepot back with her, she poured Cara another cup, then set the pot on the table and sat again in her chair.

"There's something else I wanted to tell you," Toy said hesitatingly. "About last night."

"Oh? What's that?"

"I heard what your brother said about me."

Cara frowned. "I'm sorry you had to hear that. It was vile."

"Yeah, it was." She picked at her nail and shrugged. "But I'm kinda used to it. A lot of people like to judge pregnant teenagers. They think there's something wrong with us, with our morals. You know? Anyway, I heard what you said back to him." She raised her eyes. "Thanks."

Cara leaned back in her chair and smiled. "Don't mention it. He's not a bad guy, really. He just needs a zing every once in a while to keep him honest. Julia should learn how to do it."

"Yeah. Like, what's that about?"

"What?"

"You know. He bosses her around a lot."

Cara frowned into her coffee. "Like father like son."

"You mean your daddy treated Miss Lovie that way?"

"Oh, yes. Only worse." Her face darkened and she grabbed hold of her coffee cup. "Much worse."

Toy drew back in her chair. She didn't think things like that happened to women South of Broad. "I don't believe it. Who'd ever treat Miss Lovie like that? She's like the perfect lady. So kind and sweet."

"Most ladies who are treated like that are sweet. It's the bitches like me who won't tolerate it."

Toy laughed, enjoying the sound of it again. She'd been on tenterhooks ever since Cara had arrived. "You're not a bitch." Then when Cara looked at her askance, she laughed again and added, "Well, not anymore anyway."

Until this morning, Cara's smiles were rare. Now they spread across her face frequently, even if with a rusty awkwardness.

"All joking aside," Cara said, "I don't think a woman who refuses to be hit or bullied is a bitch, actually. She has self-respect."

"Are you saying your daddy hit Miss Lovie?"

Cara's face clouded. "I'm just saying there's no excuse for

a man to hit a woman. None. Period. But verbal beatings can be worse. More insidious, in that the scars aren't visible. Words can be killers. And don't think for a minute he didn't fire those verbal bullets in a splay pattern. It was a war zone growing up. We all got hit at some point or another." Her gaze was distant and Toy could see she was remembering details. "The difference is I escaped. She stayed. I swear, I don't know how she stood it all those years."

"She must have loved him a lot." Her voice sounded very small to her own ears.

Cara looked at her for a long time, her dark eyes pulsing some message that Toy couldn't quite grasp. "That would only make it worse, don't you think?"

Toy lowered her head to pick at her nail. "You can't help it when you love someone real bad."

"You can always help it. You always have a choice."

Toy felt a surge of anger and shame sweep over her that stained her cheeks pink. When she heard things like this it made her feel like there was something wrong with her. Her friends used to ask her why she put up with Darryl's harassing her all the time, shoving her or saying cruel things in public. They asked her why she didn't just break up with him. But she couldn't, and it made her feel stupid, like she should know better. She knew they were trying to help, that Cara was trying, but it only made her feel like she wasn't good enough.

"That's easy for you to say. What do you know about what it's like to be in my place? You had problems, sure, but you were rich. You went to a good school. You had chances girls like me just don't get. You had a way out. People say things to me a lot worse than what Palmer said and I just have to take it because there's nothing else I can do. You think you're smart because you went to college and have an important job. But you just don't know."

"It doesn't take brains or money to figure out that when a man breaks a woman's spirit or beats the shit out of her—if he so much as raises his hand against her—it's not love. It's called abuse. It's some guy wanting power and control over a woman."

Toy bridled, jutting her chin out in defense. "Darryl isn't like that! He's real good to me. It only happened once and he was real sorry."

"They're all sorry afterward. But they do it again."

Toy was feeling cornered and felt tears sting the corners of her eyes. "No!" She shouted out the word. "Don't you talk about him like that. He's nothing like your father. I love him. We're gonna be a family. In fact, I'm fixing to call him today." She pushed away from the table, rose clumsily and stomped from the room to go out on the porch.

Cara, watching her flee, felt guilty for arousing such defense from the girl when all she'd intended to do was warn her. She'd known a number of women at the agency who showed up to work with bruises. In time, it always affected their performance and she had to get involved and refer them to counseling so they could keep their jobs. The hardest thing to convince these women was that they didn't deserve the violence.

Cara scratched her head and exhaled a great sigh. Though it was still quite early, she felt the need for a good stiff drink. She rose to go after Toy.

As she made her way to the porch the phone rang. Not wanting the persistent ringing to awaken her mother, she detoured to the phone in the hall, keeping her eye on Toy, who was standing with her arms wrapped militantly around her chest, looking out at the ocean.

"Hello?"

"Lovie?"

She rolled her eyes. "No, it's Cara. Her daughter."

"Why for heaven's sake. Cara! It's me! Emmi."

Cara's mind switched mental gears with a grinding crunch. "Emmaline Baker?"

"How many Emmis do you know on the Isle of Palms? I heard talk that you were back but you never bothered to call. What kind of friend is that?"

"I'm sorry. I've been sick and it's been a bit crazy here."

"Yeah, yeah, sure," she drawled. "Doesn't matter. What are you up to today? I'd love to see you."

Cara smiled faintly and leaned against the wall. "I'd love to see you, too."

She conjured up a vision of Emmaline Baker the last time she'd seen her, God, twenty years ago? She was lanky, big boned, with a wide-smiling mouth. They used to call her Carly Simon's long-lost cousin. But it was her hair that Cara always loved. Long, curly and a fiery red that Cara thought made her look like one of her wild Scottish ancestors. She had the tongue and temper to match. Emmi was smart, too. They went to different schools—Cara to Ashley Hall and Emmi to Christ Our King—and at the beginning of every summer when they came to the island they would compare report cards. Most years it was neck and neck. Though they were best friends, there was always this competition between them, in a good, edgy kind of way. Knowing that come June she'd have to compare her grades with Emmi Baker was what kept her nose to the books during the school year. What was Emmi like now? she wondered. Was she as fiery as ever? Or had age mellowed her?

"I hear you're a Turtle Lady now." There was a tease in her voice.

"Yep. Your mama finally roped me in. Took her thirty years, though." They both chuckled over the line. "Remember how she made us walk the beach every morning to look for tracks?"

"I don't know who hated it more, you or me."

"That's why I'm calling, actually. I spotted tracks this morning, right in front of your house."

"We know. We saw the mother lay the eggs last night. Mama put some shells in a pile to mark the spot."

"No kidding? Cool. Talk about beginner's luck. I've been doing this for two years and I haven't seen one yet. Those wily turtles. Is Lovie coming down to put the stakes in? The nest looks like it's in a pretty good spot."

"No. Mama's not feeling well today. Tell you what. I'll come down with the stakes and stuff and you can impress me with all you know. We could catch up."

"It's about time. I thought you'd been avoiding me the past two weeks but I told myself my old pal Cara wouldn't do anything like that." There was a pause, then she said with less bravado and more sincerity, "It's been too long, sugar."

"I know. Okay, I'll be down in a flash."

"I'll beat you there." She hung up before Cara could respond. It was an old game of one-upmanship they used to play as kids.

Cara hung up the phone with a tightness in her throat. Emmi Baker. In all her life there was probably only one girlfriend who she'd felt was like a sister to her, who she could tell anything to and not worry about it leaking out. Someone who didn't have to finish sentences to be understood, someone who could say it all with one glance, someone who was squarely on her side. That person was Emmaline Baker. And she couldn't wait to see her again.

She walked out on the porch to Toy's side, sticking her hands in her pockets as she approached. "Hi," she said in a subdued voice.

Toy turned to face her. "Was that someone you knew?"

"Emmi Baker. We were friends growing up."

Toy nodded, accepting that at face value. She seemed troubled and her distance was not so much the old aloofness as it was a new sadness.

"Toy, what I said earlier... I might have been a bit preachy. I'm sorry if I upset you. You're right. I don't know your boyfriend. I told you about my mother because I wanted you to know you aren't alone. These things happen to a lot of women, and it doesn't matter if you're rich or poor, smart or not so smart. We're not judging. We just care about you. That's all."

Toy lifted one shoulder in a halfhearted shrug. "That's okay. I know you didn't mean nothing by it."

"You aren't really thinking of going back to him?"

"Someday I am." Then, glancing over her shoulder, added with less attitude, "Are you sure you want me to hang around now that you'll be here all summer?"

Cara knew this was her chance. One word from her and Toy would leave and she'd have the house to herself and her mother. It was tempting. She looked at the girl—her protruding belly, her choppy blond hair and her kohl-lined eyes. Toy wasn't really all that different from Cara at that age. At eighteen they were both outcasts, beaten by a man with nowhere to go. Except Cara had had her self-esteem and her stubborn determination to succeed while Toy... All Toy had was her baby and a fragile dream of a family.

"I'm very sure," she replied. "Listen," she added in an encouraging tone. "Emmi is going to meet me down by the turtle tracks. Something about marking the nest. Want to come? I sure don't know what I'm supposed to bring."

"I should stay here in case Miss Lovie wakes up. But everything you need is right there in the red bucket beside the door. Emmi will know what to do."

"You're quite sure? We could write Mama a note and tell her where we are."

"I'm pretty tired myself." She met Cara's eyes, her expression one of utter defeat.

"Okay," she replied, letting it ride. "Tell you what, I'll treat us all to lunch when I get back. You pick where." She looked at her watch. "I'll be back in an hour or so. I'd better get down to the beach." She flipped on her cap and donned sunglasses, then picked up the red bucket. She stared at it in her hand and said ruefully, "I can't believe I'm getting hoodwinked into doing this turtle stuff!"

He answered the phone on the fifth ring. "Yeah?"

"Hello, Darryl?"

There was a moment's silence. "Who's this?"

"It's me."

"Toy?"

"Of course it's me. I thought I'd just call and see how you're doing."

There was a long pause during which Toy wrung the cord.

"Nice of you to call," he said with sarcasm. Then tersely, "Where the hell are you?"

"Do you miss me?"

There was another long pause. "It's been a long time, babe."

She chewed her lip. "So, how are you?"

"I'm doin' okay."

She could tell he was mad. Was that good or bad? she wondered. "I'm doin' okay, too. And the baby is, too. You'd be, like, shocked to see me now. I'm so big."

"So you kept it." It wasn't a question. His anger was easy to hear over the wire.

"I told you I was gonna. It's our baby, Darryl."

"It ain't no baby of mine. I told you that."

"You know it is. I haven't been with anyone but you."

"Hey," he said sharply, cutting her off. "Whatever. It's your bod. Your life."

She had to suck in her breath against the pain. "I gotta go."

"Hold on a minute," he said in a rush. "Toy?"

She agonized, bringing the phone back to her ear. "I'm here."

"It wasn't right what you did. Leaving me like that. I came home and you were gone. I mean, shit, Toy. What was that?"

"It wasn't right for you to throw all my stuff out on the street, neither. Denise told me you did that. I didn't even have a chance to get my things."

"I was mad and I had a right to be. We had something real good and you went and broke it."

"I didn't want to! But it got too much. I was scared."

"You were scared of me?" His voice rose.

"Not you exactly. I was scared for the baby."

"See, that's what I mean. That baby is coming between us. I told you this would happen and I was right. We don't need this shit right now. You're too young. I'm too young."

"I'm pregnant. We can't take it back. And don't even say it, Darryl! I'm not getting rid of it."

He inhaled his cigarette. She could hear him exhale a long plume. "Then that's it, I guess."

"I guess," she said softly.

"Toy, baby, think what you're doing. I've been going crazy these past few months, missing you. There was no reason for you to leave. You know I was sorry. I just got mad. Where are you?"

"I—I can't tell you."

"What do you mean you can't tell me? What do you think I'm gonna do?"

She heard the anger building again and immediately tried

to placate him. "I don't think you're going to do nothing. It's what I might do. I might see you and want to come back to you."

His voice lowered to a seductive note. "And what would be so wrong with that?"

She melted a little. "Nothing. Just not yet. I want to stay here while I'm pregnant. Then after the baby's born, I'll look the way I did before, you know? We can be together then."

"That might work."

She took heart instantly. "I know you'll love the baby when you see it. I'll take care of it and you won't have to worry about anything."

"Whoa. I told you. I'm not ready to be anybody's father."

"But Darryl, you *are* somebody's father." She heard a woman's voice calling Darryl in the background. Gripping the phone tighter, she asked, "Who's that?"

"Some girl." He didn't even try to make an excuse.

"What's she doing there?"

"What do you think? You're not here. Remember that. You made a choice."

"You pig!" Seized with a jealous fury, she hung up the phone. Her breathing was erratic and she felt small pains in her belly. She took deep breaths and made circles with her fingertips along her taut abdomen. This had gone much worse than she'd imagined.

She leaned against the wall and brought her hand to her eyes. Everything was such a mess. She knew he was mad but she'd hoped he had missed her and wanted to get back together. What a laugh. How could he already be with another woman? She probably wasn't even the first. How could she be such an idiot to think he still loved her? That's what she got for getting involved with a player.

A moment later the phone rang.

"Hello?"

"Just thought you'd like to know I have your number."

"Darryl, you can't call me here! You can't come here neither, hear?"

"Don't you go tellin' me what I can and can't do. You're mine, don't be forgettin' that. I'll come by when I'm good and ready. And when I do, you're coming back home with me. Where you belong."

"If you want me back, you'll have to want the baby, too."

But he hung up on her before she could finish the sentence. Her heart was pounding again as she put the receiver gently back. He always had to have the last word. And he usually came through with his threats.

She stared at the phone, chewing her lip. She didn't feel anger anymore. Now, she felt fear.

Whenever she thought of Emmi, Cara thought of the day they'd learned about kissing under Emmi's front porch. It was the summer after seventh grade and she and Emmi and Tom Peterson had sat on the cool earth in the dank shadowy light and played spin the bottle. She couldn't remember who suggested the game—probably Emmi—but she vividly remembered the fierce, unspoken competition between them to get the first kiss from Tom. They both had a crush on the boy, even if he was shorter, skinnier and a year older than them. But he had dreamy eyes and a smile that showed his shiny white teeth and melted them both into pools of prepubescent desire.

Not that they really understood a lot about desire at thirteen, but they did understand kissing Tom Peterson first was a prize. They sat on the dirt in a tight circle of three, she perched on her knees, Emmi and Tom Indian style. Tom went first. It was a hot day and Cara felt beads of perspiration forming on her upper lip and brow. She gave them a hasty swipe with her forearm but kept her eyes peeled to the bottle. Round and round that Coke bottle spun. Cara held her breath and clenched her hands into tight fists on the ground. She glanced at Tom. He was looking at Emmi. With her fiery hair in pigtails high up on her head and all tied up with yellow ribbons, Cara knew that Emmi looked ten times prettier. She squeezed her fists even tighter, wishing she'd let her mom pull her own long dark hair into braids like she'd wanted to. Cara said it itched her scalp and had stubbornly insisted on letting it hang all loose and scraggly.

Finally the bottle slowed. It landed on Cara. She lurched forward with triumph. Then she stopped, suddenly shy. Tom was blushing furiously and Emmi was uncharacteristically quiet, looking down as she drew circles in the dirt. Tom looked at Cara, wiped his mouth and then, in the manner of a condemned man, leaned on his knuckles toward her. Cara swallowed hard and inched forward on her knees toward him, aware of Emmi's gaze on them. Right there and then, over an empty Coke bottle which later she was sure was somehow prophetic, Cara closed her eyes and received her first kiss. To this day she could feel the zing she felt then, from her lips clear down to her toes. Yes, please!

Though it was to be years before she'd do any serious kissing, she knew at that moment that kissing was right up there on her list of favorite things to do. As for Tom, on the next spin he got to kiss Emmi and he'd been kissing her ever since. They both went to Bishop England High School and dated on and off throughout. During the summers, though, they all hung around together like the Three Musketeers. Their main objectives were to get tanned, go to the movies at night and avoid being trapped into turtle duty during the day. Emmi and Tom both went to the University of South Carolina and got married right after Tom's graduation. Cara had been a bridesmaid.

Then they lost touch as friends often do when they grow up and go their separate ways. Yet even though they never spoke or wrote much over the years, Cara learned from Christmas cards or via her mother that Emmi and Tom had moved to Atlanta where Tom was an executive at Coca-Cola. They had two children, boys, right away. Yet, unlike with other friends she'd made and lost over the years, Cara always felt with Emmi that the intangible thread between them was strong and secure.

Arriving at the beach she saw a woman sitting on a large piece of driftwood poking a stick around in the sand. She was as broad in the beam as the tree trunk she sat upon. Bits of coppery colored hair curled around the rim of her sunhat. Cara walked closer. Before she reached her, the woman turned her head and her face lit up.

"Cara!"

"Emmi!"

With a joyful laugh they closed the remaining distance and hugged tightly. In the rocking Cara felt the years peel away and they were thirteen again, pals forever. When they stood apart, Cara saw tears glistening in Emmi's eyes as they hungrily scanned each other's faces.

"You haven't changed a bit. Damn you," Emmi said, her wide mouth stretching happily across her face. On her, a smile was more than a facial expression. It was a statement.

"Neither have you."

"Oh, go on, liar."

Emmi had gained weight proportionately, though on her large frame she didn't look fat so much as big. Her face was tanned and the faint freckles sprinkling her nose and cheeks gave her a youthful look. She still had that wonderful exuberance about her and her green eyes danced in welcome.

They just grinned at each other for a moment, soaking each other in. "It's so wonderful to see you again," Cara said with feeling. "How long has it been?"

"God, *years*. Too long."

"It's terrible."

"I know. But didn't it go by quickly?" After they chuckled Emmi said, "So, you're still not married?"

"Uh-uh. What can I say? You stole Tom from me and after that..." She shrugged.

Emmi laughed, but there was a strain in her eyes that Cara didn't miss.

"How is Tom? Is he around? I'd love to see him."

"Oh boy, where is he now? Let's see," Emmi tapped her lips in thought. "He's in South America, even as we speak. He's still with Coca-Cola and he's overseeing a new plant in Peru. He's back and forth a lot, mostly forth. I got tired of sitting around the house and came here. We pretty much decided we wouldn't see a whole lot of each other in the summer." She kicked her toe in the sand. "Sort of like your mom and your dad used to be."

Cara blinked. Her mama had come to the beach house as an escape from her husband, but Emmi didn't know that. As close as they were growing up, Cara could never confide to Emmi the personal problems of the family. If there was one thing her mama had drummed into her head, it was to never hang the family's dirty laundry out on the line.

"Since the boys were born we've come here every July and for holidays like Thanksgiving and Christmas. The boys love it here and, of course, so do Tom and I. Then last year my parents retired to Florida and gave me the beach house. So here I am."

"How about your boys? I'm guessing they're surfer dudes now, bronzed and breaking hearts every week?"

"Yes and no. They come once in a while for a weekend. James, our eldest, is an obsessive-compulsive studier. He's in premed at Duke and refuses to waste his time coming to the island to hang out during the summer. So he stays on campus. John's got his friends and a job. He still fiddles around with a surfboard when he visits, which is not too often. He prefers it in Atlanta. At his age the last thing he wants to do is spend time with his mother."

"So you're living alone here for the summer?" Cara asked.

"Yes, ma'am, and loving every minute of it. I'm as free as a bird. Whoopee!"

Cara laughed to see Emmi spread her arms and flap them like the gulls overhead. "You're still as crazy as ever."

Emmi dropped her hands and removed her hat to smooth her hair. Cara found it bittersweet to see the long thick red hair she'd admired cut bluntly around the chin and mingled with a few strands of gray.

"No, sadly I'm not anymore. But I'm trying to regain a little craziness in my life. Let's not go down that road quite yet, honey. Tell me about you! I hear you're some big muck-a-muck ad executive in Chicago. I always knew you'd amount to something, Caretta Rutledge."

Cara sighed and moved to sit down on the long palm trunk that had washed ashore. She patted the warped wood and Emmi came to join her. They sat shoulder to shoulder and both stretched their long legs out before them as they did as kids. Cara's legs were lean and pale beside Emmi's tanned, thick ones.

"*Was* is the operative word," she replied, then kicked her heel in the sand. "I got canned. Just before I came here. I went to work one day with a new client on my mind and before an hour was up I was escorted out the door by an armed guard. Now *that's* an experience you never want to have, I can promise you."

"What?" she asked, sounding shocked. "Did you embezzle pots of dough or bring an Uzi into the cafeteria?"

Cara laughed. "Hardly. Let's just say it was spring-cleaning and I was a superfluous dustball. A big and expensive-to-get-rid-of bit of dust, but discarded nonetheless."

"Cara, I'm so sorry."

"It happens. More often in this business than you'd think. But," she added with chagrin, "you still never think it's going to happen to you."

"So, how are you? I mean, are you okay or are you destitute-and-on-the-streets kind of unemployed? We used to say we'd always take each other in if we had to and my door is always open." She paused. "Is that why you're home?"

She shook her head. "I'm okay," she said with a light chuckle. "At least so far. I was with the agency for a long time and the severance package was very generous. I'm far from destitute, but I wish I could tell you I've got a great stock portfolio or something. I figure with my costs set, I can afford to regroup this summer. A headhunter is already looking into things for me and I'm confident something will turn up. I just hope it's sooner than later or I might take you up on that deal."

"Anytime. We're blood sisters, remember?"

"God, do you know how lucky we are to have been kids when we were? These days it'd be crazy to share blood like that."

"We would've done it anyway."

"You think?" She kicked the sand again and her tone changed to a more philosophical note. "You know, it's providential. I realized that when I woke up this morning. If it had happened to Mama last year, I couldn't have stayed for the summer. But now I can."

"Whoa, back up. You lost me. If *what* happened to your mother?"

"My mother has cancer."

Emmi sat straight up and looked stricken. "Miss Lovie? Oh, *no*."

"I only just found out myself. It's lung cancer. Apparently it's already metastasized and there's really nothing more they can do." Her throat constricted and she abruptly stopped speaking.

"Oh no, no, no. Not her. That's just shitty."

Cara nodded. "She's asked me to stay for the summer and I've agreed. That's what I meant. I have the time to stay now because I was fired, where a year ago I couldn't have swung a whole summer off."

"Well, you could have."

"Not and kept my job. But that point is moot now, isn't it? And what does losing a job compare to losing my mother?"

Emmi shook her head sadly. "I'm so sorry, Cara. My heart is sick. The whole island will be heartbroken, too. Why, most everyone who's ever spent time here knows her as the Turtle Lady. We all saw our first hatchlings because of her."

"Remember how she used to raise a flag whenever a nest was due to hatch?"

Emmi nodded, then offered a rueful smile. "But she used to help them hatch a little, too, if you know what I mean. There are strict regulations against that now."

Cara didn't know or care about regulations. All she knew was that her mother would not be here next summer when the loggerheads returned. "It's so unthinkable to imagine that she's really dying. It's hard to accept. When I see her I think, 'okay, she's sick.' But I still can't imagine her life coming to an end. It's odd, but in some ways the summer looms so long. Yet, when I think this will be her last summer, then it seems frighteningly short."

"Imagine how it must feel to her."

"That's what's so amazing. She doesn't seem the least bit afraid."

"What is she do—"

Emmi was interrupted by the high-pitched "hello" of a woman approaching up the beach. Emmi raised her arm and waved back. "Hey there!" To Cara she said, "There's Florence. You remember Florence Prescott, don't you?"

"Of course." Cara watched the woman approach. Flo had been like an aunt to her growing up. Yet, she was ageless, too, her brilliant white hair a stark contrast to her very tanned skin. She wore a green T-shirt with a picture of a loggerhead and the words Turtle Team across the front.

Flo shook her head as she drew near and called out, "As I live and breathe, it's Caretta Rutledge in the flesh. How are you doing, darlin'?"

Cara stood to embrace the woman with the same ease she had for years when Flo walked right into their kitchen for a morning cup of coffee. "I'm fine. You look great! Oh, it's so good to see you again."

"You're looking pretty good, too," Flo said, removing her sunglasses and giving Cara the once-over with blue eyes shining like searchlights. "For someone on death's doorstep. Lovie told me you'd been under the weather since you arrived."

"I was, but I'm better now."

"The island makes you feel better. You should come home more often."

Cara heard the scold beneath the smile and nodded. "I'm here for the summer now, Flo."

Flo's expression changed quickly to become serious and her eyes flashed in understanding. "So, she's finally told you?"

Cara nodded, tightening her lips.

"Good. I'm glad. She needed to tell you as much as you

needed to hear it. Lovie needs you now, Cara. She's missed you something fierce."

Flo's voice was full of conviction and Cara shifted her weight. She'd never thought her mother needed her, much less missed her.

"It's going to be hard on all of us," Flo continued, "but we can't let on. We need to keep upbeat."

"I was thinking," Emmi broke in. "We'll have to figure out how to cover for Lovie over the summer if she can't keep up with her schedule."

"You won't be able to take it away from her," Flo replied in her matter-of-fact manner. "The turtles are her life."

"No, they're not," Cara said. "She needs to think about other things this summer and she may not be up to the task. The turtles have taken my mother away for long enough."

Flo studied her face, then spoke slowly. "You never understood about your mother and the loggerheads. And I guess there are parts of the story you never can. But trust me on this, Caretta. If you take those turtles away from her, you'll kill her faster than any cancer will. She's been doing this for as long as you've been alive and it means the world to her. Not just the turtles, but also the feeling of renewal they give her. It's a special connectedness to God, to the earth, to the best part of herself. She's earned that small bit of peace—and you know what I'm talking about."

Cara didn't reply.

"Why, you know how much she looks forward to the turtle season every year. She lives for it. Finding and marking the nests, waking early to find tracks or staying up late to sit with eggs till they've hatched. She keeps all the records, writes the newsletter, gives lectures, instructs the children, welcomes the tourists and who knows what else? She's like a mama hen worrying about each and every one of those hatchlings.

"And on top of all that, people with causes live longer, age slower, stay sharper and are just damn more agreeable." She released a quick smile that set her eyes glittering like topaz. "Even if they are a bit single-minded. Take the turtles away from Lovie and what's she got left? Just her illness, that's what. Dry rot will set in and she'll be waiting to die. I've seen it happen too often. Why, the very notion boils my blood. I say she needs to feel a part of this team now more than ever. Olivia Rutledge *is* the Turtle Team."

Emmi nodded her head in staunch agreement.

Cara, who had remained silent during Flo's fiery defense, ran her hand through her hair. "What do you recommend we do?"

Flo heard the deference and exhaled a long breath. Chewing the end of her sunglasses, she regarded Cara shrewdly. "You should get involved."

"With the Turtle Team? Me?"

"Exactly."

She shook her head. "I don't think so. Thanks for the offer, but I'm not the Turtle Team type."

Flo brought back her shoulders. "I'm not sure there is a *type*."

"Sure there is. The nurturing type."

She skewered Cara with a look. "And you're saying you are not the nurturing type?"

Cara looked her right back in the eye. "That's what I'm saying."

Florence burst out laughing. "The hell you aren't. You just don't know it yet. There's nothing like a nest of hatchlings to bring it out, too. Okay, now here's my suggestion. Just hear me out. We both know your mama wants to spend time with you this summer. This would be the perfect project for you to share. She might not be up to doing all the tasks, though, so you can take over a lot of the physical activities like getting up early and following up on the turtle track reports and checking the nests at night. Lovie can do the charts, write the newsletters and still come down to the beach as often as she feels up to it. That way, no one is taking away any of her duties."

Cara made an agonized face. "But I'll be taking *on* a lot of them. Flo, you know I've never wanted to be a turtle lady."

"Oh, come on," Emmi chided, nudging her in the ribs. "Your mama came over to my house and got me involved last summer and I have to admit, I was reluctant to have to get up early every morning, especially with the boys gone and no breakfast to make. But you know your mama. The next thing I knew I was walking the beach every morning, feeling great, and couldn't wait for the sun to set so I could sit out there by the nests with the girls at night. Being part of the team grounded me and made this island my home again. You were just saying a minute ago how the summer loomed so long. This will give it focus. Best of all, you'll have this to share with your mama."

"And she needs you now," Flo added simply.

Cara realized that this one quietly spoken statement was the winning argument. Her mind spun, trying to think of alternative solutions. But there were none. She felt herself being dragged along into this decision like a piece of driftwood in the tide.

"Will you help me? I don't have a clue what to do."

"Of course. We all will," replied Flo. "But not to worry, Caretta. You've got the greatest teacher of all."

Emmi's eyes filled suddenly and she wrapped her arms around her once again.

"I'm so glad you're home. Welcome back."

nine

---

*The loggerhead deposits her leathery, Ping-Pong-ball-sized eggs
into the nest cavity, laying two, three or four at a time.
She will lay eighty to one hundred and fifty eggs in each nest.*

On the South Carolina coast, summer doesn't begin at the equinox. Summer begins after Memorial Day when the schools open the floodgates and kids pour out onto the beach with hurrahs of triumph, colorful towels flapping like flags and surfboards pointed toward the sea. The beach houses that line the shore are rented clear through until September when the schools pull the children back in. Until then, cars cruise the boulevard bumper to bumper.

For Cara, summer began with her first day on the Turtle Team. Soon after her "induction" into the team, a phone call came in reporting turtle tracks at 22nd Avenue. When Lovie woke up to the news, she smiled like the Cheshire cat.

"Fetch the red bucket," she said, throwing back the covers.

With the bucket in tow, they headed out in The Gold Bug for the nest. It was a cloudy, introspective morning with a brisk, moist wind. Cara drove, enjoying the feel of the clutch again on a winding road after years of automatic in stop-and-go traffic. They bumped along Palm Boulevard with the top down like two teenagers on an outing. Looking to her right, she saw Lovie smiling as she held on to her cap, little wisps of fine white-gold hair flying against her small, slender hands. Sometimes she could look so young, Cara thought.

She parked along the sandy roadside, placed her hat on her head, then hopped out of the car to run around and help her mother out. Grabbing the supplies, they headed out along the twisting, narrow beach access path. The houses were so close together Cara could smell coffee and bacon coming from the kitchens. Ahead of her, Lovie was as nimble as a mountain goat, but she paused midway to cough. It sounded deep and wet and Cara recalled hearing that cough a few times around the house as well. An inner alarm went off.

"Are you okay?" Cara asked. "Maybe you're catching something?"

"No, no, it's just the dry air and sand."

"I don't know. You're supposed to be taking it easy. Perhaps you shouldn't be coming out here."

"Nonsense, I'm fine. The doctor said exercise is good for me. Come on, let's go find those tracks." She cleared her throat and with a tease in her voice asked, "You do remember what a turtle track looks like, don't you?"

"Yes, Mama," Cara replied in singsong, picking up the bucket. She was never going to live down her first disastrous day searching for turtle tracks. The day before she'd run back from the beach to breathlessly tell Lovie she'd found tracks. Lovie made the phone calls to Emmi and Flo. Then they all raced to the designated beach with probes in tow, only to laugh until tears moistened their eyes when Cara's tracks turned out to be the trash man's tractor tracks.

Chagrined, Cara was determined never to make that mistake again. Once on the beach, she readily spotted the wide turtle tracks that carved the smooth, untrammeled sand. They traveled from the high tide line to a small body pit. Not far beyond it was a huge, man-made hole, probably the remains of a massive sea castle laid low by the tide.

"Fools," Lovie muttered coming close. "A sandcastle is one thing, but a huge crater is another. Don't they know a turtle has to crawl by? She might've gotten trapped in one of these pits."

"I'm sure they didn't even think of the turtles when they were building it," Cara replied, moving on to the turtle's nest. "Not everyone is as turtle crazy as you are."

"They should be. The loggerheads have been coming to this beach for a lot longer than any of us have." She picked up a long, tapered T-handled dowel and gave it with ceremony to Cara. "This was my probe stick. And now it is yours. It's kind of a badge of honor in the Turtle Team, so don't take it lightly. Only a few people are approved to probe a nest and I'm going to teach you how it's done. So pay close attention."

She drew lines in the sand, dividing the circular body pit into four parts. Then, beginning with one quarter, she taught Cara how to hold the probe stick and balance her weight before carefully pushing the stick into the sand. Her small, slender body moved gracefully, inch by inch, up and down, sliding across the small area like a ballerina doing pliés on the beach.

"It's important not to push in fast like a drill because, if you should find the egg chamber, your probe will go through the soft sand like a knife through butter. You don't want to push hard, either, lest you break an egg. So nice and easy, like this." She probed a few more times with deliberate slowness and care. When she was done, her breath came short. "Now you try it."

Cara took the probe stick, feeling more nervous than she

thought she'd be. "At least I'll get some payback from all those ballet lessons you made me take as a child."

"No knowledge is wasted," her mother volleyed.

Cara centered the probe between her legs, bent at the knees, caught her balance, then began. Each time she pushed the stick through the sand, she was sure she was going to come crashing into an egg.

"Not so fast," Lovie admonished. "There's no hurry. Why are you always in a hurry, Caretta?"

Cara took a deep breath, then tried again.

"People always seem to be in so much of a hurry," Lovie continued as she sat down breathlessly in the sand. "Rush, rush, rush. What are they rushing toward? Life isn't some kind of race. We all cross the same finish line, sooner or later. You'd hate to get the end in sight and suddenly wish you'd walked rather than run, wouldn't you?"

"Maybe that's why they call it the human race."

Her mother laughed. "Well, we *are* all in it together. But the winner of this race gets no prize. So take your time, Cara. Move steadily and serenely at a turtle's pace. Smooth movements. That's better. Careful now. The dip always catches you by surprise. Sort of like in life."

Cara moved slowly, thinking of the tai chi exercises she'd once taken. Eventually she caught her own rhythm, easing the probe down to feel the hard resistance of the compact sand, then slowly drawing it back. Then on to another spot, and another, one after the other until she'd made dozens of small holes filling half the circumference of the pit. Just as she was getting into it, when she least expected it, the probe slipped in deep—so deep she had to catch herself or it would have gone too far in.

Cara felt a soaring elation and looked over at her mother for affirmation.

Lovie smiled, pride shining in her eyes. "Congratulations. *Now* you're a member of the Turtle Team." She rose and coughed, patting her chest, then said hoarsely, "Okay, roll up your sleeves." Coming closer with the red bucket she sank to her knees in the sand. "This nest is much too far below the tide line. High tide will destroy the eggs for sure. We'll have to move it. So, let's see what we've got."

Lovie began digging out the sand with her hands, carefully probing with fingers for the eggs between scoops. Cara watched intently, then followed suit. Before long, the eggs were visible and Cara laughed out loud with the delight of discovering a treasure trove. Gingerly, Lovie reached in and drew one out, handling the single egg as though it were made of spun glass. She gingerly handed it to Cara.

Cara held out her palm, cupping the egg, bringing it close. "It's the spitting image of a Ping-Pong ball. Only soft and leathery."

"We can only move them now in the first twenty-four hours, but we mustn't jostle them or turn them around lest the embryo tears from the shell." She took the egg back and placed it right side up into the trusty red bucket.

One by one they retrieved the eggs and carefully placed them in the moist sand nest inside the red bucket. When they were done, they moved the eggs to a chosen spot above the spring tide line where they would be safe from saltwater flooding. Cara crouched at the spot her mother chose and began digging with a cockleshell an arm's length into the sand. Then she carved out a flask-shaped chamber in imitation of the sea turtle's nest. Lovie sat beside her and supervised every step, a bemused expression on her face. Once finished, Cara began reverentially placing each of the 104 eggs into the new chamber, right side up.

"You know what?" Cara asked, turning to face her mother as she reached in the bucket for another egg.

Lovie looked at her daughter. The sun broke through the gray, pinkening Cara's cheeks as she grinned from ear to ear. "What?"

"This is fun. Who knew?"

Cara placed the egg in the nest, a look of fierce concentration on her face. Lovie remembered back to when Cara was a little girl, digging sand castles beside Palmer with the same expression.

Thank You, Lord, she whispered fervently. *Thank You for the chance to play with my daughter again.*

Dawn was causing a furor of excitement outside Cara's window. The birds were relentless in their chirping and squawking, more dependable than any alarm clock.

"Okay, okay!" Cara muttered, rising slowly. She yawned loudly and dragged herself from the bed. Just as well the birds woke her. She had to patrol her stretch of beach for turtle tracks. Quietly she slipped on her shorts and a Turtle Team T-shirt and laced up her running shoes. The house was quiet; Lovie and Toy were still sleeping. Stepping into the cool morning air, Cara stretched, took a deep breath, then headed toward the beach.

The undisturbed sand was smooth and hard, its shimmering surface broken by small crab holes, tracks of birds and a smattering of shells. As she jogged along her assigned stretch of beach, Cara's gaze wandered from the shoreline to the horizon. The sun pierced the bluish clouds with spectacular shafts of rosy light. Her spirits lifted and she got into the rhythm of the run. She'd been jogging this stretch for almost a week now. At first she'd been winded and muttered how she was only doing this for Lovie's sake. But by the end of the week she knew the morning run was as much for her own sake. As each day passed the cloud of depression dissipated a little more and she missed her computer and email a little less. Each day, she felt more fit and energized.

And each day Lovie presented a new lesson. Cara had crammed a lot into the past week. There were the tracks to measure, eggs to count, and the important art of moving a nest. She learned how to cordon off the nest with wooden stakes, tape and bright orange signs to protect it from being disturbed by feet or bikes.

An hour later, Cara finished up her patrol. A few more people were out walking the beach or collecting shells. There were no tracks here today but several pale gray ghost crabs scuttled into their holes as she passed. By the time she reached home again the phone would be ringing with reports from other volunteers and she'd be off again to check the tracks for nests. Such was her new morning routine.

And it was surprisingly fulfilling. Her life had turned upside down in a little less than a month, challenging so much of what she'd thought were fundamentals in her life. She'd grown up thinking Lovie had nothing to teach her. Yet in the space of a few weeks, she learned that her mother had a lot to teach after all.

She stopped before entering the beach house to kick off her running shoes. And as her mother's humming wafted through an open window, it dawned on Cara that, for the first time in her life, the turtles were no longer a barrier between herself and her mother but a bond.

It was half past five on a cool, overcast evening in mid-June and Dunleavy's Pub was hopping. Crowds of locals peppered with tourists overflowed to the umbrella tables outdoors. Men and women cruised inside with their dogs the way Cara re-

membered kids cruising with cars. Cara and Emmi grabbed a
small wooden table in the corner before a man and his giant
black Lab could reach it. The race was close but the dog jerked
at the chain to sniff a poodle in the lap of another patron and
the table was theirs. They ordered their Coronas with lime
and hot 'n' spicy wings. In a short while the music and laughter of the pub flowed through their veins at a mellow tempo.

Cara had forgotten how funny Emmi could be and how
plain good it felt to laugh out loud without thought to who
was seated at the next table. Cara was just beginning to get
used to this again after such a long time of work-connected
relationships. With those men and women—fun and hilarious
as they were—she was always "on." She kept a clever repartee
poised on the tip of her tongue and she excelled at delivering
just enough personal information to appear forthcoming yet
holding back on the real goods.

But with Emmi she didn't have to paraphrase comments
or fill in the missing information. They had shared histories
and secrets. They also had a radar for each other's emotions.

After the wings were polished off and they were on their
second round of Coronas, Emmi leaned across the table and
asked, "Okay, so what's bothering you?"

Cara opened her mouth to snap back "nothing" when the
truth just tumbled out.

"I spoke to Adele, my friendly headhunter today. She called
in a huff asking me what the hell I was doing still on the Isle
of Palms."

"What's her problem?"

"Me." She grimaced and looked over at a pair of English
springer spaniels gobbling up spilled popcorn from the floor.
"I told her to line up some interviews for me, but of course
that was before I knew about Mama. Honestly, I didn't expect that she'd have something so soon. When I told her I

was going to be staying here for the summer, let's just say she wasn't very happy. But that's not what's bothering me."

"You're not regretting your decision to stay?"

She sighed heavily. "No, but I am worried. Adele had some very interesting prospects that I'm likely to lose by taking so much time away from the mainstream. It's a scary place to be. While I'm sitting here on the island, I still have to make my mortgage payments in Chicago and pay the bills that come in every month. And then there's my image to think about. The longer I stay away, the more it will appear I've slunk away with my tail between my legs."

"Look, sugar, I don't mean to be unsympathetic, but are you for sure going to stay here or not?"

"I told you I am."

"And you can afford to stay? Without losing your place?"

"Not forever, but for the summer, yes."

"Then forget about that other crap. Worrying about it isn't going to change anything, is it? You're here, and for what it's worth, I think you made the best decision."

Cara exhaled a long plume of air.

"I kind of envy you, you know," Emmi said.

Cara raised her brow and looked at her friend skeptically.

"I mean it. At least you've got stuff on your table, decisions to make. For the past few years, I've felt as though I've been put on hold. I swear I can almost hear the Muzak playing in the background of my life." She stopped talking when the waitress came to collect their empty bottles and take their order.

"Emmi, honey, is everything okay?"

Emmi waited until the waitress walked away. From the pensive expression on her face, Cara knew that she'd hit a sore spot.

"I don't know," she replied with a tone that signaled her frustration. "I'm just lonely, I guess."

"I thought you were enjoying being alone."

"I am—sometimes. But it gets pretty quiet. I miss the clamor around the house. I miss being needed."

"How long will Tom be gone?"

Emmi's face stilled. "Who knows?" she replied at length.

Cara caught the undercurrent of that comment and gave Emmi a questioning look.

"Here's the thing," Emmi said. "About five years ago Tom got this big promotion that involved traveling—and I mean a lot. All over the world. He's not around much during the year and never in the summer. And the boys got to that age where they just wanted to be with their friends, play sports and get jobs. You know the routine. I was a good wife, staying at home in Atlanta in the air-conditioning all summer waiting for Tom to come home or for the boys to ask for dinner. Then I found I hung around the house the rest of the year, too. I baked a lot, ate a lot, drank a lot of wine and, lo and behold, I gained about twenty pounds."

They laughed in commiseration.

"When last summer came around and John graduated from high school, it hit me that everyone was busy making plans—except me. So I said, enough of this! I decided not to rent out the beach house and up and took it for myself."

"That sounds like the Emmi I know."

"Does it?" She laughed with her eyes sparking. "Maybe. Last summer everything was fun and new. Miss Lovie hooked me into the sea turtles and it really grounded me to being home again. But this year... Something is missing."

"Tom, for one thing."

"Yeah, well," she replied, coloring. She reached for her bottle and took a long sip. Then looking at it she said, "Do you remember when we were kids and played spin the bottle?"

Cara smiled. "Sure I do. Only it wasn't a beer bottle. It was a Coke. That should've been your first clue."

Emmi looked at the bottle in her hand and Cara could see that her thoughts were traveling years back. She set the bottle on the table and looked up again. "We had all these plans for our future back then. We were bottled up with dreams and excitement and it carried us right through college."

"What happened then? Did you ever work?"

"Work? Yeah, I worked. In the home."

"I meant outside the home. At a job."

Emmi grew defensive. "Don't tell me you're one of those boring ladies who think housewives lead empty, wasted lives. I've been very busy working and volunteering, and with Tom traveling so much someone had to be at home. At least when the boys were little."

"Hey, I'm not making a judgment here. I'm only curious. You wanted to be a biologist."

"You wanted to be a ballerina."

"That's hardly the same thing," Cara replied with a laugh.

"Maybe not." Emmi's expression changed and in a sober tone she said, "But we each went on different paths, didn't we?"

"I guess. We're not all that different, though. I went to my work, you went to your work. Years passed. And now we're both forty and we're wondering about some of the decisions we've made along the way. Time is flying by faster and faster. We're both watching our bodies soften and worried whether the sun will cause skin cancer or if we're taking enough calcium so we don't get stooped someday. We're picking out shoes with the same enthusiasm we used to pick out sexy lingerie. And we're listening a little closer to talk about yoga, estrogen, collagen, alpha-hydroxy or whatever else will defy aging. And, of course, plastic surgery, even if it's to lift our boobs and not the face."

Emmi laughed. "Yet."

"Yet. And we're both looking at girls of eighteen, trying to remember what it felt like to be that young." She looked at Emmi with affection. "And then, suddenly, you run into an old friend who makes you feel like it was just yesterday."

They clinked bottles and chuckled.

"The way I see it," Emmi said, "since you *are* here for the summer, you might as well explore a little bit. Spend a little time doing the things we missed out on back when we were dorky kids."

"Hey, I thought we were pretty cool."

"We didn't do anything fun, Caretta. Come on, admit it. We were reverse snobs who preferred theater and poetry, claiming to hate sailing, fishing, golf and all the other outdoor activities that obsessed most of the people around here, especially our daddies."

"I went out on the boat with Palmer and Daddy lots of times."

"Sugar," Emmi said, silencing all Cara's objections, "have you ever taken a boat deep into the marsh? Or gone crabbing on Capers Island?"

Cara opened her mouth to object, then shut it tight and shook her head.

"I didn't think so. Neither had I until I had sons who dragged me out there. Man alive, I didn't know what I was missing." She sat up and pointed her finger at Cara. "Do you know what you should do?"

Cara looked back suspiciously.

"Go on one of those tour boats. No, I mean it. There's a

good one that goes out to Capers and a whole slew of other places."

"Why would I want to do that?"

"Because you were born and raised here and it's shameful that you haven't yet. Besides, what else is on your calendar? You have to be getting bored sitting around all afternoon."

"I have to admit I've been pretty antsy."

"So, go!"

Cara finally raised her hands and said, "All right, already! I'll take the cruise!"

ten

While she labors, the loggerhead's eyes stream with tears.
These "turtle tears" are produced to rid her body of excess salt
from drinking salt water.

Being the tourist season, it was a slow drive along Palm Boulevard to the opposite end of the island. The Marina was a cheery place with an island shop, restaurant and docks. Most of the boats were privately owned and ranged from small powerboats and Jet Skis to big deep-sea fishing craft and yachts equipped for ocean excursions.

She followed a worn path to the docks where she spotted a small wooden office built on pilings. Over it a modest sign read Coastal Eco-Tours. Beside this was a long, covered tour boat with a dozen two-seater benches on either side. A line of would-be cruisers waited to board. It was the usual assortment: a few seniors in Bermuda shorts, assorted out-of-towners with cameras hanging around their necks, and mothers and fathers with young children in tow.

She stood on the dock with her arms crossed trying to decide if she really wanted to join this family affair. Hours stuck in airplanes with complaining children were fresh in her mind.

Suddenly, a shadow fell over her. Looking up, she saw a very tanned, very tall man with auburn, sun-tipped hair and eyes the same color as the faded blue shirt he was wearing.

She could only shake her head and laugh. "You."

His smile lifted one side of his mouth and his eyes crinkled at the corners. "If you didn't run off every time I've tried to meet you, I'd think you were stalking me."

"Hardly. But I can't seem to go near a boat without finding you hanging around."

His eyes shone with amusement. "I happen to own this particular boat."

She raised her brow. "*You're* Coastal Eco-Tours?"

He nodded.

"What about the shrimp boat? Do you own that, too?"

"No. During the off-season I earn some extra cash working on boats and clamming."

He wasn't her usual type but, despite herself, she felt the zing of attraction again. And it wasn't just his rugged good looks. His sexy restraint and old-fashioned masculinity had her blood pumping hard in her veins.

"You wanted to meet me?" she asked.

"Do you mind?"

Wearing sunglasses, she could quickly glance at his left hand without notice. There was no ring on his finger.

"No, I don't mind. I'm just a little surprised. I was under the impression you found me amusing. Or should I say, rather a joke?"

He looked puzzled.

"Every time I looked at you, you were either smiling or laughing at me."

Understanding dawned and his blue eyes flashed with amusement. He looked down at her sandals. "New shoes?"

"They weren't that bad, you know."

He didn't reply. He didn't have to.

"Not that I'm not enjoying your company, but aren't you a little busy for flirtation right now?"

He looked over to see people queuing up in front of the boat ramp. "Come on. You're here for the tour, aren't you?"

She hesitated, but he flashed her a full smile that melted any resistance. Telling herself that she was going to regret this, she followed his imposing physique down the ramp.

The line of people inched their way up the dock to board the boat. She took her place in line and watched as he casually stuffed the money into a metal box and wrote down the amounts on a piece of scrap paper. Not exactly high-tech but it worked, she thought, admiring his neatly formed letters and numbers. When it was her turn to pay he said, "No, that's okay."

Cara shook her head and pulled out her wallet. "Thanks, but I'd prefer to pay."

He hesitated, then lifted his shoulders as though to say "As you wish" and accepted her money.

She found a seat in the rear of the boat, behind two middle-aged women who giggled like schoolgirls and whispered loudly how handsome they thought the tour guide was. Cara's attention, like everyone else's, shifted to the guide as he leaped from the boat to untie the ropes, then leaped easily back with the grace and finesse of Douglas Fairbanks. Everyone was in a good mood, taking pictures, joking, excited to be out on the water. Cara felt their enthusiasm but sat quietly alone, taking it all in.

Suddenly the big engines churned, the boat rocked, then slowly backed out of the dock. They made a wide turn, straightened, then headed out full speed into the waterway. The children hugged the railing on tiptoes, transfixed by the sight of the glorious sprays of water shooting out a wide wake.

The breeze grew stronger and the mood shot skyward. They were on their way!

He was taking them along the Intracoastal Waterway, a stretch of water that went from the Florida Keys all the way north to Boston. He informed them that it was created in 1942 by joining two waterways so that ships could travel inland and safely transfer supplies during WWII. Their destination was Capers Island, a small barrier island designated as a State Heritage Preserve.

While the others looked out at the panoramic view of water and marshes, she watched the man at the wheel. He stood with his back to her in a wide-legged stance, a Viking of a man, taller by a head than any other man on the boat. The tails of his blue shirt flapped in the wind and the sleeves were rolled up exposing darkly tanned forearms and large hands. Though she sat in the rear of the boat, she sensed he was aware of her presence. The crackling of tension she felt was too strong to be one-sided.

From time to time as the boat chugged along he handed over the wheel to his assistant to talk to the group about the scenery. He introduced himself as a naturalist and it soon became evident that he wasn't just giving himself an inflated title. He spoke with authority in simple, declarative sentences, reeling off an enormous number of facts about the area, the history and all the creatures in the sea. The passengers gathered around him, fascinated. He didn't speak with the grand flourish that Palmer did. He was more a teacher than a storyteller, but he could make the molting of a crab sound every bit as thrilling as a ghost tale.

He was a pro, saving the best for last. The boat slowed to a stop in the Waterway. He reached over the side to pull up a small, bobbing, red buoy. As the tourists leaned forward in their seats, he bent low to pull at the long rope attached. Up from the water came a big, black, dripping mesh cage. The kids and women alike started squealing when they spied several blue crabs inside, their pincers out and snapping. Then he reached inside to pick one up with his bare hands. Cara gasped, kids clapped and adults grabbed for their cameras.

"This one's aggressive," he said, holding it up for all to get a good look at. The crowd gathered close but remained cautious. "It's probably a female."

The tourists chuckled, as they were supposed to. He released a short laugh and glanced again at Cara. She felt the smile widen on her face as their eyes met.

After a short while, the crabs were released into the water and the boat was underway again. He turned the boat over again to his assistant, then looked her way and gave a quick wave, indicating she should come up to join him.

Cara shook her head no.

He twisted his face in an adorable grin that said, "Come on."

The two women in the seat ahead of her peeked over their shoulders with curiosity. Reluctantly she rose and walked up the aisle, grabbing hold of the seat backs so she didn't fall over in the rocking boat into some stranger's lap. Up in the front the rush of wind was brisk and teased at her hat.

"Are you enjoying yourself?" he asked, coming near.

"Very much."

"I have to admit, you're the last person I expected to see on my boat today."

"Me? Why?"

"Well, for one thing, you grew up here. I'd have guessed you know Capers pretty well."

She looked at him, astonished. "How did you know I grew up here?"

He looked back at her with equal astonishment on his face,

then his face shifted to express chagrin. "You don't remember me, do you?"

Her mind went blank. "Should I?"

"Ouch. That cuts deep. Not even a glimmer of recognition?"

"I'm afraid not. Are you sure you've got the right girl?"

"Oh, yeah. I'm sure. It took me a minute to place you when I saw you in the bar, but it hit me when I saw you again at the shrimp boat. I came by to say hey but you ran off before I got there."

"Where? How?" she sputtered.

"High school. I used to see you around. I was kind of fascinated with you, actually. Your nose was always in some book."

"Do you remember my name?"

"Sure. Cara Rutledge. That is, if it's still Rutledge."

"It is," she replied, amazed that he really knew her. She studied his long, squared face, the deep dimples camouflaged by a faint stubble, the aqua-blue eyes, the tawny hair that curled in the wind. How could she forget a face like that? "I'm sorry, but who *are* you?"

"Come on. Venture a guess."

She drew a complete blank. "How about giving me a hint?"

His eyes crinkled as he warmed to the game. "I was a jock."

"Ah, well, that explains why I don't know you. We didn't exactly travel with the same crowd."

"I was also senior class president."

She blinked and squinted her eyes, realizing she should know that one. What was the name of their class president? Then she remembered and looked at him askance. "My class president was Mary Pringle. My, my, Mary, but how you've changed."

He laughed and his eyes glittered with mockery. "I never

said I was *your* class president. I'll give you another hint. I went to Wando."

"Now that's not fair. There were too many kids in that school. You win. I give up. Who are you?"

He made a mock grimace. "You've just shattered my ego. Does the name Brett Beauchamps ring a bell?"

Brett... Oh. My. God. Her mind reeled back to senior year high school and how every girl, not just at Wando but also at Charleston High, Ashley Hall, Bishop England, Porter Gaud and probably all high schools within their football league as well, had a crush on the dashing quarterback. Brett Beauchamps had it all: good looks, popularity, a natural talent for sports and a grade point average that had Ivy League colleges dropping scholarships at his feet.

"Of course I remember you. But by reputation only. We never met. Trust me. I would have remembered. Though I'm amazed you remember me. Guys like you didn't have much interest in skinny, brainy liberals. I seem to remember that the cute, blonde cheerleaders were more your speed."

He shrugged that off. "You were different than those other girls. A loner, but kind of cool about it. Mysterious."

"Like a shark?"

He laughed. "No, though maybe in debate. I used to watch you. You stood so straight with those big red glasses slipping down your nose. There was no holding back with you. You pulverized your opponents."

"Oh, God, those glasses! I was pitiful. But it was the eighties. I should be forgiven all fashion gaffes. I do remember being terribly jealous of you when I heard you got offered all those Ivy League scholarships, though. I thought it utterly sexist and unfair."

He shrugged modestly. "They were athletic scholarships."

She studied him, wondering if his modesty was sincere.

"But you had to have the grades to get into Dartmouth and Harvard. I'd have given my eyeteeth for either. And you turned them down! I still can't get over that. Where did you end up going?"

"Clemson. I knew I wanted to settle down in South Carolina and I didn't want to leave. I never applied to those other schools. They came to me. I always wanted to go to Clemson to study field biology."

"You never even applied," she repeated disbelievingly.

"So," he asked with disarming sincerity. "Where did you end up going? You just sort of disappeared after high school."

"I didn't. Go right to college, I mean."

"You didn't? That's a surprise. You were such a…an academic."

"You were going to say nerd?" She grinned then turned more serious. This part of her history she gave in shorthand. "I left home. Moved to Chicago. I worked but eventually I got my degree. Then my master's." With a spark of pride, she added, "All on my own."

"Somehow, that doesn't surprise me."

His smile dissolved the last hurdle of restraint and for a while they had nothing more to say. They looked out at the water as the boat made its way along the Intracoastal at a brisk pace.

"Back to work," he said when she could see the long white beaches of Capers Island in the distance. He moved to take over the wheel while his assistant readied equipment.

Cara took her seat under the close perusal of the two women who seemed put out that she had had such a long, private conversation with their guide. Brett maneuvered the boat to a small dock that led to a wooded section of the island. The group disembarked and Cara felt as if she were on a school trip as she and the others followed Brett on the walking tour.

His height made him easy to spot as they passed oyster beds in mud flats, a cluster of ancient oaks that spread a magical webbed canopy of leaves dripping with Spanish moss and alligators sunning in freshwater ponds.

They ended up on a sparkling white beach strewn with dark, fallen tree limbs called Boneyard Beach. Everyone had an hour to wander off on their own before they headed back home. Cara felt her skin tingle, not from the sun but from the certain knowledge that Brett would seek her out. She slowly walked along the sand, stopping from time to time to inspect a shell. From the corner of her eye she saw that he was trapped by the two women who seemed determined to keep his attention this time. Catching her eye, he cocked his head and smiled. The women at his side turned to look her way, their mouths pinched.

She smiled back, then bent to pick up another shell. A moment later, she saw his shadow stretch long on the sand beside her.

"That's a whelk you've got there."

She looked at the large curling shell that resembled a small conch. "I used to know the names of all of these when I was little. But I've forgotten." She shook the sand out from the center, checking to make certain no snail inhabited the shell. "Can I keep this?"

"If you like. I ask that folks only take one. And no sand dollars. People take so many of those, even the green ones, that they're becoming endangered. Come on, let's walk a bit."

"How did you get away?" She looked over her shoulder. The two women were walking leisurely toward the water.

His smile came slow and seductive. "I told them I had to go join my wife."

They walked toward the cluster of dead trees that rose from the sand in a ghostly forest, their roots curled around shells and rocks. The sun shone with exceptional clarity and the sea sparkled. Brett stopped to put his hands on his hips and look around in a proprietary manner.

"Isn't this the most beautiful place?"

She had to agree. It was low tide. The beach stretched far, far out and gulleys coursed through the sand like rivers. In the distance, a small child chased a gull along the surf. What was most captivating, however, was the quiet. The din of humanity seemed so very far away. The only sounds they heard were the gentle roar of the surf and the cry of the gulls.

"It feels a million miles away," she said. "I see a tent over there. Can anyone do that?"

He nodded. "It's open to the public. There aren't many barrier islands left for folks to enjoy. They're being sold off, lot by lot. It's a real shame. If things don't change soon, there'll be a whole lot of people who'll never get to see what you're seeing now. But here you can pitch a tent, bring a can of beans and a fishing pole and you're set." He bent to examine a shell. "It's a good place for lovers, too."

He said it so fast she wasn't sure she'd heard correctly. "Doesn't it get a bit crowded?"

He straightened, turning his head to offer a cocky smile. "When it is, I've got my own secret places I like to go. I could take you there sometime." When her brows rose, he added, "For a picnic."

"I hate bugs."

"I know where there's a nice breeze."

"Brett, are you asking me out on a date?"

"Twenty years too late. Yes or no?"

She brought up her shell and scraped the last bit of sand out from the center. It had a symmetrical shape and a lovely tangerine color. She'd give it to her mother.

"Yes."

★ ★ ★

While Cara was on her tour, Lovie sent Toy shopping.
Palmer had said he wanted to stop by and see her. In a fluster
of delight she'd invited him to lunch and prepared some of
his favorite summer dishes: shrimp salad, corn muffins, raspberry iced tea and cold baked custard for dessert. He arrived
on time, but seemed rather stiff and waxy faced. He warily
cast his gaze around the beach house.

"Is Cara around? Or that girl?"

She put on her hostess smile. "No, they're both off on errands. I wanted to have a quiet lunch. Just the two of us."

His face visibly relaxed and he seemed grateful that she
would arrange that. He removed his suit jacket and loosened
his tie. He'd always hated wearing a jacket and tie and her
heart felt a pang of sympathy that he'd had to assume the heavy
mantle of the family, in so many ways.

She led him to the screened porch where the weather ac-
commodated them with offshore breezes heavy with the sweet
scent of honeysuckle. The tablecloth fluttered prettily in the
breeze. She carried the lunch to the table while he stretched
his legs out. She saw longing in his eyes as he stared out at
the ocean.

"This sure is a nice spot. It's been such a long time. I'd forgotten just how great a view you have. Very nice."

"You sound like a real estate agent."

"Do I?" He laughed and picked up his fork.

"Remember how you used to surf your kayak right out
there? I would worry about you, sure you'd drown or be bitten by some shark, but at the same time I thrilled to watch
you. You were so lithe and brown as a berry."

He smiled and she saw the boy in his face. "Not so much
anymore. I wonder what ever happened to that kayak? I might
oughta get another one. Cooper could learn."

"And Linnea."

"She's more interested in the boys *in* the kayaks." He paused and dabbed his mouth with his napkin. "We don't get out to our place on Sullivan's much. It's always rented."

"What's the point of having it if you don't take time for yourself?"

His face clouded and he stabbed his salad. "I need the money, Mama. Things aren't so good at the firm. Nothing to worry about," he hastened to add.

Lovie wasn't so sure. She'd heard enough comments from Julia that made her worry. "Have you talked to Bobby Lee?"

Robert Lee Davis was the family banker and an old, trusted friend. "I did. He says we have to retrench. Tighten our belts. I don't agree. We need to expand. Take advantage of the growth going on here. Why, I know folks who are cleaning up on real estate deals all over the state. Doubling their money in a year."

The panther was prowling, she thought to herself. So much like his father, never satisfied with what he had or taking the time to enjoy it. Or his family. Stratton was always out to build a bigger empire. It wasn't the ambition that she found so distasteful, but the sense of entitlement. Like his father, Palmer believed the world owed him not just a living, but a grand lifestyle. Or, as he often put it, "the style to which I've become accustomed."

"Why don't you bring Julia and the children here for the Fourth of July? We could eat barbeque."

"Sorry, Mama, but I can't. We've already got three invitations to juggle."

"I just thought it would be nice to spend time together. Perhaps another time."

"Sure!" he exclaimed. "Real soon."

They lapsed into a silence during which Palmer finished

his meal and Lovie tried to put together the words she wanted to say.

"That's a fine, fine piece of property," he said, leaning back in his chair.

Lovie realized with a start that Palmer hadn't been staring at the ocean at all, but at the lot directly across the street.

"There's nothing else like it on the island," he said in an easy drawl. "Three lots in a row. Look at that," he exclaimed, extending his hand. "You are so lucky to live across from it. Even if someone builds on the lot in front of you, you'll still have a view to the left. Damn, I wish I knew who owned that lot."

"I thought you told me they were deeded to the Coastal Conservancy."

"Those two over there are. Not the one directly across from you. No, ma'am, that one is owned. And I'm aiming to buy it."

"Maybe the owner doesn't want to sell."

"Everyone has their price."

"But I thought you said you didn't have any money at the moment."

"It takes money to make money." He turned in his chair to face her. "That's what I came to talk to you about. I've got a lead on who owns that place."

Lovie dropped her fork. "Clumsy me! Excuse me."

"You okay?"

"Of course I am. I'm just getting old. Now, what was that you were saying about the property?" She clasped her hands tightly in her lap but kept her smile fixed.

"Well, we've been digging around. Seems those other two lots were deeded to the Coastal Conservancy by Russell Bennett. Do you know him? One of the Richmond Bennetts?"

She hesitated, clenching her hands tighter. "Yes, I vaguely remember meeting him and his wife. Her name was Eleanor, I believe. She was a Huntington."

"He was big into nature and ecology, that sort of thing. I gather he was a champion of sea turtles in particular." He looked to her for confirmation. "Seems he foresaw how these islands would be developed and he deeded those two lots for the protection of the loggerheads."

Still she made no comment.

"I can't believe you don't know about all this. It's right up your alley."

"I remember reading something about that in the newspaper. It was all such a long time ago. I admired him for that. It showed great foresight."

"I'm surprised your paths didn't cross more often, you being a Turtle Lady and all. And you traveled in the same social circles."

"He was a biologist and I'm just a volunteer. You said you found out who owned the third lot?"

"Not yet. But here's the thing. The lots were all purchased in the same year. We're checking to see if Bennett didn't own all three of them at one time."

She coughed, waving away his hand at her back. After a moment and a sip of water she asked, "What if he did own them? Wouldn't that mean that the land is held by his family?"

"There's no record of it."

She was exasperated and said sharply, "What possible difference could it make to you who owns it? You don't have the money to buy that lot anyway. You said yourself that business was tight. It seems a waste of time to pursue this any longer."

"We could use this place as collateral, then sell both lots. Or better yet, build on them like I was saying the other night. Mama, we'd make a fortune."

"I'll never sell Primrose Cottage," she said quietly. "It means too much to me."

His face screwed up in disappointment. When he spoke,

his words were measured. "I'm sorry to tell you this, but I'm going to have to cut back your allowance. Like I said, money is tight now and keeping up this place is becoming a burden."

Lovie's face colored as she felt the flames of indignation and fear. "That allowance was set in the will. You can't change that."

"Mama, be realistic. Costs have gone up. The dollar is shrinking. I know you don't understand any of this business talk but, simply put, the money is just not there."

Lovie shuddered and wrapped her arms around herself, closing her eyes.

"Now don't you worry, Mama. You'll always be taken care of. You'll be happy back at the big house with me and the family. We miss you." He leaned forward, studying her face, his brows gathered in worry. "Mama?"

She opened her eyes and searched for the boy she loved in the stern set of his features. She'd always thought that Cara was the most like her father, but now saw that she'd been fooled by visible traits such as height, eye and hair color. As they aged, it was Palmer who had assumed his mannerisms. He had Stratton's slump of the shoulders, the beguiling smile that did not reach the eyes, the way in which he could deliver an ultimatum with a cold swipe of the tongue. All these years she'd worried about Cara, but she'd been blind to the changes occurring right under her nose in her son.

"I'm staying for this summer, Palmer," she said, drawing herself up. He was taken aback by her decisive tone. "I won't go. Whatever you have to do, do it."

"Mama…"

"I'm staying because this will be my last summer. I've been wondering all during lunch how best to tell you this, Palmer, but you must know now. I have terminal cancer of the lung."

Palmer's face grew ashen and his eyes protruded in shock.

Lovie nodded her head.

"Hell, no! I don't want to hear this. What do you mean, terminal?"

"I think you know. It means, simply, that I'm dying."

"There are treatments for cancer! I read about them all the time in the paper. Goddammit, Mama, we've got one of the best medical centers in the country right here in Charleston. If they can't figure out what's wrong with you then we'll go someplace that can. I'm not going to sit here and listen to you tell me you're dying when I haven't even had a chance to fight this thing yet!"

"Palmer, come here." She opened her arms to her son but he angrily shook his head, rose and walked to the edge of the porch to stare out.

"I'm sorry I can't spare you this," she said. "I've been to the doctors. I've had all the tests. There's nothing you, or anyone, can do. I'm afraid it is in God's hands now. No, please don't argue. That's why I didn't tell you in the beginning, because I knew you would put up such a fuss. I simply don't have the energy to fight you on this."

He turned to face her, his own face filled with anguish. "What kind of a son would I be if I didn't?"

"A good son. A son who loves his mama and does as she asks him."

His face crumpled and he lowered his head. When she held out her arms to him again, he went to her side, buried his head in her lap and wept like he did as a child.

Later that day, Cara was sitting on the porch with Emmi, sipping sweet tea and eating berries. Emmi had stopped by with a big bowl of strawberries that she'd purchased at the market. They rocked together in rocking chairs, ate berries and yakked like old times. Cara remembered back to when they were preteens and had lounged on this same porch. Those hot summer days seemed to drag on forever back then.

"I got asked out on a date," she said.

Emmi swung her head around. "And you didn't tell me?"

"I just got asked."

"Who with?"

"Brett Beauchamps. Remember him? He's the—"

"I know who he is! When did *he* ask you out?"

"He runs the Coastal Eco-Tours you were so hot to send me out on."

Emmi gaped in astonishment. "Amazing. Who would have thought that Brett Beauchamps would end up a tour guide?" She shook her head again. "If he even managed to survive to forty, I would have bet he'd either be a billionaire or in prison. Brett Beauchamps," she repeated with sparkling eyes. "Takes me back. Does he have his tour boat souped up and beer in the cooler?"

"Actually, he's quite different than we remember him," she replied, feeling the urge to defend him. No one had been more surprised than she to discover that the popular, irascible football star had grown up to be a rather remarkable man. "And he isn't a tour guide. He owns Eco-Tours. He's a naturalist."

"A naturalist," she said, drawing out the word. "That is so hard to imagine. He was such a wild, tempestuous good ol' boy. How did you recognize him? Is he still as gorgeous?"

"Actually, I didn't recognize him. He recognized me." She laughed lightly at seeing Emmi's shocked stare. It was hardly flattering, but Cara had to acknowledge that it was unlikely. "I didn't think he even knew I was alive in high school. We didn't exactly hang around the same crowds. He's a lot mellower now, more laid-back. And yes, he's still gorgeous, but in a chiseled way. More ruggedly handsome than dreamboat, thank God."

"But my, my, my, I'll bet he's still got those football muscles."

"I've always been a brains-over-brawn girl myself," Cara said with a haughty lift of her chin.

Emmi smiled devilishly. "Brett has both."

"You're enjoying yourself, aren't you?"

"I'm simply living vicariously through you, reflecting in your glory. I have to do something since my own love life is in shambles."

"What do you expect when your husband is out of town?"

Emmi's rocking stilled. They'd suddenly moved into deeper waters and the mood shifted. "It's not just when he's out of town. It's when we're together, too."

"Oh, come on. You and Tom are the poster couple for the All-American Love Story. You were childhood sweethearts and all."

Emmi began rocking again. "All stories come to an end."

"I hope you're still joking."

"No. I'm serious. Lately, I think he looks forward to going out of town. And I have to admit, I do, too."

"But Tom loves you. He always has."

She shrugged. "I'm sure he does, but not the way he used to. I don't love him the way I used to, either." Her face grew long as her voice lowered. "It's hard to feel anything for him when he's gone all the time. We don't share any interests anymore. Not even the children. And it's not like we're hot for each other, either. I mean, after twenty years there aren't many surprises left." She stretched out her legs and wriggled her toes. "I wouldn't mind poking my toe in the proverbial pond again, just to see how it felt."

"Emmaline Baker Peterson!"

"Hey, don't look at me that way. Why not? I know he does."

The image of a shy, red-faced Tom leaning forward to plant her first kiss on her lips shot through her mind. "I can't believe that, either. Tom was so shy and so…conservative. He was the only guy we knew who didn't believe in premarital sex."

"He just believes in extramarital sex."

"No!" Cara exclaimed.

Emmi just looked at her.

"You're killing me," Cara said. "That's the third time my heart's stopped. Are you sure?"

"I've left five messages for him at his hotel. At all hours of the night. Even Tom doesn't work that hard."

The silence stretched on while Cara tried to think of a plausible excuse. She couldn't.

"It wouldn't be the first time," Emmi continued. "Of course, when he gets home, I never bring it up. We go about our lives as though nothing happened. I'm not a coward. I'm just lazy. It's easier just to pretend I don't suspect than to confront him. And the funny thing is, after a while I begin to question and doubt the whole thing. Before you know it, I let it slip out of my mind—until it happens again."

"I had no idea," Cara responded, not knowing what else to say.

Emmi tapped the arms of the rocker. "Hey, I don't want to talk about this boring old stuff."

"Are you sure?"

"I've made my bed and I'm sleeping in it. Even if it is in a different house," she added, her wide mouth stretching into a mirthless grin. "The question of the hour is, where is Brett Beauchamps taking you on your date?"

"We're going out for a picnic."

"Oh, my God. Let me guess. That's you, him, a boat and

a trip to some way-off hammock. I heard about those picnics in high school. Better put bug spray *everywhere*."

Cara laughed again, but inside she sizzled. She'd heard about Brett's picnics, too.

eleven

Her eggs laid, the mother loggerhead now uses her rear flippers
to rake sand over her nest and her front flippers to throw sand to
disguise the area. When her work is done, the mother lumbers
back to the safety of the sea. She'll never return to her nest.

Brett picked Cara up in a johnboat.

"You certainly go to both extremes," she said as he took
her hand and helped her from the dock at the marina into the
twelve-foot, flat-bottomed boat. The Eco-Tour boat next to
it looked like the *Titanic* in comparison.

"We'll need something flat to get where I've in mind,"
he replied. "Sit down now, lest you want to take a dip in the
water."

She moved in her rubber-soled sandals to sit on the flat
metal seat, holding on to the sides as he shifted a large cooler,
a fishing rod, a net, long rubber boots and thick rubber gloves
out of her way to make room in the front of the small boat.
Not the usual accessories for a date. When he sat down in the
rear he winked at her with a little boy's smile of anticipation.
After settling things around to his satisfaction, he turned to
work on the Evinrude engine.

"So where are we going?"

"A secret place."

"It won't be a secret anymore once I get there."

"Oh, you'd have a hard time finding your way back," he replied with a smug smile.

"I imagine I'm not the first one you've taken there."

He laughed. "No." He checked the fuel and oil on the motor. "I've got friends still trying to find it again. I have to come in and fetch them after they get themselves lost."

Cara cast an uneasy look out at the landscape of thick grassy marshes that seemed to go on forever. "Can we get lost in there?"

"Some folks can." He put heavy black sunglasses on, leaned back and grabbed hold of the engine. "Hold on now. We're ready to go."

As the engine sprang to life, she gripped the sides of the boat. Brett easily guided the boat into the waterway, as comfortable on the water as he was on land. "Hang on to your hat," he called out over the engine's din and they took off at full throttle. The tide was going out so the current moved strong in the opposite direction. The little boat bobbed against the choppy water and the wind tore at her cap. She reached for it, but it flew off her head. Brett caught it and tucked it in the back of the boat under the rubber boots. His own hair was streaming from his face and his squared chin cut the wind like a masthead. Traveling so close to the water in the small boat was akin to riding a motorcycle on an open road. Everything was closer, more immediate. The spray of the water sprinkled her face, cool and salty.

She'd only ridden on a motorcycle once and it was actually more a glorified moped. Yet the wind against her face and her arms tight around a man she was currently infatuated with had been thrilling and made her yearn for a ride on a powerful bike someday. This was as close as she'd ever come. She felt alive and exhilarated.

Two larger craft passed them, creating wakes that had Cara reaching again for the sides of the boat. Brett only waved nonchalantly and kept his eyes straight ahead. They couldn't talk over the roar of the engine as they bounced along. So, relaxed at not having to maintain conversation, she admired the view. She saw several long-necked egrets wading in the shallows of the marsh. Overhead, a pelican banked and flew off. A ways farther, Brett tapped her shoulder then pointed. Cara followed the trajectory and gasped out loud. A dolphin was streaking through the water only a few feet away, keeping up. It seemed to be playing with them, surfacing with a loud whoosh through its blowhole. A minute later she saw another one, even closer. She wanted to reach out and touch the sleek gray skin as it skimmed the surface only an arm's length away. She laughed out loud. Looking over at Brett, she saw his smile stretch across his face at her reaction.

He turned off the main waterway onto a narrow channel of water. She watched the pair of dolphins swim off until they disappeared. She and Brett were winding their way through the thick of the marsh where several other channels interconnected to form an enormous maze. She looked to the left and right, a little afraid. The grasses rose up high over her head, blocking out any horizon markers. In only a few minutes, she was totally lost. She only hoped Brett wasn't bluffing when he'd claimed he could find his way back.

The farther they traveled in, the more the tide moved out and the water levels lowered. In some areas it drained away completely, exposing steaming mudflats where wading birds hunted for dinner in the soggy soil. Brett slowed their pace and the engine lowered to a bubbly growl as he expertly motored through the jungle of grass, his eyes on the bank, one hand on the rudder. It was like being Katharine Hepburn and Humphrey Bogart on the *African Queen,* she thought to herself.

"Are we almost there, Mr. Allnut?"

He broke into a grin and pointed to a small hammock. "Just ahead, Rosie," he called back.

She smiled. He just bumped up a few notches for catching the old movie reference. She always found well-rounded men to be infinitely more fun.

At last he pulled up to the bank of a small, treed island. He brought the boat as far up shore as he could, then shut off the engine. Instantly, the quiet enveloped them. As quickly, Cara felt very far away from the rest of humanity.

"We're pretty far from dry land," she said doubtfully, looking off beyond a long stretch of mud.

"This is as close as we can get by boat. It's just a short walk away."

"Walk?" Cara's voice rose in disbelief. Surely she couldn't have heard right. "Brett, you can't expect me to walk through that mud! There are acres of it. And who knows what's in there?"

"That's the interesting thing about marsh mud," he replied as he kicked off his sandals. He reached for the pair of rubber boots from the bottom of the boat. "That slimy mud out there is rich in organic matter. All sorts of life forms—oysters, snails, fiddler crabs—live, breed and die in that mud. Not to mention all manner of insects and larvae."

Cara watched in horror as he pushed his legs into the waders that reached up to his knees, then gathered his gloves, a hammer and the net and threw them into a mud-stained canvas bag.

"I don't care what those critters do in that gook. I'm not joining them."

He stood up and took a step toward her. She crouched back with a short yelp.

Brett laughed and stepped out of the boat into the soft, slimy mud. He sank down to his ankles. Moving to her side, he turned his back to her. "Okay, hop on."

"You've got to be kidding."

"Nope. I'll carry you."

"You can't do that!"

"Unless you'd rather walk."

"No! Wait. What should I do?"

He looked over his shoulder, eyes twinkling. "You don't remember how to piggyback?"

"Sure. But we're not kids anymore. I might hurt you."

His eyes traveled up and down her thin frame and he snorted. "Hop on. I think I can handle it."

"Well, okay. But don't say I didn't warn you." She rose and carefully stepped across the boat, afraid it would tip, which was highly unlikely in all that mud. He stooped low and, after a tentative pause, she grabbed on to his shoulders.

"No, I can't," she said backing off. "It's okay. I'll walk."

"Honey, a Lowcountry man never lets his lady walk in the mud."

"Is that on some list of a Southern man's rules of behavior?"

"Right up there with opening doors and giving up my seat. Learned at my daddy's knee. So hop on."

"Oh, okay then. Ready?"

"Any more ready and my legs will atrophy."

She grabbed hold of his broad shoulders, held her breath and jumped from the boat on to his back, squealing when he slipped his arms under her legs and hoisted her up. His back muscles were as hard as iron and she wriggled to get a grip. She wrapped her arms around his neck, laughing as he bounced her up, gaining purchase.

"Giddy up," she called out against his neck.

"Look who's suddenly feeling spry," he said with mock indignation. He turned and reached for the canvas bag and net. "Mind holding on to this net? Thought we might catch some dinner."

What a novel idea, she thought as she reached to take the gear. "Got it. Can I carry anything else?"

"Can you handle this, too?" He gave her the canvas bag, which she looped over her arm. Next she saw him reach for the cooler.

"Good God, Brett, you're not going to carry that, too?"

"Do you have any other suggestions?"

"But it's so heavy! With me and all. Brett, isn't it too much? Can you manage?"

"Only one way to find out," he said, then, with a guttural grunt, he hoisted the cooler into his arms. Cara held her breath and tightened her grip on her parcels and him. He bounced her up once more, tightening his own hold on her legs, then began making his way through the ankle-deep mud like a bull in the harness. She held on to his broad back and tightened her thighs around his sides. She wasn't blind to the muscle power such a feat demanded but he pushed on through the steaming mud with relative ease. And she had to admit, it was fun.

"How you doing down there, Mr. Allnut?"

"Okay, Rosie," he said, half turning his head. His neck was right in front of her lips as she lay wrapped around his back and she had to fight the urge to tickle the small auburn curls with her tongue or blow in his ear. She was afraid if she tried either one the great bull would miss a beat and they'd end up in the pluff mud.

"How deep does this mud go?"

"Oh, it can get pretty deep. A couple of times I sank down to my knees."

"That's like quicksand," she replied, not liking the sound of that at all. "What did you do?"

"Only thing you can do. Just rolled onto my back and wiggled till I got my legs out."

"But I'm on your back."

"Yep."

She squeezed him with her thighs and he chuckled. It was a deep, sonorous sound that rumbled in his chest.

"Seriously now," she said, trying not to sound as nervous as she felt. "What happens if you do fall down? What should I do?"

"Stand up, I guess. And wipe the mud off your cute li'l bottom." He walked a few paces, then added, "But don't worry about the leeches. I brought some salt."

Cara stiffened, her mind reeling with visions of Humphrey Bogart covered with bloodsucking leeches as he pulled the *African Queen* through the marshes.

"You sure are a skittish thing," Brett said. "Feel your muscles, all tense. I could snap your legs like twigs. You've got to learn to loosen up."

"Please don't drop me," she pleaded. "I'm terrified of leeches."

He laughed again, obviously enjoying himself. "I was only joking about the leeches. There aren't any in here. I wasn't joking about sinking low in this mud, though. But never at this particular hammock. It's one of the reasons I like it here so much. There now. Feel better?"

Her muscles loosened and she leaned against his back with a sigh. "That's mean, to tease a city girl like that."

"Nah, I'm just having a little fun. For being so book smart, Miss Rutledge, you sure are gullible. You ought to know better, growing up here."

She'd never in all her life been called gullible. She found it oddly beguiling. "Maybe I am," she replied. "Honestly? I'm a bit scared."

He was silent for a moment. "Don't be," he said, and she didn't detect any further teasing in the tone. "I'll take care of you."

I'll take care of you. Cara warmed to the words, believing them. Had any man ever said that to her? She couldn't remember one that had. She was proudly self-reliant, not the type that men felt the need to take care of. Instinctively she knew Brett was the kind of man who took care of women. Respected them. He felt at ease in his own skin and didn't appear the least threatened by a strong woman. Which, in turn, made her feel all the more womanly. She rested her chin against his shoulder, breathing close to his ear. The silence was powerfully erotic, and she was loath to see dry land just ahead. My, my, my, she thought to herself, her mind imitating Emmi's lusty wail. She could see why Brett Beauchamps stole the hearts of pubescent girls up and down the Carolina coast.

He set her down upon terra firma and stretched his muscles, rolling his shoulders.

"For someone so skinny, you sure pack a punch," he said.

"Thank you very much," she replied, setting down the bag. "But just in case you think I'm walking back to the boat, think again. I've taken a liking to this kind of transport."

"You'd best be on your best behavior then, Miss Rutledge."

She frowned at the implication.

"I'm teasing," he chided. "Follow me. I'll show you around."

They set off again, their feet treading uphill on a path of matted cord grass toward a forest of trees. The sun was just beginning to set, bathing the hammock in a lavender twilight that was as mysterious as it was exotic. They walked through a green border of scrubby shrubs. Farther in, there were places where the trees were so dense it was like an impenetrable wall and as dark as night. Brett led the way single file, following a zigzag path through the thick, shadowy forest.

Inside the canopy of the hammock it was a Garden of Eden, filled with live oaks, hollies, pines, cedars and palmettos. Here and there brilliant red and yellow flowers blossomed in pockets of dappled light. Then, quite unexpectedly, they stepped into a wide circle of space that opened to the sky like an amphitheater. Cara stepped into it cautiously at first, like a deer at a meadow, craning her neck to look up.

"This place is magical," she exclaimed. "It's no wonder you keep it a secret."

He smiled, pleased at her reaction. "Indians used to come here to camp. I've found bits of broken pottery and shell mounds. They used to call this a *hammocka,* that's where the name *hammock* came from. Animals like it, too. Deer, raccoons, birds."

"Deer? How do they get here?"

"They swim."

"I don't believe it. From the mainland?"

"Back and forth. I've seen them do it many times. Everything they need is here—shelter, dense nesting spots and plenty of food. Fresh water gathers between dunes after a rain and on the leaves. Just being so far away from the mainland provides protection."

"I can see why the Indians liked it here. It's idyllic. And so private, like a temple. It was probably some sort of ancient ritual grounds." She glanced at him and her lips twitched. "I imagine you've developed a few rituals of your own over the years, right on these hallowed grounds."

"A few. One of which is eating miraculous-tasting food. Let's set up camp. I seem to remember I invited you to a picnic."

As she unpacked the cooler, he gathered pieces of wood,

making a small campfire in the center of the amphitheater. Then he picked up the gloves and hammer, walked to a shrub, and from there pulled out of hiding an old wooden bushel basket. He held out his hand. "Here are some matches. See if you can't start a small fire. I'll be right back."

"Where are you going? You're not going to leave me here all alone?"

"You're perfectly safe. Leeches don't climb on shore."

"What about alligators?"

He laughed and shook his head. "Relax, Cara. No gators either, though you might keep your eyes open for snakes. Most likely they're harmless glass lizards, but stay away from anything with color. I'll only be a while. I'm going to get some oysters for dinner."

"With a hammer?"

"You really are green, aren't you? They grow in clusters in the mudflats. 'Cept they're stuck together as hard as cement. I've got to beat them off."

"I'm coming with you," she said, scampering to her feet. "I feel the same about snakes as I do leeches. Maybe even more so."

"Well, come on then."

The sun was setting lower, turning the sky dusky. A welcome breeze met them as they stepped out into the open air of the mudflats. Brett moved farther out onto the oyster bar. Onshore, Cara crossed her arms and watched him work, his legs planted wide and his back bent as he hammered at a large cluster of oysters. He worked without pause, taking the large ones and tossing the small oysters back. Before long he filled half a bushel. Then he straightened with his hands on his back and, stretching, he gazed out at the setting sun. Cara stood silently looking at the dark, solitary silhouette on the dusky horizon, thinking he appeared a part of the natural scenery. Brett bent once more to pick up the bushel and headed back.

"It's getting dark," he called out as he approached. "Let's get that fire going. We're going to have ourselves an oyster roast."

In no time they were sitting around a small fire, a mound of empty shells at their side, chilled beer in their hands, their stomachs sated. They were enveloped in a smoky cloud of burning cedar. Cara lay back on the blanket Brett had spread out for them and looked up at the stars. They were just beginning to shine, pale yet pulsing. It was a classic South Carolina sky. The crescent moon was a mere white razor slash in the velvety indigo. The fire cast shadows on their faces and illuminated their eyes.

She sighed, a sound that brought him down to stretch out on his side next to her, resting his chin in his palm.

"Is the lady satisfied?"

"The lady is so satisfied she's going to burst. I didn't know I could eat so many oysters in one sitting. The saltines, however, were the pièce de résistance. I give the meal five stars." Then, looking up at the sky, she amended, "Make that millions of stars." She smiled and turned her head toward him. His face was above hers, barely a foot away. "Aren't oysters only supposed to be eaten in months with an R in them?"

"They're good all year round, but they taste better in the fall and winter. They're spawning now so it's only legal to harvest for business in those months. I've never seen anyone harvest out here, so the pickin's good all year round."

"Is there anything you don't know?"

"I was born and raised on these waters. My father is a harbor pilot and his daddy before him. He's probably guided more ships into and out of Charleston Harbor than any man alive. He knows every twist and turn, where the sandbars are and the shallows. His blood flows with the tides. It's a good living, too. He taught me everything I know about the water. Naturally, he expected me to follow into the family business. That's what it is, really. A family business. Not just anyone can become a harbor pilot. You almost have to be born into it. It's a tough job, real dangerous, and the pilots have to trust each other. No one wants to make a mistake with one of those huge tankers. Some ships run seven hundred feet or more."

"Unbelievable."

"I'll tell you, though, I've seen my daddy maneuver one of those suckers under the bridge as easily as a johnboat."

"So why didn't you become a harbor pilot? You obviously love boats and the water. It would seem a natural fit."

"I thought about it, of course. My father wanted it and you can make a good living. But pilots are on call 24/7. That wasn't for me. Besides, I was more interested in what was *in* the water than what sailed on it."

"So you went to Clemson."

"That's right. I graduated with a degree in biology—aquaculture primarily. For a long time I did all kinds of research studies on this coastline. I worked for a state agency for a while, too. I can't say it wasn't interesting. I loved the fieldwork especially. But bureaucracy isn't for me. Much as I like being with people, deep down I'm a loner. Like you. I guess that's what attracted me to you, even way back when."

She smirked. "I never would've guessed from the way you acted. You certainly didn't seem like much of a loner back then. You were always surrounded by a retinue of pals and adoring girls."

"Yeah, well. I was young. A slave to my hormones."

"And now?"

"Well, the hormones are still active, if that's what you're asking. But tempered. More under control." He looked at the fire. "As for the rest? I don't know. I started the tour company about ten years ago. It's doing fine."

"That's an understatement from what I can tell."

He shrugged. "I expanded to two sites and I'm thinking about another. For the first time I'm keen about the prospect of a little more money coming in. On the other hand, I'm not keen about getting stuck doing paperwork behind a desk."

"I noticed your interesting accounting system."

"Yeah, well," he said, scratching behind his ear. "I guess I could use a little help in that department. I've never made decisions before based on money, and I don't want to start now. It's a trade-off, I guess. Most things are." He plucked a bit of grass. "Now that I'm older, I want different things."

His words resonated deep, leaving her feeling both drawn to him and wary. She sensed that she could get close to him.

"Turning forty does that to a person," she said.

"The ol' Tolstoy's bicycle theory."

She laughed lightly and looked at him. "What's that?"

"Tolstoy wrote *War and Peace* at forty. He learned how to ride a bicycle in his sixties. It's supposed to be inspiring."

"Well, it is to me." She stretched and looked up at the stars again. "I wonder what can I do at forty that I've never done before? I suppose I could learn how to pilot a boat. Or catch a fish. Maybe even harvest an oyster." She wriggled her brows. "I know a secret place."

"You're the first one I've ever brought here who I'm worried just might find it again." He moved to his stomach, resting on his forearms to look down at her face. "So, what about you?"

"What about me?"

"Tell me about your life. The missing twenty years I don't know about."

"What do you want to know?"

"Were you ever married?"

"Were you?"

"I asked you first."

"No, I never married. Never wanted to. As you said, I'm a loner." She looked straight into his blue eyes, gauging his reaction. The firelight seemed to dance in them. "Does that shock you?"

"No. Should it?"

She'd expected some comment of disapproval, and not hearing one, she felt herself loosen. He was chipping away at her hard-shelled obstacles as readily as he had the oysters.

"It's just that most men, and women too, are not sympathetic with the concept of a woman being single and content. They think all single women are frustrated or unhappy." When he didn't say anything more, she found she was suddenly intensely curious about him. "Your turn."

"Nope. I never married. I almost married once," he admitted. "We were very young, right out of college. She wanted to settle down and have children. I wanted to do fieldwork and travel all over the world."

"What happened?"

His face darkened and he tossed the blade of grass from his mouth. "It ended."

A scuttling noise sounded in the darkness, followed by the high, piercing scream of an animal. Cara sat up and stared into the black. All she heard was the crackling of the fire and the music of tree frogs and crickets.

"Are you sure no one else knows about your secret spot?"

"I've never seen any trace of them. Not alive anyway."

"Wha— Ah yes, the Indians. So, we're really, really alone here. If anything happens to us, no one will ever find out."

A wry smile crossed his face. "Nope. Not for a long, long time."

"Uh-huh. That sort of puts me at your mercy, doesn't it?"

His eyes sparked, warming to the game, but he had the good sense not to reply.

"Be honest. How many girls have you brought here? Ten? Twenty? A hundred?" She wondered if he'd tell the truth, wondered if she really wanted to hear it.

"I haven't brought any other girl here."

"Right. Your jaunts to hammocks are legendary in these parts."

"There are lots of hammocks."

"Oh."

She felt the air thicken between them and his eyes, glittering, glanced to her lips.

"I was trying to remember," she said, lying back and bringing her arms up to tuck under her head. "Aren't oysters supposed to be an aphrodisiac?"

He leaned closer, his face now mere inches from her own. When he spoke she could feel the warmth of his breath on her face. "Well, that depends."

"On what?"

"On whether you believe in old wives' tales or not. According to them, we should both be quite randy now."

"And if I don't believe?"

"As an old oyster man once said, you've either got it in you before you eat the oysters, or you don't."

She gazed at his face. His eyes were astonishingly blue in the firelight. "So, who is right?" she asked in a strained voice. "The old wife or the old man?"

He lowered his head to kiss her neck. "I think this calls for a little field research."

She closed her eyes as shivers of pleasure swept through her blood. "Plant or wildlife?"

He moved her head to the side with his chin as his lips traveled down her neck. "Definitely wildlife."

His breath came hot along her throat and Cara felt each hair rise as a million cells tingled. She moaned, stretching her arms out from under her head to wrap around his shoulders, lowering him toward her. He stretched out beside her, slipping one arm under her back to cradle her head. Drawing her closer, he lazily stroked the length of her body.

She wanted this man. Oh yes, she wanted him badly and pressed closer, almost writhing with desire. Brett's body was solid and strong. He leaned over her, arching, moving his thigh over hers. He moved slow and easy, making her own blood race madly through her veins. She tightened her grasp as his kisses traveled teasingly, maddeningly, up her neck.

When at last he brought his lips to hers, Cara opened her mouth, ready to devour him whole. But he would not be hurried. He was deliberate, tender, exploring. Then he deepened the kiss to a passionate possession. She shivered and tightened her grasp, matching his desire. Her hands moved down to reach under his cotton shirt, then slide up along the broad muscles of his back, relishing the silky smoothness against her fingertips.

Brett drew back and raised his head to look down at her. She gazed back, welcome pulsing in her eyes.

He lowered his head again. She raised her lips.

"Come on, wild thing," he said with a quick kiss on her nose. "We'd better pack up and go before the tide comes in or we'll be swimming for the boat."

He shifted his weight and moved away from her, climbing to a stand.

Cara lay on the ground, stunned, staring up at him with her arms flat at her side and her mouth open in a silent protest.

He reached out to her.

She took his hand and with a single tug he hoisted her to her feet. She stood dazed, dusting off her pants, feeling as though she'd missed some cue. A few feet away, Brett moved quickly, dousing the fire, gathering the supplies.

What had just happened, she wondered? Did she give the wrong signals? Was she too aggressive? Was that it? Did she say or do something to turn him off? With a furtive movement, she checked her breath.

Brett drew closer carrying the gear. "That about does it. Ready to go?"

"Uh, yeah. Sure." She stumbled forward feeling awkward. "Can I carry something?"

His eyes sparked with humor. "I seem to recall that I'm the one that's doing all the carrying on this trip."

"Oh, yeah." She didn't know whether to smile or act aloof. It had slipped her mind that she'd be riding piggyback to the boat. Once again she'd wrap her arms and legs around him. Just the thought of it sent her shivering with an odd mixture of anticipation and embarrassment.

He handed her the net and gloves, then hoisted the cooler. "Come on, then," he said and began walking toward the perimeter of trees that loomed like a black wall in the shadows.

She swallowed all the questions that were poised on the tip of her tongue and hurried to follow him back to the boat.

twelve

The eggs will incubate in the sandy nest for fifty-five to sixty days, unless disturbed by a predator. Turtle eggs are gourmet meals for raccoons and ghost crabs. Dogs, cats, feral hogs and vultures will also hunt the eggs. Egg poaching by humans is common in areas, as well.

Even in the flattering pink light of early morning it was sad to see what a shambles the beach house had fallen into. Cara walked the grounds, sipping her coffee and getting a sense of the space. The sunlight cruelly exposed the chipped paint and the sagging decks. Under the porch, years of accumulated garbage, things her mother might call treasures, made the beach house look alarmingly like a junkyard. As for the yard, it was worse. One of her fondest summer memories was rocking on the screened porch listening to the bees buzz and catching the scent of wildflowers intermingled with the jasmine, honeysuckle and roses in her mother's garden. Looking around, it was clear the overgrown, scrubby lot needed a firm, guiding hand.

Cara set down her coffee, pulled out a pad of paper and a pencil and began making her list. She liked lists. The longer the better. They organized her thoughts and gave her a sense of control over chaos. She wrote down the numbers first.

One, two, three and so on. Looking around at her surround-
ings, ignoring the sense of dread at the magnitude of the job,
she began to prioritize. Her hand moved fast, trying to keep
up with her thoughts. In a short while, she had nineteen to-
dos on her list.

Crossing the *T* with a flourish, she was once again a woman
with purpose. She tucked the list in her pocket and donned
her mother's old gardening gloves. They were thick and
serious—and made her feel like a professional. She'd start with
the trash first to clear space for other projects she had in mind.

The morning passed quickly. By the end of it she'd cleared
most of the junk from the decks. The areas under the porch
were broom clean and the trash organized into two piles. The
enormous one she'd designated for a special garbage pickup.
The smaller one was made up of assorted old art supplies,
rusted garden tools, wobbly beach chairs and other flimsy
items that she was hoping her mother would okay to add to
the trash bin. She was huffing and puffing under the weight
of an old, rusting air conditioner on its way to the dump pile
when she heard her mother's voice behind her.

"You're not throwing that out, are you?"

Cara walked the final steps and lowered the incredibly
heavy unit to the ground. Still bent with her hands on her
knees, catching her breath, she turned her head to see her
mother anxiously staring at the trash pile.

"Yes, Mama," she said with dry lips. "I'm throwing it out.
It's junk."

"Oh, it still has life in it. Don't you think someone could
use it? We could donate it to Goodwill?"

"No one wants that piece of junk. It will cost more to re-
pair than to buy a new one."

Lovie wrung her hands together and stared at the pile.
"You're not throwing all that away, are you?"

Cara felt disheartened. She'd worked like a dog all morning and she'd hoped for a little thanks, not a wall of opposition. This was touchy ground, however. Her mother could be very skittish about throwing anything out. She once even had a fit when old paint cans she suspected of having a bit of useful color left in them were tossed.

"It was a fire hazard out here. Not to mention an eyesore."

Her mother went over to the pile. While Cara held her breath, Lovie began picking through rusty screwdrivers, a broken chain saw, a worm-eaten bench and an old metal bucket missing a handle. She seized hold of an old tricycle.

"Oh, I think Cooper could use this."

Cara wanted to tell her that Cooper was already too big for it and probably had a brand-new tricycle at home, but rather than start off with an argument, she obligingly rolled the wobbly, rusty trike out from the pile back under the porch. When her mother started pulling out the rotting wicker chair, however, she held firm.

"It's got to go, Mama. I'll get a new one, I promise. No, no, no, please don't tell me it has lots of life in it. Half its back is missing. Release it, Mama! Let it go!"

Lovie frowned, but left the chair in the junk pile. She stood with her hands clasped, looking at the pile with a forlorn expression.

Cara came near to put her arm around Lovie's small, slumped shoulders. "Wait till you see what I'm going to do. What *we* are going to do. Since we have the whole summer, what could be better than bringing the house back to its original shape? Wouldn't you like that? Remember how beautiful it used to be out here on a summer night? The butterflies flocked here." She extended her hand toward the yard, seeing in her mind's eye the wildflowers that used to cover the dunes. "My plan is to clear away all that ugly old brush, trim the bushes, dig up old roots, then maybe you can plant some new rosebushes. Remember your roses?"

Lovie's face softened and a small smile played at her lips. "I just couldn't keep up anymore. I tried to water…"

"I know, I know. It got to be too much," Cara said, quickly putting to rest any regrets. "I'm not sure I can do it all on my own. But what I can't do, I'll hire someone to do."

"But Cara, you're talking about a very big job." She paused to look at her askance. "You don't know what you're doing in the garden, do you? You never had much patience for it as a child. You used to moan whenever I asked you to pull a weed."

Cara laughed. "I figured it would be like with the turtles. You could teach me. Did you ever hear about Tolstoy's bicycle? It's an amazing thing. He learned to ride one at your age. Seems I could learn to plant a garden."

Lovie's eyes lit up. "Yes, you could do that. Are you really interested?"

"I thought I'd give it my best shot."

"I have a wonderful library of garden books you could read."

"I hope you have some with lots of those lovely photographs so I can identify what's what. When I read the descriptions they all start to sound the same to me. But if I see it, it's in my mind for life."

"I'll help you, don't worry."

Cara's excitement rose at seeing her mother's dismay spark into enthusiasm. "I thought I'd rebuild the porch, too. It's rotting in places and I have nightmares of you or Toy falling through. And the house definitely needs a fresh coat of paint. Do you think you could find the original shade of yellow?"

Lovie nodded and her gaze moved to the trash bin where several paint cans lay. "There should be a can in there with the paint number scribbled on it. You see? That's why I keep things. You never know when you'll need it."

Cara rolled her eyes. "These days we can find a match from a paint chip. And I was thinking of Charleston green for the shutters. Unless you want hurricane shutters?"

"All these plans, Cara. It will be expensive. Palmer has me on a very tight budget."

Cara's blood began to simmer at the thought of her brother being so stingy with their mother's own money. But she didn't want to ruin the mood with a discussion of Palmer. "Forget about the money," she told her. "I've already budgeted to cover it."

"But how? You don't have a job. Cara, I couldn't take your money. Not now."

"You're not taking anything. I'm giving it. Please, Mama, let me do this for you. It will give me such pleasure."

Lovie lifted her chin and looked out over the tumbleweed landscape. Her gaze moved on to take in the gentle lines of her cottage, the large trash pile on the driveway, and finally rested on her daughter's face. Cara's color was rosier, much better than the pallor she'd arrived with and her mahogany-colored eyes were bright from the exercise. And to think, Cara wanted to do something for *her*.

"I don't know why I was hanging on to all that junk anyway," she said. "There are a lot more important things to keep close." Her eyes took on a faraway look. "And it would be nice to see this place all spruced up once more before I…" She stopped herself and forced a smile to her face. "Well, it'd be real nice."

Cara had to turn her head lest her mother see the flash of tears. "Come over here, Mama. There's something you should see." She led the way past the trash pile to the front of the house, where a row of ancient, gangly oleanders dominated the dune. She grabbed hold of one big branch and pulled it back away from the base of the high porch.

"In the process of yanking out weeds with roots that went straight to China and getting spooked by a black snake that shot out from the grass, I found this," she said, panting to pull the branch back farther. She waved her mother over with a quick movement. "Come take a look."

Lovie rounded the beastly bush to peek in. There, along the broken slats of lattice, was a thin, rangy climbing rosebush struggling toward the sun. She laughed, high and with heart. "Why, I wouldn't have believed it if I didn't see it with my own eyes. A lone straggler. However did you find it?"

"It takes one to know one." She waited until her mother cleared the area, then gently released the branches. They sprang back in a furious rustling. "I remembered that you had roses growing here, before these oleanders got so big. I just started searching. I couldn't believe my luck to find one still alive. There's hardly any air or light back there. That's what reminded me about the pergola. You used to have roses climbing all along one that covered the whole length of the porch." She put her hand over her brows and peered at the house, remembering it as it once was. "I really loved that pergola. Whatever happened to it?"

"Hurricane Hugo made quick work of that. And most of the front porch, as you can see. I fixed up the screened porches and the roof with the insurance money. Sadly, we didn't have the place well insured. Your father had no interest in this cottage and begrudged every penny I squeezed out for it. I could only afford to replace the front stairs."

"You were lucky Hugo didn't take the whole house."

Lovie nodded in agreement. "It was the tornadoes that did most of the damage. Flo's and my house narrowly escaped. But if you look down the block, most of the others are gone.

The flooding was bad, though. Everything got a good soaking. A big boat landed right smack in Bill Wilson's front door." She chuckled, remembering the sight that was anything but funny at the time. "Still, you're quite right. We were lucky. I like to think it was divine intervention. Sometimes a place means a lot more to a person than just somewhere to live. It's like—well, it's like a touchstone. Stratton would never have let me rebuild the beach house had I lost it. I don't know what I'd have done if I didn't have this place to come to over the years." She looked out toward the sea. "I just don't know."

"That's why we have to fix it up. It's not only important to you, Mama. This place matters to me, too. And to Toy. And Palmer, even if he won't admit it. And it will come to mean a lot to Linnea and Cooper. I'm sure of it."

"Do you think so?" she asked, sounding genuinely surprised at hearing this from Cara. Then, with a different tone, one that resonated with wonder and a deep satisfaction, she said again, "Do you really think so?"

"I do."

"You can't know how much it means to me to hear you say that." She looked up at the beach house, her eyes sparkling, and said brightly, "So, what should we do first?"

The next morning, while Toy was sitting at the sewing machine trying to thread a bobbin, the phone rang. Cara and Lovie were out on turtle business so she hurried, checking the hall clock en route. It was nine o'clock, late for a call about turtle tracks.

"Hello?"

There was no reply.

"Hello?"

"Nice to hear your voice."

Her breath hitched. "Darryl, I told you not to call me here."

"What are you getting all upset about? Don't you want me to check up on you? See how you're doing? You're the one always telling me that we're having this baby."

"You don't care about this baby. You don't even care about me."

"Aw Toy, don't go sayin' that. You know you're the one I love. Haven't I always told you that?"

"Is that what you told that woman?"

"What did you expect? You left without saying a word to me, not even giving me a chance to talk to you. We coulda worked things out. Then you're gone for four months and I don't even have a clue where you are. I thought I'd never see you again. You broke my heart."

"So I suppose to get back at me you go out with other girls."

"You were gone! And a man's got certain needs. I wouldn't need to see no other woman if you were here with me." When she didn't reply, he said, "I miss you."

Toy closed her eyes tightly.

"It doesn't have to be this way. Let me come see you."

"No, you can't."

"Come on, honey. You're the one I want. You know that."

"And the baby?"

"Okay, okay, I'm willing to talk about the baby, too. Anything so we stay together."

"Do you mean that?"

"Sure I do. Why don't I drive over to where you are so's we can talk about it some. Where are you? What's the address?"

"I can't have you coming here, Darryl. Miss… They won't like that."

"Who the hell cares what they like? You won't be staying there no more anyway."

"I might. I haven't decided that yet."

"Well *I've* decided." His voice rose. She heard him inhale

deeply, then exhale. She could imagine his slender fingers holding on to the cigarette and the long plume of smoke. "Look, you're letting these people who don't matter tell you what to do. You need to be listening to *me*. We belong together. Who are these people you're so scared of that you don't want me coming over? Are they family or what?"

"No. They're just folks I'm working for."

"What kind of work?"

"You know, like a companion. I do a little housecleaning and cooking. I used to drive the old lady around, but her daughter is here now and she does most of that so I can rest more."

"I'll just bet. Do they pay you good?"

"Yeah," she hedged, not wanting him to know how much she was making. "Pretty good. But I don't have to pay for nothing so I can save for when the baby comes. They don't come free you know. And there are all these baby things I have to buy, like a crib and diapers and blankets. It'd be nice if you helped me a little. I mean, this is *your* baby."

"So, you don't want to see me but you want my money, huh? What a cunt."

"*What* did you call me?"

"If you want me to help pay for the kid, then you gotta come home. Plain and simple."

She leaned against the wall and looked at the ceiling.

"So what's it gonna be?" he demanded.

She closed her eyes tight. "I'm thinking."

"Why don't you think while I come pick you up?"

"No! I don't want you to come here!"

"Why can't I come there? Are you ashamed of me or somethin'? Is there some other guy?" There was a pause and she could almost hear his anger zoom. "That's it, isn't it? You're with another guy."

"Oh sure, like I've got all these guys after me. Darryl, I'm pregnant!"

"Yeah, well, some guys like pregnant girls."

"You're being dis*gus*ting."

He skipped a beat. "I'm being *what?*"

That tone always signaled trouble. Toy immediately tried to douse the flame. "Never mind."

"No, I want to know. You think I'm disgusting, now. Is that it?" His voice was rising.

"I didn't mean you."

"You better not be meaning me."

"I don't."

There was a long pause during which Toy felt the tears begin to flow down her cheeks. She could feel the pressure from him closing in around her; she couldn't breathe.

"Toy, you know I go crazy when you try to put some wedge between us."

"I'm not." She sniffed.

"Oh, no? What do you call saying we can't be together? Honey, can't you see? Those people don't care about you like I do. They only care about keeping cheap help. We don't need them or their stinking money. I've always taken care of you."

Toy heard the sound of footfalls on the outside porch steps. She felt panic well up, afraid to be caught. "Darryl, someone's coming. I gotta go."

"Wait! We're not finished."

"I gotta go! I'm not supposed to be talking to you."

"Shit. That's it. No one tells you that you can't talk to me. I'm coming out there and—"

"No, Darryl! I'll call you later. I promise. 'Bye." She hung up the phone just as the door swung open.

Cara walked in first, carrying a box of Krispy Kreme doughnuts and a gallon of milk. Behind her, Lovie was scraping the sand from her sandals. They both were wearing matching green Turtle Team T-shirts and khaki shorts.

"Hi," Cara called out when she spied Toy. She raised the box in her hands. "I've been naughty but I saw these at the gas station and I couldn't resist. Mmm-mmm. I just love these and they're fresh. Come and get 'em." She held the door open for her mother, then, closing it, looked at Toy again, searching. "What's the matter? Are you feeling all right?"

If Toy had learned anything from Miss Lovie over the past few months, it was to put a bright face on when times were at their worst. And Toy so wanted to be like Miss Lovie. She pushed all thoughts and worries of Darryl into a far corner of her mind, smiled and walked into the living room. "Oh, I'm fine. Just fine."

It had been three days since her date with Brett at the hammock and he had yet to call. Cara had been working in the yard like a whirling dervish, obsessed with keeping occupied. He'd made her feel like some oversexed Amazon and she was furious that she even cared what he thought. She grabbed the rusty pickax that she'd salvaged from the trash pile when her mother wasn't looking and began taking out her frustration on the roots.

It'd been a long day under a grueling sun. Her muscles trembled and rivers of sweat cascaded down her spine. She was finishing her battle with the oleanders when she heard the crunching of gravel on the driveway. Cara poked her head out from the jungle of branches to see who it could be.

The door of a white pickup opened and she spied a green baseball cap with Coastal Eco-Tours emblazoned across the top. The visor was worn low over his eyes, but there was no mistaking the broad shoulders that emerged from the cab. Oh, great, she groaned and slowly straightened, her back aching each millimeter of the way. He couldn't have waited another hour. By then she'd have had a nice shower and been all sweet smelling instead of the muddy, sweaty wreck she was now. She brushed a strand of hair from her face, succeeding only in sprinkling more dirt across it.

He spotted her, then approached slowly, looking a little sheepish with his hands tucked into his back pocket. "Hey there," he called out.

"Hello," she replied as regally as she could with mud streaked down her face.

He came to a halt on the opposite side of the oleander, grabbing hold of a branch and studying it as though it held the secrets of the universe. "I don't suppose you'd believe me if I told you the engine gave out on the tour boat? I had to work day and all night to get it fixed for today's tour." He looked up then, eyes pleading.

"I believe you." She began to pick pine needles and sand spurs from her garden gloves with staccato movements.

"And you're thinking I could have called anyway."

"Brett, you don't have a clue what I'm thinking."

His smile slipped and he looked at her as though trying to determine if there was even a shred of humor in that statement. "You're right. No excuses. I'm sorry."

It was the right answer. She lost her attitude and nodded with a half smile. "Apology accepted."

"Are you hungry? I thought you'd let me take you out to dinner."

"I don't think I have the energy for another trip to a hammock tonight," she said. "Not that it wasn't an…original first date." Her eyes indicated the piles of branches littering the lawn. "But I'm utterly and thoroughly exhausted."

"A pot of boiled crabs at my place was more what I had in mind."

It was her turn to smile. "In that case, I accept. But let me finish this first. It's war and I've almost got this sucker beaten into submission." She grabbed hold of the root and began tugging as hard as she could, muttering curses between pants. She didn't get very far. There just wasn't much juice left in her muscles.

"Here, let me help," he said stepping forward to maneuver the limb from her hands. Then, gently nudging her aside, he grabbed hold at the base of the trunk. "Rule number two," he said as he planted his feet firmly in place. "A Lowcountry man never stands by and watches a lady do manual labor."

Cara took a few steps back and watched as he took a deep breath. Then, with a low growl, he ripped out the shrub by the roots in a single tug and tossed it like a cotton ball onto the huge pile of debris. She slumped in awe.

"I'm obviously not cut out for this."

"You go on and get cleaned up while I drag all this to the end of the drive," he told her, rolling up his sleeves.

"You're all clean. You don't have to do that. I can manage."

"Yes, I do. A little groveling is in order, don't you think?"

She tried to look disapproving but couldn't stop the indulgent smile that spread across her face. "Since you put it that way, there's twine under the porch. And clippers, if you get inspired."

He was already dragging a large, fallen oak branch that she couldn't even budge to the curb. She watched for a moment, amused. He seemed to know what he was doing. She let him be, shuffling up the stairs to the house, each small movement an effort. Inside, the scent of garlic and tomato sauce filled the air. Her stomach growled and she realized how ravenous the hard work had made her. Toy was at the stove, stirring.

"Smells good," she called out.

"Thanks," Toy replied in a monotone, not turning from her sauce.

Cara passed by, pursing her lips in worry. Toy had returned to her aloof self the past few days. She did her work well and answered whenever spoken to, but she'd retreated back into her shell. At night she kept to her room, and they could hear the Singer humming as she sewed maternity clothes. Unfortunately, she wasn't a skilled seamstress. The dress she was wearing now was a hideous lime-green pattern that didn't match at the puckered seams.

"I'm going out for dinner tonight, so go on and eat without me."

"Oh, okay," Toy replied sullenly.

"Oh?" Lovie looked up from the couch, where she was resting with a book. "Going out with whom?"

"Oh, you don't know him. Just some guy I met the other day."

"Really?" She closed her book and sat up from the pillows. "A fella?"

Cara could see that her mother's matchmaking antenna was up and twirling. "I'm grossly filthy. I'll talk to you after I shower." With that, she ducked down the hall, making good her escape from the deluge of questions poised on her mother's lips.

The hot water sluiced down, washing away what felt like acres of dirt from her body. As exhausted as she felt, she was also bubbling with excitement at the prospect of another evening with Brett. With other men she'd had quick flings with in the past, she'd often hoped that they wouldn't call her again. And if they did, she usually found some way to dump them, nicely of course, but firmly. She was definitely glad Brett came back. Oh yes, she thought, turning off the faucets. Most definitely.

She dressed carefully, choosing white jeans and a sexy black silk top. She let her damp hair hang loose to her shoulders. Looking in the mirror she was surprised by how much sun she'd gotten, even under her hat and bent over like a crone. Her skin positively glowed.

"I'm going!" she called out, grabbing her purse from the hall table.

The house was deserted. Neither her mother nor Toy were anywhere in sight, despite the two place settings neatly laid out at the table, complete with napkins and flowers. Through the open window she heard a burst of laughter coming from the yard. Filled with dread, she hurried out the door.

The air was slightly steamy and insects sang in the brush. All the twigs and branches it had taken her a day to accumulate were neatly bound with twine into neat bundles and lying at the curb. Beside them she saw Brett smiling and chatting with Lovie, laughing in the manner of old friends. She hurried down the porch steps and across the lawn to their circle.

"I see you've met," she said to her mother.

"Oh, my heavens, yes. You didn't tell me that you were going out to dinner with Brett Beauchamps! Why, I've known him for years." She beamed up at him, her gaze dripping with charm. "How many years would you say?"

Brett was wrapped around her finger. "I don't know, Miss Lovie. Must be ten—fifteen years at least."

Cara was stunned. "But how do you know each other?"

"The island is really a small town," Lovie replied. "Brett used to come help Florence fix up her house every once in a while. He's really very good with his hands."

"Really?" Cara cast him a loaded glance. He arched a brow but managed to keep a straight face.

"I'm going in to check my sauce," Toy said, moving off.

Cara wished her mother would go along, too, but it was

clear from the gleam in her pale blue eyes that Lovie was enjoying her gentleman caller.

"Oh, yes," Lovie continued, eager to sing his praises. "Do
you see that lovely porch? He built that for her. And her gazebo, too. Have you seen Florence lately, Brett?" she asked,
directing the question to him. "Why, I'm certain she'd just
love to see you again. You're one of her favorite people."

"No, ma'am, I haven't seen Miss Prescott in a long time. I'll
go over and say hello. How is old Mrs. Prescott?"

"Miranda? She's doing a bit poorly now. Seeing you will
cheer her up considerably. She still talks about you. You've
stolen her heart, I'm afraid."

"There's nothing seriously wrong with her, I hope."

"Son, at ninety, everything is serious. But we hope it's just
a touch of the flu and she'll be feeling better soon. She lives
for the turtles, you know. Once the hatchlings start coming,
Flo won't be able to keep her mother from the beach."

Cara smiled, thinking of the parallels.

"Who looks after you these days?" Lovie wanted to know.
"I can't believe you haven't been snatched up yet. A good-
looking fellow like you."

A faint blush crept up his neck and feeling for him, Cara
said in a warning tone, "Mother..."

Lovie was undaunted. "Are you still living on Hamlin
Creek?"

"Yes, ma'am, I am. I was lucky to buy that place years back.
I doubt I could afford it today."

"Don't I know it. Who would have ever thought we'd be
fetching these prices? It was a wise investment. I hear tell your
business is doing real well, too. Cara gave a glowing report,
though she neglected to tell me it was *your* boat." She looked
over to smile at Cara, whose turn it was to blush. "I'm proud

of you, son. Your daddy must be, too. You're piloting boats, just like him."

"Well, his boats are a tad bigger, but I thank you all the same."

Cara looked across the yard at Florence Prescott's gazebo while the banter between Brett and Lovie faded. The porch was well designed and constructed, not at all a flimsy add-on. It looked built to withstand the harsh weather of a barrier island. And it had style. She made a quick decision, which was typical of her, and when their conversation concluded, she jumped in.

"Say, Brett, would you be interested in another job? A small one?"

His expression ranged between a grimace and curiosity. "I haven't really had the time for extra jobs in quite a while." Then considering a moment he added, "But for Miss Lovie, I'll do what I can. What's this small job you have in mind?"

"Well, it's not so small, actually. A porch for the front of a house." She looked at her mother and smiled. "And a pergola."

Lovie's eyes widened with surprise.

Her reaction did not go unnoticed by Brett. He cast a questioning glance Cara's way, then turned and walked to the front of the house at a slow gait, studying the building as he passed. The two women followed him. Standing side by side on the dune, they watched as he paced the width of the porch, carefully inspected under the house, then paced out the opposite side before returning to the dune. His face revealed nothing as he stood, arms crossed, his chin cupped in his palm, and perused the house in silence. When at last he walked back to them, his gaze was cautious yet positive.

"It could be done easily enough," he said.

"How wonderful," Lovie exclaimed.

"Do you want something like you used to have, before Hugo?"

"I can't believe you can recall that old structure," Cara replied. "That was years ago."

"Of course I remember it. Even before I moved to the island I came over in the summers to work in construction. I used to drive by your place and I always admired the roses blooming along the pergola. They were a real showstopper, Miss Lovie. I was sad to see it go."

"I was just telling her the same thing," Cara added.

"I think I know what you want," Brett concluded. "Something traditional but substantial. If you have any old photographs that would be helpful. Problem is, I'd have to do it in my free time, so it won't be quick."

"Could you complete it this summer?" Lovie asked.

He rubbed his jaw. "Well now, maybe by the end of it. Summer is my busiest time."

"It's got to be early this summer," Cara exclaimed urgently. "The sooner the better. Hire someone to help you. Order anything you need. Money isn't a problem."

His brows furrowed and Cara thought she saw a flash of anger in his eyes.

"Maybe not, but my time is."

"I'm sorry, I didn't mean to pressure you, Brett. It's just, well—" she darted a worried glance at her mother "—time is of the essence."

There was a long silence as Brett and Cara stared at each other. The fire in his eyes banked as understanding dawned. He turned to look at Lovie.

"If I did it immediately, before the season gets out of control, I could try to squeeze it in. But it would be a push and you'd have to hire someone to help, probably two if we want to get it up fast. I'll draw up the design and oversee it. I know a few people I can ask. They're good. And reasonable."

"I'm sure they are, if you recommend them," Lovie replied, eager to appease him.

Cara was more direct. "You'll do it?"

He offered a wry smile and Cara instantly knew she'd won. But just as quickly, she was on the receiving end of an exchange that told her there would be a price to pay.

"I'll do it, provided you're one of the crew."

Lovie released a short, high laugh of surprise.

"Me? But I don't know anything about wielding a hammer and nail. I'll just be in your way."

"Who said anything about a hammer and nail?"

She raised her brows, thinking maybe her luck had changed.

"I had a paintbrush in mind."

thirteen

The temperature of the sand during incubation plays a role in determining the sex of the hatchlings. Cool sand produces males, while hotter sand brings females.

"Home sweet home," Brett declared, leading the way up the crumbling cement walkway. "Come on in and I'll cook you up some dinner."

Cara just stared at the small 1960s stucco bungalow. "It's pink!" she exclaimed.

"I call it the Pink Flamingo." He pointed to a metal pink flamingo roosting in the ground near the front entrance. Catching her expression he chided, "Now, before you look at me like that, it's important to remember that you're back on the island. It might be a very different thing if I had a pink house up north. But here it's very Bermuda."

"I know that. It's just that I have a hard time picturing *you* in a pink house—anywhere." She looked at the compact, boxy structure with the gray sloping roof. Dominating the front lawn, shielding the little house from the busy street, was an ancient live oak tree that stretched its perfect-for-climbing branches across the front lawn and graced the house with shade. Her heart pinged, recalling her own favorite tree growing up.

"It's a very sweet house," she said.

"Sweet? Now that really hurts." He unlocked the door. "Come on in before you say anything else."

The interior was pure bachelor. The walls were dingy gray, the light fixtures strictly of the hardware store variety and what little furniture there was represented years of collecting whatever could be obtained free or on the cheap. A bicycle was parked by the front door and a wet suit and kayak lined the hallway. And his business office was little more than a bunch of mail, papers, books and manila folders cluttering the dining room table. Her eyes skimmed over the mayhem quickly, drawn instead to the glorious view outside the wall of sliding glass. The water of the Intracoastal was racing with the current of the changing tide. It was breathtaking and she instantly fell in love with the place.

She was standing at the glass patio doors looking out when he came up behind her. His strong arms encircled her, dwarfing her, and his big hands rested against her abdomen pressing her to him. She felt an electric jolt when he touched her and closed her eyes with a sigh. Was he making his move at last?

"Hungry?" he asked.

She told herself she wasn't going to fall into that ridiculous banter about how she was hungry for his kisses. It was too clichéd, too utterly banal.

"I'm starving," she replied, suddenly coy.

"I'm going to fix us some dinner," he said, drawing his arms away.

She watched him walk away, stunned. "You do that," she said, half smiling, half pouting. She told herself he was just throwing her off her mark. Other men would have slipped their hands up her blouse and made love to her on the spot. Dinner would have been an afterthought.

She turned her head in time to see Brett open the glass sliding door and walk off across the yard and down to the end of his dock. Curious, she moved closer to the door, resting her hands upon the cool glass. The glass was smeared with water spots and grime, but she could still see well enough that Brett was bent over the dock. A moment later, he was pulling up a crab pot. The black iron cage emerged dripping with water and filled with what she could only guess were plenty of snapping crabs. Brett appeared to know exactly what to do with them.

Who was this guy, she wondered? Most of the men she'd dated went to the refrigerator or picked up the telephone to get dinner. She leaned against the door and laughed. Brett was nothing remotely like any other man she'd dated.

Thank God.

Together they cooked the crabs in a big stainless-steel pot on a gas burner out on the back porch. Cara melted some butter in the microwave while Brett shucked corn. The setting sun cast a pink pall on the water and deepened Cara's hair to a chocolate brown that matched her eyes. She'd pinned it high up on her head; eating crab was a two-handed affair that required lots of dipping in butter and lots of napkins.

She and Brett sat in the dwindling sunlight while the candles flickered in the hurricane lamps. As they ate their sweet crabmeat and drank beer from cans, it seemed so easy to fall into a rhythm of conversation. They talked about their jobs, the latest turtle nest, plans for the porch and anything else that came to mind. As the night wore on, she found she liked Brett more and more. She liked the way his eyes focused on her when she talked and the way she could laugh readily, like with an old friend. It was comfortable—almost too. And as she watched the way his face moved when he laughed and the way his blue eyes intensified as he told a story, she wondered whether he felt the same about her or if this was merely the way Brett Beauchamps was with everyone.

After they finished clearing the empty shells and husks and returned to the table with cold beers, Cara told Brett about Darryl and Toy. He reacted exactly as she'd thought he might. His mouth set in a grim line and his large hand crinkled the metal of his beer can.

"Just let him show his hairy ass around your place and he'll be one sorry little bastard. In fact, I hope he *does* show up."

"What is it about men that they just can't wait to beat their chests and have a good fight?"

"I'm not joking around, Cara. I hate guys like that. Hitting a woman makes them feel like a man. I like nothing better than giving his type a chance to pick on someone his own size."

"I know and I agree. I just hope we don't have this little gladiator exhibition at Primrose Cottage." She reached up to stroke his arm while a flicker of worry crossed her face. "You never know about a lowlife like that. He might carry some kind of weapon. A knife or a gun."

"I can handle it."

She considered this.

"What?" he asked on the defensive. "You're looking at me funny. You don't think I can?"

"Just the opposite. When you say you can handle it, I believe you. I've never felt that way about a man before."

"Felt what way?"

"Safe," she replied, surprised she'd admitted something so personal. "My last boyfriend—" She paused and put her hand to her cheek. "God, isn't that a horrible word for a woman my age to use? *Boyfriend?* It makes me feel like I'm going steady."

He frowned. "What about him?"

His eyes were intense and she wondered with a smug pleasure whether he might be a tad jealous. Interesting.

"Well," she drawled, trying to decide where to begin and how much she wanted to divulge. Talking about old beaus with new beaus could be a tricky business, so she opted for the less is more approach.

"Richard and I worked for the same advertising firm. We could talk about anything work related and I thought we made a pretty good team. We had good times together, too. You know how it is when you find someone who shares your interests. But when it came to personal things, like my relationship with my mother or my well-being, I didn't tell him anything. I didn't consciously make the decision not to, I just never did. I'm very closemouthed about my personal life as a rule. Looking back, however, I realize it was instinct. I never really knew for certain if he'd use that information against me somehow. As it turned out, I was right."

"What happened?"

"He got promoted and I got fired. Not that I blame him for that, but he knew about it and didn't warn me."

"You got fired? When?"

"Last month. Before I came here."

"That's all you're going to tell me?"

"What more can I say? It happens. What difference could it make to you?"

"A big difference. Damn, the last thing I'm going to do is take your money when you don't have a job. Why didn't you tell me?"

"You really are too sweet. Is that another of your rules? A

Lowcountry man never takes money from a lady down on her luck?"

"If it wasn't before it is now."

"Not to worry," she replied, liking him even more. "This lady is fine in that department. I can afford a porch. Maybe not a house, but a porch, yes."

"No."

"Brett, please, don't argue," she said, stopping what she could see was a torrent of words about to spill from his open mouth. "This is something I need to do. It's hard to explain, but I need to do something to help Mama, to make her feel better in any way I can. There have been so many years of meaningless exchanges between us. I know this will make a difference to her and I want it to come from me. Whatever the cost financially, I don't care. It's the emotional cost if I *don't* do it that's prohibitive."

Brett considered this. "It won't be much."

"Oh, no you don't. No cutting any corners or pricing your time cheap. I respect hard work and value a job well-done. Though I appreciate the thought."

"You forget. I care about Miss Lovie, too." He paused then asked, "She's very ill, isn't she?"

She dreaded going into this discussion tonight yet knew it couldn't be avoided. She nodded. "She has cancer."

He lowered his head.

Cara reached out to place her hand over his. "Brett, I really want to thank you for taking the job. I realize I came on strong earlier. Maybe I was a little pushy. I'm sorry, I didn't mean to be. It's just that I felt this sudden panic. The doctor thinks she may only have this summer and I wanted to do this for her before—" She sighed. "Before it was too late."

"I thought it was something like that. She looks kind of frail."

"I know. It's hard to see her this way. It kills me when she won't eat or when she has to pause for breath. And she's beginning to cough now, too. Did you notice that? It scares me. I feel so helpless just standing by. When I see a problem I like to step in and fix it. But I can't fix this."

"No, you can't. Nobody can. It's nature." He turned his palm over to wrap his fingers around her wrist. "I hope you don't mind my speaking honestly. We all look at death as an aberrance of nature. Something that has to be fixed. Every day I see nature at work and not all of it is pretty. Life is just plain dangerous and sometimes cruel. But it's beautiful, too. We have to remember that at times like this. It's hard to watch Miss Lovie pass on because we love her. But if it's her turn, our challenge is to help her through it, not to fight it. That just makes it harder for her."

"But sixty-nine is so young. It's not fair."

"Who said life was fair? When a child dies, is that fair? Are wars or disease fair? Or even when a ghost crab grabs hold of a hatchling just after it pops out of the nest. Is that fair?"

"Oh, please," she said sharply, tugging her hand away in annoyance. "I don't want to hear platitudes. This isn't some abstract intellectual discussion."

He looked slightly wounded.

"Look," she tried to explain. "When I read in the papers about a tragedy in which someone dies I feel saddened and say, 'Oh, that's too bad.' Even when someone I vaguely know dies, I manage to go on about my business. But this is about *my* mother. I feel it intensely and it makes me so angry to feel so helpless." She brought her hands to her face. "I don't want my mother to die."

Brett came around the table to sit by her side and put his arms around her. She felt very small and leaned into him, relishing the comfort she found there.

"I'm so scared. There's so little I can do."

"You're doing a lot. You've come home, which I'm sure means a lot to her. And now you're rebuilding the beach house, which means so much to you both. It doesn't take brains to see the symbolism in that."

"It feels like everything is spinning out of control."

"Maybe it's spinning into focus."

She sniffed against his chest. "Maybe. I don't know. I'm too much in the thick of it to see clearly. I have to get through to the other side first. It scares me that it's all just beginning. I feel all alone."

"But you're not. I'll be here."

He didn't say anything more, only tightened his arms around her. When he lowered his head to hers there was no nervousness or wondering whether she'd given the wrong cues. The current between them felt as natural and powerful as the flow of the mighty waterway yards away.

The following morning when Cara and Lovie returned home from their duties on the beach, the house seemed un-usually quiet. No music blaring from the CD while Toy went through her morning chores, no humming in the kitchen. Cara saw Lovie standing rigid in the middle of the room with her head cocked.

"Listen," she whispered to Cara, waving her closer. "Do you hear someone crying?"

Cara stood still and listened to the sniffling and muffled curses coming from Toy's room. Lately, Toy had been keeping herself separate, going to her bedroom and closing the door. Meeting her mother's eyes, Cara said sotto voce, "She's been moody lately. It's probably her pregnancy."

"Moody is one thing but crying is something else entirely." With a determined tred, Lovie led the way to Toy's bedroom.

The door was ajar and, peeking in, they found her sitting hunched over a great knot of fabric that was obviously stuck in the angrily buzzing sewing machine. Toy was wearing a short, fuzzy blue robe that revealed thin, tanned legs and bare toes painted a bright violet. She looked up as they entered, her face distraught.

"It's ruined," Toy wailed, giving a frustrated yank at the fabric. "I tried and I tried and I just can't get this damn thing to work out right. I *hate* sewing."

"Honey," Lovie said, placing a calming hand on Toy's shoulder. "Why didn't you ask me to help?"

"I didn't want to trouble you and I thought I could do it on my own. It didn't look so hard when I picked out the pattern. It's this fabric. It's so slippery!" She angrily tossed the trailing piece of fabric off her lap.

"Bless your heart. You probably didn't know that's a very difficult fabric to sew," Lovie said.

"Especially for me. I'm so stupid."

"No, you are not," Cara said, jumping into the fray.

"Then how come I can't do it? Lots of people can sew."

"It's not your fault that you're having a hard time with this project," Lovie said, looking at the pattern. "Anyone would. It's also a difficult pattern. If you don't mind my asking, have you ever had sewing lessons?"

"Just the basics in seventh grade. We made a pillow or something like that. I thought I could figure it out. But all these steps… It's so hard."

"Sewing is one of my most favorite things in the world to do. It's not the least bit hard. But you can't build a house until you learn how to hammer a nail." Her gaze glided over to Cara, a sparkle in her eyes. "Isn't that right, Cara?"

Cara let it slide. "Mama's right," she said to Toy. "If anyone can teach you, she can."

Toy remained sullen and silent.

"Nothing worth doing is ever easy," Lovie continued. "I'd be pleased to teach you. And I don't think we could do any more harm to that fabric. Don't look so glum. What do you say to the idea of going to town to pick out an easier pattern? We'll find a nice, crisp cotton fabric. Something that won't be slippery and get caught in the machine."

"I'll take her for you," Cara said. "The trip to town might be a bit much for you."

"I don't need to be mollycoddled. I *want* to go to town."

Cara could see in her mother's eyes her dismay at facing the reality that she wasn't up to shopping excursions any longer.

"Oh, very well. But in the meantime," Lovie said, turning to Toy, "a little bird told me that you have a birthday coming up. Shame on you for not telling me."

"It's no big deal. I don't expect you to do nothing."

"But of course we should do something. Your eighteenth birthday! That's a milestone."

Toy's face reddened and she squirmed in her seat. "If, you know, you're thinking to get me anything at all, well, I'd be grateful if you'd get something for the baby instead. I can get by, but I don't have a thing for the baby and I need just about everything. That's what I'm saving all my money for."

Cara was moved, remembering the days when she was Toy's age and starting out in Chicago without two dimes to rub together. She would never forget that particular kind of fear.

"You'll be getting lots of things for the baby when we give you a baby shower," Cara said, privately determined to make certain Toy had whatever she needed. "But for your eighteenth birthday, you must get something just for *you*."

"Let us buy you a dress or two," Lovie cajoled. "To make you feel pretty."

"No, ma'am, it wouldn't be right. I can make my own clothes. I'm just getting the hang of it."

Lovie looked pointedly at the pitiful mess all caught in the needle. Toy, looking at it again, burst into tears.

Cara and Lovie exchanged a long look, both sure it had to be the hormones.

"There's no use arguing," Cara said with a gentle laugh. "She'll wear you down eventually. Then, of course, after she was done you'd have to go round two with me. Just say yes and let us have the pleasure of buying you a little something for your birthday."

Toy's face twisted in confusion and Cara felt a pang of sympathy for her. Her pride was kicking in and she was trying to save face. "Please, Toy," she said, coaxing. "We really won't give up until you say yes. And it will make Mama happy to do this for you."

Toy wiped her eyes and Cara saw that the tears had been replaced with relief.

"Okay," she said with an embarrassed shrug of her shoulders. "If it'll make Miss Lovie happy, maybe just one dress."

Later that afternoon, Cara and Toy sat at an outside umbrella table at Port City Java for lunch. At their feet were large bags burgeoning with several maternity dresses, shorts and tops made of light, beautiful fabrics of a quality and style unlike any Toy had owned before. She didn't even know that there was such a thing as a maternity swimsuit! There was also a brand-new layette for the baby—little tops and bottoms too cute for words.

In the back of her mind, Cara knew she should be careful with her money now that she had no income. But she didn't care. She was having a ball. In Chicago she'd been too busy to do much shopping and she'd never enjoyed it anyway. At her favorite clothing stores she had saleswomen set things aside for her to try on. For gifts, she'd found it more efficient to pick up the phone, order online or send a gift certificate.

But today had been a whole new experience for her. Toy's excited expression as she tried on dress after dress and the sound of her "oohs" over a pair of shoes were pure pleasure. Cara remembered standing in the layette section of Belk's department store. She and Toy had giggled like schoolgirls at seeing the layout of pastel infant clothing, especially the teensy knitted sweaters with adorable bears and kittens embroidered on them. Toy had wanted just to touch them. Cara had watched her stroll through the department skimming the fabrics with her fingertips, an expression of awe on her face.

"They're so little," she'd said, voicing Cara's own thought.

"Why not try one on for size?"

Toy laughed. "Pink or blue?"

"Hmm… Yellow I think. We wouldn't want to insult Baby." It was more fun than serious, rather like trying on makeup or jewelry.

"What do you think?" Toy had asked as she gingerly held up a newborn Onesie to her belly. Delicate lace and tiny embroidered ducklings bordered the soft yellow fabric. As the outfit lay against Toy's body, the reality that in the not-too-distant future a new baby would indeed be wearing the tiny garment changed the mood. Tears moistened their eyes.

Cara had bought the yellow outfit on the spot, and several more like it. The more Toy said she didn't want anything, the more determined Cara was to buy her something extra.

Cara found herself smiling at the memory and she cast an affectionate glance across the table at Toy, who was hungrily devouring her sandwich. It occurred to Cara that if she'd had a child at Toy's age, that child would be older than Toy now.

What was having a baby like, she wondered? What was it

like to bring another human being into the world? She sneaked a quick glance at Toy's belly, trying to imagine the feel of life inside her. She couldn't.

Being a mother meant she'd be responsible for that child for life. She'd have to have a job, a place to live and the means to provide. She supposed that wasn't so very different than what she was doing right now. What *would* be different was the loss of her independence because there'd be this little creature tugging at her skirts needing to be taken care of. Mama used to tell her that, from the moment she saw her firstborn's face, she never had another good night's sleep.

She tried to imagine herself a mother, holding her baby to her breast, seeing her face for the first time. Seeing a part of herself in the eyes of another being. She warmed to the vision.

Then she felt a sudden sense of loss. She'd likely never have a child.

Cara sat blinking in the afternoon sun dazed with the full impact of the realization. It wasn't that she'd actually decided *not* to have children, more that she'd been busy building her career and never got around to thinking about it. Now here she was, forty, sitting at a little outdoor bistro with an iced cappuccino, suddenly realizing that she'd *forgotten* to have children.

"I sure wish Miss Lovie could've come with us," Toy was saying to her. "She'd love this sandwich."

Cara turned her head, realizing that Toy was speaking to her. "What? I'm sorry, what did you say?"

"Maybe we should bring one of these sandwiches home for Miss Lovie?"

Cara brought her wandering mind quickly back into focus. Dragging her emotions along was a bit harder. She took a deep breath. "It's a nice idea, but I don't think Mama'd eat it. It's pretty spicy and her appetite is dwindling to nothing."

Toy put down her sandwich with a dramatic show of concern. "Don't I know it! I'm trying to cook all manner of things that she might like, but I swear, no matter what I make she picks at it like a bird."

"Don't take it personally, Toy. It's the illness. I had a long talk with her doctor the other day and he thinks she's doing pretty well, considering. Her energy level is good and her mood is up. But he warned me that it won't be long before she'll start to…" She hesitated. She didn't want to voice his word: *deteriorate*. That sounded so inhuman. Like a specimen breaking down in a lab or a piece of fruit withering in the re-frigerator. "Soon it will be a struggle to get her to eat at all."

Toy's face reflected the dismay they both felt. "I can't be-lieve it's really happening."

Cara set down her fork. "I know. It will be hard. We'll need each other then, Toy, for help and support."

Toy nodded solemnly.

"I keep thinking of her the way she was when I was grow-ing up. She had so much energy. And my, did she love to shop. This trip would have been right up her alley. She was on a first-name basis with the sales clerks in every boutique on King Street." Cara smiled remembering. "You should have seen her back then. She was such a belle. She had this tiny waist and beautiful blond hair. She always looked just so." Cara laughed in a self-deprecating manner. "What a pair we made. I always felt like the gangly sidekick. Going shopping for dresses with her was torture. When I tried things on I felt so big and gawky next to her. The nicer she was the crankier I became. She never understood that I wished I looked like her. But I couldn't tell her that, of course. I probably didn't even realize it at the time. Our shopping trips always ended with a quarrel and days of self-loathing. I think that's why I hate shopping or wearing dresses to this day."

She saw Toy's expression change to a guilt-ridden worry.

"Oh, but I loved shopping with you today," Cara hurried to assure her. "After all, you and Baby were trying on all the clothes. I got to sit back and enjoy."

Toy seemed to believe her. "Well," she said in an airy tone, "you turned out just fine. I wish I were as tall as you. You look like a model."

"Hardly, but speaking of which, Mama will ask you to model everything when we get back. Just you wait."

Toy picked up her sandwich with both hands and took an enormous bite. She started to say something else, but stopped and waited to finish chewing. Cara held back her smile.

Toy pointed to Cara's plate. "Is that all you're eating? I feel like a cow next to you."

"I'm going out with Brett for dinner, so I'm leaving lots of room."

"Again?"

For a second, Cara was caught up in her memories of the night before. She'd spent half the night trying to work out why she was so pleased with the evening when she still hadn't gone much beyond kissing. Though it was a great kiss.

"We're going to go over the plans for the porch tonight," she said in a matter-of-fact tone to quash the "Do tell!" in Toy's eyes. "He thinks he can start work by the end of the week. Can you believe it?"

"I think he'd move mountains for you."

"What do you mean?"

Toy wiped her mouth with an exaggerated demure pat of the napkin. "I've seen the way he looks at you."

Cara tried not to grin as she looked down and stirred her ice with the straw. "No, that's not the reason he's doing the job. I told him about Mama's condition and it was like lighting a match under that man. He can't get the job done fast enough. It's very sweet, actually."

"That's because he's a sweet man. Quiet but strong, you know? There aren't many of them out there, as far as I can tell."

"Take my word on it. There aren't."

"I don't think Darryl ever looked at me the way Brett looks at you."

"What do you care about the way *he* looked at you?"

Toy set her half-eaten sandwich back down on the plate. "There's something I've been meaning to tell you. I didn't want to worry Miss Lovie, so it's good we can talk about it while we're alone."

"I'm all ears."

"It's Darryl. I called him. Just to see how he was," she hurried to add when she saw the spark ignite in Cara's eyes. "We were together for a long time, you know?"

Cara stirred her ice and tried to keep her voice even when inside she was roiling. "And what did he have to say for himself?"

"Not much. He's such a creep. There was another girl with him and he didn't care if I knew it. I think he even wanted me to hear her. To punish me, you know?" She snorted. "As if."

"Still, the betrayal hurt, I'm sure," Cara responded, thinking of Richard.

Toy nodded grimly.

"Well, good riddance to rubbish, right?"

Toy shifted in her seat and kept her eyes down.

"Is there something else?"

"He must have caller ID or Star 69'd me or something 'cause he knows my number now. I mean, your number. He called me the other day—but I hung up on him."

"I see." Cara sat back in her chair while a thousand possibilities whirred in her mind, none of them good. "What do you think he might do?"

"Darryl? With him anything's possible. He thinks I, like, belong to him, you know?"

Cara felt her heart accelerate. "So, do you think he might come to the house?"

"I don't know," she said, her voice low with fear. "I told him not to."

"Okay, good. What did *he* say? Exactly?"

"I don't remember exactly. Something about how I couldn't tell him what to do, and if he comes, he's taking me back with him." Her voice was beginning to tremble. "I know when he talks like that, soft and kinda weird, that he's really mad."

"There's no point panicking. It can't be good for your baby. Why don't you drink some of your juice and then you can tell me more about the man."

Toy nodded, settling down. She sipped some juice, then followed Cara's lead and ate more of her sandwich. Although Cara's outward appearance was calm, she was very worried and fighting off the urge to run home and lock all the doors.

"What does Darryl do for a living?" she wanted to know.

"Well, what he really wants to do is play in his band. He's really good. You should hear him. It's kind of country rock. He writes his own songs, too. Wrote one about me. He keeps talking about going to California so he can get noticed. He says there's no one gonna discover him around here. All he needs is one break and he's going to make it."

Cara didn't care for the sound of pride in Toy's voice. "Does he support himself with his music?"

"No. Not yet anyway. He works other jobs. Last job he had was at Best Buy selling stereos and stuff like that. Before that he tended bar. He likes to be around music."

"Tended bar? How old is this guy?"

"Twenty-four."

"*Twenty-four?* But you just turned eighteen. How old were you when you started going out with him?"

"Sixteen, but I didn't move in with him until I was seventeen," she hastened to explain. "He said I was too young before."

"And he didn't think a high school girl of sixteen was too young for a twenty-two-year-old man? Doesn't he know the law, for Christ's sake? Toy, one false move from him and you could send his butt to jail."

"I don't want to do that! I told you, I love him and he's been real good to me. He took care of me when my parents were so mean."

All Cara could think was how utterly horrid the parents must be to let their underage daughter go off with an older man like that. "Do you think this Darryl still loves you?" When Toy only looked down and shrugged she asked, "Well, more to the point, do you think he still feels that he owns you? Because if he does, then I'd say it's likely he'll show up."

"I didn't mean for this to happen. Really. I was just lonely for him and wanted to hear his voice. I didn't think that he could trace me. Are you sure he can get the address?"

"If he wants to find you, he can. We should be prepared in any event. I don't want him bothering my mother."

"Oh, don't worry that he'll do anything to Miss Lovie or to you! He's not crazy like that. If he comes, he'll just come for me. And I'll go with him so there won't be no trouble."

"Oh, yes, there *will* be trouble if that jerk thinks we'll let him force you back." Despite her resolve, she'd raised her voice at the thought of some bully dragging Toy away against her will.

"I don't want any trouble, Cara," she said, fear in her eyes. "Maybe I should just leave."

"I know you don't want trouble," she said in a softer tone.

"That never crossed my mind. But if there *is* trouble, is there anyplace else you could go? Just for a few days? Not for our sakes, but for yours. How about your mother's? Just for a night?"

"No. They don't want me back and I'd never go back, either. That's how I ended up going to the shelter in the first place. If I don't stay here, the only place left is the shelter. Or I could just go back with Darryl."

"That's out of the question. Besides, you'd only face this situation again sooner or later." For a moment, neither of them spoke. "No, it's best you stay put. We'll work it out somehow."

"Cara, as much as I love living with you and Miss Lovie—I mean, it's as close as I've ever come to having a real home— maybe it's better that I go with Darryl now."

Cara put her elbows on the table and tapped her lips at the innuendo. At times like this she was sorry she'd given up smoking. She studied Toy's face and saw again the stubborn determination that she'd seen in her eyes the first time they'd met. "Just answer me this. Do you *want* to go back to him?"

Toy only stared back, her blue eyes limpid with indecision.

Cara shook her head. "Oh, Toy…"

"I'm so confused! I don't know what to do," she cried, bringing her hand to her forehead. "I still love him. I don't want to lose him. He's the father of my baby." She threw up her hands and sat back in a huff. "And now you're all mad at me. Or disgusted."

"No, no, Toy, I'm not mad. And certainly not disgusted. These are your feelings. And while I may not agree with them, I accept that's how you feel. What I'm most concerned about now is your safety, and your baby's safety."

"I'm scared for my baby, too. I'm not worried about what he might do to me."

"You should be, Toy. Don't forget, he's raised his hand to you once already. You can't give him another chance."

"I won't. But he won't want to do it, either."

"Do you want to take the risk with your baby?"

"No."

"Okay then. It sounds to me like you're not ready to go back to Darryl. At least not yet."

Toy shook her head.

"Then that's settled. You'll stay with us. But if he calls again, will you tell me?"

"He won't."

"But if he does?"

"I'll tell you."

"And anything else. Notes, flowers, but especially if he comes to the cottage. You have to tell me. That's all I ask."

"Okay."

Cara could only hope she would. She swore she would not let Darryl take advantage of this child again and was suddenly glad at the prospect of having Brett around the house for the next few weeks. She made a point of picking up her fork and jabbing at her salad to lighten the mood. If she ate a bite, however, she'd choke. Across from her, Toy was despondent. Cara wouldn't let that bastard Darryl ruin their day.

"I was thinking," she said, changing the subject and striving for a positive note. "If you're not too tired, let's really splurge and get manicures. The yard work has ruined my nails. I've heard raves about a salon called Shear Paradise. And since it's your eighteenth birthday, why not get your hair done? Something new. I'm told Terri is a wizard. What do you say I try and get an appointment?"

"Really? I've seen that place. Are you sure?"

Cara looked at Toy's face. A makeover was just what she had in mind, but for much more than just her hair and clothes.

Beneath the heavy makeup and bright yellow hair Cara saw an insecure young girl seeking direction. Toy had a good heart and a sharp mind. All she needed was a chance. "I'm sure."

A waitress came to take their plates.

"No, don't take that!" Toy said when the waitress reached for her dessert. Toy picked up her fork and began cutting into the pecan pie covered with melting vanilla ice cream.

Cara watched as the waitress gave Toy's pregnant belly a second look. The waitress couldn't have been any older than Toy but with her tight, cropped knit top exposing a flat belly and beaded jewelry, it was obvious that this girl lived in a different world than Toy. Cara leaned forward. "I hope you don't mind my asking, but did you get your high school diploma?"

Toy shook her head. "I couldn't. I mean, I *could* have, but my being pregnant and all made it, you know, too embarrassing. And Darryl didn't want me to. He told me I didn't need it. I just figured if I wanted to, I could get it later."

"And do you want it?"

She looked up, surprised by the question. "I guess."

"Good. Because you really should get it. Why don't we look into the GED? I'll bet if you study real hard, you could take the test by the end of summer. I'll tutor."

"Why would you want to do that for me?"

Cara folded her hands on the table. "I was just thinking. If I'd had a child when I was your age, she would be about your age. I know, I know," she said with a chuckle. "The thought surprised me, too. But after I got over the shock that I was old enough to be your mother, I thought how neat it would be if I did have a child your age. A daughter like you."

Toy set down her fork. "I never knew you thought that way about me."

"We may have gotten off to a bumpy start, but I think

we've both learned to trust each other a little bit. And like each other, too. Don't you?"

She nodded. "I got a hint after you took down Palmer for me."

"I'll probably never have a child," she said, giving voice to the realization for the first time. "Or a grandchild. So it would mean a lot to me if you'd let me help you."

Toy swiftly looked down at her belly and began to stroke it with her small hands. "It's weird, but when I was little and my mama and daddy would fight, I'd put the covers over my head and wish I could be adopted by some other family. A real nice family with a pretty house and people who smiled and talked to each other and said goodbye when they left the house." She looked up at Cara, yearning swimming in her pale blue eyes.

"I've been so happy at Primrose Cottage. It's like what I dreamed of back then, like you and Miss Lovie have adopted me. But you haven't, of course," she hurried to add, as though embarrassed for the sentiment. "I'm grown-up now. And having a baby to boot. But I want you to know that what you just said means a lot to me. A whole lot."

Cara's breath stilled in her throat as the impact of that statement sank in. She knew what it had cost Toy to make it. They'd both exposed their vulnerable spots and now everything had changed between them. Cara reached out to place her hand over Toy's. It was an impulsive move, a heartfelt gesture. But when she looked at their joined hands, Cara realized that she was imitating her mother's familiar gesture.

fourteen

Up to eighteen thousand loggerheads per season nest in the southeastern United States, the bulk of them on the eastern beaches of Florida. Sea turtles travel long distances as they migrate between their feeding grounds and nesting beaches. Although there are many theories, no one is certain how the turtles navigate their way.

Amid a whirlwind of buzzing saws, hammering and shouts, Brett and his crew managed to finish the porch and pergola by the end of June. They'd all squeezed the project in between other jobs and worked around the clock on the days they could get there. Cara hired another crew to help paint not only the porch, but the whole house as well. Everyone's spirits soared as the beach house quickly took shape. As Lovie exclaimed, it was as if God had picked up the dusty place, given it a good shake, then placed it back on the earth and smoothed out all the wrinkles.

No one beamed more than Lovie. She felt like her old self as she made decisions again. It was painful to admit, but she was beginning to feel sorry for herself. Of course, she was thrilled to see the restoration begin, but sitting in her rocker she'd felt damaged, not knowing from one day to the next if she was going to spend what was left of her life rotting in a chair and watching television. She'd given up control over her finances to Stratton, then to Palmer without much concern. Yet the home and garden had always been *her* territory. It seemed to her that she and Primrose Cottage had both been devastated—one by hurricane, the other by cancer.

When the project began she'd tried to keep out of the way. A few months earlier, Cara might not even have noticed her mother sitting alone in her rocker on the sidelines. But she noticed now—and Cara dragged her into the decision making. Cara pressed Lovie to find the exact yellow paint match for the house, to consider where the old palm trees had been before Hugo ripped them out and to choose where to place new ones. She brought her countless catalogues and had Toy drive her to nurseries to choose the number and variety of climbing rosebushes to match those that had once thrived so magnificently over the pergola. Most of all, Cara insisted that Primrose Cottage belonged to Olivia Rutledge and always would.

And her plan worked. Lovie felt alive again, in ways she hadn't in many years. When she directed the planting of the seven new palm trees around the property, she felt as she did the day she had first bought the little house on the beach. There were so few houses on the island at that time and so many trees. And though Cara did the physical labor of tilling and adding new soil, Lovie herself planted the new, blaze-red climbing rosebushes that would someday arch over the pergola.

Each morning of the three weeks of construction, Lovie awoke with a prayer of thanks to God. First, she was glad just to be waking up. She also thanked God for the simple routines that filled the days and hearts of the ladies of Primrose Cottage and brought them closer together.

Finally, on the morning the porch was finished and the workmen did not come with their hammers and saws, a quiet peace was restored. Lovie stood alone in the garden, breathing in the sweet-scented air and taking in all the changes.

Through the window she saw Toy bustling inside, cleaning the house and cooking a hot breakfast. She hummed as she waltzed through the rooms. Cara was visible across the road walking along the beach path wearing her green Turtle Team shirt, the red bucket dangling from her arm. Lovie watched her march with the confidence of a natural born leader. In addition to all her records and equipment, Cara carried with her all of Lovie's hopes and dreams.

Lovie took a deep breath, feeling as one who had run the long race and just passed the torch. It wasn't so bad being old, she thought. She didn't have to rush off anywhere to get something done. It was nice to stand back and see the wild-flowers blooming again, maybe think where she might add a few new ones. And it was very nice to stand on a hilly dune in the early morning and watch the wonder of a miracle happening right before her eyes.

The first morning of July Lovie woke up inspired. Her heart was leaping with excitement and her cheeks flushed as she called Toy and Cara to the table.

"I want to have a great Fourth of July celebration in honor of the restoration of Primrose Cottage! I want us all to be together, my family and friends, here at the beach house again."

"But Mama, it's only four days away."

"That's plenty of time. Why?" she asked dryly. "Do you have anything else planned for the holiday?"

"No, not exactly. I just thought..."

"I don't have anything planned either," Toy burst in, kicking Cara under the table.

Lovie's enthusiasm was infectious. Before the first cup of coffee was finished, all three women were gung ho. They pulled out the favorite cookbooks and old family recipes and made long lists of all the different foods to prepare, because everyone knew a holiday meal wasn't worth its salt without an impressive spread of home-cooked food.

Lovie bubbled over with ideas, every bit the matriarch again, her pencil scribbling across the paper as she made her list. "I want to fix Aunt Libby's corn bread. It's as light as a cloud. And my grandmother's fried chicken. Oh, and Granddaddy Clayton's barbeque sauce. Toy, can you make that potato salad again? It's pure heaven." She tapped her lips with the pencil. "I hope we'll have room in the icebox for all this."

"We'll make room," Toy said. "And we can always carry things over to Flo's."

Lovie set down her pencil and said with a wistful smile, "Most of all, I want to spend time with Linnea and Cooper. The darlings... I hardly see them anymore. Could we go to the beach? All of us together? Cara, I can't remember the last time I saw you in the water."

"Sure we can, Mama. We can do anything you want. But I'll have to hurry to finish painting the pergola today or we'll be eating this feast under dripping paint."

"I'll help," offered Toy.

Cara tilted her head. "Thanks. And I'll help with the food." Both women smiled in commiseration.

Lovie witnessed this and smiled, too. "While you two are busy, I'm fixing to do an errand of my own. It's too hot to do our own baking. Flo and I are going to town today, so I'll pick up a few cakes and pies. And on the way back I'll stop by Belva's for some red, white and blue flowers."

"Don't get carried away and do too much," Cara warned.

"Oh, bother. I'm feeling wonderful. And Flo will be with me." Lovie picked up her pencil and poised it over the pad of paper. "We'd best make out an invitation list first. I'll call and invite Palmer and Julia before I leave. They're always busy and it's such short notice. I hope they can come."

"They'll come," Cara replied with an iron undercurrent that implied she'd make certain of it.

"And, of course, Florence and Miranda."

"Emmi will have a hissy fit if we don't invite her," said Cara.

"Of course, Emmi! Will Tom be here, too?"

"He's still away." She met her mother's knowing gaze.

"What about her boys? Aren't they coming down for the weekend? Maybe she has plans."

"She can bring them along." Cara sidled a glance at Toy. "Her boys are close to your age. Maybe a year or two older. And last I saw them, they were very cute."

"Oh sure, like they'd be interested in me." Toy rolled her eyes but not before Cara caught the flash of hurt.

Lovie twiddled her pencil. "Do you think Brett would come?"

"I'm sure he will. He's as proud of this porch as you are."

"Bless his heart."

Toy smirked. "Like that's the only reason he'd come."

Cara shot her a glance.

"Things *do* seem to be getting thick between the two of you," Lovie said good-naturedly. "You've been eyeing each other across the porch for weeks. And, I swanny, I never saw two folks bump into each other as much as you two. Just clumsy, I suppose."

"We're friends."

When her mother raised her brows, Cara felt nettled. "Why is that so hard for you to believe? A man and a woman don't always have to be heading for the altar."

"When you find the right one, you do," said Toy emphatically. "I've got *girls* for friends. Why go through all the motions just to be friends with a guy?"

"Most of my friends are guys," Cara retorted. "And if I ever do get married, I want the man to be my friend first."

Toy stared back at her as though she'd never thought of that concept before.

Lovie smiled broadly. "Cara, I do believe that's the first time I've ever heard you mention the possibility of getting married."

"Don't get your hopes up, Mama. I was talking in generalities."

"I'm not making any plans or reservations at the club quite yet. I merely think it's wonderful that you've found a man as good and caring as Brett. I've always liked that boy. He's a giver. He thinks of others before himself and that is too rare a quality these days. You're good for him, too. For all his finer points, that's one ship that needs a solid rudder."

"Oh, for Christ's sake, Mother..."

"Cara, don't take the Lord's name at my table!"

"Okay, I'm sorry. But why do you say things like that? Brett and I haven't *found* each other. That implies we were lost."

Lovie's lips twitched. "Well, since you put it that way..."

Toy shook her head. "I think when you say you've found someone, it really means that you've been searching for the right guy."

"I'm not searching for anything, except maybe a new job."

"You just don't like that you can't control falling in love," Lovie said.

"Maybe I don't believe in love."

"But that's crazy," Toy blurted out, seemingly upset by the very idea. "There's someone out there for everyone."

"Someone or anyone? There's a difference. Anyone isn't good enough for me. I won't settle. I'd rather live alone, thank you very much."

Toy again sat back in her chair, speechless.

"Brett and I like each other very much," explained Cara,

"We are enjoying each other's company. He's a very attractive man. But neither one of us is looking for anything permanent. We accept this for what it is. At best, a summer's fling."

"One summer can change lives," Lovie said softly. She looked at her daughter. Cara's dark brown eyes were indecipherable. She'd always felt guilty with the knowledge that her own bad marriage had shadowed Cara's viewpoint. It was a pity that her daughter saw love as highly overrated and marriage as a trap that crushed a woman's spirit. Lovie prayed that this summer Cara would open herself up to allow love to flow in. She could never tell Cara how true love—the love she'd experienced for one golden summer with Russell—was like the tide that rushes in to replenish even the most arid soil. How one summer could last a lifetime.

No, she couldn't ever tell her daughter this.

"Well, then," she said, looking again at her list. "That brings the total to thirteen."

"Thirteen? Isn't that bad luck?" Toy asked.

"Not necessarily," replied Lovie. "But just in case, I'll fix up a batch of my special black-eyed peas." Her smile was bittersweet. "I'd like to make that dish one more time."

As she bent her head to finish writing her list, Cara leaned back in her chair and gazed out the window and Toy scraped with her nail at something stuck on the table. The three women quietly understood that Lovie wouldn't be around in January to make this traditional Southern dish that brought good luck to the New Year.

"Is that you, Lovie Rutledge, sneakin' in my kitchen?"

"Miranda! You're up and about again. How wonderful! That must mean you're feeling better." She went to hug Miranda who walked with a wobbly gait into the room. Her long, gnarled fingers clung to the counters for balance. Years back, Miranda Prescott used to dwarf both Lovie and Flo and she had a voice and attitude to match her size. Sadly, the past ten years had not been kind to her. At ninety, she'd grown steadily weaker and more confused. On her good days, however, her pale eyes radiated warmth and wisdom. Today was one of her good days.

"I just had myself a visit with Jesus but I'm back again for a while," Miranda replied. "This is no time for being sick. Couldn't miss the hatchlings, now, could I?"

"It wouldn't be the same at the nests without you. We're expecting our first hatching any day."

"I know it. I'm watching for it."

"We're going to start sitting on the 6th Avenue nest first. According to my chart, it ought to boil on July 6th. How's that for a good omen?"

Miranda's eyes sparkled. "You just never know. Those turtles are wily."

Since the moment Miranda Prescott came to live with her daughter on the Isle of Palms, she was devoted to "her babies." She couldn't be bothered by turtle tracks or the moving of nests or the regulations of the Department of Natural Resources. All she cared about were the hatchlings and she visited every nest on her small stretch of beach during the hatching season.

"I'm having a holiday picnic. You'll come, won't you?" Lovie asked her.

"You're what?"

Lovie raised her voice. "Having a picnic. On the Fourth."

Miranda's eyes, rheumy with age, were uncomprehending. "I hear you two girls are going to town this morning."

Lovie gave up on that question with a chuckle. She got a kick out of still being called a "girl" by Miranda. "Just a few errands. I don't imagine you'd like to come?"

"Me? Good heavens, no. Why would I want to deal with all that traffic in this heat? Plus, I don't like to go to the city in the summer. Pains me to see those horses work in this heat. I'll just sit on my porch and watch my stories."

"We're going to the bakery for some pies. I'll pick up something sweet for you, and when we come back, we can sit together and pour the tea. How does that sound?"

Miranda smiled tremulously, and with a vague uncomprehending nod, turned and began shuffling off, mumbling something Lovie couldn't quite catch. As Lovie watched her leave, she thought to herself how she wouldn't grow to be as old as Miranda.

A moment later she heard Flo's voice in the other room telling her mother in a loud voice where she was going. When she burst into the room the air seemed to crackle around her. She was dressed in a rather short khaki skirt and a vibrant red-and-white-striped shirt that showed off her tan.

"Hey, sugar! Don't you look nice in that blue dress. Are you ready to go to the bank?"

Lovie clutched her purse against her conservative sheath dress, nervous about her appointment. Despite the heat, she wore nylons, dress shoes and a sweater against the chill of the air-conditioning.

"I'm long past ready," she replied.

Flo hesitated, searching her face. "Are you sure you want to do this? After all these years, to do this *now*."

Lovie nodded, her gaze firm. "If not now, when? Bobby Lee Davis will be waiting for me and he's called my lawyer to join us, too. It's all arranged. He says it'll be as easy as falling off a bridge. The only thing I have to do is sign some papers. Besides," she added with a twinkle in her eye, "we're preparing for the Fourth of July, the day we celebrate our independence. Don't you think that's fitting?"

fifteen

Hatching time approaches. Inside the nest the baby turtle pecks at its shell with an egg tooth. The hatchling will remain underground for several days to absorb every bit of the important yolk sack for the energy to survive. It also needs to allow its curved shell to straighten.

The sprinklers were swirling all morning on the Fourth to help the garden perk up for the party. They'd rented long tables to place on the back screened porch and covered them with bright blue paper tablecloths, paper dishes, plastic forks and spoons and the fresh flowers Lovie had brought home from the florist. Nobody wanted to spend the evening washing dirty dishes when there were fireworks to be seen. Cara and Toy twisted and taped red, white and blue crepe paper and added balloons with flags on them in the corner. Cara also strung white lights around the room, something her mother had always done. She'd thought they were like stars when she was a child and hoped Linnea and Cooper would, too.

She walked into the living room in search of more tape when she spotted her mother arranging photo albums on the living room table.

"What's all this?" she asked.

Lovie looked up from her task smiling with pride. "These

are the fruits of my labor for the past few months. An ongoing project. I've gathered all the loose photographs of the family into some kind of order at last. I had no idea there were so many. They've been stuffed in shoe boxes for years. Come look," she said, sitting down on the sofa and pulling out two albums. "I've separated yours and Palmer's childhood photos, one for each of you. I thought you'd like to keep them."

Cara came closer to join her mother on the plump, floral sofa. She took the album labeled Caretta in gold and ran her hand reverentially over the fine, soft navy leather.

"Thank you," she replied, moved. "It's beautiful."

Lovie smiled, anxiously fingering the album. It was plain to see the albums meant a great deal to her.

"The rest of the photos I placed in albums and grouped them in years. It seemed the easiest way."

Cara glanced over at the albums on the table. There were at least ten and they represented decades. "So many years," she said, suddenly feeling each of her forty. "You've done an incredible job."

"I'm not done yet," Lovie replied, flushed with the compliment. She leaned closer to look over Cara's shoulder as she opened up the album.

Cara enjoyed sitting beside her mother, pressing shoulders with their hands almost touching as they leafed through the pages. They skimmed over photos of Cara learning how to swim in the surf, fishing with Palmer, performing in piano and school recitals, teary eyed but smiling as she boarded the bus to camp, and dressed up in all sorts of costumes for Christmas pageants, Halloween and Easter. Cara relived the happier moments of her childhood, years that anger had clouded.

"Look at this one," Cara said chuckling. There was a proud Palmer, not much older than Cooper was now, chest puffed out and a tooth missing, with two meaty fists clutched to the wheel of the boat. "Like father like son."

Lovie laughed too, leaning forward for a closer look. They flipped through several more pages, then moved on to other albums, slowly moving forward year by year. Cara recognized most of the photos but seeing them again brought smiles of recognition. She realized as the hour passed that her mother had done much more than chronicle her and Palmer's childhood or the family's history. She'd collected experiences and emotions for the family to remember and cherish forever.

"Who is this?" she asked, pointing to a photograph of a tall, striking man with white-blond hair that was tousled in the wind. He wore khaki shorts and had his sleeves rolled up. Most arresting was his wide, engaging smile. Lovie stood beside him in the photograph, straight and prim in a broad-rimmed straw hat. Beside her was an enormous loggerhead on the beach. "He's very good-looking."

There was a short silence as Lovie studied the photograph with uncertainty.

"I'm not sure," she replied. "I believe he was someone who came to study the turtles."

Unlike before, when Lovie had gone on and on relating a story associated with a picture, she remained silent and uneasy. Attuned to her mother's nuances, Cara looked into her face. There was a slight flush to her cheeks and she inched her fingers to cover the photograph.

"He looks vaguely familiar," Cara said.

"It was the turtle's photograph I wanted to keep," she said as she turned the page.

"Wait." Cara tapped the page back with her forefinger. "I remember him now. He came by a lot one summer, then he went away. Emmi and I were sorry when he didn't come back the next summer. He was a nice guy. He didn't ignore us or push us aside like most adults." She drummed her fingers on the album as her mind dug back. "What was his name? *R*-something. Robert? Randolph?"

"I believe his name was Russell something or other." She cast a quick, assessing glance toward Cara, then firmly turned the page. "It was a very long time ago."

"I suppose. But looking at all these photographs, it seems like yesterday, doesn't it?"

Lovie closed the album and rested her hand over the leather. Her smile was bittersweet. "Yes, it certainly does."

Julia arrived later that morning with Linnea and Cooper in tow. The children scrambled from the SUV and charged up the stairs, their flip-flops clapping against their heels and beach towels trailing.

"Grandmama Lovie! We're going to the beach!" Cooper shouted as he ran into his grandmother's arms.

"Yes, we are!" Lovie exclaimed, wrapping her arms around him.

Linnea came rushing up to hug her grandmother with exuberance.

"Settle down there," Julia called out, following them at a slower pace. "You're going to knock your poor grandmother over. Cooper, let go of her neck! Linnea, honey, go to the car and fetch those flowers you picked out special from Grandmama's garden." She reached the porch and shook her head, chuckling softly with a mother's pride. "Hey, Mama Lovie," she said breathlessly, coming close to deliver a kiss. Her hands were filled with a covered casserole dish. "Where do I put this?"

Cara stepped forward. "I'll take that for you. How are you, Julia? You look like you've been out on the golf course."

"Tennis," she replied, following Cara into the kitchen. "But it's these two hooligans who are running me ragged. They were fit to be tied all night waiting to come. I finally told Palmer flat-out that I wasn't going to force these children to make an appearance at all those parties today. We've done enough of that over the years. Today is Mama Lovie's party. I tried to talk him into coming with us, but you know Palmer and business. He's still making the rounds, but he'll be by in a little while."

"He'd better not eat at those parties," said Cara, squelching her flare of disappointment. How could Palmer put business over his mother at *this* time? She knew full well that Palmer would not show up until much later. "We've been cooking for three days."

"Mom," Cooper screeched from the porch. "I want to go to the beach!"

"Then stop your caterwauling and go get your swimsuit!"

Cara thought they looked like a circus caravan as they walked single file along the sandy path to the beach. Lovie led the group like a petite drum majorette in her red sundress and broad-rimmed straw hat trailing red, white and blue ribbons. Cooper followed, an adorable clown in oversize plastic sunglasses and wreathed in an orange floater. Behind him, Linnea wrapped herself pareo style in a towel and had a Walkman at her ears, desperately trying to be grown-up. In contrast, Toy seemed like a little girl in her cheerful gait. This was the first time she'd gone to the ocean since she'd arrived on the Isle of Palms. Once she found out that Emmi's sons had opted for surfing over an afternoon with the family, her nervous frown disappeared and she began to enjoy herself, agreeing to wear her new maternity swimsuit after all. Julia and Cara were the pack mules. They carried umbrellas, the cooler, extra towels, beach chairs and toys galore.

It was a classic family holiday at the beach, almost like being a child herself all over again. Linnea and Cooper vied with each other for her attention. Being children, they knew a captive audience when they spotted one. *Aunt Cara, look at me! Aunt Cara, try this! Come here, Aunt Cara!* The three of them swam in the ocean until their fingers and toes pruned. They built mighty sand castles on the shore and gathered shells. Julia took advantage of the free babysitter and sat under the umbrella with Toy and Lovie to read the novel that Cara had brought down.

After only an hour, however, Lovie had a coughing spell that interjected a dose of reality to the day. She waved away their concerns as she rose. "Forgive me, children, but I'll be fine if I go back to the cottage to rest before dinner."

"I'll come with you." Toy gripped the sides of her chair to rise.

"Don't you dare get up. I can certainly walk back home by myself. I've done it enough times. Now just settle back and enjoy the sun. What will you do with yourself at the house while I lie down in the bed?"

"Are you sure?"

"Of course. Tell Cara where I am so she doesn't start looking for me. Someone should be home anyway, lest Palmer arrive."

Julia waved that suggestion away with her hand. "Don't hold your breath, Mama Lovie. If he starts partying early, then who knows when he'll get here?"

Alone in the cottage, Lovie relished her solitude. Although she loved having her family around, she needed quiet time more than ever now to keep up her strength. She prayed a good deal these days, too. Not for herself, but for her children. Before she left them, she wanted to see them happy and content.

She walked out to the new porch that Cara had pursued with such energy. Resting her hands on the freshly painted white railing, she looked at the row of rosebushes and all the newly planted palmetto trees. The transformation was remarkable. Looking out, she felt as though she'd stepped back in time. But she was more pleased with the change in her daughter this past month.

Cara had arrived home with an emptiness inside her. Lovie could see it in her eyes when she looked at the sunset. Her daughter was still searching for fulfillment, spreading her energy around in countless outside tasks rather than quietly focusing inward. But the turtles would help her find her way home, Lovie thought to herself with a small smile of satisfaction. Going to the ocean every morning, putting her hands in the sand, sitting by the nests at night—all these activities would steer her on the right path.

But Palmer...

She smoothed out the tablecloth and arranged a few flowers in the vase as she considered her son. She had come back to the house early hoping to catch a moment alone with him. He would not like what she had to tell him. She slumped down into her favorite rocker and looked out over the dunes and ocean, rocking back and forth. In the waning hours of the afternoon, she prayed for the strength to do what she had set her mind to.

Palmer found her on the porch. "Hey, Mama," he called out in his boisterous voice.

She startled. She'd been so lost in her thoughts, she hadn't heard him come in. Turning, her heart melted to see her son's eyes light up at the sight of her. It had always been this way with him. She knew he'd walk through fire for her. It was just such a shame that his hot temper sometimes started those very fires. When he bent to kiss her cheek, she smelled the strong odor of bourbon on his breath. This didn't portend well. Nothing flamed the fires like a dousing of alcohol.

"Will you look at this place?" he said, craning his neck to get a good view of the new porch and pergola. "I couldn't believe it when I drove up. This porch looks just like I remember it. Cara and I used to play Monopoly in that corner over there for hours and hours." His eyes glazed and she could see that he was remembering those halcyon days when the hours were strung out before them like pearls. "Y'all did an incredible job. I am all amazement. How did you get it done so fast? Julia can't get someone in to fix a broken window."

"We've all worked hard but the job was pure pleasure."

"Whoever built this thing," he said, putting his hand to the pergola and giving it a shake, "did a fine job. It's built like a tank. It'll take a hurricane to knock it down." He gave her a wink.

"Do you remember Brett Beauchamps? The credit goes to him."

Palmer's eyes lit up. "Hell, that ol' rascal? I haven't seen him in ages. He built this? Well, I can't believe it. I remember him tearing things *down*. Talk about divine justice. What's he up to these days when he's not building porches?"

"He's dating your sister, for starters."

"Come again?"

"Brett and Cara are seeing each other." She wagged her brows. "Sparks are flying."

"They say opposites attract, but I don't know about that. How long has this been going on?"

"Only a few weeks but I have my hopes. He's quite a catch."

He shook his head. "It'll never happen. She's a die-hard

spinster. Besides, there isn't a woman alive who can catch that big ol' fish. Let me tell you, they've been angling since high school."

Lovie bristled at hearing Cara called a spinster. It was something Stratton would have said. "We'll see," was all she replied.

Palmer's gaze traveled beyond the porch to the grounds. He put his hands on his wide hips and a slow smile stretched across his face. "Yessir, this place looks all spiffed up. You've done a nice paint job, new shutters and landscaping to boot. Looks to me like you're fixing to sell it, Mama."

She saw the excitement in his eyes and hurried to tamp it down. "No, dear, that's not it at all. Quite the contrary. We did it strictly for us."

The light in his eyes quickly doused. Pursing his lips, he sat slowly down in a wooden rocking chair, gripping the armrests and rocking back and forth a few times with his eyes fixed on her. The silence was as heavy as the humidity.

"I thought we talked about this, Mama," he said at length with a weary voice that sounded patronizing to her ears.

"So we have." Lovie rose from her chair to move her rocker from the other side of the porch. Palmer sprang to his feet to carry it for her and place it right across from his. Once they both settled down again, they rocked a moment in silence, each knowing the other was merely biding time.

It was Lovie who spoke first. "I think, Palmer, since we're alone, it's time for you and me to talk about this issue one last time."

"If you want," he said in a drawl. "I don't know what more there is to say. I know you want to keep it, but like I said, the numbers just don't add up."

"It's interesting that you should put it in just those terms," she said in a calm voice. "Robert Davis used the exact words."

He stopped rocking. "What's Bobby Lee got to do with this?"

"I went to see him in his office. After you and I talked a few weeks ago, I wanted to get a clearer picture of my financial situation. Bobby's a very nice man, so polite. He took a world of time to explain things so I'd understand them. And I do. It wasn't so confusing after all. Except, perhaps, for the part about how the numbers didn't add up. I may not be as good with arithmetic as you are, Palmer, but I do know when two plus two doesn't equal four. It appears there have been many more withdrawals from my account than I ever received."

Palmer's face paled. "You don't think I'm stealing from you, do you? It's a juggling act. Sometimes I rob Peter to pay Paul, but it all comes out even again in the end."

Lovie gave Palmer a stern look. "Paul hasn't paid back Peter in a very long time."

"I can tell you where every penny went. You'll get every cent back, I swear. You don't understand business, Mama. How can I explain it to you?"

"Bobby Lee managed to explain it to me well enough. Why don't you try?"

Palmer's words were strained when he spoke again. "A transport business is a complicated animal. And, lately, it's been tough going. If I don't have the money in my accounts to pay off a debt when it's due, I get the money wherever I can. It was only temporary, of course."

"Of course. So, basically, I gave you an interest-free loan?"

He offered a humorless smile. "I guess you could say that. I thought we were all in this together. Guess I thought wrong. Do you want me to write you a check right now? 'Cause I will. This very minute."

"No, Palmer, that won't be necessary. In fact, I don't want

a penny of that money back. I don't even want to know where it all went. I give it to you, free and clear."

He sat back in the rocker, puzzlement etched on his florid cheeks.

"I can manage fine without it," she continued evenly. Then she cleared her throat. "However, I instructed Bobby Lee to transfer the rest of my funds into a new account which I will tend to myself."

"You *what?* Mama, you can't do that. You haven't written a check in forty years."

"I can and I have. Cara can help me. She has quite a good head for figures." She paused to choose her words. "I don't mean to contradict your own figures, Palmer, but Bobby Lee assured me that I do not have to move out of my beach house. I have more than enough money to stay here for as long as I need to." Her lips moved into a forced cheery smile. "Isn't that good news?"

Palmer's face mottled. "You're saying you don't trust me?"

Lovie sighed. That was the truth of it, but she couldn't bring herself to say it. It would hurt him too deeply and she loved him too much. "Let's just say I'd rather trust myself."

"That sounds like Cara's doing. It is, isn't it?" he said with a scowl. "She found out how much this place is worth and wormed her way in at the eleventh hour. I'll just bet she talked you into all this sprucing up, too. On your dime. All this time I worried it was that Toy Sooner we had to watch out for, but it was Cara setting you up against me."

"She was doing no such thing," Lovie said with a scold in her tone. "No one is against anyone. You're the only one making accusations."

"So you're saying she isn't behind you taking over your own finances?"

"She recommended it," Lovie replied honestly, then, seeing the spark of indignation in his eye, she sprang to Cara's defense. "That kind of independence comes naturally to her. You fail to recognize that she has been successful in a man's world. I don't know why you find that so threatening. But to be honest, she didn't pursue that suggestion. She didn't have to. Over the past few weeks she's shown me the courage to confront my fears. I've always found confrontations difficult, as you well know. I've been so willing to be taken care of by the men in my life. It was just the way things were done in my generation, I suppose. So don't go casting blame. If anything, you brought this on yourself."

"How did I do that? By advising you to sell? By asking you to move back in with me so I could take care of you? Was that so horrible?"

"Yes. Frankly, it was. I've told you again and again that I don't want to live in town any longer. I'm happy here in my little beach house. I need peace and solitude now and it suits me. But you only want me to do what *you* think I should do, what's easiest for you, without a thought to what I might need. Or want. Cara did all this—" she waved her hand to indicate the porch and grounds "—with her own dime, as you put it, and without a single thought for herself. She did it simply to make me happy."

"I'm just sure she didn't have any ulterior motives," he said sarcastically.

Lovie drew herself up. "That's enough, Palmer. Primrose Cottage is *mine*. I've given up everything else that's ever mattered to me. More than I can ever tell you. This little cottage is all I have left of the only time in my life I knew true happiness. I clung to it when your father tried to wrest it away from me. He knew I loved it—and why. And it made him quite cruel. But that only made me all the more determined that he should never succeed. I gave him my house, my money and,

I see now, my self-respect. But I never gave him my heart or my memories—or this beach house. And now you want me to simply give this place up to you? Now, at the end of such a long struggle? Palmer, do you think I would sit back and let you do this? Child, you forget, I've wrestled with a much bigger fish."

Palmer appeared dumbfounded. When he spoke, his eyes were wild and searching. "I don't know what's going on here. I've never heard you talk like this before! You've never spoken a word against Daddy. Why did he want to take everything away from you? You were his wife, for pity's sake. You were married for forty years."

"I counted every one of them."

"Then tell me why?"

"It's not for you to know, Palmer."

He looked hurt, then his gaze cooled. "So, there it is. I'm not to know anything. But I'll wager Cara does. I don't know what's going on, but ever since Cara came home, things have been different."

She thought to herself how true that was but for reasons entirely different than he was envisioning. "Palmer, you must stop all dreams of developing this property. I also saw Ashton Etheridge. I had him draw up the legal papers. It's all done. Primrose Cottage will go to Cara when I die. Regardless of our problematic history, she is my daughter and it is only fair and right that I leave this place to her."

A strange light came into Palmer's eyes.

"I know you think I don't appreciate all you've done for me over the years," Lovie said. "I do. I recognize that you work hard and are a good provider for your family. But, Palmer, there is more to life than material possessions. These meaningless things cannot bring you happiness. My darling, think of what your father left you when he passed on. How meaningful was it? Is that the same legacy you want to leave your children?"

She began to cough, long and hard, unable to calm the spasm. Palmer gripped the sides of his rocker, his eyes betraying terror at seeing his mother ill. When the coughing finally subsided, she wiped her mouth with the tissues she kept near and straightened in her chair, catching her breath.

"Mama, I—"

"Shhh…it's all right," she hushed as her heart gradually came back to a normal pace. She took a last, long shuddering breath. "Don't waste your time worrying about an old woman. Your children are out there, at the beach. Go on out and play with them. They need you, Palmer. *They* are your real treasures. And you need them."

"What I need is a drink."

He got up from the rocker to go fix one but turned on his heel and paced the floor instead. He seemed so distraught that Lovie wanted to rise and get the drink for him, to somehow soothe his ruffled feathers. But she could see a barrage coming and steeled herself.

"Well, I've got to hand it to you, Mama. This is one whoppin' Fourth of July party you're having. You sure know how to bring on the fireworks." He whistled sharply, bringing her back up.

"What's next on the agenda? Are we all gonna sit down at the table like some great, big happy family?"

She opened her mouth to answer but was interrupted by the sound of a man's throaty baritone at the front door. She recognized it as Brett's.

"Coming!" she called out in a cheery voice. She gave Palmer a silencing look that closed his mouth, then slowly rose and hurried out to answer the door.

"Happy Fourth of July, Miss Lovie," Brett exclaimed. His arms strained to carry a large pot of steamed crabs.

"More food? My goodness, Brett, but we've already got more than those tables can hold. The legs are going to give out. I hope you're hungry!"

"Don't you worry. I've been out on the boat all morning talking till I'm blue in the face. All I intend to use my mouth for tonight is eating." He set the crabs down on the kitchen counter and, looking up, caught sight of Palmer. His ruddy, tanned face broke into a wider grin of genuine pleasure. "Hey there, Palmer!" he said, sticking out his hand.

To her relief, Palmer brought an amiable smile to his face and shook the hand offered. He was very good at turning on the charm when called for. Lovie stepped back, enjoying the sight of two handsome men catching up. Brett was taller, his auburn hair windblown. He'd cleaned up for the party but was still in an island attire of khaki shorts and a short-sleeved shirt worn open over a T-shirt. In contrast, Palmer's blond hair was neatly trimmed and he was conservatively dressed in an expensive polo shirt and pressed trousers. She saw the way Palmer's sharp eyes studied Brett, too, now knowing how things were between Brett and Cara. They chatted for a few minutes before Brett looked her way.

"It's awfully quiet around here. Where is everyone?"

"They're all down at the beach. I was just telling Palmer that he should go on down and join them. The children are having such a good time. Why don't you two go on?"

"I'm sorry but I can't," Palmer replied in a formal tone. "I've got to make a few more rounds before the night is over. You go on down, Brett. Maybe I'll catch you a little later." He turned to place a perfunctory kiss on his mother's cheek.

Lovie closed her eyes tight against the bitter disappointment she felt in her heart. When she opened them again Palmer was already leaving the house. She quickly followed him out to the porch. "Dinner will be at six," she called to his back.

"Don't wait on me. I don't know when I'll be back."

"Palmer!"

He turned at the stairs to face her again, all traces of his joviality gone.

Her heart strained against her chest. "You mustn't miss dinner. The children will be so disappointed."

"They might as well get used to it. I had to."

She reached out to him but he turned his back for the last time. Lovie stood on the front porch and watched her son walk away, the sound of each footfall causing her to wince.

sixteen

The hatchlings remain quiet during the heat of the day,
but at night, they scrape with their flippers, plowing through
broken shells and compact sand, working as a team.
This causes the floor of the nest to slowly rise to the surface.

It had been one of those dazzling, perfect summer days that Cara knew she would keep tucked away in her memories forever. The sun shone high in a cloudless sky, the ocean was refreshingly cool and the onshore breezes kept the bugs at bay. They stayed out for the whole glorious day, catching their second wind when Brett showed up with a long-tailed kite that looped joyously overhead. The tide was high and, holding hands, Cara, Brett, Linnea and Cooper ran into the surf, squealing. They had great piggyback wars, she with Linnea on her shoulders and Brett with Cooper perched high and crowing on his. When the children grew sleepy, they joined Toy and Julia under the umbrellas to stretch out on towels. The warm air breezes gently dried them while the murmurings of the surf lulled the children to nap.

As the sun began its downward descent, it seemed as though all the people on the beach decided in unison that they were hungry and eager for the holiday feasts and fireworks to come.

Folks stood and began folding up their beach chairs and shaking out their towels, calling children in from the water. Toy and Julia scuttled away early to help get the food laid out for dinner. Brett and Cara stayed behind with the children to gather the beach paraphernalia. Cooper ran back to the surf to rinse off his feet only to find them just as sandy by the time he returned to the group. When he made too much of a fuss and kicked the sand in frustration, Cara worried that she'd kept the children out too long and that they would fade out before the fireworks. She looked up to catch Brett's eye. They exchanged a long look, smiled, then, by unspoken signal, agreed to ignore the child's outburst.

Linnea stood alone a few feet off, patiently waiting to go home. Her towel was wrapped around her slender shoulders and her teeth were chattering. Cara's heart lurched at the sight of her. She was in that tender age before hormones kicked in where girls floated somewhere between child and teen. Her white-blond hair was a sharp contrast to her pinkened skin. Cara had discovered today that Linnea was keen to see the baby turtles and she'd extracted a promise from her aunt that she could come out to Primrose Cottage for an extended visit to help babysit the nests. Cara looked forward to spending the time together and discovering more about her niece.

"I'm starving," Cooper said with a pout, leaning against Cara's leg. She looked down at the scowling tanned face.

"Are you?" she asked with a pouting expression of her own. He nodded seriously and she could feel the scrape of sand against her thigh. The poor little fellow was coated from neck to toe with salt and sand. Her heart pumped with affection. With their dark, wet hair sleeked back, their deeply tanned skin and their brown eyes fixed on one another, Cara thought someone might pass and think they were mother and son, the resemblance was so strong.

"I'm starving, too," Brett said to the boy, coming up to rub the top of Cooper's head with his hand. He rested it atop Cara's shoulder. Cooper turned his head to squint up at the tall man as though trying to figure things out.

Cara felt part of a strange tableau, one that depicted a typical American family celebrating an American holiday. She hadn't believed in such visions, or the feelings of sweetness and contentment that were running through her at the moment.

"Okeydokey," Cara replied to both her guys. "We have a mountain of food waiting for you up at the house. If everyone will just grab something to carry, we'll head up for hot showers, clean clothes and a feast. Linnea, are you ready, honey? Cooper, you can take the lead."

By the time they'd showered and changed into clean clothes, the tables were overflowing with fried chicken, steamed crabs and shrimp, corn on the cob, pickles, all kinds of greens and salads, biscuits, four pies and two cakes. Lovie lorded over the feast attending to every detail and decoration. Her wispy hair was pinned back from her face and she'd carefully applied her favorite red lipstick, which perfectly complemented her red dress.

In the twinkling fairy lights she appeared to Cara as the charming, vibrant hostess she once was. Cara thought back on all the times she'd watched her mother at the many parties her parents had given at the Charleston house. Caterers in black carried trays of delicious-smelling appetizers and champagne while her mother glided through the rooms chatting with her guests, making introductions, then whirling back into the kitchen to supervise the staff. The huge parties had been an enormous amount of work. But even though she knew her mother was exhausted, Lovie had made it appear effortless.

James and John Peterson, Emmi's sons, arrived just as they

were ready to serve. Cara greeted them warmly, trying to make them feel at ease, but they stepped into the house like condemned men. Their awkward, stiff movements spoke clearly of their eagerness to do their duty for their mother's sake, then leave as quickly as possible. Emmi's boys were tall like her and had her red hair, rangy build and green eyes. James, the eldest, was more conservative in dress and manner. He obviously spent more time in the library than on the beach because he was as bright red as a cooked lobster. In contrast, John's skin was as tanned as shoe leather and his soft hair frizzed out like an aura of spun gold.

"There you are!" Emmi called as she hurried to greet them with hugs and kisses that embarrassed them. "Toy, come on over here. There's some fellas your age I want you to meet," she called out, waving her hand to draw Toy over.

Cara felt for the girl as she ducked her head, cheeks aflame, and dragged her feet over to meet them. The boys rocked on their heels, nodded their heads curtly and mumbled their nice-to-meet-yous but their eyes glazed over. Toy kept her eyes averted and mumbled some barely audible hello.

Didn't they see how pretty she was? Cara wondered as Emmi strained to keep up the conversation. Without those bangs in her eyes, anyone who looked could see that, when she smiled, sweetness shimmered in them like the sun in an azure sky. But the two boys couldn't see beyond the bulge of her belly. They kept their gazes on the walls, the ceiling, anywhere but on Toy as she stood with her shoulders slumped and her nervous fingers plucking at her gauzy dress as though trying to conceal the obvious swelling of her belly beneath it.

Cara flashed back to a memory of being Toy's age and feeling awkward and overlooked by handsome boys like James and John—boys like Brett. The pain was still acute just to witness. She wished she could whisper in Toy's ear that it was okay, that someday it would all be different. Except she knew Toy wouldn't believe her. The sprinklers whirred in the background, emphasizing the silence that dragged on after they'd exhausted the topic of fireworks displays.

"I think it's time we all eat," Lovie announced with a loud voice, mercifully ending the torturous exchange.

Cara led the boys to the tables, away from Toy, where she removed lids and Saran Wrap and placed serving spoons in all the dishes. Once their plates were filled, the two made a beeline out of the house to the front porch where they proceeded to shovel mass amounts into their mouths as quickly as they could.

Gazing around the room she spotted Toy and Linnea sitting together on the rear porch steps—as far away from the boys as they could get. She said a mental thank you to her niece, impressed that she had sensed a wounded spirit and had the kindness of heart to keep Toy company.

Florence, Lovie and Miranda sat together on the front porch. Brett chatted with them for a while, then found his way back to Cara's side to join Emmi and Julia around the outdoor table.

As predicted, the boys left soon after eating. A cheerful, relaxed mood returned to the small group, even though everyone was aware that Palmer was absent from the family gathering. No one mentioned it, but Cara thought Lovie felt it most intensely. Something had transpired between them during his visit and she was anxious to learn what. When they'd returned from the beach she had found Lovie sitting on the porch, just staring out at the sea. Though she rallied when she saw them and made a great fuss over the children, Cara had been alarmed to see that her eyes were rimmed red, as though she'd been crying.

Julia, on the other hand, seemed to barely notice or care that

Palmer wasn't around. "Oh, he's always gone," she said airily when Cara asked her about it. Linnea didn't seem to care one way or the other and Cooper didn't even ask where his father was. He sat himself down next to Brett and allowed only this big, tall man to help him crack his crab claws. The little boy was obviously seeking a male role model. Cara wondered if Palmer had any clue as to what he was missing.

Or did Brett?

Emmi, Julia and Cara were wrapping up the last of the food and bringing out the coffee when Florence came in from the porch, her face strained with worry.

"Has anyone seen my mother?"

Cara's gaze flew about the room. "Wasn't she out on the porch with you?"

"I thought she came inside a little while ago." With a frown, she hurried down the hall to the bedrooms calling, "Mother?"

Everyone began to look for Miranda but it didn't take long to figure out she wasn't in the house. Cara felt the tension shoot skyward as everyone realized that the old woman might have wandered off in the dark somewhere. Miranda wasn't senile, but she sometimes was a bit confused.

"I'll go check my house," Flo called out as she headed for the door. "She probably just went home."

Brett went with her, but in a few minutes they returned, not even trying to conceal their worry.

"She's not there!" Flo exclaimed. "Are you sure she's not here? Have you checked everywhere?"

"I checked the grounds with the children. She's not here," replied Cara.

"Maybe we should call the police," said Emmi.

Cara heard a gasp and looked at the children's faces. The mention of the word *police* had their eyes as round as the moon. "Wait, let's just think a moment," she said, interjecting a dose of calmness. "When was the last time anyone remembers seeing her?"

"About thirty minutes ago. We were watching the sunset," answered Flo.

"Yes, she was talking about the hatchlings," Lovie added. "I remember her going on about how they like to come out an hour after the sun goes down."

"What next?"

"We came inside to get coffee," replied Flo. "I was talking with her about whether the caffeine would get her too jazzed but she wanted some so she'd stay awake for the fireworks. Both Lovie and I came in the kitchen and chatted with you a few minutes while the coffee perked—gee, not long. When we came back out to the porch with her cup, she wasn't there."

"So you didn't see her come into the house?" asked Cara.

"Isn't the first nest due to hatch any day now?" Emmi asked. "She always likes to go down and check the nests."

Relief flooded Flo's face. "That's got to be where she went. I could bean her for not telling anyone. Lord, I just hope she doesn't get lost on the way." She turned on her heel and trotted back toward the door.

"Which street is it, 6th or 27th?" Emmi asked, following her.

"She only cares about the nests on her stretch of beach, so it must be 6th," Lovie replied as she followed them out the door.

Cara hurried out to the porch to catch up. "Mama, are you sure you're up to going out again? It's been a full day and you were pretty tired."

"You bet I'm sure," she declared, her eyes dancing. "Miranda has a sixth sense about these things. If she took off like a bird dog for the nest, then I'll wager there'll be a boil tonight. Nothing can keep me away! I'll be fine. Don't you worry about me." The screen door slammed as she followed them down the stairs and disappeared around the corner.

In the house, Julia grabbed hold of her children.

"Oh no, you don't. Not without your sweatshirts. Those mosquitoes will eat you alive." When they opened their mouths to argue, she said firmly, "No sweatshirts, no go."

They weren't about to waste time arguing. They tugged their sweatshirts from the knapsacks, then ran out the door with Julia in hot pursuit.

Cara heard the swish and slam of the doors and felt a shiver of excitement at the prospect of the first hatching tonight. She hurried to the porch to grab a couple of beach blankets, her cap and the trusty red bucket of supplies. "You coming, Toy?" she called out.

"No, y'all go ahead. I think I've had enough beach for one day. I'll man the fort."

"You sure, now?" Brett asked solicitously as he passed her at the door. "You don't mind being alone?"

She blushed a bit at his concern and shook her head. "No, I'll be fine. I'm tired."

Brett caught up with Cara on the porch. Grabbing hold of the blankets in one hand, he scooped her into an impulsive, possessive kiss that set her spinning, words like lost and found running through her head.

"Been wanting to do that all day," he said with a low voice as he drew away. Then he took her hand and together they took off down the stairs, running like kids to catch up with the rest of the gang.

Cara and Brett found them all standing with Miranda at the 6th Avenue nest. Most of the holiday revelers were farther down the beach by the pier waiting for the fireworks to begin. Flo's finger was wagging as she lectured her mother about leaving without telling anyone. The children were dancing on tiptoe, getting all worked up about the prospect of seeing baby turtles. Lovie was on her knees bent over the nest, peering at it through the eerie red glow of her turtle flashlight.

"What's the verdict?" Cara asked, sinking to her knees beside her in the sand.

"See that depression?" Lovie asked, pointing her light to reveal a dip in the sand. "That's a clear sign something's going on down there. Children, do stop jumping around so close to the nest. They'll never come out if you keep that up."

Miranda came closer to peer at the nest in the light. "Why don't you stick your fingers down in there and see if the turtles are on top."

Lovie shook her head. "Let's just let them be. They'll come out in their own good time."

"Aw, go on and hurry things a bit," Julia said as she came near. "You used to help them out. The children are all excited."

"This isn't a show for the children," Lovie replied to a chorus of groans. "I used to do a few things I shouldn't have but we've all learned. Remember the time they came out with their lunch pails out? I still feel bad about that."

"You always bring up that one time." Flo was resentful since it had happened on her watch. "We covered them right back up."

"More than once…" Lovie countered.

"What's a lunch pail?" asked Cooper.

Brett patted the blanket beside him as he stretched his legs out beside Cara, who could sense the teacher in Brett about to slip out. Cooper lost no time claiming the spot beside Brett.

"Well now," he began in a slow drawl. "The lunch pail is a little yolk sack that gives the hatchling the energy it needs to make it to the Gulf Stream. If he comes out of the nest before he's eaten his lunch, he's doomed. You see, once the turtles hatch and run to the sea, they do what's called a swimming frenzy. They swim without eating for twenty-four hours. That is, if they're lucky enough not to get eaten themselves by ghost crabs and raccoons on the beach or fish and birds in the sea."

"It's like a prison break," Emmi added for the children. "The baby turtles are just sitting there under the sand, waiting for the signal, while one little guy sneaks out to check things out. Then once they get the all clear—boom! They come scrambling out of the tunnel and run madly to their escape in the sea before they get caught by the crabs."

"You mean the crabs eat the turtles?" Cooper was horrified.

Brett nodded. "Hatchlings are a gourmet meal for them. They can feel the movement in the sand and tiptoe close. Then the crab chases the little guy and nips him in the tendons with his pincers." Brett reached out to nip at Cooper with two fingers. He squealed in delight and terror and tried to wriggle away. Brett held on firm, laughing and acting out the rest of the tale. "They hold on tight as they drag the poor baby turtle down into the hole, and the very first thing they do is gobble up the eyes." Cooper squealed again as Brett pretended to be pinching out his eyes.

"Thanks, Brett," Julia said with exaggeration. "Now I'll have to deal with nightmares."

"Don't you fret. They'll be too tired to dream tonight," Lovie said.

"Well, that's one lecture I slept through in high school," Cara said with a teasing jab in Brett's ribs. "Say, Cooper, do you want to get those crabs?"

"Yeah!" His face was furious as he scrambled to his feet.

"Me, too," exclaimed Linnea.

Brett joined them. They showed Cooper how to stuff the crab holes with wrack and sand. He took to the task like the pirate he was at heart, jabbing the spartina sticks in like swords, shouting, "Take that. And that!" Linnea swept the beach clear of debris and filled ruts with graceful, waltzing movements.

"Like this, Aunt Cara?" she asked, eager to please.

"That's right, sweetie. You're doing it just right."

Soon, all was in readiness for the hatchlings' race to the sea. They gathered around the nest again to sit and wait in an expectant silence as the moon rose higher in the sky, its light shimmering brightly on the water.

Toy stood before the small mirror over her dresser and brushed her hair, her movements slow and dejected. If she just saw the top of her body in the mirror—just the head, neck and shoulders—then she didn't look all that different from the richer girls who lived around here. Her new golden-brown hair color was real natural-looking and she liked the way it fell softly to her shoulders.

She set the brush on the bureau and, looking down, traced the curve of her belly. But this was all those boys saw, she knew. In their eyes, she wasn't a teenager anymore. All they saw was someone pregnant, used up and discarded.

"Do you think I'm special?" she asked her baby, stroking the mound of her belly. She hated the tear that rolled down her cheek and wiped it away angrily. What good was crying? She had gotten herself into this mess. She might as well try to get herself out of it.

Lying on the bed were her schoolbooks. A few weeks earlier Cara had knocked on her door, then come in carrying them and a brochure about the GED program. She'd sat with Toy every night at the table and gone over the lessons while Lovie sat with her feet up on the sofa and listened. When Toy passed her first test, Cara hooted with delight. "When you graduate, you can go to college!" She'd said it like she really meant it, too. Not like she was just being nice.

Toy stretched out and opened her algebra book. She didn't tell Cara this, but she'd never even dreamed of college. College didn't hold anything for girls like her. She had a baby to take care of. She needed to get a job.

She was tired after all the party preparations and the sunshine, but she'd not done much studying in the past couple of days so she'd just better "buckle down and do it," as Cara liked to say. Toy had learned a lot of Cara's sayings. Things like "putting one's nose to the grindstone" and "not procrastinating." Toy grinned, saying the word aloud. "Procrastinate." It was one of those big words she'd always wanted to use and she liked best that it meant exactly what she wanted to say. She'd always thought big words were just for showing off, but now she knew that one right word could say what five or six little ones couldn't. And that thought helped to lift her spirits.

A while later, while solving simultaneous equations, Toy was distracted by the sound of a car pulling up on the gravel outside. She lay still, her ear cocked, but she didn't hear anything more. She felt cozy and secure in her little room and wasn't afraid. There were lots of folks parking in the road to watch the fireworks from the beach. She returned to her algebra, chewing her lip and wishing Cara was home to help her with this problem. She worked on until a short while later she heard the unmistakable popping and thunderous exploding of fireworks.

She stopped working to listen closely. They sounded real close. Maybe she'd be able to see them if she stood out on the deck. Just as she stepped outside, another boom rumbled and color exploded in the sky. She leaned against the railing and arched on tiptoe to look out over the eastern sky. The fireworks were coming from Sullivan's Island. Two more fired off in rapid succession.

"Oh, baby, if only you could see this," she said excitedly.

"All I need is to see you."

Toy startled at the voice coming from the darkness. Her heart pumped so hard it sounded like fireworks exploding in her head. She didn't need any light to tell her who it was.

"Darryl!"

She heard a shuffling in the sand and gravel and there he was, plain as day. He stood at the bottom of the porch steps with his hands in his pockets and one foot on the first step. She knew she should be afraid or mad, but all she felt was the same traitorous shiver of pleasure she always felt whenever she looked into those baby-blue eyes.

It had been so long since she'd seen him, since a man had looked at her the way he was looking at her now. Not with boredom or disgust, like those Peterson boys had looked at her, but in a way that made her feel the way a woman wanted to feel. He looked good, too. Cleaned up. His brown hair was shorter, cut in a softer style that curled around his neck and open shirt collar in a sexy way. His jeans were dark blue without any stains or holes in them and, looking at the boot on the step, she could see it had real fancy detailing in the spit-polished leather.

"You did something different with your hair," he said.

Her hand darted to self-consciously tuck a piece behind her ear and she blushed, knowing he was studying her with the same intensity. "I thought I'd try something a little more... mature." She'd almost said grown-up but thought of the better word.

"Well, it's different, that's for sure. You look, I don't know... real nice."

Pleasure washed over her, soothing her wounded pride. She remembered how nice he could be and she relaxed.

"What are you doing here?" she asked, shaking her head in disbelief. "I told you not to come."

"I didn't mean to cause you no trouble," he answered. "I have a gig at the Windjammer on the island later, and I thought I'd stop by and see how you were doing. That's all, Toy. I swear."

There was something in his eyes that drew her in. A lost, little-boy look that made her want to mother him. She thought of words like *lost* and *found,* believing there was someone out there for everyone. "The Windjammer's a real good gig."

He moved up a few steps, taking them slow. "Yeah. Me and the guys feel like it's a break. Never know who's in the audience around here. This might be the one." He was standing right in front of her now, staring down at her with his hands at his sides. He wasn't very tall, not even as tall as Cara, but in her mind she'd thought of him as big. She could smell his cologne and her stomach fluttered with desire.

"I was thinking how you were always there for me, Toy, whenever an important gig came up. My little good luck charm."

The humidity rose like a mist around them. She could hardly breathe.

"Be there for me tonight, baby."

Her eyes closed and she leaned into him.

Her belly touched him first. Her eyes flew open and, looking down at the obstacle between them, she laughed nervously. She was relieved beyond words to hear his low chuckle in the dark.

"I told you that little guy was getting between us," he said. She smiled tremulously because she didn't hear any of the meanness she'd heard before whenever he talked about the baby.

"He's getting big," she said.

"He's gonna be a big fella."

It was odd them talking about the baby—their baby—as if they knew it was a boy. But suddenly she knew it was and she saw in her mind a little Darryl. She brought her hand to her belly to stroke it. She felt a little choked up standing close with her baby and the father. It was almost like being a family.

"When's he going to be born?"

"September. Around the fifteenth. He'll be a Virgo."

"Is that good?"

"They're all good, silly. A Virgo is smart and good with details. I'm a Gemini. Sensitive."

"I hear that." He stepped closer, narrowing the space. "What am I?" His voice was husky.

She licked her lips again. "A Leo. That's the lion." For no reason she understood, that suddenly seemed terribly sexy.

"I miss you, Toy. Nothing's the same without you." He reached up just to skim her arms gently with his fingertips.

She felt the calluses from his guitar strings on her pliant skin and a flood of memories played back like the lyrics of a beloved song. "I miss you, too," she said softly, reverently.

He lowered his head and the pull was strong. She tilted hers and closed her eyes. She felt his lips cover hers and press softly, and in her heart she saw only the Darryl that loved her.

"Do you want to come hear me play?" he asked when they pulled apart.

The invitation was unfathomable. To go out. To a club. Like old times. A chance to not be old before her time.

"Just give me a minute."

She hurried to her room to brush her hair and put on some

lip gloss. Grabbing her purse from the bed, she turned off the light and hurried back to Darryl. The algebra book lay open on the bed, forgotten.

seventeen

Male and female turtles are similar except for the male's long tail and longer claws on the flippers used to grip a female during mating. Courtship is tempestuous. Males may fight with each other in pursuit of a female.
When receptive, the female accepts her suitor.

The moon was ghostly in the sky as clouds and fog rolled in. It had been a long night on the beach. The firework show had been loads of fun and they'd all oohed and aahed along with the children. Fortunately, the turtles were smart enough to wait until the crowds had left before emerging from their nest. The clouds had dimmed the moonlight and smoke from the firework shells lingered in the sky. They'd hardly been able to see the hatchlings as they scrambled down the beach into the sea.

Yet emerge they did. Cara had knelt close to the nest and counted nearly eighty vigorous baby turtles as they tumbled out. It was nearly midnight, and though her limbs were tired, her mind was alive with exhilaration.

"Caretta?"

Cara turned her head to peer through the darkness toward the tall shadowy form approaching along the shoreline. As

Brett drew nearer she could just make out the chiseled angles of his jaw and chin in the shadows.

"Is that the last of them?" she asked.

He came to stand beside her at the water's edge. "I think so."

She looked again at the sea. Even in the mist the edges of the surf were tinged white with light. "They were so cute." She laughed lightly. "I suppose *cute* is hardly the word a naturalist would use to describe a baby turtle."

"Neither is *baby,* but they both seem to apply."

She liked the way he was never patronizing. "I was thinking of the night Mama and I saw a turtle lay her eggs in the sand. The moon was full and bright that night. We could see everything as though it were dusk. She was enormous and these little hatchlings were so small. It's amazing to think that they'll someday grow so large."

"If they survive. Only one in a thousand will."

"That few? It seems so sad."

"It's nature's way."

"I suppose." Cara wrapped her arms around herself. "Sometimes nature seems rather cruel."

They both knew she was thinking again of her mother's illness and there was little either of them could or wanted to say on that matter. They stared out at the sea for a few moments. The tide was coming in and the water was stretching up to lap their toes, deliciously warm.

"Care for a walk?" he asked.

Cara looked up the beach toward the nest. Julia, Miranda and the children were already gone. Squinting, she could see the shadowy forms of her mother and Flo just leaving the nest. The night was soft, moist and inviting and she didn't care to go home. And yet...she was hesitant. Brett was an enigma to her. When she'd first felt the zing of attraction she'd expected them to fall into the usual pattern of casual sex and a quick farewell. He hadn't allowed that to happen, however. Just when she thought she'd figured him out he did something to surprise her. And that made him all the more intriguing. Not to mention he was the only man she'd ever met who could provide a meal with a bit of string and a hook.

"Okay," she replied.

He took her hand and they began walking along the surf line. She gradually matched her own long-legged pace to his in an easy rhythm. In the distance, the stretch of white lights along the pier looked like low stars in the velvety blackness.

It all seemed terribly romantic. Very much like a postcard of two lovers strolling along the beach, except, of course, they weren't lovers. Pity, she thought, as the silence became erotic. She grew intensely aware of the feel of his hand over hers, as though every neuron in her body was focused on those few inches of skin. Each time their hips bumped it sent shivers down her spine. Each ruffle of the breeze seemed a caress.

"Do you walk out here often? At night, I mean?" she asked, then felt silly for the question. "But of course you do. You live here."

"Actually, it's because I live here that I don't. I guess I take the ocean for granted. Look up there," he said, pointing to a row of houses up the beach. Even at this late hour, a number of them had lights still shining indoors. "See the gray flickering lights? They're all inside watching TV. I'm not the only one who takes it for granted."

"My condo faces Lake Michigan and I have to admit, I rarely stand at the window to look out at the lake anymore, either. But I know it's there. I sense its presence. Every once in a while I look up and really see it. It takes me by surprise how beautiful it is. Like a gift. I appreciate it then. It may only be a moment, but in that moment my life is better. I suppose it's the same for those people, too."

"Do you miss Chicago?"

She had to think about this answer. She hadn't really thought about Chicago in a while. Not since her conversation with Adele. It was as though she'd closed some mental door to that part of her life and opened the door to her life here on the island.

"I can't say that I do," she replied honestly. "I suppose I'll come to miss the city. The excitement, the variety. The pace." She chuckled lightly. "I've really slowed down. I'm still busy but I'm not in such a hurry."

"No need to be. Life is better enjoyed at a slow pace."

"I'm not surprised you think so," she said as a gentle jibe.

"Oh? What makes you say that?"

"Your general attitude. Your choice of jobs. The way you approach sex."

He stopped abruptly. "What?"

She could have bitten her tongue. She tugged on his arm to keep walking but he wouldn't budge. Dropping his hand she looked at her feet while kicking sand. He was waiting for an answer.

"Well, things between us haven't exactly been speeding along, have they?"

"I thought they'd been going pretty good." He sounded a bit hurt.

"They have," she hastened to assure him. "We're getting to be good friends. Really good *f-r-i-e-n-d-s*," she said.

Silence.

"I was hoping by now we'd be something a little more," she said.

"You were?"

That definitely was not a wounded tone. She took heart.

"What did you have in mind?" he asked, taking a step closer.

"Well," she drawled. "We've been seeing each other for a while and though I've been having a wonderful time, really, I was hoping it would lead to something a bit more...fun."

"Were you? Interesting."

He paused to look down at his foot. She saw the top of his head, his wiry hair so thick she doubted she could get her hands through it. When he raised his eyes again, his gaze pinned her. "And you thought I wasn't hoping for the same thing?"

She dropped all pretense at humor and spoke honestly. Almost shyly. "I wasn't sure. I've wondered if you find me attractive. Or whether I've come on too strong. I know I can be blunt and I was worried I might have turned you off."

"Why would you think that?" He sounded genuinely surprised.

"Well, you never... I mean—" Damn this was so hard. She could feel her cheeks burning. What an idiot she was. She'd had multiple lovers over the years and would have called herself jaded. But here she was, blushing like a ridiculous schoolgirl.

"For the past several weeks you've been kissing me but nothing more," she said straight out, wanting the horrid exchange to be over.

He stood in the darkness, just inches away, so close she could see his lips curve into a slow, pleased grin. "Cara," he said, reaching up to tuck a tendril of hair behind her ear. He let his fingertips skim her jawline, then rest at her chin. "I'm courting you."

She could only look at him in a daze. *Courting?* Had she heard correctly? Did men still court women? Anywhere today? The concept was utterly beguiling. She was bowled over. Charmed. Damn, she was grinning from ear to ear.

"You are?"

"Is that a problem for you?"

"No! It's just… I didn't understand." Then, because she felt the need to disguise her awkwardness, she said as a gentle tease, "Is that another rule of yours? A Lowcountry gentleman courts his lady?"

"Depends on the lady."

Her grin widened. She liked that answer enormously.

"What are you doing tomorrow?" he asked.

"Why?"

"Want to go camping?"

She looked at him warily. "Where?"

"Does it matter?"

"Maybe. Not to some hammock. I don't want to sleep with alligators and snakes."

He barked out a laugh. "I've someplace better in mind. Say you'll come."

She was nervous, but the way he said it, with his head cocked and his eyes gleaming, was so charmingly boyish she couldn't resist.

"Where are we headed?" Cara asked Brett the following morning as he nosed the boat out of the dock. He'd packed the small boat with even more gear than before.

"Capers Island," he answered.

Cara released a smile. Capers Island. It was where they'd gone the first time they'd met. She'd been enchanted by the island ever since and had hoped he'd take her back there someday.

The current was brisk as they headed out and the weather warm and clear. Cara felt the sun sting her exposed shoulders and cheeks as she sat at the bow. They sped across the familiar waterway toward the small barrier island tucked away along the Carolina coastline.

Capers Island was deserted. Its pristine line of beach lay before them undisturbed except for shorebirds that flocked together in the distance. Brett carried the gear up a large, flat dune that rose like a plateau over Boneyard Beach. Together they pitched the tent on a high spot that was protected from harsh winds by pines yet still caught the offshore breezes.

Neither of them was in a talkative mood, so they spent the day in a companionable peace, just lying in the sun, recharging their batteries. When the mood struck, they swam in the silky waters of the sea, then lay in the sand and let the sunshine do its work. She felt the sun melting her bones and her brain, making it impossible to think about anything for too long or too hard.

"Everything is so simple here," she said to Brett, turning over and resting her chin on her arms. "There are no big decisions to be made, no one needing me for anything or asking to have a problem solved. No money to be earned. Just complete and total bliss. Could we stay here and never return, like those two kids in that movie? You know, the one where they grow up gorgeous together and make great shell jewelry and become lovers?"

"Never saw it. Sounds like a chick flick."

She leaned over to pinch his arm. "Such a stereotype. That's like me saying men only watch movies with spy toys or lots of blood and guts."

"Yeah. So?"

"You're hopeless."

"How about *Tarzan?*"

"Good movie."

"Saw that one. And that's a movie about a guy who survived alone in the jungle," he said smugly.

"Yeah, but he didn't *live* until Jane showed up."

Brett laughed loudly and climbed to his feet. Then he took her hand and pulled her to her feet.

"Come, Jane. Tarzan hungry."

Her high-pitched laughter scattered the birds at the shoreline.

He brought her to a small creek that cut a gash into the island like a knife. She stood nearby and watched as he grabbed hold of a net with his hands and teeth. After getting a good purchase, he hurled the net into the air with a graceful, full body movement. The net opened up like a flower, spread out over the glistening water and descended with a whispered splash. It was pure poetry in motion. And as he repeated the toss, she witnessed the natural athleticism that had won him as many awards, accolades and scholarships over the years as shrimp he harnessed in the nets.

He *was* rather like Tarzan, she thought. His build, his affinity for nature, his stoicism. But was she at all like Jane? She thought not. She liked to think she could be clever and brave like Jane. And she was learning to do a few things in the wild. After all, she was camping, wasn't she?

But to stay with one man in the wilderness forever and ever? Cara didn't think she could. She was a city girl. She couldn't give up forever the civilized world of emails, lattes, movies and restaurants after work.

Nonetheless, she had fun playing out her role as she lowered a mangy-looking chicken neck by a string into the creek the way Brett had taught her. After several tosses and drags, she netted a few crabs that emerged dripping from the water hanging tenaciously to the chicken neck by their claws. It was hardly the poetry of Brett's net casting but it was very satisfying nonetheless to bring home her contribution to the feast.

When the sun began to lower, they scattered across the

beach like ghost crabs to gather driftwood for a campfire. Once the fire was raging, they boiled shrimp and crab and drank chilled wine from the cooler. And when their meal was done, and the full moon rose at last to take her place among the stars, Brett took Cara's hand and raised her to her feet.

"What are we doing?" she asked.

"Dancing."

"You're kidding. I'm not very good," she worried aloud, backing off. "I've got two left feet."

"Come on."

"Brett, I haven't danced the shag since high school!"

"It's like riding a bicycle. You never forget."

"Okay, I confess, I never really learned."

"Then I'll teach you."

He bent to turn on the tape player he'd brought along. There was a loud click, then the island's silence was interrupted by the instantly recognizable sound of beach music: "I Love Beach Music," "Sixty Minute Man," "My Girl," "What Kind of Fool Do You Think I Am?" and "Sweet Carolina Girls."

"I never danced with you in high school," he said. "I thought I'd make up for it tonight."

She laughed lightly. "I feel like I'm sixteen again."

"I'm glad I didn't know you at sixteen. You might not have liked me very much back then."

"You're very endearing when you're serious," she teased.

He brought his hand up to move a stray tendril from her brow. "I am being serious. I'm glad I waited to meet you now, Caretta."

He looked into her eyes for a long time and she felt a moment's panic that he could see through her ruse of joking and know that with him she felt uncharacteristically vulnerable and unsure. Like she was indeed back in high school and on a date with this incredible guy she'd been dreaming about

and searching for all her life, only she'd been looking in all
the wrong places.

He took her hand again and guided her in the intricate
footsteps of the shag. He was amazingly fluid for a man his
size and he guided her along the sand, humming the tune as
he moved his feet.

"Now turn. The other way! That's right," he said, lavish-
ing praise. "Who says you're not a good dancer?"

She giggled and gradually got the hang of it. Beach music
was an odd blend of rhythm and blues, band and pop music
that made her feet move and her hips sway. Between the heavy
backbeat and his lavish praise, she lost her self-consciousness
and fell into the rhythm of the music. As they danced, they
laughed and remembered details of dances they'd both gone
to in high school, but never together. They took turns calling out the names of the great groups they could still recall: the Tams, the Embers, the Clovers, the Zodiacs and the
Catalinas. Then they said the names of old friends, favorite
stomping grounds, rumors they'd heard, laughing still more
at threading together the six degrees of separation. She could
hear her mother's words echo in her brain, "Where are you
from?" As they held hands and danced and told stories, they
were knitting their separate but similar histories together—
left to right, knit and pearl—to create this perfect night under
the moon and stars.

And when at last he stopped dancing and looked into her
eyes with a message of longing and need, he didn't have to
ask. He only had to lead the way to the billowing white tent
perched high on the sand dune, nestled between the pines.

eighteen

The hatchlings are drawn to the brightest light. In nature,
this is the white ligh of the moon or stars over the ocean.
Artificial lighting can confuse the hatchlings and lead them
to death in tangles of beach grass or on busy streets.

"You gonna eat them fries?"

Toy looked down at the basket of French fries slathered with
ketchup. The baby was taking up so much room these days
that her stomach was squeezed like a pancake. Even though
she was always hungry, always nibbling, she couldn't eat much
at one sitting. She pushed the basket across the table to Darryl.

"No. You can have them."

It was a Friday night and the Burger King was crowded,
mostly with overflow from the movie and tourists with tired,
cranky kids. Toy watched as a bit of ketchup dribbled down
Darryl's chin.

"What're you looking at?"

"You've got some ketchup," she said, pointing. "Right
there." As he wiped it off with his finger, she remembered the
sandwiches her mother had made for her lunch when things
were so tough they couldn't afford sandwich meat. Her mother
had made a game of it, putting little dollops of ketchup on

white bread and calling them button sandwiches. Instead of
feeling poor, Toy had thought the sandwiches were special.

"I figure we should leave on September 20," he said, ram-
ming another fry into his mouth.

Toy noticed that he was talking with his mouth full and
that his T-shirt had a tear in it, right in the seam by the sleeve.
She noticed things like that now but didn't mention them
because she didn't want to make him mad. He was being so
sweet lately, like when they'd first started dating, telling her
how much he loved her and all. He didn't tell her she was
pretty anymore, but that was okay. She knew it was because
she was pregnant.

"Do you think you'll be ready to go by then?"

Toy frowned down at her chocolate milkshake, knowing
he was really asking whether the baby would be born by then
and if she'd be free to travel. Even though he wasn't snarly
about the baby anymore, he still said that he didn't want it.
He thought the baby would slow them down. Darryl's band
had made their first CD and were heading west to California
expecting to stake their claim to fame.

She wasn't lying to Darryl exactly when she told him that
she'd give the baby up and go with him to California. She was
just giving him time to get used to the idea of being a daddy
and them being a family. She wasn't lying to Cara and Miss
Lovie, either. Ever since the Fourth of July she'd been telling
them she was going to the movies a lot. She just didn't tell
them that she was going with Darryl. They were little white
lies that didn't hurt nobody.

Besides, she didn't know what else to do. She had this baby
coming and Cara was leaving for Chicago and Miss Lovie was
dying and Darryl was going to California. She had to have
someone to be with! Everything was such a mess, and if she
thought about it she got shaky and teary eyed. All she knew

was that she loved her baby and she'd just have to wait until he was born. Everything would turn out okay. It just had to.

"Hel-lo? Ding dong!" Darryl tossed a fry at her. "What's the matter with you tonight? I keep asking questions and you just sit there."

"I was thinking," she replied, brushing her breast where the fry landed. It lay there as though on a shelf. "It's not even August. I don't know about September yet."

"Hey, it's the end of July already, okay? September is around the corner. I gotta make plans."

"The doctor says the baby could come two weeks before or two weeks after my due date. Leaving on the twentieth is cutting it pretty close. Besides, I can't just have a baby then hop in a car and go on a trip. I'm going to need a few days to rest."

"You can rest in the car. You'll be sittin' down for a couple thousand miles. Jesus Christ," he swore loudly.

"Don't take the Lord's name in vain!"

It was automatic now; she'd said it without thinking. She darted a nervous glance up at Darryl's face.

He was looking at her like he couldn't believe what he'd heard. Then he just laughed and shook his head. "I heard that pregnant ladies start actin' all crazy and I guess it's true."

She slumped in relief and ducked her head to take a sip of her shake.

"I dunno, babe," he said with a dubious shake of his head. A brown curl slipped over his forehead. "The guys are getting anxious. They're ready to shove off right now."

"Let 'em go," she muttered.

"Can't. We're all driving together in Hal's van. Might not matter, though. Hal's got to square things with his old lady, too."

"Is Amber having a baby?"

Darryl looked at her like she was crazy. "Hell no," he said angrily. "She's not that dumb."

Toy felt a sharp pain and rubbed her belly.

"Damn, I'll be glad when this baby thing's all over," he said, shifting in his seat and stretching his arms out along the length of the booth. Then narrowing his eyes he asked, "What's the matter now?"

Toy sat far back in the booth. "Nothin'."

His sigh rattled in his chest. "Hey, I'm sorry. I'm being bad. It's just because I miss you, is all. Miss bein' with you." His gaze deepened. "A man can only eat so many fries."

She laughed a little and gently kicked his leg under the table. "I miss you, too. A lot. The doctor says we can, you know, be together a week or so after the baby's born."

"You wanna know what I really hate? I hate this dropping you off at night at some house way out there. I'm thinking... maybe you should come back with me now."

"I can't," she blurted out. "I mean, it wouldn't feel right leaving Miss Lovie. And there's less than a month till the baby's due. Anyway, you hate to see me like this. You've said so enough times. I'm only gonna get bigger and grouchier and I'll be driving you crazy."

The corner of his mouth rose in a sneer. "You got that right."

"It's only for a few more weeks. Then we'll be together. You, me and..." Her voice trailed off. She held her breath.

Darryl caught the innuendo and his expression shifted. He dropped his arms and leaned forward across the narrow table. "You and me, period," he replied, a warning in his voice. "Like it always was and always will be. Just you and me."

Toy felt a cry bubbling up in her chest and she had to sip on her straw real hard to keep it from coming out.

★ ★ ★

At the beach house, Cara and her mother sat together on the front porch, holding hands in silence while watching a particularly spectacular sunset. Cara sipped her white wine. Her mother rocked gently in the rocking chair drinking tea. Toy had gone to the Towne Center for a movie again, so they were alone.

They sat and watched the colors deepen in the sky as the daytime song of birds hushed. The sight had moved Cara into an introspective mood, as sunsets were wont to do. How strange it was to sit so comfortably with her mother, feeling a quiet peace. And how nice.

She glanced over to look at Lovie. Her mother's high cheekbones caught the shadows of the twilight making her appear regal and serene. What was running through her mind as she looked out at the sunset? Cara wondered to herself. What did a woman who faced the sunset of her life think about? Cara knew that one day her own death would be imminent. How would she handle it? The uncertainty caused her to shiver.

"Are you cold?" Lovie asked.

"No," she replied softly.

"There's a crispness in the air."

"Must be you, Mama. I'm sweltering in this heat. The bugs have been nasty on the beach."

Lovie sighed. "Hope I'm still here to see the butterflies as they come through."

"Hmm..." Cara uttered, unable to reply.

They rocked back and forth in their chairs as the ocean roared loudly in the distance.

"What are you thinking?" Cara asked after a while.

"Me? Nothing profound, I assure you. Nothing much at all. I was simply looking out and thinking how very long the pink fingers of this sunset are tonight. See? They stretch

across the whole sky, embracing it." She sighed and rocked.
"Most comforting."

"How is it comforting?"

"Why, it makes me think of God, dear."

Cara stared out as the pink slowly deepened to rose, then
purple and then slipped soundlessly into the thin black line
of the horizon.

"I'm not certain I believe there is a God," Cara said at last.

"How can you say that? You were raised to believe in God."

"It was easier to just say, 'Yes, I believe,' whenever anyone
asked. But inside, I've always wondered."

"I would find that very frightening."

"I find the thought of hell very frightening. There's the
rub."

"The solution is simple, dear. You just have to love God
more than you fear hell. My faith has been my solace and
my strength through some pretty rough times. I can't get to
church often these days but working in the garden is a form
of prayer, as is listening to music, arranging flowers, sewing
a seam or just humming."

"But what if you don't have faith?"

"Faith isn't something you wait to happen to you, Cara.
Nor is it something you can study for, or work for or negoti-
ate for at some bargaining table. Paul wrote that faith doesn't
come to you. It is a gift from God."

"We're back to square one. How can you be so certain
there is a God?"

Lovie offered an old-soul smile. "Cara, dear, look at the
sky! Sunsets are daily proof that God exists."

The August moon rose high and the ocean shimmered. On
shore, the porch lights from a few houses shone as bright and
clear as the twinkling stars.

And the Turtle Ladies were ticked off.

"I'm going to bean those people with their darn porch lights burning so bright," Flo said with a disgusted snarl.

The Turtle Team was babysitting another nest. The offshore breezes were still and the mosquitoes and no-see-ums were wicked. They all had bites around their ankles and bottles of repellent were passing hands.

"It's the same house I went to the other night," Flo went on, slapping lotion on her legs. "I smiled and told them, in as nice a way as I knew how, to please turn off those outside lights facing the beach. But look at it! Still all lit up like a Christmas tree."

"The baby turtles will head straight for it."

"Whose house it it?" asked Emmi.

"There are renters in there now."

Emmi took her turn with the repellent. "Most of the renters I've talked to about the lights are excited by the possibility of seeing hatchlings while on vacation. They're happy to do anything they can to help out. They just need to be told."

"My dander is up after yesterday," Cara snapped.

"Were the hatchlings really crawling up to the street?"

"It was a disaster. The police got a call about 5:00 a.m. from someone saying there were hatchlings getting smashed in the street. Then the police called Lovie, who woke me and Flo up, and we raced right over. It was pitiful. We searched for hours—way back in the dunes in all the grass clear up to the street. We picked up fifteen dead hatchlings and twenty or so live ones."

"Barely alive," Flo said, clearly upset. "The poor things had been scrambling for hours when they should have been swimming. We brought the live ones to the ocean but they were pretty tired and I doubt they'll make it. I hate to think how many more got snatched by ghost crabs or just died from exposure."

"So forgive me if I'm mad," Cara said, slapping another mosquito.

"Okay, I'll go up one more time and ask them to turn off their outside lights," said Flo with a groan, climbing to her feet. "We don't want to appear inhospitable. You stay here, Mother, and keep an eye on the nest for me. I'll be right back."

"I'm not going anywhere," Miranda replied.

Cara chuckled at Miranda's tenacity. This was the fourth hatching on "her" stretch of beach and she'd not missed one of them.

"The stars are real bright tonight, Aunt Cara." Linnea leaned against her shoulder. "I think the baby turtles will find their way no matter what. Don't you?"

Cara smiled down at her sweet, expectant face. Linnea had come for several visits and they'd bonded. Cooper had grown bored with sitting quietly by a nest with a bunch of ladies and opted to stay home, but Linnea liked sitting by the nests with her aunt. They'd also gone shopping together, painted their nails, baked cookies and just cuddled with Lovie at night on the cushy sofa reading their favorite books. Cara hadn't known that holding a child in her arms was one of the most fulfilling feelings in the world. Nor had she suspected that she could love a little girl so much.

"Do you think they'll come out tonight?"

Cara chuckled at hearing the question for the tenth time. "Maybe. Maybe not. We'll just have to see," she replied, stroking Linnea's silky hair.

Linnea wriggled away and crawled near the nest. She lowered her face close to the sand. "Come out, baby turtles. Everything is ready for you. *Please* come out." Turning her head she asked, "What time do you think they'll come out?"

"I don't know. Maybe tonight. Maybe tomorrow night."

"They're coming out all right," Linnea said categorically, then came back to Cara's side and tucked her coltish legs under her sweatshirt out of range of the pesty mosquitoes. "How did you learn so much about turtles?"

"I learned a lot from your grandmama Lovie. She taught most of us everything we know."

Linnea's expression grew serious and she traced squiggles in the sand with her forefinger. "Is Grandmama Lovie going to die?"

The question caught Cara by surprise; she didn't know what to say. She had no experience with this kind of thing. She looked around for help but everyone's eyes were averted. It seemed no one wanted to pursue this taboo topic. Cara looked at her niece's expectant face and waved her closer, putting her arm around the child's shoulders.

"Yes," she replied honestly. "Your grandmama is dying."

"I thought so. I heard Mama and Daddy talking about it. Except Daddy says she's not. Are you sure she is?"

"I'm sorry, sweetie, but yes. I'm sure."

Linnea thought about this for a moment. "Then why does Daddy say she isn't?"

Cara sighed, wondering why herself. "Some people have a hard time accepting it."

"Oh." She paused. "Why is she dying?"

"She has cancer."

"Does it hurt?"

"Sometimes, but not too much." *Yet,* she thought with a shiver.

"When will she die?"

"I don't know exactly. It's like with the turtle nest. It happens when it's supposed to happen."

"Oh."

"Honey, didn't your mama talk to you about this?"

"No."

"I see." Julia was apparently skirting the issue as well. Cara didn't want to overstep her bounds but it was clear Linnea had questions that needed answering. "Do you understand what it means to die?"

"Of course I do," Linnea replied with preadolescent pique. "It means she's going to Heaven."

The children went to church every week so Cara assumed that at nine Linnea had a pretty good concept of God and Heaven. But death was often a gray area in children's minds. And adult minds, as well.

"Yes, but Heaven can be very hard to understand, can't it? I'm not at all sure I've got it right even at my age."

"It's not hard," she disagreed. "Heaven is where you go after you die. Everyone knows that. Of course, we don't know *exactly* what it's like. I know it's nice. Mama told me that God's up there in the clouds and he has all these beautiful houses for us to live in. If we're good on earth we get a bigger house 'cause we've earned it. I expect Grandmama will have a great, big mansion. And there are angels, of course."

"Of course," Cara replied, envying her her child's faith.

"Do you think the turtles go to Heaven when they die?"

Cara looked to Emmi and Miranda for help, but they only smiled in that way adults do when children ask such questions. "I don't know, never having been there."

"I think they do. Grandmama would be lonely without them."

Cara was alerted by the hitch in Linnea's voice. "You'll be lonely for Grandmama after she's gone, won't you?" she asked carefully.

Linnea looked down and nodded.

Cara felt a rush of love for the girl. "Oh, sweetie, me too," she replied softly, gathering Linnea in her arms. She held her and rocked her gently and kissed the top of her head. "We have to stick together, you and me. We'll be Mutt and Jeff. You can be on our Turtle Team. How's that?"

"Could I?" she asked, her spirits shooting up.

"Of course," she replied. "We'll need you on the team." She looked over to Emmi and Miranda, and knew they were all sharing the thought that Linnea would be taking her grandmother's place on the team. Cara was passing the torch. Lovie had taught her, and now it was her turn to teach Linnea.

Linnea began to rattle off the various duties she'd observed over the summer and felt she could do all by herself now. Cara half listened, amused, paying more attention to the enthusiasm in her voice and the excitement in her eyes. Such confidence. And how quickly she could shift her emotions. Nine was a glorious age to be.

"Who's that coming?" Emmi asked, sitting up.

Cara squinted in the darkness to see the small red beam of a flashlight bobbing in the distance. Just by the color of light she knew it was likely someone on the Turtle Team. Emmi dug into her beach bag to pull out her own flashlight, then made a small wave in the air with her beam to let the newcomers know where they were. The flashlight responded with a wave. All eyes were on the two shadowy figures, one very tall, one quite small.

"It's Toy and Brett," said Emmi, nudging Cara.

She smiled indulgently, but secretly she was pleased. Brett had been so busy with the business as the tourist season reached its peak that she'd hardly seen him lately.

They welcomed the newcomers warmly, scooting over on the sand dune to make room and offering repellent. Linnea—such a flirt—leaped into Brett's arms. He swung her around like a rag doll while she let out a squeal of delight. Next he went to Miranda, who preened like a schoolgirl as he paid his respects. Cara could see that young and old alike were completely won over by him.

At last he came to sit down on the dune beside her. She loved that all he had to do was rest his big hand on her knee and look into her eyes for her to know that she was the one he came for. No public show of a big hug or a kiss. That was all—and it was enough to send her heart spinning and make her dizzy as though he'd just twirled her around, too.

"Any action yet?" Toy asked as she did a funny maneuvering act to settle down in the sand. Her belly was so big now she landed with a graceless grunt and a sigh.

Cara was glad to see Toy down at the nests again. She'd missed the last several hatchings and Cara had wondered if she'd lost interest, what with her own baby due to hatch soon.

"There's a small depression in the sand but it hasn't changed in a while."

Linnea crawled close to inspect the nest for the hundredth time. "Could you check it again? *Please?*"

Cara obliged the child, flashing the red light on the nest. A gasp of surprise escaped on seeing that the little concave hole had indeed grown bigger. They all crowded close for a look. Even as they watched they saw grains of sand slip away.

Linnea squeezed her fingers tight in a prayer and said fervently, "Come on, come on, come on!"

"Looks like they might come tonight after all," Emmi said.

"They'll come," said Miranda with a definite nod of her snowy-white head.

"Oh goodie," Linnea squealed, excitement oozing from her pores.

Way up the beach, the offending bright lights on the rental house suddenly went out. There was a muffled cheer from the gang at the nest.

"Good for Flo!" Emmi said in a whispered cheer. "Just in time."

"How many do you think are in there?" Linnea wanted to know.

"We moved this nest so we know exactly how many. There are one hundred and six eggs."

"How come the mother turtle leaves the eggs?" asked Linnea.

"Turtles have done it that way for millions of years."

"I think that's so sad," the little girl said with a sigh. "Leaving all those little babies by themselves."

Toy sidled closer. "It *is* kind of sad when you think about it. I mean, not just for the babies but for the mother, too. She has to leave her babies and never see them again."

"I doubt she thinks about it much, frankly," Emmi said. "She just follows the old call of the wild."

"It's not natural for a mother to leave her babies," Toy argued.

"It's perfectly natural," Brett explained in his easy voice. "In nature there are two types of reproducers. One is the maximum investment group. In this group a lot of time and effort is spent on a small number of offspring. Like elephants and dolphins. Then there is the minimal investment group. They have lots of offspring, then leave. It's called predator glut. The purpose is to overfeed your predators so the species will survive. Frogs, fish and turtles are in this group. In biology, the individual's worth is nothing. The species is everything."

Cara gave him a pretend sock in the arm. "I can't take him anywhere."

"What?" he asked her. "I'm just answering her question."

They all started laughing and Brett said, "What?" again with wide, uncomprehending eyes.

"But what about humans?" Toy asked with persistence.

"Humans fit into both strategies," he replied. "For them it's a matter of choice."

"Isn't that what got Adam and Eve tossed out of the Garden?" Emmi quipped.

Toy didn't smile. She looked down and scratched the sand with her finger, chewing her lip. "I think it would be better if the mother stayed with her babies. Don't you?"

Cara searched her face, tuned in to the urgency in Toy's voice. She looked to Brett.

"I really couldn't say," he replied evenly. "Turtles have survived a long time in this scheme."

Toy stilled her hand, then scraped the sand clean with a single swipe.

"There's an ancient myth that says the earth rests on the back of an old turtle and this ancient turtle mama takes care of the eggs while the other mother turtle waddles off. I find that beautiful," said Emmi.

"It's kind of like the mother turtle leaves her eggs to the Turtle Ladies' care, too," Toy said, latching on to this idea. "I guess she knows her babies will be well taken care of after she's gone."

Cara shivered in the sweltering night. She was afraid for Toy as she caught a glimpse at where the young woman's train of thought was leading.

The turtle season moved into its final phase. Cara could sleep later in the morning since no one was calling to report turtle tracks. Altogether, forty nests had been laid on the Isle of Palms and Sullivan's Island.

The mornings may have grown quiet, but the nights were jumping. Cara and the rest of the Turtle Team were babysitting nests most nights, checking for crab holes, managing small crowds of tourists, often divvying up the nests due between them. Even still, some wily turtles slipped past them unnoticed, sometimes emerging en masse after an early-morning rain or, at other times, waiting until everyone had grown weary and left for home to sneak out of the nest and make their dash to the sea. Only their tiny little tracks found in the morning—dozens of them fanning out toward the sea—gave a clue to their great escape.

For Cara, it was the summer she'd always dreamed of. She loved her routine of rising early to birdsong and all the activity on the beach. She looked forward to her solitary time along the ocean as she searched for turtle tracks. She'd never felt so at peace with herself. She loved, too, the camaraderie she felt with the other ladies as they sat on the cool sand together under the different phases of the moon and just talked about anything and everything. The sea turtles may have given the group structure and focus—there were rules to follow and problems to solve—but the real strength of the group came from the bond of mutual care and trust that grew between them. Sitting under the moonshine around the nest, Cara at last felt part of a close-knit circle of friends.

Most of all, she loved the stolen moments with Brett. Over the past few months he'd taught her to be spontaneous. They held hands and jumped into the ocean when the whim struck. They laughed until tears filled their eyes. They threw back their heads to sing out loud to a favorite song. And sometimes, while walking the beach, his eyes would gleam in the moonlight and he'd lead her far back in the dunes to a spot hidden by the sea oats. Then he'd blanket her with his body under a wide-open sky.

When she wasn't with him, she thought about him. She'd look down while talking on the phone and see that she'd scribbled his name a dozen times. He lent her one of his T-shirts at the beach one day and she kept it to sleep in at night just so she could smell his scent and dream of him. When she heard a love song on the radio, she was sure it was written for them. These feelings were all new for her, and they were all-consuming.

"Sugar, you're in love," Emmi told her one night as they sat on the beach together at a nest due to hatch.

"I am not. This is just the summer fling I never had as a kid. I'm not in love. I'm *in fling*."

"There's no such thing as *in fling*. I ought to know. I married my summer fling."

"That doesn't qualify. Your summer fling became a year-round thing. By definition, a summer fling must necessarily end at the end of summer."

"Oh, so you know the definition now?"

"Absolutely. It's already written in some song. Something about when those autumn winds start to blow. Come on, you know the song."

"Okay, okay. Let's just figure this out." She stretched out her legs and lifted her hand to count off. "You had the requisite props for a summer romance, I'll give you that. First and foremost, you had the moon."

"Not just any moon, the Carolina moon. And it was shining over a body of water. We have to get the details straight."

"Okay again. I agree." She held up a second and third finger and continued counting off. "You had the sunsets. The boat."

"Boats are a plus. Not required."

"No bonus points. What next? Um…you had the kisses."

"Oh, yes. Definitely the kisses. My God—"

"Stop it. You're killing me, Cara. I don't even want to know."

"Sorry. Go on."

"Let's recap. You've got the moon, the body of water, the sunsets, the boat, the kisses. What's missing?"

"The parent. Or the camp counselor, whichever. I qualify there, too. Mama actually waits up for me, and I'm forty years old. Can you believe it?"

Emmi tossed back her head and laughed raucously. "Okay, you win hands down. You're not in love. You're *in fling.* Are you happy?"

Was she happy? Thinking about it, Cara wished she could say that she was. It was mid-August and the tourists were heading home as schools reopened. The blissful summer was moving fast, and the thought of what fall would bring only filled her with dread.

Cara felt the full impact that her summer was coming to an end the morning she awoke to find her mother gone. Panic swelled in her chest when she saw that The Gold Bug was still parked outside the house. Hurrying outdoors, there was no sign of her mother in the yard, either. Cara raked her hair from her face, revving up her sleepy mind. Lovie was not confused like Miranda; nonetheless, Cara couldn't imagine where she might have gone. Or when.

Until she noticed that the red bucket was missing, as well. She quickly tossed her nightgown from her body and slipped into her shorts, a top and sandals. The screen door swooshed as she hurried outside once again. A chorus of birds sang in the trees and the sand in the path was damp and cool as she ran to the beach. She arrived just as dawn was rising over the ocean.

She found her mother standing at the shoreline, a slight, solitary figure with a bright red bucket dangling from her hand. Her long, white nightgown was flapping in the brisk breeze. Bathed in the misty pink-and-yellow light, she appeared a ghostly figure looking out to sea.

Cara approached her mother quietly, not wanting to star-tle her from what seemed a deep and private contemplation. "Mama?"

Lovie turned her head slowly and Cara was shocked to see tears flowing down her mother's cheeks.

"What's the matter, Mama?"

"They're gone," Lovie replied, her voice raspy and weak.

"Who's gone?"

"The loggerheads. The mothers. They're gone now, to wherever it is they go. I can feel it. It's over. And I miss them already." Her lower lip trembled as she brought her fingertips to them and tried to control her emotions. "Oh, Cara. I miss them."

Cara had no words of solace. What could she say? That they'd be back next year? There was no comfort in that. She knew her mother was feeling the pain of knowing that this was her final season. For her, the loggerheads were truly gone.

And soon, so would her mother. Cara felt hot tears flood her eyes. For the past two months she'd denied the truth of what the end of summer would ultimately mean. She'd forced it to the back of her mind as she would any reminder of the cold winter ahead while the sun still shone warm.

"I wish I could go with them," Lovie said, looking again out toward the swells. "I want to follow my instinct and swim away with them in the currents. To have it all be behind me. Wouldn't it be lovely?"

"Not yet," Cara said in a broken whisper and wrapped her long arms around her mother, holding tight. "Please, Mama. Don't swim away yet."

Her mother stroked her hair. "My own, dear Caretta. *You're* still here, aren't you? That's such a comfort."

While her mother wept in her arms, Cara experienced an odd reversal of roles, as if she were the mother, strong and capable, and Lovie were the child, small and vulnerable. It was as moving as it was terrifying.

Mother and daughter stood together on the beach as morning broke around them. The tide was going out, littering the beach with shells, wrack and sea whip. Together, they wept for all the mothers that had left, and for those that were soon leaving.

After the mother turtles departed on their solitary journey, Lovie's health declined rapidly. It was as though, in spirit, she had indeed swum off with the loggerheads. She'd been so stoic about her illness that Cara, Toy and the others had fooled themselves into believing that, with a positive spirit, Lovie could live forever. Now, however, her energy waned along with her optimism. She grew more moody and withdrawn. Whenever Cara tried to lure her down to the beach to sit by a nest, she'd just shake her head, claiming that her coughing had kept her up most of the night before and made her too tired. When Cara tried to interest her in the turtle records, or get her opinion on a nest problem, Lovie would lift her slender shoulder, then go to her rocker on the front porch and stare out at the sea. She was drawing inward, swimming in her own currents, and Cara couldn't reach her.

As Lovie lost weight and grew smaller, Toy was getting bigger as she entered her final weeks of pregnancy. She was cooking up all manner of healthy recipes to tempt Lovie's palate. But Lovie only nibbled like a mouse, then turned her head away with an apology. "It's the coughing," she'd say again, clearing her throat. "It takes my appetite away."

"If it wasn't for liquid nourishment, you'd waste away," Toy complained, tears in her eyes. "Look, Miss Lovie, I made a cheese soufflé. It's nice and soft. Try it."

"I'll try," Lovie replied as usual, without heart.

Neither Toy nor Cara could argue with her because the coughing was horrendous. One night they'd both gone running into her room, afraid she'd choke to death on her own spittle. After that night, despite Lovie's resistance, Cara put her foot down and declared they had to see her doctor.

"No, he's so busy," Lovie complained. "We mustn't bother him."

"Mama, it's his job. Besides, how can we help you if we don't bother him once in a while?"

"He's not going to tell us anything we don't already know."

Cara could only look at her mother. They were moving into dark, unfamiliar territory—and they needed help.

nineteen

The minutes spent dashing from the nest to the sea are very dangerous in a turtle's life. Ghost crabs tiptoe across the beach to attack the hatchlings. Only one in thousands of hatchlings may survive to maturity.

Three days later, Cara sat in the waiting room of the oncologist's office located inside the hospital complex. Around her, older men and women sat in a depressed silence reading old, worn magazines, some carting along oxygen tanks that clanked when they moved, a few dressed in those flimsy hospital gowns that were universally awful. Cara wouldn't touch the wrinkled, curled magazines or the arms of the chair. She didn't want to touch anything. She tried to compress herself and stared at her hands in a private misery.

She despised hospitals. They all looked the same, she thought to herself as she shifted her weight in the uncomfortable metal chair. Cold and sterile with long, narrow halls that wound around linoleum floors and passed through double doors like a maze. The worst thing about hospitals was that they were filled with sick people. Cara didn't like being around illness. She hated flying because, to her mind, it was like being trapped for hours in a giant germ bank. When someone coughed in a theater, she'd lean far away. If someone sneezed in a crowded elevator, she'd hold her breath until she escaped. Which was why Cara was convinced that her mother's persistent cough, and now the hospital visits, was God giving her a kind of purgatory for sins of the past.

Not that she was complaining. Her love for her mother was more powerful than any aversion to illness. So she quietly sat hunched over in the metal chair while Lovie underwent multiple tests. She waited, thinking every minute what a saint Toy had been for so long. While Cara was oblivious in her career in Chicago, Toy had driven Lovie to her radiation treatments and waited like this, pregnant and tired, probably having to get up to pee every ten minutes. Cara fervently believed there was a special place in Heaven for caregivers.

After two and a half hours, the nurse emerged to ask if she'd join Dr. Pittman in the examining room. Cara practically sprang from the chair to follow her through the very narrow hall. When she entered the room, she found her mother sitting on the examining table still wearing the papery green robe and chatting away with an unnatural cheerfulness.

"Look who's come to join us!" Lovie exclaimed, her eyes feverishly bright.

Lovie was trying too hard to be cheerful and Cara immediately felt on edge. She looked over to the doctor, a young, bookish man with heavy eyeglasses and a long, serious face. Dr. Pittman was writing in the chart but managed to look up briefly and smile. They'd spoken on the phone at length when Cara had first learned of her mother's illness, but this was the first time they'd met.

"Take a seat, Miss Rutledge," he said, indicating another metal chair.

"Thanks, but I'll stand," she replied, walking to her mother's side.

"So, what's the verdict?" her mother asked, again with a forced optimism.

Dr. Pittman's silence spoke volumes. Lovie's balloon of cheer deflated as his expression turned somber.

"I didn't like what we found today."

When Lovie turned her head, Cara saw that the fevered cheerfulness was, in fact, fear. She reached out to hold her mother's hand.

"The cancer has spread more rapidly than we'd anticipated. In particular, it has moved into the trachea, which would explain the coughing."

"Is surgery an option?" Cara asked.

"The trachea is inoperable. The mass is...everywhere."

Cara's stomach tightened but she tried to maintain calm. "Surely there's something we can do, Doctor."

He sighed. "We could consider initiating another round of radiation therapy."

"No." Lovie was adamant.

Dr. Pittman looked at Lovie and smiled weakly. He closed the chart and looked at Cara with compassion. "We've entered the final phase of the disease."

Cara heard him clearly and returned his gaze unflinchingly, grateful for his honesty. She couldn't have stood it if he was evasive or tried to mask the harsh realities. "I understand."

"Your mother understands that the best we can offer at this point is palliative treatment."

Lovie patted Cara's hand. "What he's trying to say is there's nothing he can do."

To his credit, he smiled. "That's right, as far as treatment goes. However, there is a great deal we can do to make certain you are comfortable, Mrs. Rutledge. There is absolutely no reason for you to suffer. Since you've decided to remain at home, I'll arrange for a visiting nurse to set up regular appointments and for oxygen to be delivered. It just makes it a little easier when you feel like you're not getting enough air. Use it. Don't be shy. We can also discuss at length the use of morphine." He glanced at Lovie. "But there's no need to do that today."

To Cara he said, "This is a process that needs to be understood so you can best help your mother. It's time to be practical and realistic as to what treatments you can manage at home and what you might need help for. Time to gather together a support group. Is Miss Sooner still around?"

"Yes. She's a great help."

"Good. But she's having a baby soon, isn't that right?"

"She's due September 15."

"I see."

"Cara can handle this," Lovie said. "She's very competent, you know."

Cara didn't miss the pride in her mother's voice and felt a chink in her self-control.

"Good," he said emphatically. "But don't take it all on yourself. Too often I see a competent daughter or wife feel she can manage it all and in the end she suffers burnout. There's no need for that. A good caregiver takes care of herself. Remember, it's important to have a two-pronged support system. The first is your medical support staff. We'll get you lined up for visiting nurses, social workers and hospice. The second you have to arrange yourself. You'll need a support group that will provide a caring atmosphere for both Mrs. Rutledge and yourself. A group of good listeners who can be counted on to help when needed."

Cara and her mother exchanged a glance.

"The Turtle Team," they said in unison.

The phone began ringing off the hook as word leaked out about Lovie's illness. Volunteers asked if they could bring over

a covered casserole, soup, anything at all from the four basic
food groups. Brett did all the lawn work. Emmi called every
time she left her house just to make sure some errand didn't
need to be run. Miranda came by just to sit beside Lovie on
the bed and keep her company while they watched TV. Flo
briskly walked in twice a day full of enthusiasm and energy,
talking loudly and bringing along something fun or interesting to read that she'd painstakingly searched out. "Got to keep
her spirits up," she said with a knowing look to Cara each day
before returning home.

Cara couldn't keep count of all the turtle paraphernalia that
arrived each day from well-wishers. Turtle jewelry, shirts, candles, wind chimes, hats, cups, flags, key rings—Cara didn't
know where folks found so much turtle stuff. Lovie was moved
and grateful for it all and tried to take the time to speak to
everyone who stopped by or called. On occasion, the visitor
would break down into tears and it was Lovie who had to
offer comfort. Before the week was out, Cara saw how her
mother's energy was sapped and she began restricting visitors.
Word was sent out that Lovie needed her rest and, gradually,
peace was restored at the beach house.

Lovie's bedroom looked increasingly like a hospital room,
though. It couldn't be helped. The oxygen tank and cart took
up a lot of space beside her bed, and the bedside table was
covered with a tissue box, a water glass and several small pill
bottles. A TV had been moved in as well as a bookshelf. Cara
tried to order a mechanical bed that moved position but Lovie
was horrified at the thought. She wanted to sleep in her own
four-poster bed, the one her mother had slept in, and her
mother before her. She refused any discussion on the matter.

Thus, in short order, the house went topsy-turvy. Lovie
spent a good deal of time in her room resting, reading, watching television and organizing the photo albums that had

become an obsession. She tried to keep involved with the household decisions and turtle affairs, but it was a struggle.

Cara also began preparing more of the meals. Toy helped but her advanced pregnancy made her slow and cumbersome in the kitchen and she had to put her feet up frequently because of swollen ankles. Several nights a week she grew antsy and said she had to get out of the house for a little while, too. Toy began going to the local movie theater on a regular basis.

That was how Cara became the official gatekeeper, cook, laundry woman, housekeeper and chauffer. She managed the meals, the medication and the complaints. She scheduled medical appointments, did the shopping and paid the bills. She had several offers to help but was reluctant to accept. She didn't like to bother folks with her problems. Besides, in her mind it was easier and quicker if she just did the job herself. There was, however, one person she felt *should* step up to the plate.

Palmer opened the door of his home and his face broke into delighted surprise. Then, as if catching himself, the warmth iced over and his smile turn stiffly polite.

"Hello, Cara."

"Hello, Palmer."

He looked healthy and tanned in his pale blue polo shirt that brought out the color of his eyes. Cara guessed he'd been boating or golfing, or both. She was dressed in plain khakis and a madras cotton shirt that made her look almost girlish compared to his sophisticated casualness. She regretted not dressing up more for the discussion.

"What brings you here?"

"I thought we'd chat about Mama."

He thought about this a minute while she shifted her weight. He wasn't going to make this easy for her.

"Come on in, then," he said with reluctance, opening wide the door.

She entered the house with a firm stride to disguise her nervousness. This was only the second time she'd visited her old home since her arrival. There had been no more invitations to dinner nor had there been any more visits to the beach house from Palmer since the Fourth of July party.

"Where are the kids?" she asked as she passed through the marble-floored foyer.

"They're out playing somewhere."

"Too bad." She was disappointed not to see them. But perhaps it was just as well, given the topic of conversation. She made her own way into the living room. When he joined her, he indicated two plush armchairs covered in a gorgeous Italian fabric.

"Are these new?" she asked, admiring them.

"No, those are the ones that used to be in Daddy's library. They had that tapestry-looking fabric on them, remember?"

"They look very different," she said, sinking into one of them. They must have set Palmer back a few pennies. "Very nice."

"It's all Julia," he replied without enthusiasm as he took the opposite chair.

"How is she? I haven't seen her in a long time. She hasn't stopped by."

"She's at some committee meeting at school. She's always doing something over there. Things are heating up now that school's started up again."

"Things are busy at the beach house, too." It was an opener and they both knew it.

Palmer nodded noncommittally.

Cara leaned forward, eager to end the polite chitchat and get to the topic at hand. "I called you about Mama two weeks

ago." She paused for emphasis. "I thought I'd clearly explained
to you what Mama's doctor had said but perhaps you didn't
understand. So I'm here to talk about it."

"I understood what you said well enough, but I don't agree."

"You don't agree? What's to agree with? Mama's got cancer. She's dying."

"I don't believe she's dying."

Cara leaned back in the chair, stunned. She hadn't been
prepared for that.

"That's denial, Palmer," she stammered.

"Says you. I talked to the doctors over there myself and no
one told me that she was dying. Hell, she'd be in the hospital if she were."

Cara stared back at him, not knowing what to believe. Either the doctors were hedging with Palmer or he wasn't listening. "Mama doesn't want to go to a hospital. She wants
to die at home."

"She's not dying," he repeated.

"Palmer, listen to me. It's bad. She needs to see you. She
asks for you all the time. And for Cooper and Linnea."

"You know we want to come out there more, but you see
how it is. The kids have got Julia running ragged with one
thing or other. And we were there just the other week."

"You mean the children came out. You haven't been to see
Mama in over a month." Her tone was accusing.

"I've been busy," he said with a flat voice. "You're the one
with all the free time. Besides, Mama's designated you as caregiver. You and that girl."

Cara's resentment knew no bounds. "I can't believe you're
treating this so lightly. Talking about kids' schedules and being
busy—at a time like this!" She felt a fury welling up against
her brother. "What are you so afraid of? The possibility that
Mama is dying?"

"Like I said—"

"Or are you angry at her?" she interrupted. His mouth shut tight and Cara knew she'd hit the truth. "I know you had words on the Fourth. You upset her, Palmer." She was relieved to see regret in his eyes. "But she won't talk to me about it and I'm not asking. I don't need to know what the argument was about. I don't care. But surely you're man enough to overcome mere pique when our mother is dying."

His jaw flexed and his eyes sparked with anger. "You let me be the judge of my own dealings with my mother. I've been seeing to her needs for a lot longer than you have."

"No one's denying that, least of all Mama. But she needs you now. I need you."

"You seem to have everything under control out there. Yes, ma'am. Things are going just the way you like."

"I'm not quite sure—"

"You're doing a fine job," he said with false bluster, rising to a stand. "Real good. I'll be by soon. And call me if there is an emergency, okay? Listen, I've got to run."

He was pushing her off! She couldn't believe it. She rose in a huff and followed him through the foyer.

"What's gotten into you?" she snapped, unleashing her frustration. "Don't you care about your own mother?"

"Don't you dare question my love for my mother!" he bellowed back in her face. "Who the hell do you think you are? You don't know what love is. Who do you think took care of her all those years while you were in Chicago? Me, that's who. You left!"

"I got kicked out!"

"Only because you forced the issue with the old man."

They stood inches apart, glaring at each other, while the memory of that night played in both their minds.

Cara stepped back and brought her hand to her temple. Her fingers were shaking.

"Hell," Palmer cursed, putting his hands on his hips and looking out the beautifully etched transom windows that bordered the front door. "I was damn proud of you that night."

"I don't see why," she replied softly. "I'm ashamed to think of it."

"I hated my own guts for being such a chickenshit. And I hated you for leaving me behind to hold the bag."

"I didn't have any choice in the matter."

He shrugged as though to shake off the heavy history.

She saw the gesture, the set jaw, the squint of his eyes, and saw him again as the wary teenager she remembered. The older brother who laughed and told a good story on the outside had held a lot of pain on the inside. "I really think you should come visit Mama. In fact, I'd come right away, if I were you."

Palmer looked at his shoes. "She doesn't need me."

"Sure she does. Now more than ever."

"Not when she has you. You've always been her favorite."

"*You* were her favorite."

His lips rose in a smirk and he said almost contemptuously, "Is that what you think? Then, honey, you don't know anything." He turned from her to open the door wide. "Go on back to her and to your damn beach house. And leave me the hell alone."

The following day an enormous bouquet of flowers was delivered along with a card that said, "Get Well Soon! We love you!" It was signed "Palmer and Julia." Cara held the bouquet in her hands at arm's length and wanted to throw it in the compost. This was Palmer's reply and she found the gift heartless. Her mother would see through the ruse and be crushed.

She dutifully carried them to the kitchen, added water and

Floralife into the cheap glass vase they'd arrived in, plastered on a cheery face and delivered them to Lovie's room.

"Look what Palmer's sent!" she exclaimed through a tight smile.

"He sent those?" Lovie asked, rising to a sitting position as her eyes lit up. She coughed with the effort as her hand reached out toward the bouquet. "Oh, they're beautiful! Such extravagance! No, no," she snapped at Cara, jabbing a pointing finger in the air. "Put them over here so I can smell them."

Cara pinched her mouth tight and moved them to the bed-side table.

"Isn't he a wonderful boy? Cara, could you get me my thank-you notes? Right away?" She leaned over to smell the flowers, murmuring, "Wasn't he thoughtful? Do you think he might come visit soon?"

When Cara came out of the room she saw Toy pounding the sofa pillows with vigor.

"Easy, girl. What's got you in such a fury?" Cara asked as she crossed the room to the small writing desk.

"I overheard. I can't believe she thinks that Palmer is such a prince. It makes me boiling mad. Don't she care that he hasn't even bothered to come by and see her? Her own son? Shoot, anybody can send flowers."

"I don't think she wants to even think that. It's too pain-ful for her to accept. I just let her be. She has enough pain to deal with now."

"What about you? Don't you get mad at him?"

Cara almost launched into her fight with Palmer the day before but thought better of it. "I can't spare the energy or the time to get mad. I'm too tired."

"I sure would be. She sings his praises and all he does is sit on his butt and send flowers while you do all the work."

Cara pulled out a drawer of the desk to find her mother's box of ice-blue, monogrammed thank-you notes. It was the same pattern she'd used for as long as Cara could remember. She traced the elegant blue swirling letters with her fingertip, recalling how her mother had always rigidly demanded that Cara sit and write a thank-you note immediately after a gift or a kindness was received. Naturally, her mother couldn't wait to write Palmer. How could he deny that he was her favorite?

Cara doubted she'd receive such a formal thank-you for all that she was doing for her mother now. After all, how do you thank someone for being the martinet and badgering her to drink Ensure and water, for scolding her to eat and take her pills, for being the mean one to enforce the doctor's orders when all Lovie wanted was peace? In her heart, Cara knew her mother was grateful and depended on her. She didn't need or even want a piece of paper to validate her efforts.

But it was just plain hard to see Palmer receive such lavish praise for so miserly an effort. Hurtful. Mama always made such exceptions for the males in her life and the pain was as stinging now as it had been as a child when her mother would praise anything and everything that Palmer did, barely noticing her own hard-won successes. His term paper with a B–was posted on the fridge while her A was accepted as a given.

She brought her hand to her forehead, amazed at the power of her anger. Her hand was shaking! It was ridiculous to still be jealous of her brother at forty years of age. She was ashamed of herself.

Cara looked over at the pillows on the sofa. With her face set she walked directly over to them, bunched her fists, then, glowering, pummeled one hard. Again and again and again. She could hear Toy laughing beside her.

"Go for it! Feels good, doesn't it?"

Cara stepped back and put her hands on her hips, nodding,

breathing deeply and feeling a release. "You're right. I *am* angry. I'm angry at Palmer. I'm angry at my mother. Mostly I'm angry that I'm caught in this damn position again. I left home to get away from this, and here I am, stuck back in the mire."

"You're not stuck. You're doing a nice thing, the right thing, taking care of your mama. When she goes, you'll know you did your best. That's more than Palmer is going to be able to say."

"I suppose," she said, raking her hand through her hair. "But it's too bad. It breaks my heart. I know he loves her."

"Maybe he just can't stand to see her sick. Some folks are like that."

"He's been spoiled all his life. First by Mama and now by Julia. He's used to letting women handle this kind of thing."

"He's a man."

"I hate stereotypes, but the social worker told me that women provide most of the caregiving in this country."

"No surprise there. Most men figure it's woman's work."

"It shouldn't be. It's the duty—no, the honor—of all children to take care of their sick parents."

"Well, I'm never taking care of mine," Toy said, her face mutinous.

"Never say never. When I was your age I would've said the same thing. But here I am, twenty years later... And I thank God. I would've died somewhere in my heart if I hadn't had this chance to tell my mama I loved her before she died."

Toy's face twisted.

"Oh, Toy, I didn't mean to imply—"

Toy shook her head. "I know. It's just that my mama had to take care of her sick daddy till the day he died. He was a terrible drunk, but she loved him. And at least she had her sister to help her."

"I have you."

Toy's eyes rounded before she looked away, wringing her dust rag. "Yeah, big help I am lately. I'm sorry I've been away so many nights. I shouldn't leave you alone."

"You need time to yourself. You're young and going through a big change of your own."

"I'm trying to figure so many things out right now," she said, appearing a bit guilty. "It's so confusing. I'm going to be a mother soon but I'm still just a kid, you know?" Her voice went higher. "I—I— What am I going to do with a baby? How can I take care of him?"

Oh Lord, Cara thought, unable to stop the grimace on her face. With all that was going on, she'd clean forgotten about Toy's situation. Not forgotten, maybe, but shoved it aside to the corner of her mental desktop, like she did a lower priority problem at the agency. Her mind was spinning as she wondered what she could do to help. Or even if she had it in her to handle one more crisis. She felt used up, sucked dry of any advice left in her.

She plopped down on the sofa and patted the cushion beside her. Toy reluctantly joined her, grabbing a pillow and tucking it behind her back for support.

"What have you got planned?" she asked, hoping the girl had given the situation some thought.

Toy took a deep breath. "Well, I'm going to take the GED test soon. I feel pretty good about that. Then, I don't know. I guess I'll start looking for a job."

She guessed? "Anything in particular?"

"Anything as long as the pay's good and I get health insurance. I don't care what."

"Do you have any skills? Experience? Anything you've done before that you liked?" Cara was grasping at straws.

Toy looked down with dejection and shrugged.

"Who will take care of the baby while you work?"

"I dunno." Her voice was barely audible.

"Have you looked into day care centers?"

She shook her head.

"Toy," Cara exclaimed, her frustration sneaking into her voice. "What *have* you looked into?"

Toy grabbed the pillow from behind her back and held it tight across her chest. "I guess I was thinking about the GED first."

Cara closed her eyes. This was much worse than she'd thought. Toy had done nothing to plan for her future. That she could be so careless was unthinkable, even infuriating, to someone as goal oriented and driven as herself. She remembered the comparison her mother had made between Cara at eighteen and Toy. She'd described Toy as childlike and Cara as someone who had always known what she wanted. Was that knowledge and drive something one was born with? Or was it something learned? But it was ironic, too. Toy could be meticulous around the house. How could a young girl who couldn't see spilled milk on the counter without grabbing a sponge stand by, her whole life lying strewn out before her, and not make a move to pick up the pieces?

Whatever the answer, she thought as she looked at the dejected pose of Toy across from her, it wasn't important now. Cara knew that it was also part of her personality to try to fix a problem.

"You know you don't have to leave the beach house right away."

"I know. But I also know I can't stay forever. Miss Lovie is…well, you know her time is limited. And I expect you'll be going back to Chicago?"

"Yes. I'll be going back to Chicago. After…" She didn't finish.

"So, I guess I have to figure out where I'll go."

Cara was filled with a spiraling panic as one more responsibility piled on to join the others. "Don't worry. We still have time. We'll think of something."

Toy nodded and plucked at the pillow.

Cara didn't see the optimism and faith that had filled her eyes at the beginning of summer. Back then, the days loomed long and they were all filled with plans. Now they'd run out of time and she only saw the same terror and worry that Cara felt in her heart.

That night, Cara had a mental meltdown.

"I'm not Toy's mother!" she exclaimed, clinging to Brett's shoulders. "I'm not my mother's mother. I'm not anyone's mother!"

"No, you're a hellcat," he chided. "Retract those claws before you draw blood."

Cara groaned and flopped to her back on the bed, flinging her arms over her eyes. "Brett, I can't take much more. I'm ready to explode or run away, whichever comes first."

He turned onto his side to rest his head on his palm and gently moved her arm from her face. She looked up at him, searching for comfort. Beside him, she felt the same peace she felt when she looked out at a mountain range with its jagged terrain and imposing breadth. There was a power in Brett's quiet strength and even-tempered goodness, just as there were hidden mysteries and dangers lurking beneath the surface.

"No one thinks you're her mother," he said in his low, rumbling voice.

"They don't have to. I feel it." She brought her palms to her face, dragging them down while her breath came short. "I hate feeling like a mother to my own mother," she confessed. "It's not natural. And it makes me feel like some kind of ogre.

Sometimes she acts like this little kid. She pouts when I give her pills or hides them under her pillow and pretends that she took them. And she has this tight-mouthed grimace—" she turned her head to imitate it "—when I bring her water to drink. I swear, I'm ready to start saying, 'Open wide for the choo choo train.' Ugh!" She grabbed the pillow and tossed it over her face. "I don't want to be like this. I don't want to see her like this."

Brett gently moved the pillow from her face, blessedly silent.

"And Toy... She thinks of me as a mother figure, too. Me! What a joke."

"Why is that a joke?"

"Look at me," she exclaimed, looking at him disbelievingly. "I'm not the least bit nurturing and I'm a loser at relationships."

"You don't think worrying about Toy and nursing your mother is nurturing?" he asked gently.

She grew annoyed that he might be nearer to the truth than she wanted to admit. "It's not the same thing. How can I take care of her when I can't take care of myself? I'm falling apart. I seem to work harder every day and accomplish less. I'm so exhausted most of the time I find myself just staring at the walls on the verge of tears."

"You're taking too much on yourself. You need to ask for help."

She laughed bitterly, still feeling the hurt and disappointment in Palmer keenly. "I asked my brother for help and he sent a bouquet of flowers. Brett, the responsibilities are endless. I can't keep up. I didn't ask to be anyone's mother."

"What spooks you about being a mother?"

"I'm not spooked. I just don't like being forced into a role I haven't signed up for." Her voice was harsh, deliberate, as though she was saying the words as much to convince herself as him. She turned her shoulder from him and pulled the sheet up higher over her chest, simmering. "I don't want to talk about this anymore."

He shifted to sit up in the bed and placed his hand on her shoulder, drawing her back to face him. "Can I say one more thing?"

"Sure."

"I think you'd make a wonderful mother someday."

She turned to stare back at him, sensing more.

"Maybe even a fine wife."

He'd said it with a smile, but she saw in his eyes that he was feeling vulnerable, venturing on shaky ground. The air grew thick with expectation. She felt as if she couldn't breathe.

"Nope, not me," she said, grabbing hold of the sheet and rising to sit.

He seemed thrown off guard. "Why not you?" he asked, reaching out again to draw her closer. She held herself rigid.

"The same reason for you. Folks like us are just not cut out for marriage. Or children. We're loners, right?"

"I don't know that I've actually sat down and decided not to get married or have kids. It just hasn't happened yet. Maybe folks like us take a little longer to come around to it."

She couldn't deal with this now, couldn't handle one more thing. She threw back the sheet, rose and began slipping into her underwear.

"Where are you going?"

"I've got to get back. Toy wants to go out to the movies again."

"I wanted—"

"I have to hurry." She didn't need to look at him to know he was watching her. Feeling self-conscious, she fumbled with her T-shirt, not caring that she'd put it on inside out.

"Wait, Cara. Don't go yet. I want to talk to you. I'll drive you back."

"I don't think I want to talk anymore tonight, Brett," she said, stepping into her shorts, keeping her head down. "And I rode my bike." She almost tripped over his sandals as she raced for the door. Turning her head before leaving the room, she saw Brett sitting in the middle of the bed. His powerful body was slanted, a sheet draped around his muscular thighs. But the expression on his face made her think an earthquake had just rocked the mountain.

When she returned home, Cara found her mother asleep and Toy in her room, studying. All appeared peaceful. Relishing the quiet, she went to the kitchen to make herself a cup of tea, then brought it out to the leeward porch. She lit a scented candle—a rare treat—feeling the need for comfort tonight. She slumped into the rocking chair, tucking one leg beneath her. Then, for no reason she could name, she began to cry.

A few minutes later footsteps sounded on the porch steps. Cara stiffened in the chair, wiped her eyes and peered through the dim light toward the noise. "Hello?" A woman's figure appeared, her white hair an aura in the candlelight.

"Hello there," Flo called out softly. "I was walking and saw the light. Is this a good time?"

"Sure. Yes. Grab a chair."

Florence dragged a chair near Cara. "So, how's everything?"

"Fine, thanks."

"Lovie?"

"She's sleeping."

Flo stopped rocking and looked directly at Cara. "What's wrong?"

"Nothing." Then, because it was Flo, she said, "Everything." She started sniffling again and reached up to wipe her eyes, embarrassed for the tears. "I feel ridiculous."

Flo reached into her pocket, pulled out a pack of tissues and handed one to her. "It's an old habit from my days as a social worker. You always seem to need a tissue."

"Oh, don't mind me. I'm just tired. It's been a hard week."

"Do you need help?"

"Thanks, really, but I can handle it."

"Yes, I see how well you're handling it."

Cara blew her nose then shook her head. "I don't know what's the matter with me tonight. If I'm not weeping, I'm snapping at someone."

"Oh-oh," Flo said with humor. "Who'd you snap at?"

"Brett."

"Want to tell me about it?"

"I don't understand it myself. We were talking about my mother and Toy and the next thing I knew we were talking about motherhood and marriage. I just panicked. I couldn't deal with where his feelings were headed. It was too intense, too much. All I wanted to do was run away."

"So you did."

She nodded.

"That's not so horrible."

"You didn't see his face. I hurt him, Flo."

"Looks to me like you're hurting, too. Do you want to end it with him?"

"No. Not at all."

"Then tell him that. Don't sit on this and let it fester. Call him. Talk to him. Tell him what's going on. He can't understand unless you open up to him."

"I'm not good at those kind of conversations. What would I say?"

Flo smiled. "You can start with hello."

The phone rang several times before he answered.

"Hello?"

"Brett, it's me. Cara. Did I wake you?"

"No. I couldn't sleep."

"Me, neither." She gathered her words in her mind like cue cards. "I've been thinking about tonight. I didn't thank you for listening to my rant. I guess I was wound up pretty tight." She was relieved to hear him chuckle. "You're the only one I can let go with and get all my frustration out," she said, then laughed nervously. "Aren't you the lucky one?"

"I'm glad you feel that way."

"It's probably a backhanded compliment, but I mean it as one. I feel safe with you, Brett. And I wanted to say thank you."

"Okay."

She waited for him to say more. When the pause lengthened, she asked tentatively, "Don't you want to talk about it?"

"Not really."

"Oh." She felt a little deflated and was about to say goodbye when he spoke again.

"We all get tied up in knots once in a while. You know," he said with invitation in his voice, "whenever that happens to me, I go fishing."

twenty

When the hatchling reaches the ocean and gets its first taste of the sea, instinct kicks in. The crawling motion is replaced with power strokes by front flippers. The turtle will go nonstop for twenty-four hours in what's called a "swimming frenzy" to reach the Gulf Stream.

Whenever turbulent weather starts churning out in the Atlantic during the months of September and October, residents of the southeast coast turn on the radios and TVs and keep watch.

Cara and Brett were driving home from their fishing expedition when they heard the bulletin. A tropical storm was forming off the coast of Africa and heading toward the Caribbean. This was the first hint of a hurricane she'd lived through in twenty years but the chill she felt running up her spine was all too familiar.

"Do you think it will form a hurricane?"

Brett didn't appear the least bit alarmed. "Who knows?" he answered with an easy shrug. He glanced at her from the wheel, a question in his eyes. "Why? Are you worried?"

"No, no," she lied.

"Right."

"It's just that with Mama sick and Toy due any day now, the timing couldn't be worse."

"Don't worry. We get these reports all the time. It wouldn't
be the season without them. At this very moment, hundreds
of people are running for the hurricane tracking charts they
got from the grocery store with smiles of glee on their faces.
The newscasters just love to get the people going. Fact is, most
of the storms die far out in the ocean long before they even
come near shore."

Cara chewed her lip and searched his face. His features
were serene; she decided to take his word for it. After all, he
knew more about nature than she did. She looked out the car
window. The sky was brilliantly sunny with only a few wispy
clouds. It didn't look like a storm was coming.

"But it wouldn't be a bad idea to get things ready anyway,"
he said. "Lay in supplies. You should always enter the hurricane season prepared."

"Great," she said with a groan. "I'll add it to my list."

She glanced at the clock when they pulled in the driveway.
It was a quarter to five. She was pretty grungy after an afternoon of fishing. Her hair was falling out of the elastic, her
shorts were damp and the suntan oil had collected sand and
dirt like a magnet. But she felt better than she had in days.
They'd caught some nice trout and stopped off at the Red and
White for a few groceries to make a feast. Her mouth watered
at the prospect of grilled fish smothered with lemon juice.

"I'll clean the fish if you'll grill 'em up," Brett said, offering the usual deal as he hoisted several bags full of groceries
in his arms. Creek fishing was one of their favorite dates and
she'd become an avid fisherman over the past months.

"Suits me fine," she replied, grabbing the final two bags
and balancing them on her knee as she closed the trunk. She
followed Brett up the stairs to the house with a heavy tread.
She couldn't wait to get into the shower and wash off the smell

of sea salt and fish. "I hope Toy has some of her famous cole-slaw leftover. I'm so hungry I—"

She stopped short, almost crashing into Brett's back. He was standing at the threshold with his arms full of groceries. Her mother stood across the room. One look at Lovie's face told her something was wrong.

"Look who's here," Lovie said in her cheery hostess voice.

Cara stepped around Brett into the room, feeling as though she were stepping onto a stage. She heard a shuffling sound to her left and swung her head to look past Brett's shoulders. In a single glance she caught sight of the last two men on earth she expected to see that afternoon: her brother, Palmer, and her former lover, Richard.

She almost dropped her groceries. The room suddenly seemed to shrink in size. She hadn't thought of Richard in months. Her brain couldn't make any sense of him being here—on the Isle of Palms—at her mother's beach house, of all places. She was left speechless.

Always at ease in awkward situations, Richard stepped forward to relieve her of her bags. "Hello, darling. I'll bet you're surprised to see me." He tugged at the bags. "You can let go," he said, chuckling.

She relinquished the bags gratefully, because her knees were about to buckle at her first whiff of his expensive cologne.

"Surprised?" he asked.

"Surprised doesn't begin to say it."

She darted a glance at Brett. He was standing rock still, the muscles of his arms bulging under the weight of several bags and the cooler. She saw him at that moment as she knew Richard would, just some laid-back local in baggy cargo shorts, old brown sandals frayed at the heels and wind-whipped hair curling around a baseball cap.—

She rallied as training clicked in. "Brett, this is my former colleague, Richard Selby. Richard, this is my good friend, Brett Beauchamps."

Colleague? Friend? Who did she think she was kidding?

Richard cracked a smile. "Any friend of Cara's is a friend of mine. I'd shake your hand but…" He shifted the bags in his arms.

Brett only jerked a nod of acknowledgment. Any harder, she thought, and he'd have broken his neck.

Cara was grateful they both had their arms filled and didn't have to go through the charade of a handshake. All they had to endure was the pretense of politeness.

Which was, apparently, too much to ask of Richard, she thought, as his glance traveled insolently over Brett.

"Been fishin' have you? I heard you good ol' boys were good at that."

Brett stared back at Richard. The blue of his eyes turned icy.

"Come along, boys," Lovie said, stepping into the fray. "You can put those groceries down in the kitchen."

There was a reluctant shuffling of feet as they followed her. In their wake, Cara shot a loaded glance at her brother. He was enjoying the scene immensely.

"Hey, don't look at me like that," Palmer said with a short laugh. "He came looking for you at my house. All the way from Chicago."

"I see," she hissed. "And you personally brought him out here?"

"It was the neighborly thing to do. Once he explained your relationship."

She opened her mouth to ask exactly how Richard had defined that relationship when suddenly he was there. He looked as handsome and polished as ever in creased dove-gray trousers, linen navy jacket and a silk, open-necked shirt. On his feet he wore tasseled shoes. Not one of his sleek dark hairs was out of place and, despite the heat, he looked as cool and fresh as though he'd just stepped from a shower. In contrast, she felt sure she smelled like a fishery.

"It's great to see you again," he said, stepping closer.

She drew her shoulders and took a step back. He understood the implication of the small movement and didn't press any closer.

"Richard, what are you doing here?"

"I should think it's obvious. I've come to see you."

"I can't imagine why."

Richard looked over her shoulder at the group of people in the room listening to every word. When he faced her again, his eyes pulsed a private message of discomfort. They used to communicate with glances all the time during client meetings. They'd known each other's thoughts and opinions so well that one look could speak volumes.

"It's a little crowded in here. Can I take you to dinner?"

"I have dinner plans."

"There's a lot I need to talk to you about." His eyes were pleading.

"Sorry."

"Cara, I can only guess what you're thinking."

"If you knew what I was thinking, you wouldn't have had the nerve to show up in my house."

He grinned mischievously, without a trace of guilt. It threw her.

"Precisely. Which is why we need to talk. Alone."

"Richard," she said with frustration, hedging.

"And just to sweeten the lure," he went on as though he hadn't heard her, "let me tell you right now that, all personal feelings aside for the moment, I've come on business."

Her interest suddenly perked up. She looked over to Brett. His brows were gathered and he was listening intently.

"I had dinner plans…"

"This is more important."

"You two go on and settle your business," Palmer said, stepping forward with congeniality. "I've been looking for a chance to visit with Mama."

Cara looked at him with irritation. They both knew his coming here had nothing to do with visiting Mama.

"Hey, Brett," Palmer called out. "What you say we cook up whatever you got in that cooler?"

"Not this time, Palmer," he said, moving toward the door. "I've got things to do. But you help yourself to the fish. Cara caught most of them anyway. Miss Lovie, it's good to see you looking so well. Toy, always a pleasure." As he passed Cara, his eyes searched hers before he put on his sunglasses.

After he left, she turned to Richard. "If you'll wait till I get cleaned up, I'll hurry."

It was as though she'd returned to another life. The candlelight of the downtown restaurant glimmered seductively as she traced the thin crystal bowl of her wineglass with her fingertip. Around her she was aware of the gentle buzzing of conversations and the clinking of glasses. For the first time that summer she was wearing the slinky black dress that she'd packed in that hastily gathered assortment of silks she'd arrived with. Sizeable pearls around her neck and at her ears had been pulled out from the back of her drawer, as well as the Cartier watch that replaced the Timex she wore on the beach.

"You look marvelous," Richard said, his eyes glowing with appreciation. "You're so tanned and fit. Are you playing golf?"

She laughed. "Hardly. I'm a Turtle Lady."

He looked puzzled. "A what?"

She gave him the shorthand version, knowing he wouldn't

be the least interested in the loggerheads. "I walk on the beach a lot. And I've been gardening, fishing and boating."

Now it was Richard's turn to laugh. "You? I can't believe it. You hate the outdoors."

It irked to be described like that. It was no longer how she saw herself. "No, I don't. The lifestyle here is quite different. You might like it."

"What's not to like? It's a beautiful city, the weather's great and there are world-class golf courses here. And the restaurants are superb. I read about this one in *Gourmet* magazine. Five stars."

"Would you be surprised if I told you this was the first time I've eaten in the city since I arrived?"

"You're kidding. Poor darling, you must be starving. You hate home cooking."

Cara thought of all the fresh crabs and shrimp Brett had harvested and boiled or grilled for her, of impromptu picnics on the beach, of Toy's experiments with healthy cooking and Mama's family recipes and smiled, thinking she'd never eaten better in all her life.

"How's your mother?"

"She's dying, Richard. How do you think she is?"

His smile dropped and he drew back his shoulders. "I'm just trying to be friendly."

"Don't bother. Look, Richard, I can't sit here and pretend we're having a friendly dinner together. The last time I saw you, you kissed me goodbye and flew off to New York. I seem to remember that you were apologizing for having forgotten my birthday, but what you really forgot was the little detail about my getting canned the next day. Or was that your idea of a birthday surprise?" Her smile was so brittle she thought her face would crack.

"I did have to go to New York. And I couldn't tell you

about the layoffs that night. It would have been a breach of confidence."

"Oh, please."

He held up his hand to gesture for more time. "Cara, listen. Give me a chance to explain. I never wanted to hurt you."

"Right. Well, you did. I took a major hit with no backup. You just left me hanging in the wind."

"I didn't expect you to leave town! I've been going crazy these past months wondering where you were, how you were feeling. I tried to call you at home. On your cell phone. You had to have gotten my messages! Why didn't you call me back? You could have spared me months of agony and I could have spared you all these months of wondering what happened."

"I caused you months of agony? How delightful."

"If it makes you feel any better, I suffered. Okay? You left word that you'd call me when you got home. So I waited by the phone for several days that turned into several weeks. Then I started trying to find you. No one knew where you were. It was like you'd dropped off the face of the earth. I didn't panic. I knew how much you loved travel and I figured you'd taken some time away. And I knew you were royally pissed off at me." He had the grace to look sheepish.

Cara wasn't falling for the illusion that he really cared. He wanted something from her and she just had to wait it out to discover what. Her foot wagged in agitation under the table, but at eye level, she appeared calm and in control. He seemed to take her quiet fury in stride, having expected it. But he was holding a trump card.

"That all happened a long time ago," she responded coolly. "It's ancient history."

"Okay, I admit it. But when you were gone for the summer I was damn scared I'd lost you for good. I put feelers out everywhere. I even considered hiring a private detective.

Do you want to know how I finally found you? I had lunch with Adele. She told me you were still with your mother in Charleston but she wouldn't give me your number. So I went straight to my office, looked up Rutledge in the Charleston phone book—by the way, do you have any idea how many Rutledges there are in Charleston?—and I finally reached your brother's house. And here I am."

"That's quite a story. And I'm only left to wonder why you bothered?"

He narrowed his eyes for a moment, then spread his palms open on the table and shrugged. "Darling, I know you're angry. I'm sorry for not telling you about the layoff. I really am. But you have to believe me. I planned all along for you to come back. It was all a matter of timing. And that's what I've come to tell you." His dark brown eyes glowed in the candlelight. "That fast-food campaign you were working on? It went over. We got the account. And they want Cara Rutledge to head the campaign. So do we. We want you back. We need you back." He paused for drama. "As Senior Vice President and Group Director of the account."

Cara's foot stopped wagging and she dropped her shoe. "You can't be serious," she said, searching his face.

He leaned back in his chair and grinned. "Can't I?"

She paused for only a moment. "I want it in writing."

"Cara…"

"I want a contract specifying all that you just told me and all that you haven't gotten around to telling me yet. FedEx it to me. No faxes. I don't have a machine. And if it looks good, I'll let you fly me to Chicago, put me up at the Four Seasons and wine me and dine me. And then, if after the few days of negotiating I like what I see, you've got me back."

He returned a wry smile, half admiring, half annoyed. "You're not joking are you?"

"I never joke about money or my career. I don't lie, either."

He laughed then, a high, grating sound, and she wondered what she had ever found so attractive about him. But business was business and she knew that, regardless of her personal opinion of him, the offer was valid if he'd come all this way to woo her. She gathered her purse and rose to stand.

"Where are you going?"

"Our business is completed. I really don't see the need to continue this any further. It was good to see you, Richard, and I look forward to seeing you again in Chicago. At the office."

"But dinner…"

"I hear the food is marvelous here. Enjoy. But I've got some trout I'm just dying to taste. Oh, and I hope you get that round of golf in while you're here. You look a little pale. 'Bye!"

She tucked her bag under her arm and sauntered from the room with the glorious knowledge that he was watching every move she made as she walked away from him.

Cara felt so high she thought she was flying across the connector to the Isle of Palms. She'd put the top down on the Saab, turned the music up loud and was tapping her fingers on the steering wheel as she zoomed home. It seemed as though the weight of the world had been lifted from her shoulders. She wanted to shout out to the universe, "I'm back!" And not just to a job but a whopping promotion. They must really want her to have sent Richard begging and she planned to translate that into meaningful negotiations before she was through with them. As the wheels of her car turned, her mind spun with the names of good people from her team who'd been laid off who she could hire back. Oh, it was sweet to have a job and money coming in again. A future to look forward to. Cara Rutledge was back on track, she thought, then laughed out loud again as she reached the top of the connector and saw the ocean sparkling under the still-shining sun. She was soaring!

Inside the beach house, it was quiet.

"Hello!" she called out, setting her purse down on the table. The kitchen was sparkling clean. Sniffing the air, she didn't catch the scent of fish. "Where is everyone?"

Toy came out from her bedroom. It was only seven-thirty and the sun was still out, but she was already in her pajamas, tying the sash of her robe as she came down the hall. "Oh, hi, Cara. How did it go?"

"Fine. It's so quiet. Where's Palmer?"

"He left a little while after you did."

"And Mama?"

"I'm in here!"

Cara and Toy walked into Lovie's bedroom. The windows were wide-open and there was a steady breeze blowing in from the ocean, but Cara could still smell the stench of medicine and illness in the room. The wastebasket beside her mother's bed was filled with crumpled tissues, an oxygen mask covered her mouth and nose, and the TV was on. She put on a smile and went directly to Lovie's bed.

"Hey there, Mama," she said, sitting on the bed and giving her a kiss. "How are you feeling?"

Lovie reached up to remove her mask. Toy hurried over to turn off the oxygen.

"Oh, fine, fine. I just use this to help me out a little." She used it more and more each day but hated to admit it. "Well, look at you!" Her eyes brightened at seeing her daughter dressed up and Cara felt a flush of pleasure at her approval.

"How was your visit with Palmer? He didn't stay long."

"A little of this and a little of that. He likes to keep things light. He had to leave and, honestly, that was fine with me. I can't take long visits anymore." She sat up a little higher on the bed, coughed long and hard, then settled again, smoothing the sheet across her chest. "Toy, be a darling and turn that thing off, would you?" she asked, pointing to the TV. Then she turned to Cara, her nose pointed like a bloodhound. "So, what did *he* want?"

Cara laughed and felt the tingle of excitement stir again. "You won't believe it," she said, settling on the mattress beside Lovie for a good chat.

Lovie's eyes were sparkling with anticipation.

"He offered me my job back. With a promotion! Remember that fast-food account I was working on before I left the agency? Well, it flew and now they want me to come back to head the account." She smiled to herself, the wonder of it all just beginning to sink in.

"Wow, that's great," Toy said in a breathy voice.

Cara turned her head to acknowledge the girl's words.

"I worked very hard for that account. Oh, Mama, this is such a big deal for me."

Lovie looked puzzled. "You mean, that young man flew all this way just to offer you a job?"

Cara's smile slipped. "Yes. What did you think he came for?"

"Well, I suppose I thought he'd come to propose marriage."

"Marriage?"

"Why are you looking at me like that? That's the usual reason a man comes storming in unannounced like that. At least in my generation." She lifted her slight shoulders. "In your generation, who knows? Everything is so different. I thought you were quite taken with the young man. Wasn't he your fella for several years?"

"Yes," she replied slowly. "We had some good times. But trust me, Mama, I'll never be Mrs. Richard Selby."

"Why do you say that?"

"Because I know now that we don't want the same things out of life."

"How about Mrs. Brett Beauchamps?" chimed in Toy.

This time, Cara didn't rise to the bait. "I've wondered about it sometimes," she said, surprising everyone. "But the moment I heard Richard offer me that promotion, I knew what I wanted. I said yes."

Lovie made a face. "Brett is such a fine man and you two seem to get along so well. Are you sure you know what you really want?"

"As much as anyone, I suppose."

"But to live alone, Cara. That's so hard on a woman. Every woman needs a man to love her. To provide for her. You're not getting any younger." She tsked and shook her head with worry. "If only you could find yourself a good husband."

All the soaring elation Cara had been feeling crashed to the earth. She felt a familiar clutch inside her gut and her first instinct was to let the iron wall fall between them again. But she'd had enough of the old patterns. She took a deep breath and looked at her mother long and hard.

"Mama, you really don't understand, do you?"

"Understand what?"

"How things are today for women like me. And Toy." She looked over to include the young girl in the conversation. "You've lived a privileged life. It's not like that for us. There isn't anyone out there who's going to write a check to cover our health bills or the rent or to put gas in the car. If we even have a car. We have to provide for ourselves. You know, sometimes I think you forget that I've always taken care of myself."

"What do you mean?"

Cara looked straight at her. "You and Daddy didn't put me through college. You didn't set me up with my first home. You didn't contribute one dollar to my well-being after I left

Charleston. When I was eighteen. Toy's age," she added, driving the point home. "There were more years than not when I was running one paycheck away from the street. I've worked very, very hard for many years to get to the point in life where I'm offered a position like this one." She took a ragged breath. "It's a *big* moment in my life."

Lovie looked at her with wide, uncomprehending eyes.

"And all you can say is that you wish I'd find myself a good husband?"

Cara stood and walked to the window to look out. As always, the sea rolled in and out in its monotonous, never-ending rhythm. She turned to face her mother again, crossing her arms tightly around herself. "Mama, do you even know how you've just dismissed me?"

"I did no such thing! I simply said how nice it would be for you to find a husband, someone to provide for you. Is that so wrong to wish for my child?"

"Oh, Mama, I'm not saying I wouldn't like a relationship with a man. Even marriage—maybe. But I'm not looking for a man to provide for me. I'm not going to settle for marriage just to be married or to find security. That's a pipe dream I can't count on. I'm counting on myself."

Instead of drawing herself up with indignation or lowering her shoulders in a sulk, as Cara expected, her mother lay back against her pillows and studied her as though she were seeing someone she hardly knew.

"I'm so sorry," Lovie said softly. "I didn't know… You always wrote such positive, upbeat letters and told us how well you were doing. I wanted to believe that. You've always been so capable that it was *easier* to think everything was fine." Her eyes filled with tears, which she hastily wiped with a tissue from the box by her side. "I didn't know."

Cara watched her mother weep and felt ashamed for her

outburst. Why hash this out now, she asked herself? Her mother was dying, she had enough to deal with. Besides, after all these years, what was the point? She came closer to stand at the bedside, wishing she could just drop the whole subject.

"Oh, Mama, never mind. It doesn't matter anymore. I didn't come in here tonight for a row. I shouldn't have told you. I just thought you'd like to know about the job offer, that's all."

Lovie wiped her eyes and sniffed in the tissue. "No, I'm glad you told me. I didn't mean... It's just that I've always believed a woman is happier being married."

"Can you honestly tell me that you were?"

Lovie looked up, her eyes red rimmed and watery, and opened her mouth to respond. But no sound came out. She seemed to be struggling with an answer that left her mute.

"Does that mean you'll be leaving for Chicago soon?" Toy wanted to know.

Cara turned to face Toy who was standing by the door. She looked as if she were halfway in the room and halfway out.

"I'm not going anywhere until after you have that baby!" she said, pointing her finger and interjecting a little enthusiasm into her voice. She saw relief blossom on Toy's face. "But, after that, I'll have to go to Chicago for a series of interviews. It should only take a few days. A week at most. I imagine you can hold the fort for that long if I bring in help. And Flo's promised to be on call, but we all know she just wants to hold that baby. I won't dally. I'll hurry right back."

Cara sat on the edge of the mattress again and took her mother's hand. She squeezed it and said with intent, "I love you and I won't leave you. You understand that, don't you?"

Lovie mustered a weak smile. "Of course I do."

In the pause Cara could almost hear the subject drop. She had never felt the role reversal so strongly as she did at that moment. The responsibility for these two lives—one about to depart life, the other about to bring a new life forth—fell squarely on her shoulders.

"Are you okay?" she asked Lovie.

Lovie nodded feebly.

"Did you eat dinner? I don't smell any fish."

"We just weren't up to cleaning fish," Toy replied apologetically. "So we ate the leftover tuna casserole from yesterday and a little fresh pea soup."

"It was delicious, dear," Lovie said, distracted.

"Can I get you some?" Toy asked Cara.

Cara's stomach growled. "I didn't eat and I'm starving. But don't get up. I think I'll scrounge around in the fridge after I change into something more comfortable."

"You look quite nice in that dress," Lovie said. She was eager to make amends.

"Sexy," added Toy. "I can't remember the last time I wore anything like that. Or high heels."

"Me, neither," she quipped as she left the room.

As she kicked off her heels and changed into jeans and a T-shirt, Cara wondered what Brett was up to. She picked up the phone and dialed his number. It rang several times but there was no answer. It was just like him to forget to turn on his answering machine. He was probably out on the dock, cooking up some shrimp. Her stomach growled again and she decided to go right over. Tying her tennis shoes, she thought how much she wanted to see his face again after staring at Richard's.

"Mama?" she called out, grabbing her purse. "I'm going over to Brett's. Don't wait up."

"Okay," Toy called out over the television noise in Lovie's bedroom. Before closing the door, Cara heard the weatherman announcing that the tropical storm in the Caribbean had been upgraded to a hurricane.

twenty-one

*The hatchling swims from the dangerous, shallow water
near its natal beach to the deep water of the Gulf Stream.
Once there, it will hide and feed in the relative safety of
enormous floats of sargassum weeds and flotsam.*

Cara pulled into Brett's driveway and found him in a black
leather jacket standing beside a big, mean-looking black Har-
ley motorcycle. The leather made his shoulders appear even
broader and lent him a dangerous air. He turned his head toward her when she parked.

"I didn't even know you owned a motorcycle," she said,
coming close. Her gaze was glued to the gleaming bike.

"I don't ride it much anymore. Don't have the time."

She caught the crispness of his voice and looked up. There
was no easy smile of welcome, no sweet kiss or arm around
her shoulder.

"I'm starved," she said. "Have you eaten yet?"

"I thought you were going out to dinner with what's-his-
face."

"Richard? I did. Or rather, I went to the restaurant with
him. But our business ended quickly and I left before I ate."

"Business? What kind of business?"

"He offered me a job."

Brett digested that without a word. He turned back to his motorcycle and checked gauges.

Her excitement fizzled as disappointment settled in for the second time that night. She'd hoped at least for a lame question about the job, or even a polite acknowledgment.

She tried again. "I was hoping I'd find you boiling up some shrimp."

He shook his head. "I just grabbed a frozen pizza."

"Oh." She was deflated. She stood for a moment trying to decide if he was angry with her for not cooking up the trout for dinner or whether he was jealous. She preferred to think the latter and tried one more time.

"Are you going out for a ride?"

"Yep," he replied, still not looking at her. He walked into the garage and returned a minute later carrying a black helmet.

That did it. Now she was mad. She didn't deserve this treatment. "What is your problem?" she asked angrily.

"My problem? I don't have a problem."

"No? Then why am I getting the cold shoulder?"

He put the helmet on the seat and stared at it for a moment. "You're right," he said, looking up. "You didn't do anything to deserve this. I'm just feeling a little edgy tonight."

"Because of Richard?"

He didn't reply.

"Brett, I didn't know he was coming. I certainly didn't invite him. There's nothing between us anymore, for heaven's sake. At least on my side. That became perfectly clear tonight."

He looked at her but she couldn't decipher his thoughts in the feverishness of his pale blue eyes. He surprised her by turning and going back into the garage again, this time emerging with another helmet. This one was smaller and white. When he approached, he handed it to her.

"Put this on."

She exhaled with confusion, but obliged him while he put on his own helmet. Then he swung his leg around the bike and grabbed firm hold of the handlebars. He'd changed into long jeans and the heavy, sun-bleached boots she remembered seeing him wear on the shrimp boat at the beginning of summer.

"Come on, then."

Cara was filled with curiosity about where they were headed. She swung her leg around and slid forward on the slanted seat so that her thighs and knees hugged his hips. She wrapped her arms around his waist, locked her fingers together and tucked her tennis shoes onto the pegs.

"Hold on."

"Where are we going?"

"There's something I want to show you."

"Okay."

She felt his arm move and the powerful engine roared to life. Her heart skipped a beat and she tightened her grip around his waist. She didn't have time to tell him that this was her first ride on a motorcycle, not counting the moped. Fear mingled with the thrill of excitement as she leaned against his back. They took off in a spray of gravel and a guttural roar out of the driveway and down Palm Boulevard. They crossed the connector as the red sun lowered into the purpling marsh and she rested her chin against Brett's shoulder, slumped in awe. She'd traveled around the world, but nowhere on earth did the sun descend into the horizon with such panache as in the Lowcountry.

It was a great night for a ride. The moon was near full and illuminated the roads. She felt as if she were riding a bullet pushing through silken wind, and clung to Brett for dear life in an embrace more passionate than any they'd shared before. The engine vibrated beneath them, its roar filled their ears. The night smelled of leather, damp earth, green grasses and the sea. Out in the open, so close to the road, she felt the same visceral connection with the landscape that she did on the small johnboat speeding down the Intracoastal.

They crossed the bridge to James Island where the road opened up and curved along the water and under huge oaks dripping with moss. Moonlight poured through the leaves like magic through lace. They leaned to the left as they took a curve, straightened, then leaned to the right for the second, moving as one body. When the bike surged forward, they felt the force pushing against them as an invisible hand. When the engine slowed, their muscles slackened again. They had traveled for nearly an hour when they came to a winding stretch with several sharp curves. Brett slowed the motorcycle and came to a stop.

"This is it," he said, turning off the engine.

She loosened her arms from his waist and took off her helmet, shaking her hair loose. The engine still roared in her head and the vibrations stiffened her tender inner thighs. But after she'd climbed from the bike and stood still for a few minutes, her blood seemed to slow back down and she heard the night music of insects and frogs. Brett removed his helmet and hung it from the bike, then he walked a few yards along the side of the road to where a small white cross was erected in the dirt. He came to a stop before the cross, reached inside his leather jacket, pulled out a flattened yellow rose and laid it in front of the cross. She didn't approach him, giving him the space she sensed he needed.

He stood there for a long time, his head bent. The night grew chilly. Several cars sped past them, the beams of light flashing over Brett's features like the bright searchlights of a prison. At length, he turned and waved her over.

The gravel crunched beneath her feet along the road, then

the ground turned soft as she crossed the earth to his side at the foot of the cross. She drew near and was comforted when he wrapped his arm around her waist and pulled her closer.

"Her name was Ashley Carter," he said. "We met freshman year in an intro to fisheries and wildlife class, and dated on and off through college. She was real smart and not a party girl. Kinda like you were. She wanted to be a forester. Her idea of a date was going out to take samples from the marshes." He laughed without humor then paused, lost in his own thoughts again. Cara waited without speaking.

"You didn't know me back then," he continued. "I wasn't so much a bad kid as I was dangerous. I took risks, pushed things to the limit. I didn't think twice about jumping off a bridge. I didn't give a damn if I flooded my truck or wrapped it around some tree while mudding, as long as it was fun. It's what gave me the edge in sports. I drove my boat too fast and too close to those monster ships than was smart—even for a bullheaded teenage boy. I could've gotten sucked into the wake in the front or caught in a whirlpool in the back any number of times. My dad got word of my antics from one of the harbor pilots who spotted me. That was the only time he ever laid a hand to me. And I deserved it. I wasn't alone in that boat.

"But I wasn't always lucky. Broke a leg once. An arm twice. A couple of toes and fingers. But did that stop me? No. It only made me feel more invincible. I thought I was immortal. I don't know how I survived high school, but by the time I got to college, I was drunk most nights. I honestly believed I was *good* at driving drunk. Thought I had a skill for it. That kind of crazy ego scares the shit out of me now that I'm older.

"But Ashley never saw that part of me. When I was with her, I was different. The irony of it all is that I wasn't drinking the day of the accident. We were coming home from a field session at the DNR labs. It was broad daylight and I wasn't in any kind of hurry. I took the turn at an easy pace, but a truck coming the other way took the curve too wide and came right for us. I swerved to avoid it and spilled. The wheels slid out from under me and I got dragged along with the bike into the grass. But Ashley got thrown off.

"If she'd just landed on the ground, she would have been hurt, but alive. Except fate turned the deck on us that day. She was thrown against that big old oak over there. I'm told she died on the spot."

"I'm so sorry, Brett."

He nodded in acknowledgment, then looked off at the oak. His jaw moved as if he were grinding his teeth.

"You can't blame yourself. It was an accident. You said yourself you weren't drinking."

"Easy to say. I blamed myself for a long time, figured I'd just used up my quota of luck. I'd pressed the limit so many times and escaped that, this time, no matter what, I had to pay. Only I didn't pay. Ashley did. I know I'm damn lucky to have a life at all, but I know my day is marked just as surely as Ashley's was marked for September 2, 1984."

"That's today."

He nodded. "Yeah. I wasn't so bothered by that Richard guy showing up. But he showed up *today*. I felt threatened. Not by him, but by fate. I thought I was going to lose again someone—" he stopped, exhaling long and hard "—someone I cared about."

Cara reached up to unzip his leather jacket, then she slipped her arms around his neck and held him, pressing herself as close as she could against him so he could feel her living, breathing warmth. His big arms reached up to encircle her and squeezed so tight that she felt they were merged again into one body, one heart. He buried his face in her hair. She tasted salt on his cheeks.

A car zoomed by, whisking her hair and crunching gravel. Against the noise, she thought she heard the words, "I love you."

He took her back to the Isle of Palms. They changed into their swimsuits and went for a swim in the ocean, then spread out on towels in the sand. She lay in the crook of his arm with one leg lying across his and her fingers toying with the hairs on his chest. They heard the scritch-scritch of ghost crabs scurrying along the sands and the rattling of sea grasses in the wind.

"Cara, when we were together at the cross," Brett said, stroking the damp hair from her neck, "I wasn't completely honest with you."

"Oh?"

He took her hand from his chest and played with her fingers, his brows furrowed.

"The reason I wanted to go there wasn't just because it was the anniversary of the accident. I went to put my past to rest. I've made an important decision, but I was scared. I am scared. And seeing that Richard guy didn't help. I tried to tell you this once, but you didn't want to listen then. I hope you're ready to listen now."

She sensed what was hovering at his lips. Her heart rate accelerated and she was grateful the darkness masked her face. "Brett..."

He took a breath. "I love you, Cara." He blurted it out like an admission. "It's crazy, I know, to fall in love after all these years of swearing I never would. The only explanation I can come up with is that I was meant to fall in love with you when we were sixteen but neither you nor I were ready for it and we had to go on our separate ways before meeting up again. Now. At forty."

It came out in a long rush, a recitation of love not memorized and practiced, but ripped from the heart. Once the words were spoken, however, he looked at her, unsure, like a little boy. "It's Tolstoy's bicycle again," he added, grinning, delighted with the comparison. Then, quite quickly, his expression turned very serious. "I love you, Cara. And I want to marry you."

Her heart stopped and she could only look back at him, speechless.

He cocked his head. "Are you shocked?"

"Totally."

"Didn't you see this coming?"

"I might have caught a glimpse, but I never thought... Brett, you've said so many times you were a loner."

"I was wrong."

"Were you?"

"You said the same thing about you."

She took a breath and slipped her hand back from his. "Brett, I was right about me."

It took a moment for him to accept what he'd just heard. The light in his eyes clouded. "What are you saying? You don't want to get married?"

"I don't think so. Not yet. I'm sorry."

"I thought..."

"It's not that I don't love you. I do." She rose to a sitting position, crossing her legs Indian style. Her skin was bare and she shivered in the cool night air. He reached over to grab his shirt and slip it over her shoulders. It was little gestures like this that made her love him—and made what she was about to say so hard.

"You don't want to marry me," she said. "I'm not easy to

live with. I'm crabby before my coffee. I like to work late at night. And I'm not much fun, really. All I know how to do is work. And I'm a terrible housekeeper. My mother can tell you what an absolute pig I can be. I'm forever shrinking something in the dryer. And cook? Forget it. I burn water. Run while you can, Brett."

"I've been cleaning my own house and cooking my own meals for a long time. That's not what I'm looking for." He reached out to put his hand around her neck and draw her face closer to his. "Why do you always have to do everything the hard way? Just say yes."

When his lips covered hers, they were filled with hunger and need and were incredibly persuasive. She moaned and pulled back, half laughing, half crying.

"You aren't making this any easier."

"Good."

It wasn't good. It was breaking her damn heart. She raked her hands through her hair, clenching it in fists at her neck. How could she avoid breaking his?

"Do you remember when I said that Richard had offered me a job? I was a little surprised when you didn't ask me what that job was."

Her tone had changed and he answered in kind, drawing back. "I didn't want to know."

"Well, your instincts have always been good," she said cautiously. "I was a little hurt that you didn't ask."

He moved his body to join her in a sitting position. The ribs and muscles of his chest were illuminated by the moonlight making him appear as inflexible as stone.

"Okay, I'm asking now. What did he offer you?"

"He offered me a big promotion. And the biggest lure was that it was for the account I'd worked so hard to get. *My* account. I got it—and they want me!"

"*I* want you."

Her face fell. "I told him I'd take it."

His face closed and he looked away. "Congratulations."

He was the only one to offer her the accolade, but it fell flat.

"Why does this have to be so damn sad?" she argued. "We're not breaking up. We can go on as we are. I'll be back here a lot. And you can come to Chicago. Just because we're not married doesn't mean that we can't see each other anymore."

Brett shook his head and the finality of it frightened her. "No. That's not good enough for me. I've gone too far to settle for that."

"How can you say it's settling? What's wrong with what we have right now? It's working. We both love our independence. We enjoy having our own space. Tell me, honestly, what's the advantage of getting married? Certainly not taxes. Marriage is highly overrated if you ask me. People like you and me, we do better alone."

"Then let me ask you this. Why are you always comparing us to famous movie couples? Mr. Allnut and Rosie. Tarzan and Jane. Those two kids on the island. They're together because they're stronger and happier together than apart."

"Those are movies. That's not real life."

"How do you know it's not like that in real life if you won't give it a chance? Let me tell you something about real life. Animals come together all the time and mate for the survival of the species. Most of the time it's just rutting. But did you ever see what happens when the male sticks around and he and the female help each other watch over the young? It does something to you because it's so damn beautiful."

"And rare."

"That's what makes it all the more precious."

"But you forget my name is Caretta. I'm named after the loggerhead. She's a solitary creature."

His brow furrowed and he looked totally defeated by that argument. He reached for his clothes and climbed to his feet. She saw him step into his shorts, heard the hum of the zipper.

"Where are you going?"

"To sleep under the stars." He slipped into his sandals and took a few steps.

"Don't go." When he wouldn't stop she called out, "Why do you have to be this way?"

He stopped and turned his head angrily. "Be what way?"

"Stubborn."

"Cara, I'm sorry if I'm not doing this right. But you're the first and only woman I've ever asked to marry me and you just turned me down. If you don't mind, I'd like to be alone." He narrowed his eyes. "Isn't that what you say we're so good at?"

"Wait. If I said yes—I said *if*—would you come to Chicago with me?"

"Chicago? Why would we have to go there?"

"Because I have a job there."

"I have a business here."

"I see. Right. So, the answer is no."

"Cara…"

"Why is it okay for you to say no and not me?" She saw him struggling for an answer and pushed on. "Brett, why can't we just keep going with what we have?"

"Because I can't."

She was so frustrated she wanted to scream. "So, you're saying it's got to be your way or no way?"

He looked so sad, so defeated, she wanted to weep.

"I've said all a man can say. And you've answered my question. Good night, Caretta."

"Brett…"

She watched him walk away into the darkness. He was right. There wasn't anything more to say. She reached out to pull the towel up over her shoulders. It was still warm from his body. The ground felt hard and lumpy. The night air was cooling quickly. All around her, the night was alive and the noises no longer seemed soft and gentle. From somewhere in the dunes she heard the scurrying and rustling of the hunted and the sharp cracking of twigs. All around her was the incessant high-pitched hum of insects. Beyond, in a booming crescendo, was the rhythmic pounding of the surf.

She slowly rose to her feet, shook out the towel, gathered her things into her bag and slipped her feet into sandals. She was beyond exhausted. The day had been too long, too much had happened. Suddenly her limbs felt as if they couldn't make the short walk home. Nonetheless, she doubted she would sleep. It would be, she knew, the longest night of her life.

twenty-two

---

*The hatchlings are carried by the North Atlantic system of
gyres to the islands off West Africa where the dinner plate
sized loggerheads may remain for a decade or more.
When seen again along the eastern seaboard, the juveniles have
grown considerably in weight and size.*

They named the hurricane Brendan.

Unpredictable as these storms often were, Brendan was
changing course and weakening one day, gaining strength the
next, causing havoc for weathermen and rattling the nerves of
everyone living on the eastern coast. On the Isle of Palms, the
weather was still clear but there was a new heaviness in the
air, thick and expectant. Cara had spent hours waiting in long
lines to buy sheets of plywood, nails, batteries, bottled water
and other emergency supplies and provisions. Just in case,
she told herself. Long lines of cars bearing license plates from
North Carolina, Ohio, New Jersey, Illinois and other states
were crawling across the connector back to the mainland.

"At least he's still a category one," Emmi said between pants
as she helped carry a sheet of plywood to the front porch of
Lovie's house.

"But a category one is still seventy-four-miles-per-hour
winds," answered Cara, struggling with the other side of the

wood. The rough edges were digging into her palms. "If it hits
at high tide, we'll get flooding." She grunted as they reached
the top step. "There's a reason they call these the barrier islands, don't forget."

"I know, I know. I hate this!"

"It's the price you pay for living in paradise, kiddo."

"What's the latest report? I heard at the hardware store that
it's going to go out to sea."

"Mama and Toy are listening to the radio for updates."

They set the heavy piece of wood down while they gathered their own strength.

"This is the last window, thank God," Cara said, stretching her arms.

"What about the side windows?"

"We'll just close the wooden shutters at the last minute.
Otherwise it would be like living in a coffin." Cara shuddered
at the unfortunate image and looked out at the ocean for the
hundredth time that day. Everything out there in the distance
looked serene but a dingy gray. It was deceiving. No matter what the weather reports said, she could feel the coming
storm in her bones. It was nothing she could identify, not the
temperature, the wind or the humidity. It was more a heaviness in her chest that she couldn't shake and made it hard to
breathe. And it was the quiet of the birds. Even the insects
were silent. The stillness was eerie.

She shook off her wariness and focused her attention on
the tasks at hand. There was too much to do to dawdle. "Rest
time is over. Alley-oop!" she said, grabbing hold of the sides
of the plywood again.

"Why are we doing all this work now?" Emmi complained
as she investigated a long white scratch down her arm. "If it
misses us, we'll just have to take it all down."

"Consider it insurance. If this is what it takes to strike a bargain with the gods, it's worth it. Come on, now. Just one more. Lift on the count of three. One…two…three." They hoisted the plywood over the front window, their muscles straining while Cara moved quickly to hammer nails into the corners. She slumped against it when she was finished. "There, that's it. The last one. We're done."

Cara lowered the hammer but could still hear hammering throughout the neighborhood. Many people had hurricane shutters these days, but the die-hards still relied on plywood and taped windows to get them through such storms.

"You *would* pick a time like this to break up with Brett," Emmi said, bent over with her hands on her knees, catching her breath. "We sure could've used his muscles now."

"He called and offered to help."

"And you turned him down? Again? Girl, you really are nuts."

"I didn't. Mama did. He talked to her."

"Oh. I see."

"We couldn't very well have him come over here to do work after I'd just refused his marriage proposal. That wouldn't have been right."

"I suppose not."

"Besides, he's got his own worries. He has to batten down the hatches and take his boats out to safe water. He's already long gone."

Even as she said the words, she heard the double entendre. She cast a quick glance at Emmi, whose expression told her she understood all.

Cara walked over to retrieve the two glasses of iced sweet tea, as much to cover her discomfort as to quench her thirst. Toy had set out glasses, ice and even little sprigs of fresh mint. Cara smiled at seeing it. Toy was becoming a mini-Lovie, she thought as she carried the glasses back and took a seat beside Emmi on the front steps.

"Drink up."

"Thanks." Emmi took a long swallow. "Mmm," she said with relish. "Nothing like sweet tea."

Cara drank thirstily. The tea was as thick as syrup and so sweet it made her teeth hurt. But on a hot day, when she was working hard, Southern sweet tea packed a punch.

Emmi turned to look at Cara and her eyes were shrewd. "You okay about all this?"

"I think so. We've got all the windows done. Emergency supplies and medical records are packed. And Mama's putting all her photograph albums and important papers in a plastic bin to take with us."

"I'm not talking about the hurricane, you idiot! I'm talking about you and Brett."

"Oh." She frowned and rested her elbows on her knees. "Well, there isn't a me and Brett anymore, is there?"

"That's nuts. Anyone can see the two of you are crazy for each other."

Cara only stared down at her sweet tea and stirred the ice with her finger.

"Lordy, your mama must be going bonkers that you said no to a marriage proposal."

"It's weird. I expected a long lecture on the horrors of spinsterhood but she hasn't said a word. Not a whisper."

"Really?"

Cara thought about this a moment then said, "Wouldn't it be just my luck to have finally reached an understanding with my mother right before she dies?"

They looked at each other and smiled.

"Better before she dies than not at all," Emmi said.

Cara swallowed hard. "I'll miss her terribly."

"And you'll miss Brett," Emmi said with feeling. "Sugar, why are you doing this to yourself? You shut yourself off from any chance at happiness."

"How come everyone thinks the only way for a woman to find happiness is to wear white and walk down a church aisle? I just *feel* that I don't want to get married. Maybe I'm afraid to give up everything I know. Maybe if I'd met him at thirty instead of forty I'd be more malleable, more open to change. Maybe…it's just too late."

"For heaven's sake, we're not dinosaurs, you know. Forty is still young. Women are having babies at forty all the time."

"Oh, please, let's not start talking children. That will really put me over the top."

"You don't want children? Not ever?"

"It's funny but I've really never thought about it much before this summer. But now that I have, no. I don't think so. Don't get me wrong, I love children. I absolutely adore Linnea and Cooper. But I just don't have this need to have any of my own."

"Really?" Emmi thought about this a moment. "Well, just because you don't want children doesn't mean you can't get married."

"Brett might want children."

"Have you talked to him about this?"

"No."

"Well?" Emmi said, with a tone that said, *why not?*

"There's no point talking about children when I don't even want to get married, is there? Besides, having children is not the main issue. I have a career. A home in Chicago. A life I'm used to."

"It sounds like you've got that answer down pat."

"I'm just not cut out for marriage."

"What have you got against marriage? Your mother and father were married for umpteeump years."

Cara closed her eyes. She and Emmi had grown closer over the summer and Emmi had been candid about her own troubles with Tom. They weren't children anymore snickering over kisses. They were women with adult issues. She couldn't see the point of keeping her history a secret any longer. When she opened her eyes again, she gave Emmi a knowing look.

"I hate to break it to you like this, but my parents' marriage is one of the reasons I don't believe in the institution."

"What do you mean? They were the happiest couple around."

"It was a farce. All for show. They made each other miserable."

"Come on. True?" she asked, shocked. When Cara nodded, Emmi stared back, her mouth agape. "And you're only telling me now?"

"I wanted to tell you, lots of times. But loyalty in the family meant not talking outside the family about such things." She took another sip of tea, trying to decide how much she dared reveal. "I don't know if they were always unhappy. I don't have any memories of them fighting when I was little. They seemed pretty Ozzie and Harriet then. But about the time we became pals, back when we started spending whole summers at the beach house, things began to change. Daddy never came here anymore and he started being cold to my mother. He didn't listen to her and he spoke sharply to her, as if he were angry or even disgusted. Then the abuse started."

"No! I don't believe you. Not your parents."

Cara spoke these things aloud for the first time, needing to get it out, to tell someone she trusted before she burst with it. "It wasn't physical abuse. It was more insidious. He broke her spirit. He was always implying that she was stupid or slow, especially about money. Not just her, but the whole female sex. That was his stance. Men were dominant and women were born to serve. Can you believe it? Whenever she ventured an opinion, he mocked her. Or he blew up if she said something 'wrong.' Finally she just stopped talking much at all."

"But she's so open and lively."

"Only here at the beach house. You didn't see her when my father was around. She was like a different person. I didn't know it then, but he began a campaign to take all her money and property away with the excuse that business was a man's work, that kind of crap. And he was so cheap with her, doling out small amounts of money, always forcing her to have to ask him for more. He was so controlling. And he'd do weird things like check the gas gauge on the car, or the odometer to see how far she'd traveled."

"I hate to say it, but that's the kind of thing someone does when they suspect their spouse is having an affair. I should know."

"Mama? An affair? Aside from being too ridiculous to consider, how could she have had one? She never left the house unless it was for some social or charity event that Daddy approved of. No one would ever think Olivia Rutledge was isolated. She had parties and guests in the house all the time and she was very active in the community. But it was always to serve his needs. She didn't have any real friends, except for Flo. Not even her daughter." Cara paused for a moment as she had a small epiphany.

"My God, I just realized how alike we are. I don't have any real friends, either, back in Chicago. It's like I deliberately isolated myself with my work."

"Why?"

"Haven't a clue. I'm sure a psychotherapist will have a field day with it someday."

Emmi was still working this out. "But why did she put up with it? Your mom's a sweetheart and all, but I never thought of her as weak."

"That's the million-dollar question. It couldn't have been easy. As Daddy got older, he became a mean old man. His threats weren't so subtle anymore. Especially when he started drinking. We could hear him yelling at her downstairs, calling her all sorts of vile names. And he'd accidentally, on purpose, break something she loved. Oh, nothing too dear. More like a piece of Chinese export porcelain or a teacup, always something from her side of the family. All those years I thought she put up with it because she loved him. And now she tells me that she hated him all that time."

"I don't believe it," Emmi said again.

"Believe it."

Emmi leaned far back against the porch. "Well, there goes another role model down the drain. Whenever things got rough between me and Tom, I used to think of your parents. I thought they had the ideal marriage. It just goes to show you never really know what goes on behind closed doors. Makes my problems with Tom seem pretty small."

"Infidelity is hardly a small problem. You should talk to him before you lose what you have together."

"Look who's talking! You're giving up what you have with Brett because you're both too stubborn to pick up the phone."

"It's not at all the same. We don't have a commitment to each other like you and Tom do."

"Commitment? He's fooling around. What kind of a commitment is that?"

"You're married. You said vows. You have children together. You grew up together. Those are the ties that bind."

Emmi looked at her hands and fiddled with her wedding band.

"Maybe that's what I like about being single," Cara said. "No ties. I'm free to walk whenever I want." She paused, staring out as another thought hit hard. "Shit," she muttered.

"Let me guess," Emmi replied. "You're thinking that you don't want to get married so you won't get stuck like your mother did. Right?"

Cara's silence spoke for her.

"Honey, if anybody needs to start talking, it's you and Lovie. You've got a lot of history to mine through. And you better be quick about it."

The humidity was thick and the flies were biting. Cara swatted a pesky fly away. "I don't want to upset her. Not now."

"This isn't about upsetting your mother! You need to think of yourself for a change."

"I don't want to be selfish at a time like this."

"It's not selfish. It's time to put yourself at the top of that to-do list you're always making! You've given everything to your job. Now you're giving everything to your mother. When are you going to take a minute to stop and look at what you need to give to yourself? Something's askew here and if you keep up that I-don't-want-to-talk-about-it stance it'll never get straightened out. Talk to your mother, for both your sakes. And when you finish with her, go talk to Brett."

Cara raked her damp hair and took deep breaths. "I can't breathe. It's this storm coming. The air's so thick!"

"It's anxiety. Been there, done that."

"Oh, Emmi," she said, leaning against her broad shoulder, feeling better just at the touch of her sweaty T-shirt. "What would I do without you?"

Emmi sighed. "Sugar, I have to admit, I don't know what I'd have done without you this summer, either. Sitting at the nests at night and talking to you about my mess with Tom helped me a lot. I couldn't talk to anyone else." She smirked.

"You aren't the only one with that loyalty thing." She grew suddenly serious again. "Having a secret like mine and no one to talk to can be isolating, too."

They looked at each other, understanding. Each felt the bond between them strongly.

"You know, you're the sister I never had," Emmi said.

"Me, too." Then Cara laughed lightly. "But Palmer would warn you off."

"Palmer…" Emmi said with a commiserating smirk. Having lived three doors down from him every summer, Emmi knew Palmer as well as anyone.

They both laughed, breaking the tension.

Cara put down her glass, stood and walked to the porch's edge. "Let the storm come!" she shouted to the sea. "We've got each other to get through." Grinning, she turned back to look at her friend.

Emmi made one of those half-grimace, half-smile faces that made Cara think, *Uh-oh*.

"I've been waiting to tell you this," Emmi said. "I've decided to pack up and head back to Atlanta right away. Before the storm hits."

Cara felt like she'd just been knocked over by a category four. "You're leaving? For the season? But I thought you'd decided to stay till after Thanksgiving."

"Tom called last night. He finished the job in Peru ahead of schedule and is coming home in two weeks. He sounded real excited, too, like he couldn't wait to see me." She shook her head and shot off a self-deprecating laugh. "I felt as giddy as a schoolgirl."

Cara stared back at her, speechless.

"Oh, don't look at me like that, Cara," she said in a groan. "I talk a good game about leaving Tom, but the truth is, I never will. We've been together for twenty years and most of those were good ones."

"What about the other women?"

Emmi avoided her questioning stare.

"You can't keep looking the other way."

"No, I can't," she said soberly. "You helped pull my head out of the sand. No more hiding. Tom and I will have to talk when he gets back."

"Will you?"

She looked pained. "Try to understand, Cara. Tom isn't just a summer fling for me. He's the whole year, every year, forever and ever. He's my husband. We took vows. Like you said, we have a commitment. I love him too much to let go. And after being alone all summer, I've decided I'd rather suffer with him than suffer without him. I'm not like you. Even when we were kids, I had to work hard just to keep up with you. Deep down, you're stronger than I am. I'm not cut out for being alone."

Cara stared at her best friend. Everyone was leaving her. Letting go and moving on to a husband, job, baby, even death. This glorious summer was truly over. It was all too sad. "I'll miss you."

Emmi's expression changed and Cara could see remorse at leaving her childhood friend behind to face the storm. When Emmi hugged her in her warm, motherly-sisterly arms, Cara didn't want to be alone any longer. She held on tight.

"I'll be back at Thanksgiving. I promise," Emmi said in her ear. "You'd better be here, too. Dinner at my house. Three o'clock sharp. No excuses."

"I'll be there," she whispered back.

Then, pulling away, she wiped her eyes and looked out again at the narrow line of clouds gathering at the horizon.

Cara looked at Emmi and they shared a knowing glance, one that all islanders shared at just such a moment.

"Provided we have houses to come back to."

That evening, Toy stood on the porch and, like most people along the coast, looked out at the sea. The sunset backlit the storm front. Eerie, hallucinatory blue clouds stretched ominously over the water in layers with thin, fiery, red-orange clouds. The tapered edges streaked across the sky like fingers grasping out at the island. She shuddered. Everything seemed all out of proportion.

Toy took deep breaths and stroked small circles over her belly. Her mind was whirling faster than the hurricane. She'd run out of time. She had to make a decision. Tonight. Darryl had called the house frantic, yelling over the phone how a big mother hurricane was coming straight for Charleston and how the guys in the band had decided to head out before the storm hit.

"Those fuckers don't care about nobody but themselves. But I'm not like that. I care about you and I'll be damned if I'm going to let you stay out there for one more minute, hear? I want you off that fucking island. There's a goddamn hurricane on its way! So you just pack up your things. I'm coming out to get you and we'll just see if some old lady is going to stop us."

Toy breathed deeply, feeling another twinge shoot straight down from her sternum to her uterus. The humidity was as thick as a wet blanket and she could really feel the pressure pressing hard. Her due date was in two more days but this storm system was having an effect on her baby. The little guy hadn't moved around much today and she felt like a bowling ball was lying between her legs. Or maybe it was just her nerves, she told herself. Oh, God, what if she had her baby in the car?

She could feel the tears welling up for the millionth time since Darryl had called. She had to go with him. She had no one left but Darryl. He was the father of her baby and she had to at least try to give him a chance, even if she didn't love him anymore. She was going to try with him the way Miss Lovie had tried with her. Besides, she didn't have no choice. *Any* choice, she corrected herself.

Across the porch she could see slivers of light escaping the edge of plywood covering Miss Lovie's bedroom window. Walking over, she put her ear against the wood. Lovie and Cara were watching the weather forecasts on TV. The weatherman was talking on and on like he'd been doing all day about Hurricane Brendan. It was upgraded to a category two hurricane and was currently hammering the Bahamas. His voice was high and staccato and it made her jumpy just to hear it. But she got really scared when she heard Cara say with alarm to Miss Lovie, "They've issued a hurricane warning now for Charleston County. Wait. Damn, they're calling for a mandatory evacuation of all the barrier islands."

"There's no need for panic. We have plenty of time," she heard Miss Lovie say. Her voice was real calm compared to Cara's and the weatherman's.

"We'd better go first thing tomorrow morning," said Cara.

Toy stepped back. So, that's what Darryl was so freaked about, she thought, crossing her arms in a protective gesture over her baby. She was so afraid. For herself, for her baby, for Miss Lovie and for Cara. She wanted to go inside the house, to join them on Miss Lovie's bed and hear them tell her that they were all leaving together. That everything was going to be okay.

But there'd be no more talking between them. No more yakking over morning coffee or giggling at night out on the porch. No more Miss Lovie gently correcting her speech or

Cara helping with her studies. They had a way of teaching her things in a real nice way that always made her feel good about herself, not stupid. Toy laid her hand upon the wood and leaned forward.

"Goodbye, Miss Lovie," she whispered. "Goodbye, Caretta Caretta."

She wished more than anything that she could say the words to them in person. To thank them and say *goodbye* the way real families did.

But, of course, she couldn't do that. They weren't really a family. They wouldn't understand why she had to go with Darryl to make a family of her own.

Toy walked quietly over to pick up her suitcase. Then, grabbing hold of the railing, she walked slowly down the stairs to the roadside where she set the load down and waited. The wind was really picking up. The palm leaves were clicking like castanets and she could smell rain coming in from the ocean. Somewhere out there the roaring of the surf was loud and threatening. She shifted from one foot to the next, feeling so nervous she had to pee. She didn't wait long. She spotted headlights piercing the misty gray, then recognized Darryl's white Mustang. She waved. He slowed to a stop beside her and stuck his head out of the window.

"Hop in. I want to get the hell outta here." His eyes looked out toward the pounding surf. "Shit. Look at that monster out there," he said with a jerk of his head. He took a long drag on his cigarette and his eyes narrowed over the curl of smoke. "It's just lying there like a growling dog, waitin' to pounce. Come on, babe, hurry up."

Toy tugged open the rusty door with a yank, lifted her suitcase and, with a shove, pushed it up onto the back seat. She slammed the door shut, cringing when it creaked loudly. Worried that someone might have heard, she hurried around the front of the car and clumsily slid into the front seat beside him.

"You're as big as a house," Darryl said with a quick glance her way.

Toy didn't say anything, didn't even ask him to put out the cigarette that was making her queasy. Silently, she turned to look out the back window for a final glimpse of the little yellow beach house on the dune. Inside she knew she'd left the kitchen all orderly and sparkly and the floors vacuumed. She'd carefully wrapped up all the china that she'd enjoyed using so much and stored it in the closets with Miss Lovie's favorite vases and pictures. And on her neatly made bed she'd left a note for Cara and Miss Lovie.

As they pulled away, she felt the finality of her decision. The beach house, where she'd been so happy, was all boarded up and shuttered. Closed to her forever.

twenty-three

Hatchlings are two inches long when they emerge from the nest. Adults weigh in at 250-400 pounds and the shell length can measure more than three feet in length. It takes 20-30 years for them to mature and reproduce but no one knows for certain how long they live. It could be as long as 100 years.

Hurricane Brendan was gaining power and speed as it set a course directly for the Isle of Palms. Cara tossed and turned most of the night, terrified after an evening of being glued to the weather channel. She awoke groggy and hearing a high whistling in her ear. She groped for her alarm clock, then gasped when she saw it was nearly nine o'clock. How could she have slept so late? she wondered, waking quickly and throwing back her covers. How could it be so dark? Was the power out?

Then she remembered she'd boarded up the windows. For the first time that summer, the birds did not awaken her with their chatter. She slipped into jeans and a T-shirt, aware as she dressed that she'd be wearing these clothes to evacuate the island. That realization sliced fear into her resolve. She chose socks and tennis shoes instead of sandals, and laid out a sweater on the bed along with her purse.

There was a stuffy, closed-in smell in the opaquely lit house and the mood was ominous. She unlocked the porch door and swung it open. A gust of wind laced with biting drops of rain slapped her face. She caught her breath and stared, shocked, at the change in the weather. All trace of blue was erased from the sky to be replaced by a sickly jaundiced hue. Over the ocean, closer now, the looming clouds were a battle gray and the sea threw waves fast and high. In that moment she lost any hope she'd harbored that they were going to escape the punch from this one. She should've known. The hurricane was named after some guy. Brendan was shaping up to be another bully, just like Hugo and Andrew.

Everything was aquiver. The red rosebushes were fluttering from their ties to the pergola, throwing petals into the wind. Beyond, the new young palms they'd planted were swaying. The air swirled around her, a strange mixture of warm and cool, humid and icy. Unlike in the Midwest where a tornado spun from the sky without warning, a hurricane gave you plenty of notice to get the hell out of its way.

"Mama! Toy!" she called out. "Wake up! We've got to get moving."

"I'm awake," Lovie called out from her room.

Cara felt a jolt of adrenaline. She began carrying the rocking chairs and small tables in from the porch at a fevered pace. "Toy!" she called out again, miffed at the silence in both bedrooms. Then it hit her that Toy could be in labor. She set down the basket of hats, making a beeline for Toy's room. She knocked on the door. "Toy?" She knocked again. When there was no answer, she slowly pushed open the door a crack to peek in.

Even in the dim light she could see that the bed wasn't slept in. She pushed open the door and flicked on the light. The room was pristine. Toy's maternity clothes hung neatly in the closet. The topaz ring that Lovie had given her lay in a bowl on the dresser. On the maple bed lay a white envelope.

With her heart in her throat, Cara reached for it and tore it open.

Dear Miss Lovie and Caretta,
I've gone with Darryl to make a family of my own. I'm sorry I had to sneak out like this. I never meant to. I wanted to say goodbye, but the hurricane speeded things up. Darryl was leaving and I promised you I wouldn't make any trouble.

   I can't thank you enough for all you did for me. I'll al-ways remember you and the things you taught me. Most of all, I'll always love you.

   Please don't worry about me and forgive me.

   And try to understand.
Love,
Toy Sooner
P.S. I'll send you pictures of the baby.

Cara stared for a minute at the letter, disbelieving. How could she have done that to them? Now, of all times? Her heart hammered in her chest as she sprinted to Lovie's room. She found her mother dressed in the same outfit she'd worn the day Cara returned home, only now the denim skirt and white blouse hung loosely from her gaunt frame.

"Mama, Toy's gone."

Alarm flickered across Lovie's face. "What's that? What do you mean, gone? To the hospital?"

"No. With Darryl!"

Lovie teetered back with her skinny arm out for balance. Cara rushed forward to grasp her, afraid she'd pass out in her weakened state.

"Toy, Toy, Toy," Lovie keened in distress. "Why would she run off with him, Cara? Why?"

"Because she's young and she thinks she loves him. Here, sit down and read the letter for yourself while I think of what to do."

She went to the hall phone to call the police, but the line was dead. Staring at it, a new whip of fear slashed through her. Without a cell phone, they had no connection to the outside world.

"The phone is dead," she exclaimed, hurrying to Lovie's room. "I can't call the police. Even if I could, what would I tell them? We don't even know Darryl's last name. Or what kind of car he drives. Mama, we don't know anything about him except that he's a creep."

"She made her decision, Cara," Lovie said calmly, sadly. She held the letter loose in her lap. "We have to let her go."

"There's got to be something we can do."

"She knows where to find us."

The front door swung open and they heard Flo's voice. "Hello! Hello?"

"In here!"

Flo came rushing in wearing a bright yellow slicker. Her face was frantic. "Thank God you're still here. I'm trying to shove off but it's Miranda."

Lovie rose to rush into her friend's arms. They gave each other a reassuring hug. "What's wrong with Miranda? Has she run off again?"

"No, she's plumb crazy, that's what she is. She's crying and fretting about that last nest in front of the house. Says we can't leave it to get flooded by the hurricane."

"There are a lot of nests still out there. What does she think we can do?" asked Cara.

"She wants us to move it."

MARY ALICE MONROE

"*What?* We can't do that. It's against DNR's rules."

"Not really," Lovie spoke up. When they turned her way she said, "The regulations state that the nests can be relocated by a permit holder when there is danger of the nest being destroyed by high tide."

"Only with permission." Cara was a stickler for rules. "And not off the beach."

"Okay, then call Sally for advice," said Flo.

"The phones are dead."

"I'll try my cell phone."

They waited in a tense silence while Flo tried to reach the Department of Natural Resources offices. But there was no answer, only a recorded message.

"No one's going to be there," said Flo, closing her cell phone. "Everyone is getting the heck out of Dodge. As we should. The roads are already backing up."

Cara's mind clicked off their options. "Do you think the nest is in mortal danger?"

"No doubt about it," replied Flo. "At least that one is. The tidal surge will completely flood the area, probably even erode that dune clear away. The other nests...well, they're farther back. That's the best we can hope for. Nature has to take its course."

Cara looked at Lovie. "We can't reach Sally. What do you want to do, Mama?"

"I don't know...."

"Mama, it's a yes or no decision. There's no going back."

Lovie lifted her chin. "Yes. But just that one nest. And I'll be the one to do it. It's my responsibility," she said, her eyes flashing a warning that she was not to be argued with. "Y'all can just keep away."

While her mother was moving the nest, Cara took the final steps to close up the beach house. While she worked, she kept a close watch on the television for up-to-the-minute reports on the weather and traffic. The front room looked like a warehouse, the porch furniture and clutter stacked in every spare inch of space. The flowerpots and tools she'd locked securely in the shed under the porch so they wouldn't become flying missiles. Suitcases and plastic bins filled with important papers and photographs were lined up by the door to be carried to the car.

A short honk brought her out to the porch. It was Flo and Miranda and their Buick was packed to the gills. An orange tabby cat stretched out in the back window.

"Just want to say goodbye and give you our travel plans," called Flo. "The name and number of our motel is in there. Better give me yours, too."

Cara went to her Saab and scribbled down the name of the motel in Columbia, where she'd made a reservation, and the route she planned on taking.

"Here." She handed her the information. "We'll give you a call when we arrive."

"And the nest?" Miranda asked. She leaned to clench Flo's arm with birdlike fingers, her pale, cloudy eyes entreating.

"We're taking care of it, Miranda. Don't you worry."

"Aren't you leaving yet?"

"Almost. I'm still waiting for my mother."

"You're what?" asked Flo, aghast. "Don't tell me she's still out on the beach!"

"I'm about to go right out and fetch her."

"Do that! And git! That wind is getting strong and they'll be closing the bridge before long." Flo took a last long look at her house. Cara saw the creases of worry and longing carved deep into her tired face. "I wonder if I'll ever see it again."

"This can still veer off and miss us," Cara said, trying to sound reassuring.

Flo tsked loudly and released the emergency brake. "I don't like this," she said with a slight tremble in her voice. "Not one little bit."

"None of us do. Off you go. Drive safe now, hear?"

Toy waited in the front seat of his car as Darryl loaded up the Mustang for the trip west. They'd spent a horrible night on an air mattress in Darryl's empty apartment. It was so hot and muggy inland that she couldn't breathe much less sleep. He'd sold the window air conditioner with the rest of his furniture so the only relief from the thick humidity was a creaky, rusty fan whirring back and forth. She couldn't believe it when his hands started reaching for her. Her with a baby due! A few weeks earlier she might have gritted her teeth and tried to go along with him. But last night her belly had felt as tight as a drum and she was sticky with sweat so she slapped his hand away. Now he was banging things around like a sulking kid. Above them, the sky was swirling gray soup. If they were going to make it out of town, they had to hurry.

Suddenly she felt a pain shudder through her, straight up from her pelvis along her spine, causing her to stiffen and hold her breath. She'd had pains all night long but not like *this*. When the pain eased and her muscles relaxed, she took a deep breath and glanced at her wristwatch. She'd read that she had to time the pains. She rested her head in her palm and tried to keep her breathing steady, thinking of the ocean as it rolled in and out, in and out. She imagined she was floating under a hot sun when she was hit by another pain, every bit as hard and demanding as the last one. She began whimpering.

Darryl got in the front seat, slammed the door and wiped his brow. "Damn, it's hot. I'll be glad to leave this hellhole." He swung his head around. "Are you cryin' again? *Toy.*" He whined the name to make each vowel a syllable. "What's the matter now?"

"I'm having these pains."

"What's that supposed to mean? You're not having the baby now, are you?"

"I don't know. I've never had a baby before."

"But aren't women supposed to know?"

"I just told you, I don't know!"

"Take it easy." He put the key into the ignition and started up the engine. "Maybe they'll just go away."

She couldn't believe he could be so stupid. "I think you should take me to the hospital."

"Now? But we're leaving! Shit."

She could feel her face get red with heat and the fear that another pain was building up like the waves she'd imagined before. She shouted at him, "I'm not having this baby in a car!"

She didn't know what gave her this maddening strength, but she'd get out of the car and walk to the hospital if he didn't drive her.

He must have seen something in her eyes because he only muttered, "Okay," along with a lot of other things she didn't catch.

As he pulled away from the curb she felt a sudden burst of water leaking between her legs. It was warm and she couldn't control it. Scared, she started to shriek.

"What? What the hell's the matter?" Darryl shouted, turning his head and looking at her with a frightened look.

"Something's happening. I'm leaking!" She tried dabbing at the seat between her legs with her dress but it wasn't doing much.

Then she remembered reading about how the water always burst before the baby was born and she stilled while relief flooded her. She felt stupid but incredibly excited.

"Oh, my God. It's really happening! The baby's coming. Darryl—" She reached out to touch his arm.

He shook it off. "It's about fucking time," he said, pulling a pack of cigarettes from his pocket and dragging one out with his teeth. His hand shook so badly he could hardly light it.

Toy shrank back in her seat, dragging her hand back to cover her belly. The streets rolled by in a blur of tears and, above, the storm clouds whirled thick and ominous. But inside the smoky car, Toy saw her world with crystal clarity. She was alone in this. She couldn't count on Cara and Miss Lovie. She couldn't count on Darryl. The only one she could count on was herself.

Lovie crouched down in the wind and gingerly laid the last egg in the bucket. She'd been especially careful not to jostle them so late in the incubation period. She also added extra moist sand along the bottom and sides of the red bucket to form a nestlike setting. When the last egg was in place, she covered all eighty-two of them with more moist sand, up to the rim, and gently patted it down, then covered it with a towel. The bucket was heavy and her arm shook as she lifted it, but she walked with a slow, steady tread, determined not to shake her hatchlings any more than was absolutely necessary. She sang to them as she walked, songs from the nursery any mother would sing to put her babies to sleep.

The wind teased her like a naughty child, lifting her skirt and pushing her forward with a gust. She stopped to steady herself so as not to rock the bucket. At least the rain had stopped, she thought, then said, "Thank you, Lord." She didn't want to ask God for any more favors, though she was tempted to drop to her knees right here in the sand and howl off a litany of requests. An inner voice told her to be calm and to accept whatever came.

"Mama!"

Lovie took heart at hearing Cara's voice and looked up to see her trotting along the path. She set the bucket down, shaking now with fatigue.

"Where have you been? You scared me to death!" Cara had to shout to be heard over the pounding surf and the wind. "Look at you. You're soaking wet."

"It took a long time with the waves rushing. And with all my coughing."

"Let me take that bucket. Here, lean on me."

"No! Don't touch the bucket. If you do, you'll be implicated."

"Oh, hell, you're in no condition to carry it. And I'll be damned if I let you. Where are you taking them, anyway?"

"To the house."

"You can't do that!"

"Caretta, I don't have time to argue. The tide has already crumbled the dunes. There's no safe place here on the beach to put these babies and we don't have time to go searching for another spot farther up. I have no choice."

"Oh, hell," Cara muttered again, bending to lift the bucket with one hand and grabbing hold of her mother's arm with the other. As she straightened, the wind slapped her face with cold drops of rain. "Come on, Mama. It's starting to rain again. Let's hurry."

They walked facedown, cutting into the gusts of wind and the sleets of rain. As they rounded the house, Cara squinted through the mist and saw a figure step away from her Saab.

Brett. He was dressed in jeans and an olive poncho. Strips of hair lay flattened across a face grave with worry. Her heart leaped to her throat. She was so relieved to see him she wanted to drop the bucket and go running into his arms.

But his face was scowling and his heels cut into the sand as he barreled toward them. "What the hell are you still doing here?" he roared. Then his eyes spotted the bucket and his face stilled.

"We had to move it," she shouted, her eyes glittering with challenge. "The dune was crumbling." She shouldered past him toward the house.

"I don't want to know about it!" he shouted back, but he bent to take Lovie's arm as gallantly as though he were escorting her up the stairs to a ball. "You should be long gone, Miss Lovie."

"It's my fault," Lovie said, leaning against him. "I was so slow and I'm the one who decided to bring the nest up to the house. Cara's been packed and ready to go for hours."

"You don't have to defend her to me."

"Don't I?"

She looked up into his face but it was as shuttered as the house.

Back inside, the noise was thankfully muffled. "I gather Florence and Miranda are gone? I got no answer when I knocked."

"They've gone," replied Cara. She saw Brett walk from window to window, checking out the plywood and shutters. "Don't worry. I put plenty of nails in." Then turning to Lovie, "Mama, I'll put these eggs in a safe place. You hurry and change. You're soaked through."

Brett followed Cara into the kitchen where she was moving pots and pans from a lower cabinet. Then, very carefully, she placed the bucket into a spot where it was dry, dark and warm.

"Sleep tight," she said, closing the cabinet softly. Rising, she wiped the hair from her face and sighed. "I feel like some criminal."

"You *are* some criminal."

"So we broke a few rules," she said defensively. "I don't have time to worry about that now."

"I've done nothing but worry about you since the moment I saw your car still in the driveway. No, since the moment I last saw you days ago."

They stood a few inches apart in the small galley and she felt a greater pressure between them than from the hurricane outdoors. She looked up, uncertain. His hair was spiked where he'd pushed it off his face. Drops of rain trailed down his forehead and one hung on the tip of his long lashes.

"Are you all right?" he asked.

She slumped against the counter. "Toy's gone. With Darryl. We found a note this morning."

Brett's eyes shone with restraint, then a scowl formed as the situation sank in. He began to pace the narrow kitchen. "Are you certain she's left with him? Have you called the police? How long have they been gone? Isn't she due any day?"

Of course his instinct would be to protect.

"She wrote in her letter that she went with Darryl. They could have left anytime last night or this morning. We don't know. And there's no point in calling the police because we don't know anything about him, not even his last name. I've never even laid eyes on him for a description. All I do know is he's twenty-four years old, in some band and he hits pregnant women." She brought her hands to her face. "God, it's all my fault. I've been so caught up with my own problems that I didn't take the time to reassure her. Of course she went with him. She figured she had nowhere else to go."

Brett stopped his pacing in front of her, but he didn't touch her. "You can't blame yourself."

"If not me, who? I knew she was afraid. Knew she needed guidance. She tried to tell me, but I didn't listen. I wanted her to make some decisions for her own life. Then I just got so caught up with mother, my job, the hurricane. She must have been frantic, getting closer and closer to the baby being born. I—I thought I'd have time. We'd figure something out. Wing it. But I wouldn't have abandoned her!"

Brett's eyes were feverish and he clenched his fists at his sides, helpless to console her.

"I'll find her."

Cara grabbed a paper towel, swiped the tears from her cheeks and sniffed loudly. "How can you? We don't know where she went."

"The traffic is backed up, and in her condition, I doubt she could have gotten far. I'll check the shelters. I've got connections. I'll make some calls. Tell me where you'll be staying."

She fumbled with gratitude. "Is this another of those rules of yours? A Lowcountry man never leaves a lady in distress?"

He didn't reply for a moment, then said reluctantly, "Something like that."

She grabbed a piece of memo paper and wrote the name of the motel they'd be staying in and the route they'd be taking. "Here, Brett," she said, handing him the paper. "Even if you don't find her, thank you. It means a lot that you tried."

He took the paper. "I'm off then. Turn off the electricity and gas before you go. And *go!* Now. No more delays. I'll call to check on you and Miss Lovie tonight."

Then, with a final parting look, he went out into the storm.

She stared at the closed door and wondered for a fleeting moment if she was crazy or if, when she'd handed the piece of paper to him, she'd really felt the connection as his fingers took hold.

A short time later Cara finished loading the car. She'd squeezed all she could into every inch of space then, glancing at her watch, groaned. Two o'clock already, though it seemed

more like night. The storm was building as quickly as her fear.
They'd delayed too long, Brendan was already at their heels.
The surf was pounding so loudly she could feel the percus-
sion in her head, and fear snaked along her spine as she fought
her way up the stairs.

"Mama!" she called on entering the house. "Mama, hurry!"
She ran into her mother's room to find Lovie stretched out on
the bed, a blanket wrapped around her legs.

"Come on, we've got to go!"

Her mother shook her head and brought her knees up to
her chest. "You go ahead."

Cara stopped abruptly. "What?"

"I'm staying."

"You're *what?* Oh, no you don't. This is ridiculous. We
don't have time for this. You're going."

"I'm not! I'm not leaving the beach house. Not ever again."
Her voice began to rise with emotion but she checked it, strug-
gling to maintain her dignity. "But *you* have to go. So hurry.
Please." She smiled stiffly.

Cara could only stare at her mother while panic whirled in
her chest. She knew that look. She'd seen it enough times over
the years. It was the narrow-eyed, teeth-bared look of a cornered, beaten dog. If she was going to move her, she'd get bit.

It was the last straw. Cara threw her purse down on the
floor, wiped a damp lock of hair from her face with an angry
swipe and glared at her mother with mounting fury.

"Well, screw this!" she shouted. "I've had it. If you're not
going, then I'm not going!"

Lovie looked stunned and her composure collapsed. "But—
but…you have to go!"

"I'm not."

"Cara, don't do this!" Lovie cried, her voice rising. "I'll

be fine here. This house has withstood lots of storms, even Hugo. It will stand up to this one, too."

But Cara didn't move; she steeled herself against her mother's growing hysteria.

"I have to stay," Lovie cried, wringing her hands. "Someone has to stay with the turtles!"

Cara crossed her arms across her chest. "I'm not going."

Suddenly there was a thunderous cracking of a tree branch outside the house, followed by the horrid creaking of the bathroom shutters as they were torn off their hinges. After a crashing thud, the broken branches battered the window glass like pounding hands.

"Go, Cara!" Lovie screamed. "For God's sake, go! I don't want to leave. I want to die here. I'm not afraid for myself. Please go!"

Cara felt the lid of her emotions rip off like the shutters. She was eighteen again and a great, howling pain clawed out from her chest. Words suppressed for too many years shrieked from her in a maelstrom, as uncontrolled as the wind.

"Once!" she cried. "Just once I wish you'd think about *me* for a change!" She took a deep breath that hiccupped in her throat as she stood, arms rigid at her sides, her hands in fists. "Do you want to know why I ran away at eighteen, Mama? Do you?"

Lovie clutched her shirt close to her chest with her small hands. "Oh, Cara—"

"It wasn't just because of Daddy. I knew he didn't love me. It was because of *you!* I couldn't forgive you for not protecting me. Or Palmer. Not even yourself. That night I ran away, he beat me hard. You let him hit me, Mama! You could've stood up to him. You could've defended me. You could've defended both of us. But you just stood by and let him hurt me. Why?"

Cara angrily swiped her face and took a deep, shuddering

breath. "I know why. To protect yourself. And now, again, you're thinking only of yourself! Or the turtles!" She felt the hurt taking shape in her chest, swirling painfully. "Why not me? Mama, why don't I matter enough?" Then the hurt erupted, gushing out with tears. "Why have I never mattered enough?"

"No, Caretta, no! That's not the way it was at all!" Even as she said the words, Lovie realized that they weren't true. She hadn't protected her daughter. But Cara didn't understand *why*.

Another loud, shuddering crash exploded in the room as the branches succeeded in catapulting through the window. Lovie screamed and Cara crouched low to the ground, her head ducked, her arms crossed over her head as shards of glass splayed like bullets. Cara felt a terror as starkly horrifying as it was familiar. Only once before had she been so afraid for her own safety. That moment flashed in her mind.

She was just eighteen, crouched in the corner of the entrance foyer to their house in Charleston. She held her arms protectively over her head, heard the whispered whoosh and snap of a leather belt as it cracked like a bullwhip against her skin. It stung like hell but it was the shock of being hit by her father that she felt the most. Even while she screamed for him to stop, she felt a deep shame that he could do this to her. His face was ugly and contorted with rage that she'd defied him and she saw in his eyes that he was glad to see her put in her place. He was shouting words at her that she could only understand in phrases like, "last time" and "I'll teach you" and "do as you're told." She begged him to stop, growing hysterical.

Until she saw her mother. From a small space under her arm she saw Lovie clutching the door frame of the foyer. Her mother didn't rush forward to stop him or stand in front of her child. She only watched, her face pale and her eyes wide with horror. Cara stopped crying then and rose to stare boldly at her father while he hit her. She stood straight until she shamed him into stopping. The hurt inside had made her numb to the blows.

Cara huddled in the corner, crouched in fear, while the hurricane's wind shrieked like a ghost. Then she felt her mother's hand on her shoulder.

"Cara?" she said. Then, more firmly, "Cara, look at me."

Cara turned to look up at her mother. Despite the wind swirling in the room, Lovie stood straight, her shoulders back in resolve.

"Yes, I saw him strike you that night," Lovie said. "And I knew at that moment you had to get out of that house. For your own safety. It broke my heart when you left, but I didn't stop you because I loved you more than myself. I knew the path I'd traveled and I didn't want you to follow. Maybe I should have left with you, but I can't change what's done. I can leave with you now, though. I love you, Cara. You *do* matter."

"Mama—" Cara cried, leaning against her mother's legs.

"My little Tern," Lovie said, stroking her daughter's damp hair. "Now come, take my hand," she said firmly, guiding Cara to her feet. "I have much to explain but we don't have time now. We must go."

Holding hands, they went out into the storm. Brendan's breath was on them but his real strength was still a ways off. Cara held on to her mother's waist and they cut through the wind to the car. No sooner had they reached the road than the rain began to dump bucketfuls. Even with the windshield wipers going full blast Cara could hardly see the road ahead. She leaned forward, gripping the wheel tight and squinting, heading straight for Palm Boulevard at a snail's pace. It was a ghost town; the streets were deserted. Most of the houses were boarded up. She was careful, taking it slow, on the lookout for fallen wires or flooded streets. She worried about the wind conditions on the connector.

"Goddamn, will you look at that?" Cara peered through the sheets of rain. Not far from the connector an old oak had split and fallen across Palm Boulevard. Her mouth went dry as she came to a stop. The enormous branches stretched from one side of the road to the other. She stared at it with disbelieving eyes as the wind rocked the car and rain pelted the windows.

"Can we get around it?" her mother asked in a thin voice.

"I don't think we should try. The power lines are down and the small roads are already flooded."

"Then don't try. If the water's rising we could be washed away." Her fingers shook at her lips. "What about the Ben Sawyer Bridge? Can we back up and take that?"

"I heard on the radio that it's already closed. It fell into the water during Hugo, remember?" Staring at the blocked road through the clicking windshield wipers, Cara felt a crack in her thin shell of composure. "We're trapped here. What should we do?"

"Cara," her mother said in a strong, firm voice that drew her attention from the street. "Drive home. We'll be all right in the beach house."

"If there's flooding—"

"It's a high lot and the house is on pilings. We can't stay here—and we have nowhere else to go. But we *must* get out of this car. If flooding starts, it will be a coffin."

Cara was spurred on by that frightening image. Her hands shook as she shifted gears and turned the wheel away from the evacuation route. They were on their way back to the beach house. Only one local radio station was audible over the crackling static and the whistling wind. Turning it up, she heard that the hurricane had not gained power.

"Thank you, God! Maybe we can ride this one out."

"I'm praying, Cara. I'm praying hard."

"You do that, Mama. You've got better connections than I do."

"Now's not the time to be proud. Now's the time to fall on your knees."

"I intend to, just as soon as I get out of this car."

As Cara navigated through the rain-slicked streets, she squinted through the sheet of rain and clicking wipers to make certain she didn't drive into water. If the car stalled, she knew they'd have to get out quick and climb to higher ground. Her knuckles were white on the wheel and her jaw hurt, she was clenching her teeth so hard. She was more scared than she'd ever been in her life. But she recognized the feeling of that steely wall dropping again, the one that separated her from the outside arrows, the one that kept her emotions in check. It had served her well over the years in times of emergency and stress and she counted on it now. They needed to get out of the storm and prepare for the worst.

By the time they reached the beach house they could see the waves already hammering far past the dunes and lapping the pilings of the front-row houses. Sea spray shot high into the air. Flooding from tidal surge was her worst fear. They'd be trapped in the house with nowhere to go but up on the roof. Still, she breathed easier knowing that, if the hurricane hit, it would be at low tide. She parked the Saab under the rear porch behind The Gold Bug. If flooding occurred, the engine would be shot. Then she pulled out the plastic bin full of important papers.

Facing the wind and rain Cara said, "I swear, the next house project, if there is a next project, will be to build a covered staircase into the house."

"Just one more appendage to blow away," Lovie replied, climbing from the car with Cara's help.

Her mother gripped her arm for support and they braved the wind a final time, catching sight of palms already leaning against the storm, their fronds rattling in frenzy. Cara raised her eyes, squinting against the wind. The little cottage stood strong on its perch high on the dune. "Keep us safe," she whispered as she struggled with her mother and the heavy bin up the porch stairs.

Once inside, the house was humid, dark and still. The phrase *silent as a tomb* ran though her mind but she quickly shook it away.

"I'll light the lanterns and you can change into something warm. Again," Cara said to Lovie, striving for levity.

Her mother coughed and smiled at the same time, keeping up the front. "At this rate, I should put on layers that I can peel off."

"I'm going back out for the oxygen tank before it gets too late," Cara said, opening the door. A gale rose up, and with a sudden ferocity, it tugged the screen from her hand, slamming it back against the house and tearing the top hinge out from the wood.

"Leave it!" Lovie cried out in a panic. "I won't need the tank. I forbid you to go out in that again. It's too dangerous."

"I can get it," she cried back and dashed out into the wind. Thankfully, the tank was in an easy access spot on the back seat. She yanked it out and groped her way back up the stairs.

"Foolish girl!" her mother cried out in relief when she returned.

Cara felt triumphant. She pulled the screen shut then ran to grab her hammer and pouch of nails. With a few sound whacks the door was secured. "I guess that's it," she said, slumping against the door. Rainwater dripped from her hair and down her face. "We're in for the duration now."

"May God protect us," Lovie whispered.

While Lovie changed, Cara lit the lanterns and placed one on the kitchen counter and brought the other to Toy's room. With the windows boarded and outdoor furniture and supplies crowding, the house looked like a storage facility. She lugged an extra piece of plywood into her mother's bathroom, then boarded up the broken window. Next she began moving the plastic bins full of bottled water, medical supplies and dry food into Toy's room. Lastly, she moved the oxygen tank. She was moving Toy's clothes out from the closet when Lovie walked in carrying her Bible.

"Why are you moving everything in here?" she asked.

"If the wind gets too strong, this will be the safest spot. The pressure will push the windward windows in, but the leeward windows will pop out. And, if we have to, we can jump into this closet."

"Lord have mercy."

"We'll be fine," she said, mustering up reassurance that she didn't feel.

"Yes, I'm sure we will," Lovie replied bravely but looking lost.

"You might as well make yourself comfy on the bed, Mama. We'll be here for a while. I'll get the radio and some books. Anything in particular you'd like to read?"

"I've brought my Bible. If you don't mind, I'd like you to read from this."

Cara released a small smile. "I'd like that."

Hours passed, and though the hurricane veered north, the beach house swayed back and forth on its pilings as the storm drew nearer. Inside the small bedroom, however, the lantern cast a warm yellow light over the Bible as Cara read aloud. Her voice was a low, soothing counterpoint to the constant whistling of the wind. Lovie had chosen Ecclesiastes and they both found comfort in wise King Solomon's insights at the culmination of his life. When a gale-force wind rattled the house, Lovie squeezed Cara's hand.

"Rest your voice for a spell and turn off the radio, dear. That incessant chatter about the hurricane is only making us more nervous. And I think it's time—" She paused and took a deep breath. "Cara, I'd like to talk to you about something that's been preying on my mind for some time."

twenty-four

Hatchlings dine on small snails, macroplankton and invertebrates. After they reach adulthood, their powerful jaws can crush heavy-shelled crustaceans and creatures that reside in reefs and rocks. Jellyfish are like candy treats.

"Do you remember when I wrote to you about clearing out the years of accumulation?" Lovie asked.

"Of course I do," Cara said, closing the Bible and turning toward her mother.

"You thought I was referring to all that junk cluttering up the Charleston house."

"We talked about this, Mama. I know you meant us."

"I did. But I haven't even begun to shake out all the dust. Oh, Caretta, I've been going back and forth on this for months, one day thinking I'd made up my mind, then the next doubting the decision I'd made. I only hope I'm not too late and the good Lord isn't taking that decision away from me."

She cast a worried look at the windows. The wind seemed to be prying at the surface, seeking a way in. Lovie took Cara's hand in both of hers.

"You asked me why I took all that abuse from your father for all those years."

"Mama, you don't have to—"

"Yes, I do. So, please, just listen until I've finished. I've a lot to say." She licked her lips and, after gathering her thoughts, began. "First you have to understand what it was like to be a wife in my generation. Not just a woman in the South, but a woman in my era. Our accepted roles were different. I daresay our attitudes were, as well. There was men's work and women's work. A woman was responsible for the home and children. It was where she belonged. For a woman to pursue a career as you did reflected as a failure upon her husband's ability to provide.

"My mother raised me as her mother raised her—to believe that a husband's word was law. I was taught never to refuse his needs. To stand behind him." Her lips turned up in a wry smile. "Preferably two steps behind. And I was to bolster his self-esteem, not fluff up my own accomplishments."

Cara leaned forward, trying to understand. "Are you saying you let him treat you so badly just because he was a man?"

Lovie shook her head, perturbed. "No. I'm trying to give you some background so you can understand what I'm about to tell you."

"I'm sorry. I won't interrupt again. Go on."

"I was thirty-nine that summer—not much younger than you are now. Stratton was already quite successful. He was only too happy for me to spend my summers at the beach house with you children while he stayed in the city or traveled. He traveled quite a bit to expand the business then, especially overseas. I suspected he played with skirts a bit but I learned to look the other way. At any rate, here on the island there was no Turtle Team back then, no one who kept watch over the nests or maintained any records. There was only me."

Lovie released Cara's hand and, leaning back against the pillows, closed her eyes.

"And a man by the name of Russell Bennett."

Lovie smiled briefly, enjoying the simple pleasure of saying his name aloud to someone else after thirty years. Hearing it made it all come alive again, real and not imagined.

"Russell? The man in the photograph?"

"Yes. He came to the Isle of Palms that summer to do research on the loggerheads. Russell was a naturalist. He was involved in his family's interests, too, but what he loved most was just being out in the field doing research. Brett Beauchamps reminds me of Russell. Not so much in looks. Russell was tall like Brett, but lanky and fair. The contrast between his white-blond hair and his leathery tan was really quite dramatic. He was more like Brett in his personality. Quiet but intense and bright. Dedicated to the environment. I found that...very attractive.

"It was our interest in the turtles that first brought us together. I was the only one on the island at the time who took an active interest in the loggerheads, as clumsy as it was. I'd read everything I could get my hands on, articles, Archie Carr's book, whatever. Looking back, I didn't do too badly. Word got out that I was helping the turtles and Russell came to see me. When he looked at my records I could tell that he was impressed. And honestly, Cara, it was the first time I was ever proud of a project that had been totally my own.

"That summer we worked together. He taught me so many things about the loggerheads and how to help them. I learned so much..."

Lovie lifted her hands as though to make a point, then let them flop into her lap with a sigh of frustration, shaking her head.

"No, no, no. Cara, this isn't what I mean to tell you. This isn't about the turtles at all. I'm still covering up and I want to be completely honest with you. I must if I'm to tell this right."

She faced Cara and saw dread in her daughter's eyes. She

hesitated, shaky and unsure how to proceed. She closed her eyes and from the darkness conjured up Russell's face. There, deep in her heart, where her love for him resided, she found what it was she wanted to tell her daughter. Opening her eyes again, she bolstered her resolve and pressed on with more feeling.

"Do you know what it's like to meet someone, to look him in the eyes and know, without a doubt, that this person is your soul mate? That's what it was like for Russell and me. I remember it as if it were yesterday. We were on the beach with a number of others, all gathered to hear him talk about the loggerheads. It was a hot day. The sun was bright and I raised my hand to shield my eyes. The gesture drew his attention and our eyes met. I looked into his gray-blue eyes and for a moment it seemed as though we were the only two people on the beach. In the universe. I remember thinking to myself, *Oh no. Please God, no.* Because I knew at that moment that I would love him as I'd never loved any man before. Or since.

"We were both very polite, amusingly so. For several weeks I met him at dawn on the beach, strictly professional. I'd bring a thermos of hot coffee and we'd watch the sun come up. Then we'd get on our bikes and ride around the island in search of turtle tracks. Every moment I spent with him was a gift. Every word he spoke, I thrilled to. We tried so hard not to let our feelings show at first." She chuckled lightly. "We were able to hold back until we began sitting at the nests together at night. Then—" She sighed. "We were desperately in love, Cara.

"We became lovers. Does that shock you? It's an odd thing for a mother to be telling her daughter. But it happened—as I daresay we knew it would. We met most evenings on the dunes right across the road, in that lot that Palmer is so desperate to buy. Only, you remember what it was like back when our property was beachfront, don't you? Before the road was built? The dunes used to stretch all the way up to our house. It was very quiet and sheltered then. A lush haven." She smiled again and cast a slanted glance.

"I thought you were checking the nests!" Cara's face reflected betrayal.

"I did. Faithfully. But I couldn't very well tell you that I was also meeting the man I loved, now, could I? You were only ten years old. And I knew that this affair could not last beyond the summer. You must believe that, Cara."

"But why did it end if you loved him so much?"

"This is the hard part to understand. It's why I tried at the beginning to explain who I am. Who I was raised to be. You have to remember I was married. And Russell was married. We both came from families where a divorce would have been a scandal. It just wasn't done in our circles. And more, we both *felt* our responsibilities and commitments. I could no more leave Stratton than he could Eleanor. At least in the beginning."

She couldn't restrain the surge of coughing that seemed to take more and more out of her every day. There were times Lovie believed she wouldn't live through the next cough. Cara quickly turned on the oxygen for her and Lovie pressed the mask to her face to take a few breaths. While she settled her ravaged lungs, she heard the wind howl at the windows like ghosts rattling their chains. *Oh, go away, Stratton. Your howling will do no good anymore. This story must be told.* She set down the mask and gestured with her hand for Cara to turn off the stream of oxygen. Then, sinking back into the pillows, she ignored the peevish wind and began her story again.

"As the summer came to an end, our feelings were too strong. Russell wanted me to fly in the face of our families, to divorce Stratton and marry him. It was a heady dream and

I wanted it. Oh, Cara, you can't imagine how I wanted to do as he asked. Saying goodbye to Russell was the hardest thing I've ever had to do. At the end of August, we were together for the last time on our dune.

"It was one of those perfect nights that ripens in memory. I still see that full moon and the way it spread its silvery light far out across a stretch of sand, transforming it into something otherworldly. It was dazzling in its serenity and thus all the more poignant. The air was still, as though the night were holding its breath, waiting, watching to see how the final few moments of our summer would end. The only movement was the dancing of the waves along the shore, the only sound the beating of our hearts in rhythm with the breakers. We held each other tight as we wept and swore our undying love. We were every bit as tragic and full of emotion as any star-crossed lovers I'd read about in books. For that's how I felt, like some tragic heroine forced to give up the love of her life for duty and honor. Yet, despite all our noble intentions, it seemed impossible that we'd never see each other again.

"So we made a last, desperate promise. We would wait six months. And if at that time one or the other of us wanted to leave our spouse, we would come to the beach house. There would be no pressure. No recriminations. If either of us didn't show up, the other would never call again. We set a date. It was a ribbon of hope to cling to, and it gave us the courage to say goodbye.

"As I walked back along the sandy path to the beach house, I felt as buoyant as though I were bobbing about in the sea. I knew—*I knew*—I would keep that date. I would settle my affairs as tidily as I could, asking nothing from Stratton but my freedom, and I would return to Russell, free to be with him. My heart was like the moon that night, overflowing with light. I was aglow, laughing aloud as I waltzed along the path. I'd made my decision. I'd thought the worst was behind me.

"I didn't know the worst had yet to begin. When I entered the beach house, Stratton was waiting for me. I can see him now as clearly as though it were yesterday. He was standing wide-legged in the middle of the room in a dark business suit. His face was pale with restrained fury and his hands were meaty fists at his thighs. He never came here and seeing him caught me by surprise. I held on to the doorframe, in part to steady myself, in part because I was but a breath away from running. A million thoughts raced through my mind in seconds but uppermost was relief that I'd come back alone. I couldn't imagine how he could know about my affair, and yet I felt certain that he did. It was the way he looked at me, his dark eyes narrowed and his teeth showing like one of his hunting dogs when it catches the scent. I once saw those dogs rip a rabbit to shreds with their razor-sharp teeth and Stratton's eyes were bloodthirsty as he watched them do it. That was the expression I saw in his eyes that night and I was very much afraid.

"'Where were you?' he had ground out.

"I raised my hands to pull back my hair, trying to seem nonchalant. 'I was at a nest,' I replied in a voice that sounded anything but. 'I go out to check them most nights.'

"He glared at me with his dark eyes. 'All alone? So late?'

"'Of course. It's quite safe.' I slipped out of my sandals and moved into the house, brushing away sand from my shorts. I froze. I saw that my wedding ring was off my finger. My eyes darted to his, and in that second I saw that he'd noticed, too. His gaze penetrated right through my defenses. I should have kept quiet, but like a guilty fool I began to babble.

"'I never wear my diamond to the beach. It collects too much sand. And if I have to dig a nest it—'

"'Who is he?' His voice was low, like thunder, and his eyes flashed like lightning.

"I shivered. And then I lied.

"'Who?' I replied. Even as I asked, I knew it was pointless.

"Only now, in retrospect, do I see that I missed my one chance for salvation. If I'd owned up to the truth at the very beginning, if I'd been strong enough at that moment, if I'd trusted Russell enough, trusted our love, then everything that came later might have been different. But I was afraid, a coward. Too timid to confront him. So I slipped into the lie that condemned me.

"To this day I don't know how he knew. Whether he saw us together or whether someone told him, or whether I'd left some telltale item in the house that he'd found. Perhaps his hunting instincts were so honed that he knew the scent of another man on my body. But he knew. And when he demanded that I name my lover, I refused.

"That night was the first time he hit me. He broke two ribs, my wrist and my spirit. A part of me died that night. But I never told him the name. Never. Not to anyone. Until this night."

Cara felt the blood drain from her face. She reached out to place her hand over her mother's, as much for her own comfort as for her mother's. "I didn't know," she said, barely a whisper. "I'd always wondered if he hit you."

"You and Palmer were away at friends' houses that night— a small blessing I'm grateful for. I was able to hide the bruises with some story about a fall."

"I remember now. Oh, Mama, how could I have been so naive?"

"You were a child. How could you have guessed? Stratton never hit me before or since that night, but that beating was enough for me to see his violent nature. I knew it was there and I lived with the fear it might come out again. Especially with you. I knew how strong-willed you were. It was only a matter of time till you reached the boiling point."

"You should have reported him to the police."

"My darling girl, no. You don't understand. I felt that I'd deserved my beating."

"You can't mean that."

"I may not have broken his heart but I did break my marriage vows and the trust. It was the knowledge that I'd wronged him, Cara, that compelled me to bear it for so many years. It was the guilt that shamed me to silence."

"But why did you stay with him?" she cried.

"He told me that he would never grant me a divorce. That he'd take you and Palmer away if I tried to divorce him. That he'd expose me as an unfit mother and the whore that I was. It was blackmail, made all the more powerful by the fact that I absolutely believed him. Stratton was a prominent citizen with connections and women had little recourse at that time, especially ones who had sullied their reputations. Even my own mother advised me to maintain my dignity and my silence. When I took into consideration how my action would affect all the people I loved, I made the only decision I could. And Cara," she said with finality. "Knowing what I did about him, I could never leave the marriage and let him have custody of my children."

Cara stared back at her mother, clutching her hand as the wind howled outside the windows. So many questions had been answered.

"So when six months passed," Lovie continued, "I did not return to the beach house. It was a blustery March day, dreary and cold, befitting the mood. Oh, I remember it so well. I had to lock myself in my bedroom that day. I didn't trust myself not to listen to my instincts and flee straight into Russell's arms.

"Afterward, I just went through the motions. You and Palmer were the only joys in my life and I tried to make you happy. I tried to shield you from the truth, but children have an instinct for these things. No amount of crepe paper and ribbon can create happiness. I could see the truth in your eyes especially, Cara. But you didn't know *why* and I couldn't tell you."

Cara's eyes filled and she brought her hands to her face. "I wish I'd known. All these years I thought you were so weak. And that Daddy was so cruel. Why didn't you tell me? It's all such a complicated mess."

"Most lives are if you live long enough, my darling."

"I've been angry at you for so long. I stayed away, not because I didn't love you, but because I loved you too much."

"Don't be angry any longer! Cancer is eating away my body, but anger will eat away your soul. Don't let it destroy your chance for happiness. It took years, but I clawed my way back to where I could find peace again. Only here, at the beach house, could I feel free from despair and sadness."

Her eyes scanned the small room, shabby in the dim light and crammed full of supplies. "This little place was my oasis. Stratton knew what it meant to me, and why. He tried to take it from me like he'd taken everything else, but it was in my name, and no matter how furious he was, I would never give it up. Stratton would never come here, and I couldn't stay away. So we more or less worked out a silent agreement that, for the summers at least, I would come here with you children while he had his time alone in the city. It was, after all, a socially acceptable arrangement."

"But didn't Daddy think you'd see Russell here again? I'm surprised he let you go."

"He knew he'd won. He saw something die in my eyes."

"I don't understand. You never saw Russell again?"

Lovie shook her head.

"So neither of you kept the date?"

"The following May I read about Russell's death in the newspaper. He was flying in his plane along the shoreline, as he often did at the beginning of the turtle season, and his plane went down. It was a headline article with photographs of him with his wife and two children. I wanted to die myself. I was inconsolable for months. That was the summer your grandmother Linnea came to stay with us at the beach house. Do you recall? I believe she thought I was going quite mad. I wandered the beach at all hours. I learned later that he'd kept our date and waited for me at the beach house all that night." Tears flooded her eyes. "I'm haunted to this very day by the pain he must have suffered thinking I didn't love him enough."

She was seized by a coughing spell. Cara held her shoulders and stroked her back, thinking to herself how little she really knew this woman. How wrong she'd been about her, how unfair she'd been to judge her. They were mother and daughter, yet in so many ways, they were strangers to each other.

When the coughing subsided Cara asked, "Do you want to rest awhile?"

Lovie placed her hand on her breast, took a short breath and shook her head no. "I need to finish," she said in a raspy voice. "Come, put your feet up next to mine." They settled back against the pillows, stretched out upon the bed.

"That fall," Lovie continued, "a strange man came to see me here, just as I was closing the beach house. His name was Phillip Wentworth and he was an administrative officer of Morgan Grenfell Trust Limited in the Channel Islands. I didn't know what he could possibly want with me, but I invited him in and offered him tea. He was British, a very proper sort of gentleman, very precise. Yet even in his clipped English, I had difficulty understanding exactly what he had come to tell me.

"You see, Russell came from an old, moneyed family in Virginia committed to preservation. Mr. Wentworth informed me that Russell had already bequeathed two beachfront lots on the Isle of Palms to a land conservancy. Russell and I had talked about this several times over the summer and I was so pleased that he'd carried out that dream. Russell saw what was happening on the island. He'd seen developments occur all along the eastern seaboard with little thought to the impact on marine life or the environment. Granted, those few lots were a small dent in the eight hundred or so being developed on the far side of the island, but I believe he'd hoped to set an example.

"I didn't know that he'd left the third lot, the one across from my beach house, in a trust for me. Mr. Wentworth informed me that Russell had also set aside monies to pay for the taxes on the land so that my reputation would not be compromised by the risk of mail, tax forms or any legal documents being directed to me. Under Channel Island law, the trust cannot reveal who the owner of the land is. Thus, Mr. Wentworth was instructed to pay me a personal visit upon Russell's death."

Cara's breath exhaled in a gasp. "You own that lot?"

"Yes, dear. I have for some time now."

She let out a short laugh. "Palmer will just die when he finds out."

"He's *never* to find out, Cara," Lovie said and her eyes were so filled with serious intent that Cara could only stare back speechless. "No one is ever to find out. That's what I'm leading up to. Oh, Caretta, don't you understand yet? The monetary value of the land never meant anything to me. Nor did the value of this beach house. Despite Palmer's constant niggling about it, I've never sold either of them because they were my refuge. You mustn't laugh, but I often go just to sit on the dune and talk to Russell. I feel close to him there. When his plane crashed into the Atlantic they never found his body. I like to think he's out there, with the turtles, just waiting for me."

She sniffed and reached for one of her tissues. "I do go on. But you do see why I love that land so much, don't you?"

"Of course I do, Mama. How horrible it must have been for you to give him up."

"I know now that I've been blessed to have known that kind of love."

Lovie saw tears filling her daughter's eyes. She didn't want to get maudlin before she got to the heart of the matter. Outside, the rain began coming down in fierce torrents. They could hear it thunder against the roof.

"We should turn the radio back on," Cara said with worried eyes looking at the ceiling. Water stains were dampening the west corner and the sound of dripping came from the other room.

"Wait one moment," Lovie said, reaching out to hold back her daughter. "Cara, this is my dilemma. I've gone round and round on this. What's to become of the land when I'm gone? I have to decide and I need your advice. Naturally, I've thought about leaving it to my children or to my grandchildren. Sometimes I think I owe it to you all for having failed you in life.

"But if I do, then the questions would begin. Where did the land come from in the first place? I read once of a woman who had stuffed her mattress with the letters she'd received from her lover over the years. I chuckled to myself when I read it. Imagine. Sleeping with her husband atop all those passionate declarations of love. Closing her eyes and thinking of her lover when her husband…well, never mind. The point is, the letters were discovered after her death and her secret was out.

"That mustn't happen to me. It's my life, my secret. Far too many people would be hurt. I've paid the dearest price already to prevent that. I couldn't bear to have it all come out after my death. Is that too selfish?"

"No, of course it isn't. You've paid the price for that secret many times over."

"Yet so have you. So has Palmer."

"You owe us nothing. Mama, what do you *want* to do with the land?"

Her face became wistful. "Russell left the land to me to help me gain freedom should I need it. And in its own way, the land did give me that freedom. But I won't need it anymore." She gripped Cara's hand and looked into her eyes beseechingly. "I want to leave it to the conservancy, as it was always intended from the beginning. I'd like to know that my children, my children's children, and children everywhere can enjoy that small stretch of dunes and beach as I have. And, of course, I should like very much to die knowing that there is a patch of beach left on the Isle of Palms for the turtles to return to and lay their nests undisturbed."

"Then that's what you should do."

"Do you really think so?"

Cara smiled into her mother's eyes and nodded her head. "Absolutely."

"I'd hoped you'd agree. I couldn't do it without one person I could totally trust with my secret. Someone competent who could notify Morgan Grenfell Trust of my decision. Would you act as my trustee when I die, Caretta?"

"I'd be honored to."

Lovie sighed wearily, the last of her energy seeming to slip away. "Thank you. You'll find a paper in the box with my photograph albums. It has Phillip's name and phone number on it, that's all. But you know now who he is. Phillip Wentworth is no longer at Morgan Grenfell, of course, but whoever is in charge will handle everything discreetly, you can rest assured. They're quite good at that sort of thing. I can't tell you what a relief it is to have made that decision! It's been such a burden."

"Don't worry anymore, Mama. I'll take care of everything."

"Oh, one more thing. There will be a bit of money left after the transference, from the monies he set aside. Not much, but enough to help with the taxes on the beach house for several years."

"The beach house?"

"But of course. I'm leaving it to you."

Cara was taken aback. "But I thought... Well, I don't know what I thought. I didn't think about it at all, actually. I supposed... I imagined it would go to Palmer."

"Palmer? Cara, you mean all this time..." She sighed and held open her arms. "Come give your mama a hug." She relished the feel of her daughter's head against her breast and her arms around her shoulders.

"What a funny girl you are," Lovie said. "Always have been. So brainy in some things, and so oblivious in others. But never selfish. That has always been a quality of yours. And a strength. Your ability to walk away is something I've always admired about you. It shows you have good instincts, Cara, and you heed them. I worried about you when you were in Chicago. You worked so hard and with such deliberation. You didn't have any relationships to balance out your life. I thought perhaps you no longer heard your inner voice in all the noise of the city. But when you stood up to Palmer and told me not to sell the beach house, when you fixed up this old place just to please me, and when you took care of me and Toy, I knew your inner voice was still very strong."

"I only did it because I love you."

"Precisely. Cara, when a parent passes on what little they have, be it a piece of land or a grandfather's wristwatch, it's done with love. He or she tries to think which child would most cherish that particular item. Palmer might think of the dollar value but my mind doesn't work that way. I'm not good with numbers, though I do try to keep things fair. I love you both and I've tried to think what would make each of you happiest. When I gave the Charleston house to Palmer, I had in mind to give the cottage to you. I'd planned this for many years, long before the value of this land shot up as it has. I simply knew that Palmer loved the city house and the life-style. And I knew that you didn't and had been happy here.

"Cara, you're my child, my baby," she said, gentleness flooding her features. "You might think you've been out of my thoughts all those years that you were away but you were always here." She pointed to her forehead. "And here." She moved her hand over her heart.

Cara's eyes moistened. "That's all I ever wanted. Just to know that I wasn't forgotten. That I mattered enough to be considered."

"You silly, precious child," she said again. "The beach house is yours, Caretta. It's already been arranged with Bobby Lee. That's what I told Palmer on the Fourth of July."

"So that's what he's been stewing about."

"Don't let him pout too long. He really has a good heart when his mind isn't clouded with dollars and cents. He needs the beach house more than he knows, but it's yours because you understand the magic better than I ever did. It's not so much a place as a state of mind. Listen to me, Cara. The beach, the ocean, solitude—these are only a means to help you travel to the true peace and joy inside you. You must carry the magic in your heart, wherever you go. We had a lovely summer, didn't we? So many wonderful summers. And I hope you'll have many more here. But if you find you have to sell it, then do so. It's your life, Cara. Don't let anyone or any thing hold you captive from finding your heart's desire."

"Oh, Mama… How will I know what that is?"

She cupped her daughter's face, and in the woman, saw the little girl. "You'll know, my precious. One day you'll look up and see it—and just know."

twenty-five

Loggerheads are air-breathing reptiles. They can sleep under water for several hours, but stress and activity can markedly shorten the time they can hold their breath. This is why sea turtles drown when tangled in shrimp nets and other fishing gear.

Cara awoke to the spasm of her mother's coughing fit against her shoulder. It was pitch-black in the house. The lantern had gone out and the house was shuddering. She wiped the perspiration from her brow, unable to see her hand. Everything felt damp. The humidity was like a wet blanket lying on her lungs.

"I'll get your oxygen," she said in a croaky whisper. She rose up sleepily and swung her legs over the edge of the bed.

Her feet landed ankle-deep in water.

"My God!" she choked out, yanking them back up. Her whole body shook as her mind snapped awake and wildly tried to figure out what was going on, what she should do next. She sat with her legs to her chest, shivering, her eyes wide with terror and her heart pumping hard. All around her in the darkness she could hear the sound of water rushing, the clunk and clatter of things banging against each other as they floated, the creaking of wood as the house swayed and shuddered against the wind and surge. They were going to die, she thought numbly.

The hell they were.

"Mama! Mama, wake up!"

"What? What is it?"

"Water. There's water in the house."

"What!" she cried out.

"Don't move." The darkness made her fear palpable. She needed to get some light. Her hands were shaking so badly she could barely make them function as she groped clumsily on the bedside table. Outside there was a tremendous roar that sounded like something was being ripped off the front of the house. Her mother whimpered at her side. Cara fumbled in the dark, trembling. At last her fingers rested on the flashlight. She clutched it like a lifeline. Flicking on the light, she felt a bone-deep relief at piercing the horrid blackness and being able to see.

She beamed the light across the room. The bed was an island in a black and swirling sea of water, several inches high. She could only stare at it, openmouthed in numb horror. Her shoes, the plastic bins, clothes, chairs—all were bobbing about like little toys in a bathtub.

She felt her mother clutch her arm. "It must be the storm surge," she said. "Is the tide high or low?"

Cara licked her dry lips, not knowing. The water was still shallow, but even as she watched, it was rising inch by inch. "We've got to get out of here."

"Where can we go? We can't evacuate."

"The attic."

"We don't have an attic. It's only a crawl space."

"Then we'll crawl! Come on, Mama, we don't know how high this is going to get. We'll pray we don't have to climb on the roof. Let me think…" She moved her beam of light around the room, looking for her supplies. The suitcase was bobbing, but with luck, some clothes would still be dry. She climbed on all fours and stretched from the bed to grab hold of it and drag it back to the island bed. Then she reached for another flashlight from the bedside stand and handed it to her mother. "See if you can pull out some dry clothes. I'll try to find my tools and whatever else I can get up there in time. Hurry!"

"The eggs. Cara, the turtle eggs!"

"Yes, okay. I'll get them."

She looked over the bed at the swirling black water, poised to step off. For a crazed moment she wondered about getting electrocuted and snakes. She thought back to Brett's warning. Yes, thank heavens she'd remembered to turn the electricity off at the main switch. As for the rest…well, she couldn't do anything about it.

"Be careful, Cara."

She nodded, then, taking a deep breath, she stepped into the black.

The water was blood warm. It reached high over her ankles, halfway to her knees, swirling with a strong current.

"Wait here," she told her mother as she faced the bedroom door. Visions of opening a door to a tidal wave made her knees watery but she said a quick prayer and, holding her breath, yanked it open. She felt a rush of water around her calves but thankfully, no wave. The hall was a tunnel of watery darkness. As she waded through, she felt as if she were in some horrible amusement park waiting for something slimy and creepy to jump out at her at any moment. She almost wept with relief when she reached the rope to the trap door. She pulled down the ladder, then went back for her mother.

They huddled together in the stifling, cramped crawl space. Beside them on the dirty plywood flooring was the red bucket of turtle eggs, a battery-operated radio, a pile of dry clothing, the green plastic bin of papers, her tools and a first aid kit—all she could carry up before the water hit her knees. Above them, the wind shrieked like a madwoman, plucking and tearing at their roof. Below, the black water rose like a menacing beast.

As she stared down into the black water, she prayed simply for another chance to enjoy a sunrise. To walk along the beach. To listen to Toy and her mother chatter about marinades. To laugh with Emmi. To lie in Brett's arms. She prayed for the chance to enjoy all the simple pleasures of the Here and Now that she'd taken for granted. Just one more chance.

The nurse was real nice, Toy thought as she sipped hot, sweet tea from a foam cup. She was lying on a gurney in the hall of the hospital's emergency level. They'd had to bring everyone down to the shelter during the worst of the storm but the nurse told her in a cheery voice that they'd soon be able to bring everyone back upstairs. Then she'd get a real bed to lie in and something to eat. All the nurses were running back and forth between the patients like crazy. There weren't enough of them to go around since a lot of women had had babies tonight. Something to do with barometric pressure.

Toy wasn't complaining. She felt a strange new peace inside, though not as powerful a relief as she'd felt after the baby finally slipped out of her body. Lordy, she doubted she'd ever feel anything like that incredible, bone-deep sense of *Ahhh* again. This was a quieter peace, like the way she felt when she was looking out at the ocean, only much deeper still. She'd felt it the moment she looked at her daughter's face and the feeling lingered. Toy knew that this feeling would last the rest of her life.

And her baby girl was really something special. A girl—not the boy she'd been so sure it was. She was wrong about a lot of things, she'd realized. When they first put her baby in her

arms, she was all pink-faced and screaming as if she were mad
at having to leave such a nice, warm place. But she didn't keep
bawling like the other babies around them. Her little girl just
opened her eyes real wide and blinked slow and heavy, like
she wanted to get a good look at this new place she was in.

Toy was smiling just remembering it when she spied Darryl
walking down the hall past a long line of gurneys and people
sitting in chairs. His face was pale and his hair was flattened
to one side. He looked as if he'd been sleeping on the floor,
which he probably had. When he drew closer, she felt a ping
in her heart seeing the worry in his eyes.

"Hey, darlin'," he said, coming closer. He leaned against
the gurney to give her a kiss, but jumped back when it started
to roll. "Whoa!"

She giggled. "They didn't put us in real beds yet."

He recouped, putting his hands in his back pockets. His
arms stuck out, thin and gangly.

"Did you see her?" she asked.

"Who?"

"The baby, silly!"

"Oh, yeah. I mean, no. No, I didn't."

"She's so beautiful. She has soft, yellow, fuzzy hair like a
baby chick and big, wide eyes. I think she has your nose. We
have to give her a name."

"Name her whatever you want."

"Don't you want to give me some ideas?"

"It don't matter to me." He turned his head to look down
the hall and jerked his shoulder, like a man about to run. When
he faced her again he seemed impatient. "Look, how long do
you think they'll keep you in here? It's hotter'n Hades."

"I don't know. Not long. I've got to rest a little bit. They
put in these stitches. You know, down there. They itch something fierce."

"But when can we leave? The weathermen gave the all-clear sign. Folks are going home."

Home. She heard the word and clung to it. "I'd like that, Darryl. The doctor's checking the baby now. As soon as they say she's fine we can—"

"Why do we have to wait around? Won't somebody, you know, come for it? A social worker or something?"

She felt a panic rising up in her at hearing him call the baby *it*. "Darryl, just go look at her. Take a peek."

"What for?"

"Go on. Please. When you see her you'll love her."

"Drop it, okay?"

"Darryl, look at her!" she shouted.

"I don't want to look at her!" he shouted back.

The women in the gurneys next to her looked at them nervously and a nurse rushed over from around the corner.

"We can't have any of that," she said, her stern look traveling from Darryl to Toy, then back to Darryl.

"We won't let it happen again, ma'am," he said. "We're a bit wore out is all."

Toy could see the woman's anger melt at the power of Darryl's smile.

"All right, then. Just keep it down." The nurse walked away, too busy to deal with this minor problem any longer.

When Darryl faced her again, she expected him to be angry or frustrated. He surprised her by being contrite.

"I'm sorry, Toy, but I don't want to see the baby." He rubbed the stubble on his chin and paced the few feet of space they had between the gurneys. Then he came closer so that he could talk soft so the other ladies couldn't hear him.

"I told you," he said in a pleading voice. "A thousand times. I'm not ready to be anybody's daddy."

"You really will leave her? Without a single look?"

"If I look at her I might not want to leave. And I've gotta go. This is my big chance to make it. You know how hard I've worked for this. How long I've waited. If I don't go now I'll always wonder what might have been. And that's a woeful place to spend the rest of your life."

Her mind slowly spun into focus as she opened her eyes and saw an amalgamation of pipe dreams unravel and dissipate like smoke. Toy opened her mouth. She felt her tongue move to touch her teeth, her lips move and the air expel. "Then go."

He hesitated. "You're not coming with me? How can you tell me this now?"

She closed her eyes and felt the hot tears leak around the corners and down her cheeks. "Darryl, I can't make this turn out the way I dreamed it would. All the time I was lying here waiting for you I was having this conversation in my mind, imagining all the things you'd say when you came. You'd tell me how you'd seen our baby and fallen instantly in love with her. How you wanted to be a loving husband and father and take us home to be a family." She opened her eyes and saw Darryl's drawn and weary face a few inches from her own.

"I had that dream a lot, but I knew when I saw your face today that you were never going to say those things. I shouldn't have expected you to. You were always straight with me about the way you felt. It was me who was lying all along—to you, to Cara and Miss Lovie, and to myself. I guess I was lying to my baby, too. But do you want to know something amazing, Darryl? I see things real clear now. When I held my baby in my arms I knew for sure and certain what was really true. I'm her mama now and I'll never abandon her. She means everything to me. I've depended on other people all my life but no more. I don't know how I'm going to do it, but I'm going to give my child a good life. She might not have a lot of things, and she won't even have a daddy, but she'll have me and I'll have her. And that'll be enough."

By 2:00 a.m. the radio reported that the storm had skirted the South Carolina coast and was heading north toward Wilmington, North Carolina. By dawn, the water had receded from the house and they could come down.

Cara led her mother across the soggy flooring to the living room. They were exhausted, wet and chilled despite the soaring heat. Cara was desperate to get some fresh air and light in the stuffy, sour-smelling house. She settled her mother on one of the dining room chairs, then hurried to the front door, pushed away the barricade, unlocked the bolts and swung it wide.

The air still felt stormy and the pewter ocean still pounded the shore with huge steely waves, but the screaming wind had at last quieted. A few birds ventured out to chirp and the palmetto trees stood straight again, ragged but intact. A pale pink light pierced the ethereal, gray morning.

The storm was past.

But Hurricane Brendan had done his damage. Lying on the front dune, twisted with canes of roses and bits of roofing, was the pergola. The deck stairs were damaged, the screens shredded as though ripped by thousands of razors and the screen door was halfway to Flo's house. The cars below were flooded. But it could have been a lot worse. The beach house was sound, and more importantly, they'd survived without harm.

Lovie tottered up beside her, pale and worn to the bone. Yet her eyes were glowing with gratitude at seeing another dawn. She reached out to take Cara's hand in hers, lifted her face to the sky and, in a clear voice that rang with exuberance, gave thanks with a psalm.

"For lo the winter is past; the rain is over and gone;
The flowers appear on the earth;
The time of the singing of birds is come,
And the voice of the turtle is heard in our land."

After the storm, Cara's chief concern was her mother. She didn't like the pallor of Lovie's skin or the shallowness of her breathing. Sitting slump-shouldered and wan on the rocker, Lovie seemed to be sliding downhill very fast and Cara felt a panic, wanting somehow to stop the inevitable, knowing she could not.

Exhaustion cloaked her like a heavy winter coat in the warm sun, but there was more work to do than she could shake a fist at. Everything was wet or soggy, inside and out. She dragged herself out of the chair, stretched her arms high over her head, yawned loudly, then rolled up her sleeves.

First Cara pried the plywood off the windows, opened them wide and let the fresh air circulate through the beach house again. Then she scrubbed Lovie's bedroom and bed with oil soap and the water she had carefully saved in the bathtubs before the storm. She swept up the broken glass from the bathroom window, washed the sheets and hung them to dry. The bed was an old mahogany four-poster that stood so high off the ground Lovie used a small, embroidered footstool to climb into it. This was a blessing because her mattress had escaped the water. After a few hours Lovie's room was almost free of the mustiness that permeated the rest of the house. At last Cara could settle her mother in a comfortable spot. Lovie took mincing steps and needed help climbing into the bed. As Cara tucked her mother under the sheet and smoothed her wispy, fine white hair across the pillow, she was amazed at how small she appeared, as slender and delicate as a child. And as vulnerable.

The sun cooperated, coming out midmorning to dry the earth, the house and all the sheets and pillows she'd hung on a makeshift clothesline between two palms. She pulled the wool carpets off the floor and hung them over the porch railings, then scrubbed the filth off the heart pine floors, but it would take quite a lot of time for them to not feel squishy as she walked across them. She didn't do much to clear mud from below the house after she spotted a water moccasin slink out from under the car. There was a dead dog at the end of the road and a cat meowed piteously on a neighbor's porch. She brought it some canned tuna to eat, careful to keep her distance, but sure enough, the sweet-looking calico followed her home.

She was sweeping wrack off the porch when she heard car wheels skid to a halt in the gravel in the back of the house, the slam of a car door and a man's voice urgently calling her name.

"Cara! Caretta Rutledge!"

She recognized Brett's voice and her own leaped from her throat. "Here!"

He came tearing around the corner, took the stairs two at a time. Before she could sputter a hello he swept her into his arms, kissing her soundly. She went limp with surprise, clutching one of his shoulders with one hand, the broom handle with the other as she tilted on one foot. He kissed her until she dropped the broom and wrapped her arms around his neck, kissed her until she kissed him back just as hard.

When he pulled away his expression was fierce. "Don't you ever scare me like that again. Last night I called your motel and they told me you hadn't checked in. You weren't to be found at any motel or shelter in a fifty-mile radius. I know because I called or went to every damn one of them!"

His face was haggard with fatigue and covered with dark stubble. His tawny hair was tousled and his clothes lived in.

He looked as if he hadn't slept a wink. Cara smiled, realizing she probably looked just the same.

"I couldn't reach you," she replied simply. "I couldn't get in touch with anyone." Then, in a soft voice she added, "I was scared."

"You should have been. You risked your life." His voice lowered and she saw worry, relief and something else she was afraid to put a name to in his eyes as he hungrily studied each feature of her face. "You risked my life, too. Don't you know that yet? Damn this craziness. Cara, we don't have to get married. I'll move to Chicago. I don't care. That's just geography. But last night was the longest night of my life, wondering if you were okay, if I'd see you again or hold you in my arms again. I love you, Cara. I don't want to live without you."

"I love you, too," she blurted out.

His big arms held her close and at last she felt she could let go. She felt safe in his arms, secure against any danger that might come howling at her threshold.

When he pulled back, he was smiling. "I've brought someone to see you."

"Flo?"

"Wait here."

He released her and went back down the stairs and around the corner. She heard again the slam of a car door, then the crunching of gravel and the soft murmur of voices. She bent to pick up the broom. After leaning it against the wall, she slapped the sand from her hands and lifted her head in time to see Toy round the corner. In her arms she carried an infant.

Cara blamed it on her fatigue, the stress of the hurricane and the worry about her mother. She'd been as strong and stalwart as she could be for hours—weeks, months, really. Whatever her excuse, she brought her hands to her face and began to sob. Great, heaving sobs that were embarrassing in front of people she wanted to be strong for. But she couldn't stop herself.

Toy and Brett came around her, murmuring words of affection and comfort. She felt arms around her shoulders, and through the blur of tears, she saw Toy's smiling face and the peaceful face of a sleeping, beautiful baby.

Then a horn honked in the driveway.

The baby startled and commenced wailing. Cara sniffed and burst out laughing. She wiped her face with her palms as a grin stretched from ear to ear at seeing Flo and Miranda trudge up the stairs. They swooped down on Toy and the baby with squeals of joy and surprise. A minute later, Lovie appeared on the porch, tottering and weak but her eyes were as bright as a sparrow's at all the commotion. When Toy saw her she hurried with the baby to rush into Lovie's outstretched arms. The baby continued squawking at all the noise and fuss but the women only laughed and exclaimed how utterly adorable she was.

"Come, everybody, sit down," Cara said, ushering them toward the porch chairs. "Y'all must be exhausted. We'll have to sit on the porch, I'm afraid. The inside is all soggy and dank. Come, Toy, here's a rocker for you, Little Mama." Then, taking hold of Lovie's arm, she guided her to the rocker beside Toy. "I guess that makes you Big Mama, now," she said with a laugh that masked her worry at seeing her mother more frail than Miranda. Brett hustled to pull out chairs for Miranda and Flo.

"Just a few minutes to chat, then the two mamas have to get back to bed," Cara announced.

"Absolutely," Flo replied, picking up the cue. "We need to open up our house, too. It doesn't look too bad from the outside. A few shingles are gone."

"I'll help you ladies," Brett offered. "We don't want any injuries after the storm."

"Oh, Brett," Lovie said mournfully. "The pergola…"

"I saw," he replied. "I can always build another. You and Cara are safe. And Flo and Miranda. And Toy and the baby. Hey, we're all fine. That's all that matters."

"Amen to that," Flo agreed. "I about had a heart attack last night when you two didn't show up at the motel."

"And the nest?" asked Miranda. "Is it all right?"

They all chuckled at the older woman's one-track mind.

"It's safe and sound," Lovie replied gently, reaching out to pat Miranda's hand. Then she looked at Cara anxiously. "We've got to get the eggs back into the sand. As soon as possible."

"Back into the sand?" Flo asked, brows raised.

"Don't ask," Cara replied, holding up her hand. Then to Lovie, "I'll take care of it. You don't have to worry."

"We'll get them in today," Brett added.

"Oh, no," Lovie said to Brett with a warning tone. "You can't get involved."

"Worried that will make me an accomplice?"

Cara replied with amusement, "Now we'll be Bonnie and Clyde."

He snorted and shook his head, acknowledging the private joke between them. "You do remember what happened to them, don't you?"

"I'm quite serious, Brett," Lovie said.

"So am I, Miss Lovie."

"On that note, let me get something for us all to drink," Cara said, turning to leave for the kitchen.

When Brett followed Cara into the kitchen to help, she tugged him closer.

"Okay, now tell me everything. Where did you find Toy?" she whispered heatedly.

"At a hospital. I exhausted the shelters first, then someone told me that if she was having a baby, they'd likely send her to a hospital even with a hurricane warning. So I started combing the hospitals. I found her on the third try. By that time she'd already had the baby."

"Poor thing. And all alone."

"She wasn't alone. She was with Darryl. Apparently he stayed with her till she delivered. That was decent of him, at least."

"Oh, please. So, what's become of him? Is he still lurking?"

"Toy didn't say much, but I gather he went to California this morning after all. Something about an important gig his band had lined up."

"Yeah, right. Him and a thousand other bands. At least he's gone. We won't have to worry about him coming around here anymore."

"For the time being anyway. They tend to come back, sooner or later."

"He didn't hurt her, did he?"

"No. Oddly enough, it might have been the other way around. He wanted her to go with him, but without the baby. Toy refused. She wouldn't leave her baby behind."

"Really? Good for her. Poor girl, I'm sure that was a tough decision."

He tugged his earlobe. "I don't know. She didn't seem too heartbroken when I found her. She was eating a big breakfast and had this ear-to-ear grin on her face."

Cara chuckled, envisioning it. "You know, I'd thought for a while that she was going to leave the baby with me. There were little hints, odd questions and looks sprinkled over the summer. When I put them all together, I wondered."

"Would you have wanted the baby?"

She saw that he was anxious and knew he'd take her reply very seriously. "In an odd way, yes. I fancied what it would be like being a mother. I didn't think I would ever be one and the thought that a child—not just any child but *this* child that I'd helped care for—would be given to my care was very tempting. But, of course, I'm delighted that Toy has decided to keep her baby. It was the best decision for her and for the child. But it won't be easy for her to handle. Her whole life has changed."

"I wonder how she'll manage."

"She won't have to worry about that for a while. Right now all she has to do is take care of that baby. This is her home. Down the road I'll help her make the best decision. I won't let her down."

"I never thought you would."

She looked at him, grateful that he always saw the best in her. From out on the porch she heard Flo yell, "Do you need any help in there?" She was reluctant to go. She wanted to lean against him and talk about the thousand and one thoughts that had coursed through her mind as she'd sat in the crawl space and watched the black water rise.

"I'd better get these drinks out there," he said, grabbing several bottles in his hands.

"Yes. They're waiting for us." Then she lifted her hands to his sides and leaned forward to kiss him softly on the lips.

He looked down at her with a perplexed smile. "What's that for?"

"For the Here. And Now."

His gaze kindled and he lowered his lips to hers for another, longer, lingering kiss that was gentle yet ardent and full of promise. When he pulled away, a soft sigh escaped her lips.

"We'd better go while we still can," he said, but his eyes

revealed he'd been shaken every bit as much by the kiss as she had.

She gathered the plastic cups and followed him out to the porch where they sat among the ruins and toasted the new mother and her baby with bottled water and juice.

"Have you given that precious darling a name yet?" Flo asked Toy.

Everyone stopped talking and turned toward Toy with interest.

Toy's face brightened, and despite the mess that surrounded them, she carefully set her plastic glass on the coaster on the table. Then she looked at Lovie with shining eyes.

"If it's all right with you, I'd like to name her Olivia."

Lovie's face bloomed into a radiant smile.

"What did she say?" asked Flo. "Olivia? Oh, how wonderful. It's perfect."

Cara smiled her approval and gratitude at Toy.

"Here, you can hold her," Toy said. She gingerly settled the sleeping baby into Lovie's thin arms, slowly removing her hands until she was sure that Lovie had a firm grasp. Still, Toy hovered over them both like a worried hen.

Miranda nodded grandly. "Little Lovie," she said in her serious manner, giving her approval of the name and securing her nickname forever.

Everyone observed the sight of the two Olivias with smiles. It felt right, like maybe life did have a way of coming full circle after all.

Lovie had rested fitfully, able to sleep for only a few hours before violent hacking coughs woke her. She was weak and exhausted by the struggle, so it stunned Cara when Lovie insisted that she oversee the return of the turtle eggs to the beach.

"I must," she said softly.

"Mama, I can do it. You've trained me well."

"It's not an ordinary move," she argued. "Everything must be done perfectly and it's my responsibility."

"But the coughing... You're exhausted."

"Caretta," she said, and though her voice was little more than a harsh whisper, Cara heard the firmness underlying the use of her full name. "I *want* to do this." Then her face softened and she said earnestly, "Do you understand?"

Her mother's face was pale yet her eyes burned with intent. Cara nodded, then looked to Brett for support. They exchanged a pained look.

They ventured out along the sandy, inclined path to the beach. Brett half carried Lovie, while Cara carried the red bucket. Broken tree limbs, palm fronds and bits of trash littered the path and they walked at an agonizingly slow pace, not only for Lovie's sake but also so the eggs would not be jarred. When they finally reached the beach they stood in the soft sand in a collective silence, stunned by how badly the dunes had been battered and the beach reconfigured by the power of the storm. The tide was going out. The glistening wet sand of Breach Inlet stretched farther out than Cara had ever seen it before.

"I wonder how the other nests fared?" she asked in a worried tone.

"They probably won't make it," Lovie answered matter-of-factly. "This nest most likely won't, either. Nature can be harsh. But we tried our best, didn't we?"

"That we did."

Lovie walked slowly along the beach in search of the best possible location for the nest. Her long rose-colored robe fluttered in the evening breeze, and with her mincing, hunched-over steps, Cara thought she looked like a petite Japanese geisha. Lovie stood for a long while in front of a small, washed-out dune.

Cara came to her side. "Mama?"

"My dune is gone," Lovie said sadly, her lower lip trembling.

Cara surveyed the property that lay in front of their beach house. The high dune that had once been a place of refuge for her mother and Russell had been severely flattened. She put her arm around her mother's shoulders. There was so little left of her. She was being whittled away as surely as her dune.

"You don't need the dune anymore. Remember what you told me? The magic is what you carry with you in your heart."

Lovie turned to look at her daughter and Cara saw hope shining in her eyes.

"You're right. How silly of me to have forgotten."

Cara held back her hair and looked across the windswept, reconfigured shoreline searching for a safe haven for the eggs. "I dunno. Where do you think we should put the nest?"

Lovie looked at the dune again and half smiled. "It's serendipity. My dune was always too high and steep for a nest. But now it's really quite perfect. It's far enough back and the mound slants nicely toward the sea. This is the spot."

Lovie swayed with fatigue as she oversaw the efforts. Under her watchful eye, Cara and Brett dug a new egg chamber to the same depth, size and shape of the original. One by one they carefully transferred the eggs into the chamber, and after all the eggs were settled, Cara covered them, then gently patted and smoothed the sand with her palm. She marked the site with stakes but Lovie stepped forward to place the orange nesting sign on her final nest.

Straightening again, Lovie suffered a long spell of coughing that racked her frail body and left her gasping for air. Cara and Brett could only stand beside her, helpless, holding her frail body while waiting for the spasm to pass.

Cara couldn't bear to see her mother suffer so. She seemed to be drowning inside her own body. Lifting her chin, Cara looked out to the sea with anguished eyes and called out in her heart to Russell, who she sensed was waiting in the swells.

What are you waiting for? The summer is over. Please, don't let her suffer anymore. If you love her, come for her!

At last the coughing subsided and Lovie nearly collapsed against Brett's chest, breathing in shallow gulps. "I'm sorry... but I don't think I can make it back on my own."

Cara put a hand to her trembling lips.

"I'd be honored," Brett replied. With a gallant flourish, he lifted Lovie into his arms as if she weighed no more than a child. "Now, Miss Lovie," he said with a broad grin as he began walking up the beach. "Did Cara ever tell you about the time she rode piggyback through the pluff mud?"

Lovie's eyes sparkled with delight and Cara could see she was enjoying the novelty of being carried in the arms of such a handsome man.

"No!" she said in her hoarse voice. "But you will!"

And he did, all the way back to the beach house. Cara followed, dangling the empty red bucket, treasuring the sound of her mother's soft laughter as it floated back on a breeze.

twenty-six

Sea turtles have few natural enemies. Sharks are known to attack but humans are their greatest predator. Coastal development and eroding beaches result in loss of nesting habitat. A significant number of deaths is caused by drownings in fishing and shrimp nets, injuries from boat propellers and floating debris in the ocean.

The Isle of Palms was graced with crisp, after-storm breezes. All day the sound of hammering and chain saws echoed throughout the neighborhoods. Cars cruised down the streets and the music of children's laughter, birds chirping and dogs barking returned to the island.

But by evening, the island once again fell quiet. At the beach house, lanterns and candles glowed yellow in the twilight, lending coziness to the home after days of chaos. Toy had temporarily moved to Flo's house. Her second story was spared the flood's damage and everyone agreed it was much better for both baby and mother to sleep on dry beds. Brett had gone to determine the damage to his boat, but promised to return the following morning with more supplies. The sweet calico cat was the beach house's only guest and she sat curled on the cushion of a wicker chair.

So it was just Cara and Lovie again, two Rutledge women sitting outside on the porch, on their rockers, enjoying a sunset as they had so many nights before. They didn't speak. They didn't have to. Their held hands eloquently expressed everything that needed to be communicated between them.

Cara looked over at her mother. Lovie appeared peaceful as she sat with a wistful expression on her face and stared out at the sea and the pristine stretch of beach that she loved so dearly. Cara saw her eyes dancing and knew that memories were more alive in her mother's mind now than the present. She knew, too, that they called to her. The tug and pull was palpable and Cara clung to her mother's hand.

"Mama, it's getting chilly. Would you like to go in?"

Lovie shook her head. Just a small movement, and a slight squeeze of the hand, but Cara understood.

"I'll go get you another blanket, then. I'll be right back."

"Caretta?" Her voice was raspy.

"Yes, Mama?"

"You're a good girl."

Cara closed her eyes tightly and took a small breath. "Thank you, Mama."

She wasn't gone long. Just enough time to walk into her mother's room and pull a cotton blanket off her bed. Then a quick stop in the kitchen to grab another bottle of water. She turned off the radio. They'd both heard enough talk about the hurricane.

When she came back to the porch Cara instinctively knew something had changed. She stopped at the threshold, held the blanket close to her chest and stared. Her mother sat still in her chair. Her Bible had fallen to the floor.

Cara was aware of the details. The chip of paint on the tip of the rocker, a dime-sized hole in the screen, a page of the Bible lifting in the wind, the delicate curve of her mother's hand half-open in her lap. She walked slowly over to kneel at her mother's side. Her hand was still warm. The breeze was tugging a yellowed, crumpled piece of paper from her fingers. Cara picked it up and held it under the golden light of the lantern. It was a letter, the fine script slanted and elegant.

My darling Olivia,
I don't blame you in the least for not coming to meet me. I know better than most the complicated bonds that tie us to our responsibilities. Yes, I confess I had hoped that you would come. I waited at the beach house all night, masked by the dark like the thief I was, hoping against hope to steal you away.

I don't doubt for a moment that you loved me. Love me still. But you have made your decision. As promised, I will respect it.

But if you should ever change your mind, or if circumstances occur where you should ever find your life untenable, I want you to have the freedom to leave—even if you should not choose to come to me.

You carry my love within you. A day will never dawn nor a sunset slip into the horizon when I will not think of you. I accept that the mind often dictates the heart. Yet I believe that the heart is the truer guide.

So, if in the course of time you should want to come to me, do not hesitate. Know that I will be waiting for you. You will always have my heart—my love.
Always,
Russell

Cara closed the letter and placed it in the crisp, thin pages of her mother's Bible. Then, holding it close to her chest, she stood and looked out at the sea. A gray mist hovered over the water and from the harbor she heard the low, sonorous bellow of a foghorn, again and again, like the tolling of a bell.

"Go to him, Mama," she said, tears streaming down her cheeks. "You're free! Don't worry anymore about us. We'll be fine. I'll take care of Toy. I'll look out for Palmer. And I'll pass the torch to Linnea and Cooper. Go! Don't let anyone or anything stand in the way of your heart's desire."

Mourners overflowed the church for the funeral of Olivia Rutledge, known to everyone who loved her as Lovie. Her family tree was extensive. While only some of the family gathered yearly for family reunions, at funerals they showed up in force. Brett and Toy remained close to Cara's side while Flo and Miranda sat with the rest of the Turtle Team. Emmi and Tom Peterson had flown in from Atlanta with their two sons. Generations of turtle volunteers, young and old, came to pay their respects to the woman who had worked so tirelessly for their benefit. There were also scores of friends who had known Olivia since school days, as well as families that had been connected to hers for many generations. Charleston could be a small town in this way.

After the funeral, Cara stood beside Julia at the rear of the church and accepted the condolences with sincerity. But she kept her eye on her brother. Palmer sat hunched over in the front pew, his eyes red and his face blotchy as he stared disbelievingly at the coffin. He looked like a man who'd just been hit by a bullet and hadn't yet fallen.

He'd been this way since she'd called to tell him of their mother's death. Expecting him to rant and rave about letting their mother get stuck on the island during the storm, she'd braced herself for scathing blame that she'd caused Lovie's early death. Instead he'd been too stunned, bereft, shocked beyond speech.

As the last of the mourners left the church, Julia turned to Cara with panic in her eyes.

"Cara, I'm afraid he'll make a scene at the interment. You've got to do something. He's been crazy with grief. He's frightening the children."

"He wouldn't be the first one to cry at a burial. And he hardly speaks to me."

"You're the only one he *will* speak to. He's devastated, Cara. He's your brother. He needs you. And I've simply got to get back to the house to prepare for the lunch. More food is arriving by the minute. I swear, I can feed the multitudes."

Cara sighed but nodded her head. "All right, you go on with the children. I'll go see what I can do."

The scent of incense was heavy as she walked the long church aisle to her brother. The coffin had just been taken to the hearse for the final journey to the cemetery. Palmer, however, continued to stare at the vacant space between dozens of flower arrangements. Cara noted a gorgeous, expensive one that had been sent from her agency.

"Palmer?"

He didn't move.

She put her hand on his shoulder. The wool felt hot and scratchy. "Palmer, it's time to go. They're waiting for us."

Her brother took a long, shuddering breath then rose slowly, like an old man. Julia had done her duty and seen to it that his black suit was clean and pressed but he looked disheveled nonetheless. His hair was tousled from running his hands through it and everything from his tie to his gaze seemed askew. When he turned toward her and looked into her face, his bloodshot eyes were those of the little boy who had sat on the stairs with her at night, clutching her tight as they listened in fear to their father's yelling downstairs.

She opened her heart and her arms to him, as their mother had done. When he stepped into them and hugged her, weeping, all the cross words that had created a cold, hard wall between them melted away.

"I didn't get to say goodbye," he cried, brokenhearted. "I didn't get to tell her I loved her. I thought I had more time!"

At that moment Cara realized how truly lucky she had been. If she hadn't responded to her mother's letter, if she hadn't sorted through those years of accumulation, she, too, would have been left to live with the regret that Palmer now suffered.

Gratitude gave her compassion and she began that day to reconcile the rift between them.

twenty-seven

---

*Only a small percentage of hatchlings will survive to maturity
to repeat the nesting cycle. Research indicates the number of sea
turtles worldwide are continuing to drop. Turtles have existed for
millions of years. Only time will tell if the efforts of professionals
and volunteers will protect the loggerheads from extinction.*

Cara stood on the small dune outside her house and faced
the sea. The moon was but a silvery shadow in the purpling
sky. This had once been the site of rendezvous for Lovie and
Russell and it was now a permanent green space for generations to come. She felt closer to her mother here than in the
cemetery where she'd been buried in the family plot beside
her husband. That was where her body lay. But Cara knew
her spirit was here on the dune where she'd stood for so many
years staring out at the sea.

And in the beach house. Cara had slowly come to terms
with her grief in the past several weeks. There was an ebb and
flow with the pain of loss. Yet as Cara slept in her mother's
room, in her high bed, sometimes she could sense her mother's
presence floating in the soft breezes that caressed her brow.

But her mama was gone now, and with her death, Cara
was free to leave. Another turtle season was over. Most of the
tourists had already left for home. The turtle volunteers had

dispersed until the next season. The nests that had remained in the sand during the hurricane did not hatch and the nest that they'd moved was unlikely to so late in the year.

It was October. Cara always thought it the most beautiful month on the island. With the cooler evenings and the shorter days, a whole new array of wildflowers blossomed. Migrating birds were on the wing, passing through the Lowcountry on their journey south.

Cara was heading north. Dressed in her city clothes, she already felt as out of place on the beach as she had when she'd first arrived. Early that morning she'd laid her clothing out on the bed with ritualistic care, mentally preparing herself for the shift in lifestyles. In a few more hours Brett would drive her to the airport.

When she'd received her travel arrangements from the agency, she was a little spooked. She'd hardly left the Isle of Palms in the four months that she'd been here. She, who had traveled from Chicago to Los Angeles or New York on a regular basis for years, was suddenly apprehensive about getting on a plane and facing crowds again. Her life here on the island had been so insular. And yet oddly enough she'd established closer ties with more people in the past few months than she had in the past twenty years.

Clothed in her ceremonial armor she stood facing the shoreline one last time. Around her, the sea oats clicked in the breeze like snapping fingers. She felt pensive, unsure of what her future held. Why was she questioning her resolve at the eleventh hour? she wondered, peeved by her lack of resolve. Everything was in the ready. Her bags were packed and lined up by the door. It was decided that Toy would continue to live in the beach house with Little Lovie. Brett had agreed that Cara should settle in her new job at the agency before they worked out the details of his trip north. She'd made peace with her past, her future at the agency loomed bright and her relationships were on solid ground. She should be content.

Yet, the truth was, she hated to leave. She'd grown accustomed to life at a slower pace. She enjoyed waking up and knowing the day was hers. Her mother had told her that one summer could make a difference and she knew now it was true.

She turned from the ocean to look at the small yellow beach house. *Her* beach house. Although a bit shabby again after the trials of the hurricane, it still stood proud and strong perched high on the dune. Purple and golden wildflowers sprinkled the dunes with a vivacity that rivaled the colors that had welcomed her in a spring that seemed years ago. This little beach house on the Isle of Palms was her home. This barrier island was where the people she loved lived. This small place of earth was where she was *from*.

Yet she was leaving again. She felt the contradiction in her marrow. Russell's words to Lovie played in her mind. *I accept that the mind often dictates the heart. Yet I believe that the heart is the truer guide.* Was she repeating her mother's mistake? Was she making what seemed the right choice for all the wrong reasons?

The sky was darkening. Lifting her wristwatch, she saw it was time to go. With a heavy sigh, she began walking away. A sudden breeze swept over her, cool and sweet smelling. She looked up but the sky was cloudless. It would be a good night for travel, she thought. She caught sight of the turtle nest, the one they'd returned to the sand after the hurricane. For sentiment's sake, she detoured to say a final farewell to the turtle season that had helped to reconcile her with her mother.

The lone nest appeared as a deserted outpost on the windblown dune, just a small triangle of space marked by tilting wooden stakes, drooping orange tape and a plastic sign. She bent on one knee to remove the stakes and officially end the season. But as she reached out, she noticed a pronounced concave depression over the nest. She blinked, not quite believing what her eyes were telling her. Bending lower, there was no question. This was a live nest. And it was hatching!

Her heart pounded with happiness and she leaped to her feet. "Mama, it's hatching!" she cried, then ran up the sandy path. By the time she reached the house she was breathless.

"Toy!" she called out as she ran inside. "Toy!"

"What?" Toy called back, stepping from the kitchen with a dish towel in her hand. She looked slim and girlish again in shorts and a T-shirt, her hair pulled back in a ponytail.

"You won't believe it. The nest. Lovie's nest. It's hatching!"

Toy squealed and twirled around on the ball of her foot.

"I'm calling Flo. No, wait. Brett."

"You call Brett. I'll run over and get Flo. It'll be quicker."

Cara's fingers shook with excitement as she dialed Brett's number.

"Honey, hurry over. The nest is hatching."

"You're kidding? A reprieve! Maybe we'll get time off for good behavior."

"Just get over here, quick!"

She hung up and was about to run back to the beach when an inner voice told her to call Palmer. Mama had said he needed the beach house. And it would be one step closer for the two of them. She picked up the phone and dialed his number. After a few rings, she heard his gruff voice.

"Palmer! Mama's nest is hatching."

There was a stunned pause.

"Big brother, this is Mama's last nest. The one she personally saved. Linnea would love to see it. And so would Cooper. Mostly, I think *you* should be here. Are you coming?"

"Hell, yes!"

She felt her grin stretch across her face. "Well, good! Now hurry up and get your sorry butt out here. These babies won't wait!"

The moon rose higher in the sky. It was low tide, and arcing watermarks scored the sand in wavy lines. On the dunes, sea oats dangled their golden seed heads in the breeze. Cara, Brett, Toy and her baby, Flo, Miranda, Palmer, Julia and their children all clustered around a small, widening opening in the nest. They watched with rapt attention as the sand collapsed around the perimeter. A turtle's little flipper broke through, then its head. Catching its first breath of night air, it wiggled, broke free of the sand and, in a frenzy of flipper movement, began its dash to the sea.

"Is that all?" Cooper asked, clearly disappointed.

"That's just the scout," Linnea answered in a know-it-all voice. "Now, hush."

Cara and Brett shared a commiserating look of amusement.

Moments later, the circle of sand seemed to heave as though being pushed upward from a force below. The sand erupted and the eighty-plus hatchlings bubbled out of the nest, flippers waving in the night air, bodies squirming and pushing as they climbed one over the other. It was a true boil!

The reflected moonlight on the sea and the phosphorescence of the breakers called the hatchlings home. They raced frantically, comically, down the slope, then fanned out in the direction of the sea. The hatchlings climbed through vegetation, around rocks and ruts, and swam through the long narrow tidal pool, doggedly following the voice of an instinct over one hundred and twenty million years old. The silvery beach seemed alive with tiny sea turtles.

Cara stayed at the nest to count the hatchlings as they emerged while the others walked the hatchlings to the shore, guarding against marauding ghost crabs. When it appeared the last turtle had fled, she rose again, wrapped her arms around her chest and peered out across the beach.

Toy was walking slowly beside a hatchling, Little Lovie resting securely in her arms. Not far beyond were Flo and Miranda, arm in arm, keeping watch over a few hatchlings that had wandered off too far. Linnea inched her way down the beach, heels together in a V, guiding a chosen baby turtle along its way. Palmer stood with Cooper, one hand on his son's shoulder, one arm pointing out toward a hatchling. His suit trousers were folded up to the calf, his feet were bare and he was bent at the waist speaking into Cooper's ear. Down at the shoreline, she saw Brett's powerful silhouette, in his usual hands-on-hips stance.

Cara stood on the dune and felt her mother's presence beside her. She heard Lovie's voice in her ear. *One day you will look up and see it—and just know.*

Cara looked out at the scene unfolding before her and knew.

She would not return to Chicago. She loved this Lowcountry man and would not ask him to leave this place where they both belonged. She would stay in the beach house with Toy and the baby and help them begin their new life. She would make peace with Palmer and be there for his children. She would nurture all her relationships as she had nurtured thousands of hatchlings over the summer. She would be a kind of wife, mother, grandmother, aunt and sister. It might not be the traditional family—but when had she ever been traditional?

With her heart filled with silvery light she walked from the dune. Brett turned his head from the sea to follow her solitary journey across the beach to his side. He stretched out his hand to her and she took hold.

They gathered in a semicircle around the last straggler hatchling as it made its way to the surf. Cara saw it get its first taste of the sea as the fingers of a wave slid up to caress it. The sand washed from its back revealing the gleaming, reddish-brown color of its shell. The hatchling raised its head, straining high, seemingly to sniff out the direction home, or perhaps, hearing the ancient turtle mother's call. With a renewed surge of energy it dashed forward once more, only to be pushed back up the beach by a second wave. Undaunted, the hatchling scrambled forward again.

Another white-crested wave approached. Cara squeezed Brett's hand. The wave engulfed the hatchling, sending it somersaulting in the surf. This time, the turtle's instincts kicked in. It righted itself and burst into a frenzied swimming stroke.

Cara bade a silent farewell to the last vestige of a glorious season. She watched as the turtle caught the outgoing tide, dove and disappeared into the vast sea. Then she smiled. In twenty years' time, when the hatchling returned, Cara knew that, God willing, she would be here on the Isle of Palms, waiting to welcome the turtle home.

★ ★ ★ ★ ★

acknowledgments

For sharing knowledge of sea turtles and friendship, heartfelt thanks to Mary Pringle, Island Turtle Team.

Barbara Bergwerf's incredible photographs of so many aspects of our efforts with the loggerheads were inspiring to me as I wrote during the "off" season. Thank you!

Love and thanks to Julie Beard for her critiques, to Angela May for edits and assistance, to Marguerite Martino for helping me get to the hearts of my heroines and to Charlotte and Ken Tarr for their help with important plot points.

A special thanks to Shane Ziegler of Barrier Island Eco Tours, Isle of Palms, for sharing his invaluable insights and vast knowledge about the Lowcountry. And the tours are fabulous!

Thanks to Martha Keenan, a brilliant editor, for bringing out the best in the book.

Special thanks to Sally Murphy of the South Carolina Department of Natural Resources, Wildlife Diversity Section, for an education on sea turtles, for editing chapter headings and for her friendship.

Thanks, too, to Du Bose Griffin, Meg Hoyle, Charles Tambiah and James Spotila.

Love and gratitude to Kelly Thorvalson, Jason Crichton and everyone at the South Carolina Aquarium.

In memory of Florence Johnson, one of the first "Turtle Ladies."

Toy Sooner's story continues in Swimming Lessons
by New York Times *bestselling author Mary Alice Monroe*
Keep reading for a sneak peak!

one

Last night, Toy Sooner dreamed again of the turtle. It was always the same dream, one so vivid that when she awoke she was tangled in her sheets, disoriented and filled with a great, nameless yearning.

Toy sat on the precipice of the sand dune looking out over the wave-scarred beach. Another day was ending. Around her the sea oats were greening and above, a nighthawk streaked across the slowly deepening sky. The tide was coming in, carrying seashells, driftwood and long-harbored memories tumbling to the shore.

She identified with the loggerhead sea turtle in her dream. Was it merely that the turtles were on her mind? She searched the restless sea that spread out to forever under the vast sky. Out in the distant swells, the sea turtles were gathering for the nesting season. Toy sensed the mothers out there, biding their time until instinct drove them from the safety of the sea to become vulnerable on the beach and lay their eggs.

It was an emotional time of the year for her. Each May when the sea turtles returned to the Isle of Palms, she felt the presence of her beloved mentor, Olivia Rutledge, returning with them.

She hugged her knees closer to her chest. This small dune on this empty patch of beach was her sanctuary. She came often to this sacred spot—to think, to remember, to find solace. She felt closer to Olivia Rutledge here—Miss Lovie to everyone she'd met. This dune had been Miss Lovie's favorite spot, and on some nights, especially when the sun lowered and the birds quieted, as now, Toy imagined she heard Miss Lovie's voice in the sweet-scented offshore breezes.

It had been five years since old Miss Lovie had passed. Five years spanned a good chunk of her life, she thought, considering she'd only lived twenty-three. After Olivia Rutledge died, Toy had worked hard every day of those five years to make a better life for herself and for Little Lovie, her daughter. That had been a vow made at Miss Lovie's gravesite and a promise to her infant daughter.

"I did my best to keep my vow," she said aloud to Lovie Rutledge, feeling her spirit hovering close tonight. "I finished college, got a good job and I've made a nice home for Little Lovie. All tidy and cheery, with flowers on the table, like you taught me. I want so much to be a good mother." She rested her chin on her knee with a ragged sigh as the longing from the dream resurfaced.

"So, tell me, Miss Lovie. Why don't I feel that I am? Or content? I'm still like that turtle in my dream, swimming toward someplace I can't seem to get to."

A high pitched cry shattered her thoughts. "Mama!"

Toy's gaze darted toward the call. Her young daughter sat a distance from the shoreline surrounded by colorful plastic buckets and spades. Her long blond hair fell in salt-stiff streaks down her back as she bent over on hands and knees before the crude beginning of a sand castle.

"What do you want, Little Lovie?"

"Mama, come help me with my castle!"

Toy sighed, sorely tempted. "I'm working, honey."

"You're always working."

She saw a scowl flash across Little Lovie's face before she ducked her head and went back to her digging. Mingled in the muffled roar of the ocean she heard Olivia Rutledge's voice in her mind. *Stop what you're doing and play with your child!*

Toy desperately wanted to play with her and enjoy each precious, fleeting moment with Little Lovie. She felt an all too familiar twinge of guilt and paused to allow her gaze to linger on her daughter. Little Lovie was carefully molding another tower with her chubby hands.

That child was happiest when she was at the seaside, Toy thought, her heart pumping with affection. Whether collecting shells, digging castles or rollicking in waves, as long as she had her toes in the sand she was content. She was only five years of age, yet Little Lovie was so much like Miss Lovie Rutledge that Toy sometimes believed the old woman's spirit had returned to settle in her namesake. For Toy, the sun rose and set on her child. And it was *for* her child's future that she gathered her discipline.

"Let me finish this report," she called back. "Then I'll come help you finish that sand castle."

"You promise?"

"I promise, okay?"

Her daughter nodded and Toy resolutely brushed away grains of sand from her notebook and returned to the report that was due by morning. She was an Aquarist and had been placed in charge of her own gallery at the South Carolina

Aquarium. It was her first break and she needed to prove that she was capable of the responsibility.

The noseeums and mosquitoes were biting in the sticky humidity and blown sand stuck to her moist skin but she worked a while longer, determined to finish in the last of the day's light. A short while later she closed her notebook and raised her gaze toward her daughter. Another lopsided tower had been added to the castle.

But her daughter was gone.

Toy's breath caught in her throat as her eyes wildly scanned the beach. "Lovie!" she cried out, leaping to her feet.

"Mama, look!"

Toy swung her head around toward her daughter's voice. Little Lovie was arched on tiptoe at the water's edge. The bottom of her pink swimsuit was coated with a thick layer of damp sand and she was pointing excitedly toward the sea.

Toy ran across the beach to grasp hold of her daughter's slender shoulders. "You know you're not supposed to go near the water," she scolded, even as her eyes devoured her child and her hands gently wiped sand from her face. "You scared me half to death."

The five-year-old was oblivious to her mother's concern. Instead, her large blue eyes were riveted to something in the surf.

"It's right there," she cried, wiggling her pointed finger urgently. "I see it!"

"What do you see, a dolphin?" Toy turned her head back toward the Atlantic to peer into the rolling surf. Then she saw it. A large dark object floated at the surface not more than fifty feet out.

It wasn't a dolphin. She squinted and moved a step closer. Could it be a turtle? The dark hulk appeared lifeless in the waves. "You stay right here," she ordered in a no nonsense tone, and this time, Little Lovie didn't argue.

Toy rolled her pants higher up on her slender legs, coiled her shoulder length blond hair in a twist at the top of her head, then walked into the sea for a closer look. She felt the chilly spring water swirl at her ankles, calves and then dampen the hem of her shorts as she waded forward, intrigued by the shadowy object bobbing on the waves.

It *was* a turtle! It had to be at least two hundred pounds— and it looked dead. What a pity, she thought and she wondered if this was a nesting female holding eggs. It was always a shame to lose an adult turtle, but to lose a nesting female was a tragedy. The loss was one of generations.

A wave carried the turtle closer and Toy's stomach clenched at the sight. It looked like she'd been floating for a long time. She was badly emaciated and the shell was dried and covered from tip to tip with barnacles.

"Poor Mama," she muttered. There'd been too many dead turtles washing ashore in the past few years. "Barnacle Bills" the turtle team called them, and this was another to add to the list. She'd call and have DNR pick the carcass up in the morning. Toy was about to turn back when she saw a flipper move.

"She can't be…" Toy bent forward, squinting. A breaker smacked her legs but she kept her eyes peeled on the turtle. A flipper moved again.

"She's alive!" she called out to Little Lovie.

The child jumped up and down, clapping her hands. Toy hurriedly waded closer to Little Lovie to be heard. "Honey, I'm going to need some help. Run up to Flo's house and tell her to come right quick, hear? Can you do that?"

"Yes, ma'am!"

The child took off like a shot for the dunes. Just beyond was the white frame house of Florence Prescott, the leader of the island's turtle team. Flo was very active in the community and always out doing something for someone, but she was usually home at the dinner hour. At least Toy hoped she was today.

She turned back toward the turtle. The inert creature was floating with her posterior up, like a lopsided rubber raft. She'd have to haul her in. She sighed and looked at her clothes. Well, they were halfsoaked anyway, she thought as she began wading toward the turtle.

The pebbly sand suddenly dipped and sliding down, her toe was sliced by the sharp edge of a shell. White pain radiated up her leg and looking down, she saw the murky water stained red with blood. The turtle was drifting farther away in the current. Ignoring the pain, she kicked off to swim to the floating hulk.

The big turtle was in much sorrier shape than she'd first realized. As she drew near, the turtle's dark, almond eyes rolled in her large skull in a mournful gaze.

"Don't be afraid, big girl," she said to the turtle, feeling an instant connection. "I'll get you out of here in no time."

A small wave slapped her face as she swam around the turtle. Her eyes stung and she spit out a mouthful of saltwater. Once behind the rear flippers she could get a good handle on the shell. Then, using the carapace like a kickboard, she began kicking and pushing the turtle toward the shore.

She was making good progress when she caught a quick silvery flash of movement in the corner of her eye. Her breath hitched as she scanned the vista. The water's surface was turning glassy in the brilliant colors of the setting sun. She hesitated, not fooled by the serenity. Dusk was feeding time for sharks.

Toy knew she was in a vulnerable position. The predator would be curious about the sick turtle—an easy prey. With her toe bleeding she knew the smart thing to do would be to leave the turtle and get out of the water.

Then she saw it again. This time it was unmistakable. The slim, v-shaped dorsal fin broke the surface, heading her way in a lazy, zigzag pattern. Toy froze as the shark neared, then swiftly veered off. The turtle's instinct flared and her flippers feebly stroked in the surf. The shark surfaced again, but this time farther out by the inlet.

"Well, no one ever said I was smart," she told herself, gripping the turtle's shell. With a grunt, she pushed with all her might, propelling the turtle forward. She repeated this twice more before her feet hit sand. The shark was closer again, circling in a pattern of surveillance.

That bull shark was four feet of sleek danger and she knew it could attack in shallow water. She hurried to the front of the turtle and grabbed hold. "We're not home yet," she muttered and began tugging the enormous turtle in. Behind her on the beach she heard Florence Prescott calling her name.

"Hurry, Flo!" she cried over her shoulder.

With athletic grace that belied her advanced years, Flo ran straight into the water, her tennis shoes still on.

"Drag her out of the water," Toy cried with urgency. "We've got company."

Flo looked over her shoulder. "God damn," she muttered.

Little Lovie ran into the surf, arms reaching for the turtle. "Let me help!"

"Lovie, you get back on the beach this instant!" Toy ordered.

"But I want to help!"

"Do as your mama says," Flo told her. "Sharks nibble hatchlings in ankle deep water and your toes are just the right size. Go on now, git."

Little Lovie scrambled out of the ocean.

Flo grabbed hold of a side of the turtle's shell. Her deeply tanned arms spoke of many years spent in the sun. "On the count of three…"

With a heave-ho, they shoved the turtle up the final few feet to the edge of the beach. Out of the water, the full impact of the huge turtle's weight was felt. It was like pushing a boulder and it took all they had to get the turtle to scrape sand till only the tips of the incoming tide caressed her rear flippers.

The turtle remained motionless. Toy plopped down on the sand beside her and lifted her foot to check out her wound. She was shocked to see that the cut in her big toe was deep and bright red blood trickled in a steady flow. And it hurt like hell. It hit her how reckless she'd been to stay in the sea with a bleeding wound. Raising her gaze, she looked again out at the sea. The shark had already disappeared beneath the murky water. She started to laugh with relief.

"What are you laughing at?" Flo asked. "Is that a cut you've got there?" She swooped down like a mother hen.

"It's nothing."

"I'll be the judge of that. Those shells can be like razors. Let me see it."

"Really, Flo, I'm okay."

"Bring it here." Flo bent and, grabbing hold of Toy's foot, studied the toe closer. She clucked her tongue. Little Lovie hovered nearby, mesmerized. After a quick perusal, Flo released the foot and rose to a stand. "Put some antibiotic ointment on it and you'll live."

Toy looked up at her daughter with a reassuring smile.

"I can't believe you went out there with a shark trailing you," Flo said. "You know better."

Toy took the scolding with good nature. "I didn't see it when I swam out and I wasn't sure I was bleeding." She snorted and added smugly, "But I got her in, didn't I?"

Florence Prescott usually had something upbeat to say about most things, but she looked at the turtle with a frown and shaking her head said, "I'm not sure it was worth the risk. This turtle looks barely alive. And she's covered with gunk. I've buried strandings that looked better than this one."

"No, she's beautiful. That gunk is merely leeches, algae and barnacles. We just have to get her someplace where we can clean her up."

Before they could discuss this further, their attention was caught by calls coming from up the beach. "Well, thank goodness the cavalry's here," Flo said. She stretched her arm overhead and waved, calling out, "Cara! Brett! Over here!"

Toy turned toward the dunes and saw an attractive couple in khaki shorts and green *Barrier Island Eco-Tour* T-shirts. Toy's spirits soared and she grinned from ear to ear as she lifted her arm in a wave.

A tall, lean woman strode toward them in a long-legged, no-nonsense manner. Her glossy, dark hair whipped in the breeze and behind her smart, tortoise sunglasses, Toy knew Cara's brown eyes were sparkling with excitement at the prospect of a live turtle on the beach.

Behind her, Brett's broad shoulders and height towered even over Cara. Though he wore the same T-shirt of the tour company they owned, on Brett the clothes were faded and worn, giving him the disheveled appearance of an island boy.

Little Lovie yelped with excitement at seeing them and ran into Brett's arms for a quick hoist high up in the air.

"It's a turtle, see!" she cried out.

"I see it!" Brett's blue eyes brightened against his weathered tan as he grinned wide and swung Little Lovie around, her legs flying behind her. Then he tucked her on his hip with a hug of affection.

"What've we got?" Cara asked, walking directly to the turtle. She bent over the sea turtle to get a closer look.

"Probably a nesting female," Flo replied as she quickly moved to Cara's side. "She's covered with barnacles. And look, leeches too. Ugh, the horrid blood suckers are all over her."

Cara grimaced at the pitiful sight. "She must've been floating for weeks."

"Weeks? Longer than that," Flo replied. "These poor floaters can't dive to hunt and this old girl likely hasn't eaten in months. Her neck is so thin…she's all skin." She clucked her tongue. "I don't know if she's going to make it."

"She's not gone yet," Toy said, joining them at the turtle's side. She felt fiercely protective of the turtle she rescued. "I've been amazed at how resilient sea turtles can be. I'm not giving up on her."

"She's certainly a big girl," Brett said, drawing near with Little Lovie in his arms.

"Let's see how big she is." Cara pulled a measuring tape out of her backpack and made quick work of measurements. She called out the numbers to Flo who scribbled them down in her notebook. Little Lovie scrambled out of Brett's arms to hover closer, half curious, half repelled by the condition of the turtle.

Toy tucked her fingertips into her back pockets. The early evening's chill seemed to go straight through her wet clothes.

"From tip to tip of the shell, I've got forty inches," Cara called out. "I'm guessing she's well over 200 pounds."

Flo slapped the sand from her hands. "Well, that's that. I guess I'd better call it in to DuBose at the Department of Natural Resources to come get her."

"I could call the Aquarium," Toy piped up.

Cara checked her watch. "It's after six o'clock. DuBose won't be in her office."

"No, but there's the DNR hotline number," Flo replied. "Someone will come out."

"Tomorrow, most likely," said Brett.

"DNR doesn't do rehab," Cara said, zipping up her backpack. "What will they do with a live turtle?"

Flo shrugged. "Do you have any better ideas?"

"I could call the Aquarium." Toy said again, a little louder. The two women turned their heads toward her in swift unison.

"The Aquarium?" asked Flo with doubt. "What will they do? They don't take in sick sea turtles."

"Well, actually, yes they—we do," Toy replied. "At least, the Aquarium took two in before. A few years back. They didn't do the rehabilitation, but they held the turtle until it could be moved to a vet. I don't know…it's just a thought," she added hesitatingly.

"Even so," Cara replied. "No one will be at the Aquarium at this hour either. Why do the emergencies always happen after business hours? It's like some unspoken law."

"But we *can* still call the Aquarium," Toy persisted. "We always have someone on call."

"Really?" Cara asked, interested. "Then, I suppose that is a possibility to consider."

"The DNR still has to be notified," Flo said with finality. "Anything to do with turtles is their jurisdiction."

"Sure, but then *they're* stuck with trying to find a place to rehabilitate it," Toy argued back.

Cara shook her head. "Flo, don't get worked up. We'll call DuBose."

While Cara and Flo argued the point between them, Toy limped off, her heel digging half moons into the sand. She went to Little Lovie's lopsided sand castle, noticing the bits of

shells and sea whip that Lovie had decorated it with while she
stuffed the buckets and spades into the canvas bag.

"You okay?"

Toy turned her head surprised to see Brett standing by her
side. His broad shoulders blocked her view of the women at
the shoreline.

"It's just a scratch from a sea shell," she said and returned
to stuffing her bag with toys.

"You know that's not what I'm talking about."

She tossed a sandy spade into the bag and rested her hands
on her thighs, then she looked up again. He was standing
with his hands on his hips and a calm and a patient expression
on his face. It was so typical of him. Surrounded by volatile
women, Brett was always a steadying force for them all. She'd
come to look up to him as the big brother she'd always wanted
and he'd steered her straight through some pretty rocky waters over the years.

"Do you really think the Aquarium will take the turtle
in?" he asked.

She shrugged. "Honestly, Brett, I don't know. I've heard
talk of taking turtles in this season, but nothing's been decided.
It's certainly not up to me." She hesitated then said with feeling, "But at least it's a possibility."

"And a good one. Do you know who to call?"

A smile twitched her lips as she nodded.

"So, what are you waiting for? Make that call. You sure
don't need our permission. And it sounds to me like you've
got the best idea going."

Toy pulled her cell phone from the canvas bag, dreading
the task she'd set for herself. After all her bluster, she couldn't
back out now. Brett crossed his arms and waited while she dialed the number of her supervisor at the Aquarium. She told
herself it was the cold, not nervousness, that made her fin-

gers stiff but the pounding in her heart was proof that it took nerves for her, a low-level staff member at the Aquarium, to be calling the Director of Animal Husbandry. She shivered as the wind gusted.

Jason answered the phone after two rings. The phone connection from the beach wasn't good and she had to repeat sentences, but she managed to quickly sum up the situation. After a few minutes conversation she closed her cell phone and looked up at Brett, eyes wide with triumph.

"Jason said to bring her in!"

"Well, hey! Good work, kiddo."

Toy felt a surge of satisfaction at the congratulations Cara and Flo gave her when she delivered the good news.

"The only problem is," Toy added, "the Aquarium is locked tight until morning."

"What are we supposed to do with the turtle till then?" Flo asked.

"When I interned at the sea turtle hospital at Topsail," Toy replied, "Jean Beasley told me about the first sick turtle they found. She was a big loggerhead, like this one. They found her floating, too. It was late in the day and they didn't have anywhere to take her, so they carried the turtle to Jean's garage on the island, washed her off, wrapped her in warm wet towels and watched her through the night. The next morning they drove her to a veterinary hospital. That same night the turtle was released back to Jean's garage." She smiled. "And *that* was the beginning of the Karen Beasley Sea Turtle hospital."

"You thinking of starting a hospital, now?" Flo chided.

Toy smirked and shook her head. "Maybe someday. But right now I'm thinking we need to stop talking and get this turtle off the beach. The sun is going down and Little Lovie is cold, I'm cold, and that means the turtle is cold, too."

As if to punctuate her statement, the turtle made an effort

to take a labored breath. It was feeble yet enough to prompt the group to action.

"Well, if they could do it, so can we," said Cara. She bent over to grab hold of the turtle's shell. "Okay, everyone, grab a side."

Brett moved alongside the turtle and took hold. Toy followed suit.

"Whoa, gang. Where are we taking her?" asked Flo.

"Where else?" Cara replied with a crooked grin. "To the beach house."

Don't miss Swimming Lessons
Available wherever MIRA books are sold!